To Mr
E...
...
Ava
x

Once Upon A Lie

Ava Ming

The
X
Press

Published by
The X Press
PO Box 25694
London N17 6FP
Tel: 020 8801 2100
Fax: 020 8885 1322
E-mail: vibes@xpress.co.uk
Website: www.xpress.co.uk

First Edition 2005

Printed by Bookmarque Ltd., Croydon, UK

Distributed in the UK by Turnaround Distribution
Unit 3, Olympia Trading Estate, Coburg Road, London N22 6TZ
Tel: 020 8829 3000
Fax: 020 8881 5088

Distributed in the US by National Book Network
15200 NBN Way, Blue Ridge Summit, PA 17214
Tel: 717 794 3800 or 1-800-462-6420
Fax: 1-800-462-6420
custserv@nbnbooks.com

ISBN: 1-902934-39-3

This book is dedicated to Sharon Jeffers and Beverley Selby, my Sisters in Spirit: Gone but never forgotten.

Acknowledgments

Special thanks to:
Steve and Deborah Pope and Helen Lloyd - for constant encouragement and valued critique; Cecil Maynard for encouraging my early love of words; Naomi Jones of Walsall libraries for the word 'Romance'.

Love to:
My son Lucian, Stafford the first influential man in my life, Lucille and Denise, Wayne, Lisa, Dale and Scott Brooks.

Thanks to the following talent for lighting the way:
Emma Hargrave at Tindal Street Press, Norman Samuda Smith, Courttia Newland, Benjamin Zephaniah and his lovely mom, Avril and Roy Bartholomew.

To Kwa'mboka - let it flow!

ABOUT THE AUTHOR

A classically trained musician Ava Ming directed gospel choirs, before touring as a backing singer for Motown legend Edwin Starr. As well as being a qualified Social Worker, Ava also spent six years as a broadcaster on BBC radio. She has published several short stories and written numerous articles for a variety of newspapers. Currently she divides her time between scriptwriting and work on her second novel.

"Many waters cannot quench love, nor can all the floods drown it."
–Song of Solomon

PROLOGUE

JUNE 2001

"...TO HAVE AND to hold, to love and cherish, forsaking all others from this day forward till death us do part." The groom cushioned his solemn vows with a slow smile at the woman beside him.

"Renford and Celia by the power of God invested in me I now pronounce you man and wife." Glancing at the seated congregation the Pastor indicated for the bride and groom to turn around announcing as they did so; "Ladies and gentlemen I now present Mr and Mrs Shango!" A spontaneous round of applause erupted. Smiling broadly Shango nodded to friends and well wishers, then, turning Celia towards him, he lifted her veil and drew her close. Deep eye to eye contact preceded a loving kiss from man to wife.

The organist piped the Wedding March as the couple made their way down the aisle, thankful that his second wedding had passed without a hitch. He peered over the side of the organ and noted that they weren't even halfway along, it seemed as though each person wanted to congratulate them before they made it out of the building. He'd thought that was why people had receptions.

In the church grounds Shango and Rafi, his best man, stood aside while the photographer fussed over Celia and her bridesmaids. Shango silently absorbed the events of the day so far, not quite believing that he'd finally married Celia Clare Barrett, adopted daughter and only child of Martin and Angela. She was educated to doctorate level with an amazing brain that always seemed to be two steps ahead of him and she was the only person he knew who could read a four hundred page book in less than three days and remember virtually every word.

Shango couldn't fathom whether Celia's radiant beauty was because of her expensive designer gown, her elaborately done hair and make up, or her unconfirmed pregnancy.

"Everyone will guess if you keep staring at her belly," Rafi broke the silence between them.

"Why should I care?" Shango said proudly, "that gorgeous woman is my wife and if marriage isn't about procreation then what's it for?"

"I thought it was about having sex on tap and someone to pick up after you," Rafi replied without a hint of irony.

"There's no hope for you, man." Shango laughed.

Rafi chuckled while catching the eye of Paula, one of Celia's bridesmaids. He was attracted to her golden skin, slim hips and her bust, which was shown off by the low cut neckline of her dress. He wondered what his chances were as she gave no hint as to whether or not she was interested in him. Shrugging, he decided to bide his time, sure that an opportunity to get closer to her would present itself later in the day.

• • • • • •

Celia and Shango walked hand in hand onto the dance floor as the Master of Ceremonies began the evening celebrations. They made a stunning couple. Celia's lightly toned skin contrasted beautifully with Shango's rich ebony hues and her size sixteen curves rested comfortably against his svelte frame. As Shango pulled her towards him, her French cut, silk, off-white dress gently swished around her. The tiara she wore amongst her curls added to the regal picture she presented.

Around the hall the elder ladies wiped their eyes with pristine embroidered handkerchiefs admiring Celia's beauty while the younger women kept their eyes fixed on Shango, the most handsome and desirable man in the room. His black morning suit fit perfectly with his Kente waistcoat, neckpiece and pocket handkerchief. His immaculate dreadlocks were tied neatly at the nape of his neck and his toned figure moved easily to the slow beat of the Commodores' *Three Times a Lady*.

As their song played Celia snuggled closer enjoying the moment she'd dreamed of for so long, the time when Shango had no one and nothing else on his mind except her. It hadn't been easy getting to this day. She'd had to shake off her own doubts and persuade him to overcome his. His father, Ira, was initially wary of her racial heritage, her adoptive father was white and her adoptive mother was black while she was African and British, but Celia had won Ira's respect by simply being herself. Now she was prepared to do whatever it took to keep Shango at her side for life.

As they reached the end of their first dance as Mr and Mrs, Shango felt a familiar constriction in his chest. Fearing the onset of an asthma attack he instinctively pulled away from Celia and took a deep breath.

"Is it your asthma; shall I get your inhaler?" Celia offered.

Shango exhaled, and pulled Celia back into his arms.

"I'm okay baby," he reassured her giving her a lingering kiss before the dance floor filled up with guests who were ready to party.

As Shango led Celia back to the top table he noticed immediately that Paula was missing. He looked around for Rafi but he'd also disappeared. Shango smiled to himself guessing that they were probably together.

While the bridesmaids fussed over Celia, Shango went outside to get some fresh air. He breathed deeply as he walked along the side path that led to the car park.

June had given them three weeks of beautiful weather so far and the summer's evening felt almost tropical with the scent of flowers from the gardens at the back of the building. With his head down and deep in thought about the events of the day Shango didn't notice the woman rushing towards him until they collided on the narrow path.

"Sorry I was miles away." Shango apologised.

"I tried to step around you."

"I should have been concentrating." Suddenly they both stopped talking as realisation followed recognition.

"Shango?"

"Sandra! What are you doing here? Where are you going? How have you been?"

Sandra laughed out loud while Shango quietly appraised her. It occurred to him that her demeanour hadn't changed. She was still shy, graceful and intelligent, with an aura that made him want to wrap her up and protect her from the world. Shango's eyes travelled up the length of her body. He guessed she was still a slim size twelve but her hairstyle took him by surprise. He couldn't remember how it had been the last time they had met but now it was cut into a sleek shiny bob. As he looked into her face, Shango noticed that Sandra was actually speaking. He smiled to give the impression that he was listening while inside his heart pumped faster, a reminder that this woman still had an elusive addictive magic that he'd once craved.

"Still asking questions ten to the dozen," she was saying.

Shango nodded at the remark while drinking in the sight of his beloved Sandra, close enough to touch on his wedding day of all days.

"You're all dolled up, what's the occasion?" she continued.

"I'm at, I mean I'm getting, I'm....it's a wedding!" Shango blurted out. The back of his neck flushed hot at his lie. Before he could explain a man came from behind him and took Sandra's arm.

"Sandra we're cutting it fine, they're probably just about to start."

"I was just saying hello to an old friend. Mark, this is Renford Shango. Shango, this is my partner Mark."

Shango looked fully at Mark as they shook hands and exchanged greetings.

His smile faded as he considered Sandra's words. Had she really said 'my partner?' Was she seriously in a relationship with a long, skinny, white guy?

"Nice meeting you, Shango."

"Bye Shango," echoed Sandra as she followed Mark to the conference rooms on the other side of the building. Shango nodded, relieved. At least they wouldn't be at his reception party but what meeting were they going to at eight-thirty on a Saturday night? Confused thoughts rushed through his mind. Just who was this Mark and what did Sandra mean by partner? How long had they been together and what exactly did she see in this ordinary, curly haired, big-eared guy? Were they married? He'd forgotten to check for rings. Did she love him? Did they have children? Did they live together? Shango shuddered involuntarily at the idea of Sandra being in love with another guy. As if!

Shango continued his walk around the building glad to be out of the stultifying atmosphere of smoke and alcoholic smells that played havoc with his breathing. He was weary of the constant good-natured ribbing about the joys of his wedding night. Glancing at his watch he saw that they had two-and-a-half hours left before they were due to check into Birmingham Airport for their flight to St Lucia, but now he was considering whisking

Celia away early.

As he sauntered along the grassy path that circled the community center, a coarse voice stopped him in his tracks.

"You had to do it, didn't you? You had to go ahead and give her, her big day, just to make me look a fool in front of everybody. Well you're stuck with her now! Or didn't you realize that's what till death do us part means?"

Shango stiffened as the tapping of high heels came closer but he kept his back turned to the words that fired into him like bullets.

"You could at least look at me!"

Shango reluctantly faced Sensi, the mother of his eight-year-old son, Kai.

"You gave her what she wanted, a big show of commitment in front of the whole world, but what did you do for me today? I've got your son!"

"There's no need to shout, Sensi, come inside, say hello to everyone, have a drink, just be happy for once." Shango spoke gently but his eyes were cold.

"Just because you married that light-skinned snob with her degrees and speaky spokey accent doesn't mean you can just forget about me. I was here first and you need me, because without me, what happens to our son? What happens to Kai?" Sensi refused to be placated.

Shango rolled his eyes. It was always the same with Sensi. Their relationship had fizzled out when he'd tired of her immaturity and refusal to look beyond the latest stereo system, wide screen TV and designer dress. He'd become weary of her running him down too many times to her friends and family simply because material things held no interest for him. He was passionate about uplifting black people and uplifting himself. He wanted to teach and inspire and he'd made plans to return to college and go on to University.

All Sensi had wanted to do was have more babies and let the future take care of itself. Kai had been a surprise but since they had split up Shango had always regularly supported Sensi and seen his son. He determined that not even his marriage to Celia would change that. Now he looked Sensi straight in the eye and his expression softened as he realised that in the face of his commitment to another woman she was simply fighting for survival. He put his arms around her, in return she laid her hand on his chest and her head on his shoulder.

"Celia are you okay? You don't look too good." Michelle, Celia's best friend and chief bridesmaid was at her side. "Honey, what's wrong?" Leaning closer she whispered, "Is it the baby?"

Celia flashed her a look of irritation. "No one knows remember!" A sharp sting in her side caused her to double over, her face creased in pain.

"Celia when was the last time you saw Shango or Rafi?" Michelle looked out over the room.

"They're probably at the bar...or.....outside...chatting," Celia panted trying to smile at nearby guests.

"Girl, you're looking worse by the minute. I'm going to find Shango."

"Don't leave me!" Celia grabbed Michelle's arm, "Send Paula or one of the others."

Michelle knitted her brows as she continued to scan the room which was filling up with more revelers arriving for the evening dance. She'd noticed Rafi and Paula flirting earlier on and now they'd both disappeared. Michelle reasoned that if she found Paula, she'd probably find Rafi and then Shango.

"Two minutes," she promised Celia as she swept away.

"Michelle, where are you off to, is everything all right?" This time it was Angela that caught Michelle's arm.

"Shango's disappeared, I'm just going to remind him of the time." Michelle spoke lightly, omitting the fact that Celia seemed to be in pain. She didn't want Angela to worry unless it was absolutely necessary.

"Can't you send Rafi?" Angela asked.

"Good point, I'll just get him, stay with Celia for me?"

"Okay."

The blackened windows of the bridal limousine had steamed up. Passing guests looked twice to confirm they'd heard passionate panting. Rafi had gotten his wish. Paula was finally in his arms, succumbing without protest to his heavy kisses and wandering hands as they sat side by side in the large rear interior of the car. The leather seat made a squelching sound as Rafi pulled Paula roughly onto his lap, her long bridesmaid's dress hitched up around her thighs.

Paula ripped at Rafi's shirt and tie. She wanted to feel his skin beneath her fingertips, to discover if his broad chest had straight or curly hair and to know if his nipples were sensitive to the touch of her long nails. All afternoon she'd felt him eyeing her and now she wanted him to live up to his unspoken promises.

Rafi grabbed Paula's buttocks. He felt his nature rise and enjoyed the sensation. Paula was turning out to be more than he anticipated. She obviously knew how to handle him and he guessed she probably had a reputation as being loose. That turned him on even more. Every move she made seemed calculated to please. She bit him playfully on his neck, causing him to gasp with pleasure.

"Do it again," he murmured.

"I'm sorry I didn't hear you," Paula teased deliberately leaning away from him.

"Bite me!"

This time Paula willingly obliged. As she sank her teeth onto his neck she wriggled her hips forward and pressed down onto his manhood now straining inside his trousers.

"Mm seems like someone's ready to come out and play," she whispered in Rafi's ear. In response, Rafi pulled at her zip. Paula raised her hands over her head and rocked on Rafi's lap, her moans more insistent as she neared orgasm. She wasn't sure how much more foreplay she could take without exploding.

Rafi slid his hand down to Paula's thighs. He fumbled under her trussed up dress to reach her knickers but stopped when all he met was bare flesh. Where were the damned things, he wondered. How could he get them off if he couldn't find them? Still kissing Paula's breast, ears and neck he tried again. This time his hand felt soft pubic hair.

"Surprise!" Paula announced and laughed at the shock on Rafi's face as he realised she was knickerless.

"Don't let go." Sensi was enjoying the warmth of Shango's arms. Bright red four-inch stilettos heightened her slender five-foot-two frame. Shango grimaced as he looked down at her toes which were coloured in a a dazzling assortment of sparkling varnish, clashing with the Jamaican flags painted on her fingernails and garish pink lipstick. He blinked as he realised those lips were coming closer to his own, then he pulled Sensi close and pushed her head back down onto his chest. No way was he kissing anyone but his bride today.

"Call an ambulance!" Angela tried her best to catch Celia as she slid sideways off her chair and onto the floor. "Martin!" she called out, "Find Shango, or Michelle or Rafi! Somebody do something!" Panic filled Angela's voice and she broke out in a sweat as she tried in vain to see Shango through the crowds. A voice in her head shouted, *Where the hell is he!* He should have been at Celia's side, it was their wedding day for God's sake. People converged on the bridal table in response to Angela's screams. "Get back!" Angela struggled to be heard above the growing din. "She needs air, someone call an ambulance, please!"

Outside, halfway along the grassy path that circled the building, Sensi grabbed Shango's hand and placed it firmly on her bottom. Taking advantage of his surprise she pulled his head again towards her lips, willing him to concede that she knew best and that he'd made a mistake in marrying Celia.

In the limousine, Rafi and Paula panted their way to an erotic climax. Knees apart she straddled him as he at last pushed deep inside her. With slender fingers Paula tugged at his hair and pressed her hands into his shoulders. Rafi gripped her thighs, his mouth searching for her moist lips as he thrust harder and harder. She was good, better than he imagined. He knew he'd be coming back for more.

Michelle hurriedly crossed the car par thinking that she might find Shango asleep in the limousine. At the car she heard the cries of a couple in the throes of sex. She reached for the handle ready to expose the shameless pair but stopped short as she heard sirens They seemed to be getting louder, surely they weren't coming to the community centre? she wondered. Michelle left the car and continued her circuit towards the hall. She turned the last corner in time to see Sensi grab Shango's head and plant his lips firmly on hers. Michelle watched in silent rage as Shango resisted for just a moment before returning Sensi's kiss ardently, one hand on her behind, the other caressing her neck before sliding down onto her firm, full breast.

The reception hall was a scene of chaos.

"Thank God you're here! She's my daughter," Angela greeted the medics who moved through the crowd quickly and efficiently. "I don't know what happened. One minute she was okay, then she slumped onto the floor. She just got married, but we can't find her husband," Angela rambled on while the paramedics checked Celia's vital signs and edged back the crowd. "She's never fainted before. Is she okay? Should I do anything?" Angela's mind was a tangle of confusion. Why was

Celia unconscious? What was that red mass staining the beautiful satin of her gown and where was Shango?

As Rafi and Paula satiated their desires, Michelle watched her best friend's new husband groping another woman. Martin had managed to fight his way through the crowd to reach his wife. The assembled guests mumbled amongst themselves in whispers as Celia left the hall alone on a stretcher, her blood soaked dress confirming the paramedics' fears. This pregnant bride had lost her baby.

CHAPTER ONE

JUNE 2002

WHY DIDN'T YOU call?" Celia held back angry tears.

"I meant to, time just ran away from me today." Shango tried to pacify her as he entered their new home and walked through the hallway to the cloakroom.

"I was expecting you hours ago! Where have you been?" Emotion flooded Celia's words. She hugged herself in an effort to stop waving her arms around, but she still demanded Shango's full attention.

"Let me just hang up my coat, put down my bag and then we can talk, okay?" Shango spoke calmly knowing that he should have been home much earlier. "Is the water on? What about the central heating? Did they plumb in the washing machine and connect the cooker? Have you managed to fit all the light bulbs?"

Celia put her head in her hands in despair. What she needed was Shango to hold her and whisper sorry for leaving her to deal with the move. One more question about fixtures and fittings and she knew she was going to lose it.

Mistaking her silence for thoughtfulness, Shango unwittingly pushed the final button, "Did they put the boxes in the right rooms? I know you labeled them all."

"I don't care about the bloody boxes or the stupid light bulbs! The appliances aren't a problem, but you are! Where the hell have you been all day?" Celia screamed, her arms finally akimbo.

The stress of moving from a one bedroomed cosy flat to a three bedroomed semi-detached house without a single call from Shango finally took its toll. She'd had enough of dealing with removal men who had no initiative and wouldn't work unless they were constantly watched. Their resentment of her was obvious and she'd even heard them calling her names behind her back. And after putting up with all that, who told Shango that he could just stroll in after ten pm and ask if the cooker was connected? What was he hoping for, Celia wondered, a roast dinner?

Startled by Celia's outburst, Shango stopped looking at the clutter of boxes and misplaced furniture and focused on the worry lines across her forehead and the weariness in her eyes. Her clothes were covered in dirt and dust and she looked as though she'd been through hell. Touched by her fragility he drew her to him.

"I'm sorry sweetheart, when I got to University I told them I couldn't stay but they asked me to cover for an absent lecturer and I said it would be okay. Then I ended up in one meeting after another. I had no idea what you were going through. I've been foolish and inconsiderate, don't cry. I knew you could handle it but I should have been here to help you. Please forgive me."

He covered her face with kisses before leading her to the leather settee which stood isolated in the middle of the lounge. "Where's the rest of the suite?" he asked.

"Who knows, probably upstairs in the bathroom."

Celia laughed lightly through her tears. Shango laughed too as he placed her legs up on the sofa and encouraged her to lie down.

"Are you hungry?"

"Starving."

"Fish and chips or Chinese?"

"Yes, please."

"Fish and Chips and Chinese it is then!" Shango laughed at Celia's response. "Don't move I'll be right back." He kissed her softly and she kissed him back, glad that he was finally home.

Shango stood at the end of a long line in the chip shop. As the queue moved slowly forward he called the Chinese takeaway from his mobile phone. "Cantonese beef steak and King Prawns with large egg fried rice, please," he ordered. Aware that people in the chip shop were staring he asked, "What?" kissed his teeth, and then ignored them.

Twenty-five minutes later Shango returned home. "Food!" he sang out as he walked through to the kitchen. He placed everything on a tray with a napkin, added a plastic rose for romantic decoration and entered the sitting room with a flourish. Celia lay exactly as he'd left her, only now she was fast asleep.

The next day, feeling refreshed, Celia dialed a familiar number as soon as Shango had left for work.

"Hi Michelle, you're the first person I've called from my new phone in my new house!" Celia giggled down the line whilst wriggling on the bare floorboards of the lounge.

"Hey, you're in! When did you pick up the keys?"

"Yesterday."

"And the phone's on already, you didn't waste much time."

"I've got my priorities in order."

"Where"s the man of the house?"

"Gone to work. When he gets back we'll christen each room."

"Christen?"

"Yes, *christen*, in the way God intended! Got to go, boxes to unpack, mortgage to pay... you know how it is for us homeowners!"

"Congratulations Celia, enjoy your new place."

"Thanks, bye love."

Celia looked around with satisfaction. After living in cramped conditions in Shango's rented flat they'd finally gotten a foot on the property ladder. She envisaged how the house would look when they'd made it their own. Shango's carvings of African Gods would be displayed in the bay window and all of their books would sit neatly in the alcoves of the lounge. The small box shaped third bedroom would be ideal as a study until the patter of tiny feet. Celia shook her head. As far as babies were concerned *if* was probably more appropriate than *until*.

Since the horrific miscarriage on her wedding day the year before, she wasn't sure if she'd ever be brave enough to try again. She remembered how helpless she'd felt realizing that her baby was slipping out of her. The awful sense that she was too weak to fight against nature and incapable of holding onto the tiny life that had formed inside of her.

Even now she couldn't pluck up the courage to ask Shango why she hadn't seen him until it was almost over. Initially she'd been in too much pain to notice how long it had taken him to get to the hospital. Angela and Martin had held her hands and wiped her brow, then when Shango finally appeared, he'd offered no comforting platitudes, no kisses of love and reassurance, no soothing embrace. Instead, his strong shoulders bowed to the weight of his anguish and tears rolled down his cheeks. He was grief stricken and Celia had hated herself as she'd watched him weep. The safe haven of her womb had turned like Judas and killed the very thing it was made to protect.

Since then they'd buried themselves in work. She wrote freelance articles on educational psychology and Shango lectured in African History at Birmingham University in the south of the City. He'd recently been discussing his plans to further his career by gaining a doctorate and eventually applying for a professorship within his faculty. Working so hard meant they didn't have to face up to the difficulties that lay between them. But, Celia reflected, perhaps now that they had a place that was big enough for personal space, yet cozy enough to be intimate, they could begin to eradicate the underlying tensions in their marriage.

Abruptly Celia decided that the tedious task of unpacking boxes could wait. She threw on her coat and drove to Marks and Spencers to get a packaged chicken meal for Shango's dinner.

•••••••

Sensi sat on the carpet outside Kai's bedroom and listened to her son's rhythmic breathing. He inhaled and exhaled deeply, smooth strokes of sweet smelling child breath that reassured her that the most precious thing in her life was safe while he slept.

Breathing in time with Kai, she closed her eyes and pictured Shango. Even after twelve months she still couldn't believe that he'd really gone ahead and married Celia and turned his back on everything they'd shared and built together before and since Kai's birth.

Sensi remembered the times when Shango had been as interested in light-hearted gossip as she was, the days when they used to hang with a crowd of like minded people, pull scams to avoid paying for things, and worry when one of their friends had been arrested and taken to the police holding cells to "cool off."

They'd wasted time window shopping and fantasizing about coming into money and buying whatever they wanted. The highlight of their week had been the Friday night dance which set the tone for a weekend of partying till the early hours and sleeping until late the next day. Sensi had truly believed she'd found her soul mate.

Then Shango had made a surprise decision to go back into education - to fill a need - he'd said. He stopped smoking their nightly spliff saying he needed a clear head for the next day's classes and he spent weekends and evenings pouring over his books. At first, Sensi had tried to show an interest in the things he was becoming so passionate about. But the black politics and conspiracy theories he spent hours discussing with his college peers meant nothing to her, and his new friends were dismissive of talk about clothes and TV soaps.

Sensi saw the changes as a rejection of her and she slyly did her best to distract Shango from his new lifestyle. When this failed she lashed out, trying to get him to see that he was leaving her behind. But Shango saw her harshness as immaturity. He encouraged her to read and even attend lectures with him, but Sensi felt out of her depth. She just wanted things back to the way they were. She didn't like change and in her opinion, ambition only led to broken dreams.

Inevitably they'd drifted apart. Sensi refused to give up the life she felt at home in and Shango held stubbornly to the new life he was embracing. His love for Kai saw him through a final loveless year with Sensi during which they argued unceasingly. Sensi accused Shango of having ideas above his station, while Shango was too far along his new path to see the hurt in Sensi's eyes. In the excitement of pursuing his goals Shango had been oblivious to the fact that Sensi felt a failure because she didn't fit into his academic world.

Now he was married to Celia who spoke to Sensi as if she was thick. Sensi wondered just what it was that Shango saw in her. Could Celia cook Caribbean style kippers and plantain for breakfast or did she just offer him dry cornflakes? And how could she know that when Shango had a headache a slow massage between his shoulder blades after a hot bath was the only thing that eased the pain? Sensi couldn't understand why Celia had to pick Shango and worse still, why he had to pick her. Apart from books she couldn't see what else they had in common.

At least she would always have Kai, Sensi reflected. He was the most beautiful, most perfect thing in her life and all he had to do to make her happy was just breathe. In and out, in and out, in and out.

Sensi looked up at the hallway clock and saw that it was nine thirty pm. Not too late to ring Shango and tell him her news. She hoped Celia didn't answer, she wasn't in the mood for her hoighty toighty ways.

● ● ● ● ● ●

Michelle curled her legs beneath her on the black leather sofa. She inhaled the mild nicotine from her cigarette and flicked on the CD. American a capella group, Sweet Honey in the Rock, filled the lounge with heartfelt singing and enveloped Michelle in their rich music. She poured a shot of vodka into a tumbler, added a dash of cola and swung the glass from side to side gently mixing the two liquids. As the women crooned their uplifting songs, Michelle drank and with each sip her melancholy faded. Soon she drifted off to sleep with her arm hung over the edge of the settee, her head thrown back, her long legs askew and her beautifully kept hair a tangled mess.

In sleep she dreamt of the life she should have had. The life where God guided her into a baby's body with a smile and a gentle nudge instead of a kick and a soulless guffaw. In her dreams she was born into a family that nurtured and encouraged her academic aspirations instead of scorning her high ideals. A cultured family that valued books, great music, fine art, good wine and all of the other things she loved, instead of one that considered West Indian Saturday soup to be the height of great culinary skills and TV Times magazine sufficient reading for the week ahead. She dreamt of a family of aspiring role models instead of a matriarchal line of lone parents all proclaiming, "*Men are only good for one thing!*"

As Michelle's fantasies rushed to their conclusion the tumbler spilled onto the laminated wood floor. Her eyelids fluttered as she dreamt of a long corridor that opened slowly. She waited eagerly knowing that on the other side stood the love of her life. Just a crack more and the light would shine brightly, exposing her true love. He would at last embrace her and life would finally be complete.

The sound of the alarm clock brutally assaulted Michelle's senses and her brain sluggishly dragged itself awake. She eyed the clock. It was nine am on Sunday morning. Michelle hated the weekends. She was convinced they were God's way of reminding her how sad and dull her life was. She'd spent Saturday night on the settee with only alcohol and a pack of twenty Bensons to keep her company; another long, lonely Sunday loomed before her.

She stretched her way to the bathroom and set the shower on hot. Afterwards as she dressed and drank a cup of coffee she decided to make a surprise call on Celia and Shango. Even though she couldn't forgive Shango for his betrayal with Sensi on his wedding day, she had no choice but to tolerate him if she wanted to be around her best friend. She'd been tempted to tell

Celia what she'd seen, but reasoned that it would do more harm than good. As far as she knew the incident had never been repeated so she'd decided to leave it alone.

Rummaging through her fridge she packed eggs, bacon rashers, mushrooms and kippers, remembering that Celia never had any food in the house. The offer of a cooked breakfast would explain her impromptu visit and interruption of their cherished Sunday morning lie-in.

As she pulled away from the kerb in her smart Volkswagen Golf, Michelle smiled wryly to herself. If she wasn't having sex this morning she didn't see why Shango and Celia should be.

• • • • • •

"I'll see you between six and seven, what are you ladies going to be discussing all afternoon anyway?" asked Shango as they pulled up outside Angela's house in Edgbaston, West Birmingham.

"Just women's stuff. Don't worry your handsome self about it. See you later, husband."

"See you later wife." Shango kissed Celia as he held open the car door for her. Turning to Michelle who'd followed them in her car he joked, "Want a kiss as well?"

"In your dreams, Renford Shango!" Michelle fired back, waving to Angela who'd come out to greet them.

"How long have you got?" Angela asked her daughter as Shango drove off.

"As long as we like. You know Shango, he's never on time," laughed Celia.

• • • • • •

Shango turned into the small cul-de-sac in Handsworth where his dad, Ira, lived. He drove all the way to the end and followed the gentle curve back down again before someone pulled out allowing him a parking space. He clicked the alarm on his BMW and tapped on Ira's door before letting himself in with a key.

"Dad, what you up to? It's me, Shango!"

"I can see that. I'm not blind or deaf," Ira greeted Shango in the small hall.

"How are you Pops? Ready for six love?"

"I'm not in the mood for dominoes today son and I can see that it's you."

21

"Is there any dinner left? I had to eat Michelle's cooking again, she's definitely got something against calories."

"I don't fancy dominoes today, man, you should play with Celia."

Shango frowned as Ira went into the living room and sat in his usual chair opposite the television, can of beer to hand. For a moment he seemed different in a way Shango couldn't put his finger on, but then he realized what it was. Ira was normally fastidious about his appearance but today he hadn't washed or shaved. Shango passed through the old-fashioned glazed glass and wooden interior doors into the adjoining kitchen diner. He was surprised to see that there were no pots on the stove filled with mouth watering cooking. Ira had been an army chef and could still rustle up a sumptuous meal. With Shango's older brother Palmer living in Atlanta and his mom, Ruby Katherine dead, their late Sunday afternoon dinners were a chance for them to spend quality time together. But unusually today, nothing had been prepared—no meat, rice, yam, or sweet potato.

Shango looked back at Ira who sat, pipe in hand, watching a western.

"You hungry dad?"

"Yes man." Ira's eyes never left the screen.

"Dinner won't be long."

Shango put frozen chicken breasts in the microwave to defrost. He turned the oven on to warm and put pots of water to boil while he washed rice and chopped sliced vegetables. Soon he was singing along to reggae classics from the small radio that was tuned to the local community radio station. Meanwhile Ira watched John Wayne.

An hour and a half later just as Shango was about to serve the dinner of roast chicken, rice and peas, yam, sweet potato and cornmeal, the doorbell rang.

"It's Preston," Ira said with half a smile.

Shango opened the door and, sure enough, a hungry looking Preston waited expectantly.

"Is dinner finished?" he blurted out.

"Dad's fine, thanks for asking, why don't you come in we're just about to eat."

Shango's sarcasm was softened with a smile. He genuinely liked Preston and found his down to earth manner endearing. Preston always said exactly what was on his mind which frequently got him into trouble. He'd known Ira from schooldays

22

back in Jamaica and since coming to England they'd shared a common bond of hardship and racism which became the seal on a long lasting relationship.

The men took their places at the table and Preston immediately bit into his chicken leg.

"Preston wait till we say grace!" Ira looked reprovingly at Preston before continuing, "Thank you Lord for this food. Bless the hands that prepared it and let it fill we up 'cos we hungry amen!"

All three men chuckled as they started their meal.

"You're a good cook son, your mother would have been proud of you. It's a shame she didn't see you become a lecturer at that University, she always said you'd do well. Ruby Katherine, now she was a real woman, you know what I mean, Preston?"

When Preston and Ira lapsed into humorous memories of women they'd known over the years, Shango grew thoughtful. Normally so sharp, his dad was oddly mistaken. Ruby Katherine had died eighteen months earlier of a stroke at only fifty-nine, but she'd attended his graduation when he received both his BA and his PGCE. Shango couldn't understand why Ira spoke as if his mom had died before all of this. Maybe Ira was coming down with something. He decided to keep a closer eye on him and schedule a check-up if necessary.

"I've got to jet, Dad, I'll call you tomorrow or the day after."

"Are you going to keep that beautiful wife of yours warm?" Preston teased.

"Don't you worry about my beautiful wife," Shango teased back. "I'm passing by Rafi's, can I give you a lift?"

"Preston's not done eating yet!" Ira laughed. "Kiss Celia for me and tell her to come to lunch next week." He waved Shango goodbye at the door.

● ● ● ● ● ●

Rafi lived alone in a terraced two-bedroom house on the southern side of Handsworth. His furnishings were an eclectic mixture of IKEA and MFI. The African Arts shop three miles away in Erdington had supplied brilliant paintings and wall hangings, which made the house warm and comfortable.

The two men touched fists. Rafi was relaxed in a faded red tracksuit, a small Afro comb jutted from the top of his head.

"Where have you been?" Rafi complained, "I told you married life was going to mash us up!"

Shango smiled. "You make it sound as though we're married to each other. Anyway, from what I hear you've got your hands full with Paula. What's up with you two these days?"

"Man, I couldn't tell you. I hear she's running with some guy or other and when I check her about it she says she's lonely because I never have time for her."

Shango nodded whilst easing himself into Rafi's comfy chair.

"Sit in my chair, drink my Red Stripe, wear my slippers, why don't you?" Rafi rolled his eyes and muttered under his breath as Shango made himself at home.

"Does Paula know how things are?"

"She knows everything she needs to know."

"Be honest with her, tell her what the deal is otherwise you might lose her."

"It's not that simple. The truth could just drive her away."

"You won't know until you try, what have you got to lose?"

"I see you've finished my beer, want another?"

"Safe. Draw up the dominoes, Dad wasn't up to his weekly game today. I have to give *somebody* six love before I pick up Celia."

"How is my darling?"

"Sweet as a nut. Is that Capelton on the system? Turn him up! I've got an idea for a group for black men!" Shango shouted above the loud toasting of the Jamaican reggae star.

"What?" Rafi shouted back.

"A group for black men!" Shango struggled to be heard above the heavy bass drums resounding from the four-foot speakers in Rafi's small lounge.

"Can't beat the Temptations."

"What?"

"The Temptations, best group ever!" Rafi hollered, his mouth full of peanuts.

"Turn that down and pay attention." Shango was becoming exasperated. "Thank you, now I can hear myself think! Not a singing group, an empowerment group. A bettering yourself organization. I'm thinking of calling it the En - Blacken Yourself Network."

Rafi looked at him blankly. "The blacken up what?"

"En - Blacken, you know as opposed to en - lighten. The En Blacken Yourself Network. A consciousness raising, empowerment, support group for black men."

"Not one of them come and find your inner joy things?"

"Behave yourself, it's going to be the best thing since the Million Man March, listen."

The day slipped from afternoon to evening and on towards night as Shango outlined his plans and ideas. At nine pm the phone rang. Shango looked around, dominoes were strewn across the table and empty beer cans lay on the floor. The television was on with the sound muted and Sanchez sang sweet ballads from the stereo. Rafi was studying the number on the portable phone display but Shango already guessed it was Celia.

"Don't answer!" he hissed just as Rafi said, "Celia darling, how are you? Long time no see...Yes he's right here, I mean, no he's just gone, actually he's been gone a long time, what he's not with you yet?" Rafi was trying to decipher Shango's frantic gesturing. The frown on Shango's face and the annoyance in Celia's tone told him he wasn't pleasing either of them. "Missus," he addressed Celia while pushing Shango out of the door, "...your man soon come, when you see him the two of you sort each other. I love you very much, come see me soon and bring that pretty Michelle. Kiss, kiss, bye-bye."

Shango smiled and bibbed his horn as he drove away. He was already thinking of ways to placate Celia and tomorrow he would start to build the En Blacken Yourself Network, he'd call it EBYN for short.

CHAPTER TWO

IS THIS THE biggest risk I've ever taken?" Shango was thinking out loud.

"For the fortieth time everything will be fine. You've planned, checked, double checked and tripled checked. Don't worry."

"Okay, yes you're right."

"Except for an act of God!"

"What!"

"I'm just kidding. You've worked really hard, now just enjoy it."

Shango rubbed his palms together for the tenth time. Celia handed him a hanky soaked in Bay Rum. He wiped his face and hands then handed it back.

"Did I tell you, you look beautiful this evening?" Shango whispered into Celia's ear.

"Only a hundred times already! She laughed back. She'd had both of their outfits handmade for the event. She wore a green and gold African suit with matching bubba while Shango turned heads in his black, green and gold African outfit.

Elijah, one of Shango's university students approached him. "Mr Shango, we're ready for you now."

"See you soon." Shango kissed Celia on her cheek.

"Knock 'em dead gorgeous," she encouraged him before taking her seat in the front row beside Michelle.

"How is he?" Michelle asked as Shango walked across the stage.

"Nervous as hell," Celia whispered.

"Ladies and gentlemen, distinguished guests, welcome to the launch of the En Blacken Yourself Network. Before I introduce you to our Founder I'd like to say a few words about the background of the organisation..." Elijah spoke clearly and confidently with a maturity that belied his youth.

As Shango rose to begin his speech, Celia moved discreetly around the hall so she could gauge the atmosphere and note the audience reaction as he spoke.

"...We expect American rappers to mind our children," Shango was saying as Celia beamed at him filled with pride. "We frown as our teenage boys wear their pants around their hips thinking they are the epitome of cool. We do nothing as our teenage girls spend their wages from their part time jobs on the latest hair-do, instead of guiding them to save for their future and that of their children. We don't question why our youth crave designer goods instead of knowledge about their history and the benefit of their forefathers' experiences. We stand silent as middle class America steals our fashions and then sells them back to us. We make no protest as their wallets grow fatter with the gains from our economy. They hide behind the darkened windows of their limousines and snigger to themselves, *'It's so easy to make money off these blacks.'*"

It was soon apparent that Shango's magic had worked again, as the crowd sat riveted throughout his address.

The network had hired hall eleven in the International Convention Center for tonight's launch. The black and gold EBYN logo adorned all the walls and swung from banners hoisted from the high ceiling. Brightly coloured balloons proclaiming the network's motto: *"En Blacken Yourself - Why Not?"* festooned the hall which throbbed with excitement and glamour as beautifully dressed guests of all races mingled.

The International Convention Center was part of the prestigious Brindley Place complex in the heart of Birmingham. Some members of the organizing committee had doubted that they'd be able to fill such a large hall but Shango and Rafi had insisted on thinking big. They'd refuted suggestions of merely holding preliminary meetings in Shango's front room and spreading the news by word of mouth. They'd argued that EBYN should start as it meant to go on, with great expectations. So far the launch had been a triumph and EBYN was on it's way.

Celia directed the photographer to the VIP table which was decorated with red, gold and green ribbons and bows, and then back to Shango who posed in front of a black backdrop with the EBYN logo in large gold lettering. Meanwhile Michelle checked the media enclosure and was pleased to see tape recorders held aloft as reporters waited for sound bites. Celia smiled as she caught the eye of the Lord Mayor of Birmingham and made a mental note to get him to pose with Shango for official photos.

After the speeches Shango smiled and shook hands with the head of Birmingham's African Caribbean Self-help Organisation; they held the pose while photographers snapped. Guided by a calm and competent Elijah, Shango moved to the next person on the list, words of congratulations ringing in his ears. Rafi, as always, was by his side.

Across the vast hall Shango saw Celia and Michelle speaking to members of the committee, but he couldn't get near them, there were more photographs to take and the after party to attend.

Shango was carried along by a wave of adrenaline. He'd never anticipated that his simple idea would be received so favourably by so many people and he was overwhelmed by the sheer amount of goodwill he'd experienced throughout the night.

After a while Shango stepped away from the photo-call and interviews in search of a cold drink. His throat was dry and his chest was tight. In the hall he discreetly took two puffs from his ventolin inhaler, hoping to offset a bout of coughing.

"Shango I really enjoyed your speech, you had the whole room in the palm of your hand." A warm voice wrapped itself around him.

"Sandra, I didn't know you were here!" A smile spread across his face as he turned to her, "What's it been, a year?"

"About that. How have you been?"

"Fine, just fine." Shango remembered that he'd last seen Sandra on his wedding day. Did she know now that he was married, he wondered?

"Tonight's been fantastic," she continued. "What's next? International links, your own political party?"

They laughed together, Shango appreciating a few minutes to relax. He realized that he was enjoying her in a way he hadn't enjoyed anyone for a while. She looked so good to him, toned and fit and gorgeous in her cream linen dress and matching jacket. At the back of his mind was a constant reminder that he'd treated her badly but even this couldn't stop the surge of longing he felt as he fought the urge to draw her close, fold her into him and just hold her.

"Sandra, we're leaving, do you still need a lift? Great speech, Shango, really inspiring."

"Thanks." Shango held in his annoyance at being interrupted by this unfamiliar woman.

"Same time next year!" Sandra joked as she followed the woman towards the exit.

Shango watched her go and suddenly felt inexplicably cold and empty inside.

"Hey, you look like somebody stole something from you!" Rafi's exuberance burst through his dark mood.

"Have you got the guest list?" Shango ignored Rafi's playfulness.

"Why?"

"Get it for me." Shango was still sombre.

"Okay." Rafi was puzzled but wisely decided to ask questions later.

●●●●●●

Held in the heart of multicultural Handsworth at Steele's nightclub and wine bar, the EBYN afterparty was open to all. The venue was a landmark in Soho Rd a mile out of Birmingham city centre, with it's huge green awning and hoisted Jamaican flag. The members of EBYN had thought it important to return to their roots and share the launch with people who would never have gone up to Brindley Place.

The owner, Tony Valentine, welcomed people personally. He stood to make several thousand pounds this evening between the door takings and the bar, but he would have done it for a lot less. EBYN espoused principles he had long believed in; black men taking responsibility for themselves, their women and their children, creating solidarity in the community and aspiring to build a sound financial base.

Like Shango, Tony recognized that organized efforts were more productive than going it alone. He relished the opportunity to lend his establishment and his name to such worthy ideals.

"Let me in!"

Tony peered through the hatch at the sound of the familiar female voice. He eyed the woman with amusement.

"Why are you making me pay? I work here for God's sake!" Sensi shouted at the new doorman who didn't know her.

"All right, let her in." Tony chuckled at Sensi's outrage.

"Ten minutes late, just ten minutes and you lock the door on me!" Sensi struggled to stay calm. "What's so funny?" she asked and that was all it took to send Tony over the edge. He collapsed laughing as Sensi gave him a dirty look.

"Calm down, have a drink on me before you get started."

Tony had a soft spot for Sensi. Despite her tough outer layer he often felt that she needed protecting, maybe from herself. He'd met her recently through a mutual friend and been impressed by her, despite her short skirts and funky painted fingernails. He'd offered her a job collecting money and issuing door tickets. Her no-nonsense approach worked well and she'd quickly developed a rapport with many of the more difficult customers. She was professional and kept her home life separate from work, another plus in her favour. This evening Tony planned to offer her the job on a more permanent basis. Her trial period was over and she'd done exceptionally well.

"You look sweet tonight, did Andrea dress you?" Sensi teased, beginning to relax as the alcohol worked its way through her veins. It was impossible for her to stay angry with Tony for long.

"Actually I dressed myself, Andrea just laid out the clothes on the bed."

"How does your poor wife have time to look after three kids and sort you out as well?"

"You can ask her later she's coming up tonight. By the way you'll need these." He handed Sensi two ticket books as she sipped Martini and lemonade. She raised her eyebrows.

"Busy night," he explained, "after party for the launch of the En Blacken Yourself Network. It's a kind of support group for…"

"–I know what it is," Sensi cut him short, her good mood vanishing. She hadn't realized that Shango would hold the after party at Steele's. She'd assumed Celia would insist on some upmarket venue in the city. Now Shango would find out what she'd been trying to tell him for weeks. She wished she'd tried harder to get him to listen to her. He'd been so busy with preparations for the launch and end of term exams, he hadn't even been spending as much time with Kai as usual. She knew he wouldn't be pleased when he saw her working there. Subdued she walked over to the booth.

Tony eased his way through the crowd pleased at the excellent feel-good vibe the DJ, Ranking Red Dread, had created as he threw himself into his work. Dressed completely in bright red-including his shoes-his whole body gyrated as he chanted over the mike. Beaming from ear to ear Ranking nodded to Tony as he cued up the next record.

Back in his vantage point in the VIP area, Tony laughed and joked with his guests. Celia and a playful Michelle had joined him. Tony noted that Michelle looked sophisticated, if a little dull, in her neat but unoriginal black trouser suit and high heels.

Outwardly he smiled and had fun, inwardly he marvelled at how far he'd come in just over two years.

He'd never actually planned to go into the nightclub business. Unable to resist its potential, he'd bought a huge empty shell on a large plot of land. He'd considered opening up a laundrette or an arts center and in the end tried running a restaurant, but that turned out to be more of a liability than an asset. Eventually, the natural choice seemed to be to run a nightclub. When he'd mentioned his new plan to Andrea she'd offered to drive him to the therapist herself. But he maintained that he'd know how to handle any problems.

The main drawback had been the long hours he'd had to put in to enable the club to thrive. All of the things he and Andrea had shared, including spending time with their three children, she'd been left to do alone. At the weekends, after being on his feet for nearly eight hours through the night, Tony often ended up sleeping for most of the following day and their kids, Natalie, Romeo and Omar had started calling him "that man."

However, the income that the club provided improved their lifestyle considerably and Andrea was able to go home to Jamaica several times a year. She also didn't have to work but was able to concentrate on her goal of becoming a magistrate. Tony and Andrea had been together for fifteen years through some very good times and some very bad times. Now it seemed their marriage was going from strength to strength.

In hindsight, Tony reflected that with all of the negatives associated with his club- the weed that people sometimes smoked openly, the constant fear of gun crime and the occasional fight- perhaps he could have done better in a different location. But at the end of the day, Tony knew that his customers were the same people he'd grown up with in Jamaica and he understood their thoughts and desires. There'd been times when he'd almost lost it all but he loved the challenge of making a success. Nights like this, when the club was full to overflowing made it all worthwhile.

• • • • • •

It took a while for Shango's eyes to adjust to the dim light inside the club. He blinked, wondering if he'd seen Sensi across the dance floor. He knew that Steele's was her kind of place.

"Got something in your eye?" Rafi asked unconcerned.

"It's so dark in here. Black people really don't like to have light shining on them."

"Especially the ugly ones!"

Shango doubled up helplessly at Rafi's comment.

"Is that Sensi?" He nodded across the densely packed room.

"Why would she be here? Have you seen Paula yet? What the hell's the matter with your eyes? I look like I'm standing next to a crazy man!" Rafi complained.

Shango, who was still blinking, gave him a brief look of disdain before replying, "Who's looking at you when I'm standing right here?"

The usual rivalry between the two men had started up again, but they were both right to be slightly vain, most women in the club had been checking them out all night, only Shango's gold wedding band made the women keep their distance.

"Take that ring off you're cramping my style," Rafi insisted.

"And have Celia kill me?"

"Paula! Precious, darling, come here. Me love you like good food!" Rafi made a beeline for the girl he'd been hoping to see all night as she sauntered past.

Alone again, Shango remembered that he'd been trying to determine whether or not Sensi was in the room. If she was here, he mused, then who was looking after Kai? Please Lord, not Hope, the grandmother from hell, he prayed silently.

Sensi's elderly mother still hadn't forgiven them for not getting married when Sensi was expecting. She'd been unable to live down the shame of her gossiping church companions and unfortunately she took out her bitterness on Kai as well. Shango decided to let his feet do the walking as he checked out what was going on.

Celia stood in the cordoned off VIP area next to Michelle who was flirting with Tony Valentine. Wound up tight from the stress of the launch she was only half tuned into their conversation. She could have done with a stiff rum and coke to help her relax, but she knew one would lead to another and she probably wouldn't stop until she'd had three or four. It was best to stick to light spritzers. She wasn't an alcoholic but some reason she could never hold her drink, it just went straight into her blood stream. Tonight was Shango's night, she determined to be strong and sober, for him.

"Finally! I thought you weren't coming!" Tony eased out of the corner that Michelle had backed him into -forcing her to remove her arm from around his shoulders- and hugged his wife.

"The kids wouldn't settle," Andrea explained, "I had to make sure they were all asleep or they would have run rings around the babysitter. How do I look, really, gorgeous or just beautiful?" She spun around giving them all a view of her long, white floaty dress with sheer matching baggy trousers and white and gold sandals. Her relaxed hair had several false pieces expertly attached creating an impression of luminous curls and tresses while her slim, dainty fingers held a matching sequined handbag.

"Darling, you look absolutely stunning. Don't worry about the kids. I'm glad you're here." Tony kissed her tenderly on each cheek, her neck and then her lips while Michelle and Celia watched silently.

Michelle felt scruffy and unkempt in her slim fitting black suit. Hot and uncomfortable she wished she'd worn less make up, she also wished that she was in Tony's arms instead of Andrea. Her face contorted with jealousy and her heart turned to stone, but she couldn't tear her eyes away from the couple. Moments later when Tony was distracted by customers, Andrea leaned in towards Michelle.

"Do you have a problem?" she whispered, a cold smile on her face

"I, I..." Michelle stuttered taken by surprise.

"You will do if you put your hands on my man again." Andrea's voice was harsh but her smile was bright. Anyone looking at them would have thought that they were having a fun girly chat.

Humiliated, Michelle wandered off onto the dance floor. Meanwhile Celia tried to remember the last time that Shango had been so tender in public. It had been on their wedding day when they'd danced to his favourite song. Looking back over the past year she realized that when they were out he hardly ever held her hand, they always seemed to end up in separate circles and Rafi commanded an awful lot of his attention. No-one watching them would think that they were still newlyweds, she conceded, her eyes still on Tony and Andrea who were laughing at some shared intimate secret.

Where was Shango now, she wondered? When was the last time she'd seen him? Why hadn't he come to look for her and why didn't he seem to need her like Tony needed Andrea? Celia felt complete when he was around but it dawned on her that Shango seemed complete without her.

She sighed. She was at a party and all she wanted to do was relax and have fun, not worry why Shango didn't seem to love her the way she thought he should. Celia licked her dry lips, torn between her conscious and her desires, she knew she couldn't really handle the strong stuff but she was tired of being the only sober person in the room. One little drink couldn't hurt, she reasoned, and it would certainly stop her melancholy thoughts. Signaling the barman she ordered a double rum and coke, downed it in one and ordered another.

CHAPTER THREE

IT WAS GETTING hot inside Steele's and people drifted outside for a breath of fresh air. The lawned area at the back offered patio chairs and tables, a place to relax and have a private moment with your partner or someone you were trying to get to know better. Conversely the people who stood outside at the front of the club in smart colourful suits aimed to see and be seen. They strolled over to parked cars chatting, smoking and enjoying the warm summer's night.

In her snug booth Sensi was hot, sweaty and dying for a cooling drink. She knew Shango must be around, although she hadn't actually seen him yet. He would have entered the club through the VIP entrance and he would stay until the end. Sensi couldn't avoid him by leaving early, she'd already spent the night's wages and Tony never paid her until the club closed. Her common sense told her there was nowhere to hide, she would have to face Shango, it was just a matter of time.

"The DJ said I must tell you, you look beautiful from you head to you foot."

"Don't you have any original lines of your own, Rafi?" Paula was bored. She leant back against the pale lilac walls and sipped her bottle of Canei, the revolving light illuminating her sweat stained face. Her hair hung limply and her lipstick, like her perfume had evaporated, she looked tired and drawn, but all Rafi saw was the rare sight of a woman whose sexual desire matched his own.

"Have you heard the one about the man who tried to cut his grass with a pair of scissors?" he tried again, adding a seductive half smile.

"Now you're insulting my intelligence." Paula turned to walk away but Rafi stopped her by grabbing her bag.

"Do you have something for me?" she asked.

Rafi was silent not knowing how to answer such a loaded question.

"I didn't think so. If you want someone to play with, Rafi, get a toy. Hey Skipper, long time no see!" Paula shouted out to a man who was passing by.

"Hey baby girl, looking sweet tonight!" Skipper put his arms around Paula's waist and drew her close. His eyes flicked lasciviously over her body.

Over his shoulder Paula flashed Rafi a dirty look. Ever since Shango and Celia's wedding she'd been waiting for him to make a move. Their passionate time in the limousine embarrassed both of them when they realized that Celia had suffered a miscarriage but Paula still felt they had the beginnings of a full relationship, even if it had begun with a wanton sexual fumble.

Rafi seethed as the burly Skipper held Paula tenderly. He was desperate to say something honest and sincere that would make her leave the big oaf in the flowery shirt and orange pants who was pawing her.

"I missed you more than I thought I would," he heard himself say. The shock of uttering something so endearing made him turn around to see if it had come from someone else, but the way Paula was staring at him, her beautiful brown eyes so intent, assured him that he had finally said the right thing at the right time.

"What did you say?" Paula asked leaving Skipper staring after her as she left his arms.

"I said every time I stand still I miss you." Rafi frowned, wondering briefly if he'd got his words mixed up but he soon realized that whatever he'd said was perfect.

Paula flung herself against him, her short yellow silky skirt rising up as Rafi lifted her off the floor. Her full breasts, wrapped only in a matching halter-top, rubbed against his chest and once again, Rafi felt the familiar stirrings in his pants that occurred whenever he was around her. He nuzzled her neck, enjoying her musky erotic smell. Soon they were the only the couple on the floor slow dancing to a raucous bashment tune.

"Are you hot?" he asked as the song ended.

"A little." Paula thought he was going to offer to buy her a drink.

"Let's go outside."

"Rafi, why is everything always about sex with you?" Paula pushed him away and tried to weave through the crowd.

"No, that's not it, listen Paula." Rafi struggled to keep her attention. He grabbed her arm just before she disappeared and pulled her wordlessly to the back entrance. Once outside he slipped his hand over hers and they kept on walking until the trees and bushes hid them. Paula looked up at him questioningly. Rafi placed a finger on her lips then kissed her. His kisses grew more demanding and soon his trousers were unbuckled and around his thighs. He ripped at Paula's g-string, her breath came in short spurts as his fingers quickly brought her to orgasm. Seriously aroused he turned her around and ran his hands over her breasts, along her hips and onto her bottom. When it was over they sank down onto the dry grass and Rafi held her close. He bit back the urge to say *"I love you"* even though he knew it was what she wanted to hear.

Shango mopped the sweat from his brow with the same handkerchief that he'd used earlier at the International Convention Center. It's spicy scent reminded him that he hadn't seen Celia for at least an hour. He spotted her in the VIP area with Tony and Andrea, she was in good company but she didn't look too happy. The double rum and coke at her elbow was not a good sign. Shango apologetically wended his way through the crowd towards her.

"Hello wife," he kissed her on the back of her neck and hugged her.

"Do I know you?" Celia responded turning around. "You look just like a man I once loved. We even got married but he kept deserting me to be with his real true love, Rafi, and in the end, I just got fed up. So, handsome, what's your name and can I take you home tonight?"

Shango laughed. Celia had been a rock for him all day and she still looked radiantly gorgeous. She was obviously a little tipsy but he supposed he only had himself to blame for that.

"Let's dance," he suggested as Ranking Red Dread threw down Beres Hammond's hit, *Rock Away*. It was a good excuse to get her away from the bar and for him to continue looking for Sensi.

"Tony!" Sensi shouted as he moved past her booth.

"Problem?" he stopped to ask.

"I'm dying of thirst, got to get a drink."

"I'll get Andrea to cover the door, don't be long."

Shango saw Sensi clearly as she pushed her way through to the bar. Freakishly painted fingernails, a knitted top that barely covered her assets, batty rider shorts and high-heeled sandals. As usual her hair was a variety of colourful add-on pieces. Shango grabbed Tony when he came near.

"Do me the honours please." He drew Tony and Celia together on the dance floor and headed for Sensi.

Celia's heart sank. Shango had left her again right in the middle of their dance, he obviously had more pressing things to do with his time than spend it with her. Picking up on her disappointment Tony spun and twirled extravagantly in time with the music encouraging Celia to do the same. He laughed, made jokes and sent himself up. His humorous mood was contagious and Celia started to enjoy herself again.

Sensi felt a hand on her shoulder. Shango stood in front of her, eyebrows raised. She closed her eyes wishing she was somewhere else.

"What?!" she snapped.

"That's a good question," Shango said quietly, forcing her to move closer in order to hear what he was saying.

"What are you doing here and where is my son?"

Sensi felt small and powerless before him. She tried to compose herself but all of her instincts were defensive. "You wouldn't return my calls. I tried to tell you. It's not my fault if that cow didn't pass on my messages."

"What are you talking about woman?! How long have you been here and where is Kai?" Shango was finding it hard to control his anger. Sensi was almost incoherent and it was too hot in the club. He leant closer, his arm firmly gripping her shoulder, determined to get answers.

"Tony offered me the job and I needed the money," Sensi mumbled.

"What job? I don't know what you're talking about."

"On the door, collecting the entry fee. Tony says I'm very good, he wants to make it permanent."

"So now you're working in a nightclub in the middle of Handsworth. Where's my son?"

"He's with his Nan."

"Hope!" Shango's voice rose, he was very angry, "Hope, who can't stand him, you left Kai with her?"

"Just for tonight." Sensi's lie came too easily.

"If you want to work in this place and wear clothes that make you look as if you're free and easy that's up to you, Sensi, but as far as Kai's concerned we're not done. Believe me I intend to deal with this properly."

"Shango I didn't want you to find out like this." Sensi hugged Shango briefly before he strode away back to Celia.

Celia was not where Shango had left her. Instead, she stood between Andrea and Tony at the bar, complaining loudly about how other women's husbands had to buy her drinks because her own was never around. Smiling gratefully at Tony and his wife, Shango pulled Celia to him with a reassuring, loving hug. She drew back but he held her tight.

Celia looked over to where Shango had come from. It was near the end of the night and the club was emptying. Across the room Celia saw Sensi glaring at her before nodding at Shango's back and winking. Celia recoiled from the message that Sensi sent, all those times during the night when she didn't know where Shango was, he'd obviously been at Sensi's side. Celia pulled away from Shango and gathered her wrap from a nearby chair.

"May I have the car keys please?" She glanced at Shango as he handed them to her, then walked towards the exit.

"I'm right behind you Celia, meet you outside in two ticks."

Take your time, Celia thought as she unlocked the door of the BMW, climbed in and drove home. Take your time.

• • • • • •

Celia didn't realise she was alone in bed until she woke up at midday. It was Saturday and fortunately she'd scheduled a day off from writing. She didn't think she'd be able to face pages of script after all the excitement of the launch. She shivered, surprised by her nakedness. Normally she'd only be naked in bed with Shango, but she didn't even know where he was. In fact, she didn't seem to know much at all about this morning.

The laminated wood floor felt chilly under her feet as she pulled on her dressing gown, padded into the bathroom and splashed cold water over her face. When her eyes were finally fully open she saw her clothes in a heap in the bath, and scratched her head trying to remember how they got there. Then she looked back at the bedroom wondering where Shango was and why everything about late last night was such a blur.

Downstairs, behind the frosted glass door that led to the lounge, Celia made out two figures sprawled across each of her settees with her crushed velvet throws over their faces. She yanked the curtains open and was met with loud protests from

Shango and Rafi as bright sunshine flooded the room.

"Rafi, what are you doing here?"

"Morning Celia, nice to see you too." Rafi yawned, sat up and rubbed his eyes in one movement. His words continued to trail out in slow motion, "It really was no problem driving all the way out here to bring your beloved home after you left him stranded in the inner city. And, I'd like some bacon, eggs and coffee please." Rafi waited for Celia's thanks until he caught the murderous flash in Shango's eyes as he looked at his wife.

"On second thoughts, I'll just help myself…anybody want some?" he finished lamely as he stretched and made his way to the kitchen at the other end of the corridor.

"What the hell were you playing at last night?" Shango began, now fully awake. His face was like thunder and his tone made Celia wary. Desperately she tried to remember exactly what had gone on but her mind drew a blank. Shango wore only his boxer shorts and his beautiful, dark smooth skin and toned muscles distracted her.

"It was nice of Rafi to…" she began softly trying to find the right thing to say.

"–to rescue my humiliated ass after you drove off and left me standing there," Shango interrupted.

"I did?"

"If that was a joke it wasn't very funny. You weren't even in any condition to drive, you were practically drunk."

"Drunk? Was I?" Celia couldn't manage long sentences.

They sat in silence, Shango fuming and Celia willing herself to remember to how they'd ended up coming home separately. Rafi entered the room with a tray of two cups of strong coffee and left swiftly. The smell of his bacon and eggs frying drifted down the corridor from the kitchen and turned Celia's stomach.

"Sensi," she said at last.

"What?" Shango's face was still dark and angry.

"You spent the night with Sensi." Celia's brain was gradually waking up.

"When?"

"Last night at Steele's. I hardly saw you because you spent most of your time with Sensi or with him." She nodded towards the kitchen. "Once again, after you'd finished with me and my services you chose to be with others. But why Sensi of all people?" Celia's tone was bitter, "Don't talk to me about feeling humiliated, you don't even know the meaning of the word."

"I spoke to Sensi for less than five minutes. I wanted to know what she'd done with my son since she'd started working as a cashier for Tony Valentine. Perhaps if you'd bothered to pass on her messages I wouldn't have had to haul her up in public like that."

"You care more about embarrassing stupid Sensi than your own wife's feelings? You left me alone nearly all night. I felt like I was some spare part that you were trying to get rid of!" Celia's voice rose as once again she experienced the painful reality that Shango didn't need her as much as she needed him.

"You're so wrong. I was apart from you because so many people wanted my time and attention. After seeing Sensi I was naturally concerned about Kai. You promised you'd stay away from the bar but instead you've made us both look stupid in front of a lot of people. I just hope your actions haven't undone all of the good work that we achieved during the launch."

"It's not all my fault! Tony works hard and yet he never leaves Andrea's side. Why do you always put everything and everyone before me, Shango? Sometimes I think I don't mean anything to you!"

"Listen to yourself, Celia! Yesterday wasn't about me showing my love for you. I did that by marrying you. Yesterday was about the start of something significant. EBYN could have a positive impact on a huge number of men and their families, that's why we have to start it right. I thought you understood that yet all I hear from you is poor me!"

Rafi hovered outside of the lounge door. Every time he'd thought it was safe to enter, Celia or Shango had started shouting, forcing him to retreat back to the kitchen. He was starting to feel ridiculous wandering up and down the hallway. He just wanted to retrieve his car keys and jacket, go home, have a bath and get some sleep. Later he might call Paula for some more of her *va va voom*. He decided to try again. He cleared his throat, opened the door and went in.

"Shango and Celia had their backs to each other leaving Rafi with no choice but to stand between them unsure of which way to face.

"I'll catch up with you later," he said awkwardly to the room in general.

"Wait, I'm coming," Shango said suddenly before sprinting up the stairs to grab some clothes and wash his face. Celia bit her lip, she was on the verge of tears.

"Excuse me, Rafi," Celia edged past him to the dining room,

Rafi followed her.

"A little time apart is probably what you both need right now," he said as Celia sat down heavily at the table. Don't stay by yourself, call Michelle. You're young, you're beautiful, have fun, go shopping, spend money! Don't worry about moody upstairs." Rafi smiled and in spite of her heartache Celia smiled back.

● ● ● ● ● ●

Lionel Richie and The Commodores drifted from the speakers in Rafi's kitchen. The soft voices of the American super group gradually became louder as Shango chopped onions, sliced tomatoes and kneaded flour. The saltfish was already soaking in the pan. If Rafi hadn't stuffed his face earlier he could be chomping on some sweet saltfish and fired dumplings, Shango mused. A few minutes later the music was so loud he thought his eardrums were about to shatter.

"What the–" Shango said out loud despite not being able to hear himself. The last time he'd seen Rafi he was on his way upstairs to take a bath. Shango went into the hallway and shouted up the narrow stairs.

"Hard ears, what's with the music?"

"What!"

"I said what's with the music!"

"Hey you shouldn't shout in my ears like that, it could be dangerous!"

Shango had found Rafi getting dressed in his bedroom. "What's dangerous is you blasting out this song like it's the end of the world or something."

"Point being?" Rafi asked innocently.

"What's going on?" Shango poked him in the chest with a floury finger.

"I was just reminiscing about you and Celia dancing to this on your wedding day, a picture of marital happiness, how it seemed nothing would ever tear you apart or make you want to spend your Saturday afternoon with me instead of her."

"Forget it Rafi. Celia almost ruined everything last night. Backfire! Me dumplings a bun up!" Shango ran down the stairs three at a time, breaking into the patios his father used whenever his cooking was under threat.

Rafi ejected the CD and put in singer Anthony B, at a lower volume. He smiled when he heard Shango singing along from downstairs. All of his speakers were wired from a central system enabling him to hear the same music throughout the house.

"Me know you love your car and your bling-bling, but put God above everything!" Shango sang as he laid the table.

●●●●●●

At seven pm Rafi looked over at his best friend. Shango was slumped on the sofa in front of the fake coal fire which was switched on despite the warm summer's evening. Rafi liked to watch the red and black colours swirl around behind the plastic shield. They'd played dominoes and backgammon, watched WWF wrestling, drunk too many Red Stripes and solved the problems of black people the world over. During the course of their conversation Shango and Celia had been married and divorced several times and Paula and Rafi were now millionaires, directing an army of valets, maids and chauffeurs while their five children attended private school. Life was certainly easy when big ideas were all you needed to live on.

"Shango will you go home now, please." Rafi realised he hadn't had a chance to call Paula.

"There's one thing I need from you first."

"Haven't you had enough? You drink all my beer, zap my remote control till it's tired, take up space, eat my food! I'm just a poor black man trying to make his way in the world!"

Shango looked hard at Rafi checking that he really had lost his mind. "The guest list that you promised me," he reminded him.

Rafi looked blank.

"From the launch!" Shango was becoming exasperated.

"Didn't I give it to you already?"

"The sooner it's in my hands, the sooner I'm a ghost like Casper."

"It's right here!" Rafi immediately dragged it out from underneath his chair.

Shango examined it carefully, while Rafi dialled a familiar number on the portable phone. Shango was so engrossed in his search that he didn't hear Rafi speaking. Halfway down the alphabetical list he spotted her name. Ms Sandra Samuels & Guest from Birmingham City Council Arts and Marketing Dept. Alongside it a contact number and an e-mail address. Perfect. The sound of a car horn interrupted his thoughts.

"Taxi for you," Rafi said.

"What are you up to tonight?" Shango queried his eyes still on the list.

"I'll go wherever the wind blows me. Hopefully straight to Paula's."

In the taxi Shango clung to his piece of paper. He'd had Sandra on his mind all day, remembering how beautiful she looked and the palpable disappointment he'd felt when she left the launch. His need to see her again was growing. He had to find out if she felt the same way.

CHAPTER FOUR

"WELCOME TO THE house of sin and temptation." Ira shook the hand of each young man who knocked at his door. It was late Sunday afternoon a week after the launch and the En Blacken Yourself Network were holding their first official meeting at Ira's.

"Welcome, welcome, come in." He continued, "This is a place of lust and debauchery!"

"Pops!" There was a stern warning in Shango's voice as he approached his dad.

"It's just fun!" Ira protested good-naturedly.

"Chat to everybody and give the guys a soft drink but no more talk like that please."

"All right, son."

"Thank you all for coming." Shango was beaming. Ira's lounge was packed. Men sat on chairs, stools, the settee, the floor, and spilled out through the doorway and into the corridor. Shango felt humbled at the show of support.

"I've tacked a suggested motto on the wall. Let's all stand as we repeat it," he suggested.

"I don't think we should be sitting down while we're saying it either," Rafi piped up. Everyone laughed, but as usual, Rafi didn't notice the irony in his words.

Shango smiled. "Let's begin."

We are Black Men. Created to fulfil a special and unique roll. We pledged from this day to honour God, our ancestors and our spiritual leaders. We promise to love our women and give unceasing support and guidance to all children of the black Diaspora. We are Black Men. Proud and privileged members of the human race.

The deep and vibrating resonance of the men's voices was very moving. They'd spoken with conviction as if the words were already familiar to them.

Shango looked around the room, Rafi's hand was up, so Shango nodded to him.

"Shouldn't it rhyme?" Rafi asked innocently and then looked around puzzled as once again all the men laughed.

An hour later the men sat drinking tea and eating rum cake. Ira was in the kitchen preparing chicken when Shango popped his head around the door.

"How you doing Pops?"

"Cooking on gas." Ira smiled.

Shango smiled back and headed toward the men. It had been a highly productive afternoon and they'd earned a break. They'd appointed people to vital posts within the organization, formally elected Shango as President and Rafi as Press Officer, decided on an official venue for regular meetings and now Ira had thrown down the challenge to all comers for a game of dominoes.

"Let's remember that EBYN had a great start," Shango addressed the room, "mainly thanks to the hard work of us all and especially Rafi and Elijah who sat with me for long hours, discussing, planning, preparing and trying to foresee any possible problems. They've done an excellent job." The men clapped their agreement. "Once you mention that you're affiliated to EBYN, your behaviour will be a reflection of all of us so strive to always walk good and act with purpose and determination. Only if you commit fully to the principles of EBYN can we grow and make a difference for our people in the Western world."

The artist Mutabaruka was pumping out conscious lyrics from the speakers when Shango realised that he hadn't seen Ira for a while. He glanced up at the landing just in time to see Ira leaving the bathroom wearing only an open dressing gown and vest.

"Where are you going dad?" Shango intercepted him near the top of the staircase.

"Shango, when did you get here?"

"Dad are you okay?" Shango was confused.

"I'm going to make some breakfast, you want some?" Ira asked.

"Dad it's evening. You've just given everybody chicken. Don't you remember?"

"Yes I cooked for all your friends here."

Shango was relieved.

"But what about your mother? You think she's hungry?"

46

Shango's heart sank. "Maybe you're tired, Dad. Come and lie down for a bit."

"I can't lie down, I've got to talk to the guests!" Ira protested.

"Dad, you've got no shorts on," Shango whispered conspiratorially in Ira's ear.

Ira checked his waist, "Better put some trousers on." He laughed as he went into his bedroom.

● ● ● ● ● ●

By eight o'clock all of the men had left. Rafi and Shango sat at Ira's small dining table. Shango flicked through the an edition of *Upfront* magazine while Rafi lit up. Shango couldn't really take the scent of the cigarettes but he remained quiet knowing that Rafi only smoked when he was stressed.

"How's things with Paula?" Shango eventually asked.

"She's lovely."

"I know that. How are you two getting on?"

"It's difficult."

"Only if you want it to be. Things can be as complicated or as easy as you make them."

"She's a bit too lightweight."

"She's not good enough for you?"

"Behave yourself!" Shango's sarcasm wasn't lost on Rafi. "That's not what I meant."

"You're just looking for excuses. You carry on like this and you'll lose her."

Rafi took another long draw, "Want me to check on Ira?" he offered.

"In a bit. When was the last time you saw Melody?"

"Yesterday."

It's a long drive from here to Chelmsley Wood but you get over there quite a lot," Shango noted.

"If I had to drive from the Midlands to Scotland to see my sister, every day I'd find a way. Her little face lights up every time she sees me. Bless her. I'm thinking of bringing her home soon."

"For real?" Shango raised his eyebrows and tilted his head, "Will you be able to cope?"

"They refer you to all kinds of meddling professionals, a support package they call it, so I won't be alone."

"Does she have fewer seizures now?"

"Some weeks are better than others."

"Paula does some kind of care work doesn't she? Maybe she

could help you out?"

"Melody's my responsibility."

"What about your job with the AA?"

I might take a break for a few weeks, so I can get Melody settled into a routine."

"It's not going to be easy, you know, man."

"I'm not looking for easy, Shango."

"When Melody comes home, you call me anytime; day or night."

Rafi nodded his appreciation.

Shango was the only person he discussed Melody with. No one else knew about his ten-year-old baby sister who lived in a home for disabled children on the north side of the city and suffered with chronic epilepsy and learning difficulties.

By the time Melody was born their father had already left them and Rafi was fifteen. A slow developer, Melody was three years old when she'd had her first fit. Rafi had heard strange noises coming from her bedroom and even now he could still remember how terrified he'd felt on seeing her body go rigid and watching her frothing at the mouth. The hospital had kept her in for two nights before releasing her with a bag of medicines and a folder of leaflets about the learning problems they thought she had. Melody had consequently spent several years in and out of children's homes and special schools.

When Melody was five, a drunk driver had turned sharply into their road just as their mother, Rema, stepped off the kerb. She was killed outright and the driver had been given a paltry two years custody and a fine.

It had broken his heart every time Melody asked when her mom was coming back and even now Rafi didn't think she understood that Rema was dead. Rafi's greatest desire was to look after Melody at home. He felt he owed that to Rema and although he rarely admitted it he missed Melody more and more every day.

"Have you noticed anything different about Dad?" Shango changed the subject.

Rafi stubbed out his cigarette into a wet plastic cup and stood up. He stretched before sticking his hands into his jeans pockets and pausing to think about Shango's question.

"How do you mean?" he countered leaning back against the counter top.

"A few weeks ago, I came for Sunday lunch, an institution in this house, but nothing was prepared."

"Maybe he was tired, it's okay to have a day off every once in a while."

Rafi's comment was reasonable but Shango was still perturbed. He rapped his fingers on the table and frowned.

"What else have you noticed?" Rafi guessed there was more on Shango's mind.

"He kept talking about mom as if she died years ago, but it's only been eighteen months."

"Maybe your Dad's still grieving?"

"Could be, but two hours ago he was talking about cooking breakfast and it was almost like he didn't understand why the guys were here, even though he welcomed them into the house."

"This is a place of sin and debauchery!" Rafi mimicked Ira's voice and both men laughed.

"Seriously though," Shango continued, "something doesn't feel right."

"Talk to Celia when you get home, she might be able to give you a fresh perspective on things."

"You're right. I'll call her in a bit and get her to pick me up."

"Will Ira be all right when he wakes up alone?"

"Preston normally shows up about now for his supper."

"Does Preston do anything else except eat?"

Rafi and Shango moved between the lounge and the kitchen, automatically clearing away plates, cups and scraps of paper as they spoke.

"How come Celia always has control of that slick BMW driving machine? For someone who works from home she gets out a lot."

"Saves me from having to buy her her own motor, keeps the peace and besides she looks good in it."

"Can't argue with that," agreed Rafi. He tossed the sponge to Shango, "you wash, I'll dry."

"Only if it's Fairy Liquid." Shango held the washing up bottle to his cheek, "It's so much softer on my hands." He laughed.

CHAPTER FIVE

LYNDON PAID MORE attention to that damned slinky that he did to me!"

"What's a slinky?" Celia looked up from a pile of reference books.

"A coiled metal thing that goes downstairs." Michelle gestured with her hands," he said it was his favourite childhood toy."

"It just went downstairs?"

"Yeah."

"Did it come back up?"

"I don't think so."

"Oh." Celia looked back at her books none the wiser.

"Mrs Woman!" Michelle threw a pink fluffy slipper which lightly hit Celia's head.

"Ow, what?"

"You're as bad as him, am I talking to myself here?"

"Yes, I'm working but you just twitter away in the background."

"Bitch." Michelle smiled.

"Bigger bitch," countered Celia.

Poised elegantly on the small brown leather settee that stretched along one wall of Celia's study, Michelle examined her long fingernails. They were immaculate as always.

"There's a mirror in the bathroom," Celia murmured engrossed in cross -referencing her notes.

"I was checking my nail polish, not my reflection," retorted Michelle.

"Makes a change."

"Where's that other slipper?" Michelle laughed. Unable to keep quiet she asked, "Are you comfortable in those dungarees?"

"If I wasn't comfortable I wouldn't be wearing them."

Celia's mind was only half on the conversation. It was Monday evening and Michelle was bored and lonely. As always Celia had a tight deadline to meet but she didn't have the heart to turn Michelle away when she'd arrived unexpectedly that evening.

"Whenever I wear dungarees I always end up looking like I'm about thirteen."

"That should make you happy," Celia slurred with a pen sticking out of her mouth. She picked up a thick book and began to thumb through it.

Michelle ignored her sarcasm. "Last time I tried on a pair I lost my bust and all of my bum."

"Hm, hmm," said Celia scribbling on her notepad.

"That yellow colour looks nice on you, although the way you're sprawled across the floor makes you look like a big fat elephant about to give birth."

Celia didn't respond, so Michelle continued, "This is a lovely mahogany desk, think I'll just throw myself across it and make mad passionate love to your husband, would you mind filming us?"

"Yeah, that's okay."

"You don't even know what you're agreeing to, do you?" Michelle poked Celia's shoulder.

Celia looked up at her as if she'd only just realized she was there. Michelle was smiling at her. "I'm sorry love, I got engrossed in all of this information. I'll take a break and you can tell me all about luscious Lyndon," Celia conceded.

"We left him behind ages ago, but you should stop for a bit, you've been at it for hours."

"You're right." Celia stretched, "Hungry? Don't look at me like that I'm not completely hopeless in the kitchen! Well all right, maybe I am!"

"What are you and Shango up to tonight?" Michelle asked as she watched Celia tidying away her books and papers.

"Nothing. The EBYN executive committee is meeting in preparation for a couple of radio interviews tomorrow. They've got their knickers in a twist at the thought of nationwide exposure."

"Where are they meeting?"

"One of the university staff rooms."

"All evening?"

"More or less."

"So we're free to go on the razzle?"

"On the *razzle*?"

"Yeah, there's a new arts club for singers, writer's, poets, you probably know some of the performers. It's opposite the cinema

ONCE UPON A LIE

on Broad St. We could pop up there for a bit and then get something to eat after."

"Sounds good."

"Just promise me one thing," Michelle was serious.

"What?"

"Don't wear those dungarees."

"You just want them for yourself!"

An hour later they were cruising down Broad St slowly enough to see and be seen. At one end of the long road was the International Convention Center where EBYN's launch had taken place. Further down, glitzy nightclubs sat next to cozy restaurants, which nestled in between brasseries and fast food joints. The traffic was limited to one lane only in both directions forcing buses and black cabs to compete with private cars for road space. Porsches rolled smoothly in front of shiny convertibles and just-washed jeeps hogged the road from "babe magnet" sports cars. Scantily clad girls and guys spilled out of the clubs and milled around deciding where to go next. In the middle of all of this Michelle drove and Celia posed.

"Good job you cleaned your car." Celia nodded her head to the beat of Jaheim's *Just in Case*, feeling extra cool in her Ray-Bans.

"Tell me about it, dust stands out on this like white on rice. Remind me not to get a black car again."

The two beautiful black girls - Michelle with coiffed hair and elegant light green silk shirt, Celia with her short afro, gorgeous complexion and charmingly pretty face - fitted right in with the carnival atmosphere of summer on Broad St.

Michelle pressed a switch and the car roof unfolded automatically enabling them to make the most of their surroundings. The road was so busy that pedestrians were often close enough to touch them. Caught up in the festival-like ambience Celia extended her hand.

"Hey, old married woman, put your hand back in before we get arrested!" Michelle was shocked.

"Arrested for what, having fun?" Celia laughed.

"No, for trying to touch that guy's bottom!"

"I didn't hear him complaining!"

•••••

"I'm sorry I can't let you in, we're full." The lady at the entrance to the arts club was apologetic but firm.

"Do you know who this is?" Michelle gestured at Celia who was peering over the woman's shoulder trying to see in inside.

"No." The woman glanced at Celia.

"This lady," Michelle was determined to make a stand, "is one of Birmingham's foremost writers. Nearly every week she has an article in one of the broadsheet newspapers."

"Really?" the woman was intrigued as were the people behind them. "What's your name?" she asked turning toward Celia.

"It's okay, I can see that you're full," Celia wasn't that bothered. "We should have come earlier."

"This is Mrs Celia Shango. A journalistic expert on education and black youth," Michelle interjected. The people behind looked away disappointed that Celia wasn't a famous singer.

"Your name sounds familiar but I still can't let you in."

"Who's in charge here?" Michelle was becoming more ardent.

"Let's go." Celia grabbed Michelle's arm and pulled her away, "Thank you very much." It was a placatory offer to the woman who looked pleased to see Michelle leaving.

"They had some really good names on the programme. We could have got in if you'd just given me a chance!" Michelle protested as they pushed through the crowds towards their car.

"Woman, I can't take you anywhere!" Celia replied.

Michelle drew her breath ready to give Celia a piece of her mind but stopped at Celia's laughter. "I think that woman was afraid of me," she said now laughing herself.

"So was I!" said Celia.

"Want to see a film?" Michelle asked as they joined the slow flow of traffic on Broad Street.

"It's too nice to stay inside."

"Food then?"

"Sounds good to me."

The waiting area in Xaymaca Caribbean restaurant on Bristol Rd, a five-minute drive away, was overflowing. When Michelle and Celia were told of the hour wait to be seated, they decided to call it a night and spin over to Slaughter's takeaway in Hockley for some food to go.

●●●●●●

"Are you telling me that you two dressed up to the nines, drove practically all around Birmingham. stayed out for three hours, spent God knows how much on petrol and all you have to show for it are these dry chicken feet?" Shango had Michelle and Celia in stitches as he summed up the evening. They were eating their takeaway food at the kitchen table.

"More or less, not forgetting they wouldn't let us in the arts club even though the lady said she knew Celia," Michelle added.

"She definitely knew me after you threatened to thump her!" Celia wiped tears of laughter.

"Sounds like fun." Shango cleared away their plates and cans of ginger beer.

"Speaking of fun, I've got work in the morning so I'd better be going." As Michelle spoke suddenly all of the house lights went out.

"What's that?" Michelle asked squinting in the blackness.

"*That* is the third time this week. *Now* can we get some work done on the wiring?" Celia asked as she edged past Shango to the hall table in search of a torch.

"I'll get Roger to come tomorrow and have a look at the circuits."

"Roger!" the women spoke simultaneously.

"What's wrong with Roger?" Shango was bewildered, Celia shone the torch on his face illuminating it from the side.

"Didn't you get Roger to look around *before* we moved in?" she reminded him.

"Exactly, he's the best person to sort it out."

Michelle and Celia groaned. Roger's claims to have been a carpenter, an electrician, a top chef and a carpet layer back in Jamaica were legendary.

"Rather you than me babe," Michelle whispered as she hugged Celia goodbye.

"See what happens when I leave you alone for too long? That woman gets you into all kinds of mischief," Shango chuckled as he fiddled with the fuse box in the cupboard under the stairs, "Shine the light here for me."

Celia aimed the torch on his hands. "We had fun," she agreed. "It was good to take a break from the books and I think Michelle just wanted some company."

"That's better," Shango said as the lights came back on.

Back in the kitchen Shango ran soapy water into the sink. Celia hugged him from behind as he washed up their cutlery, glasses and plates. Her fingers gently squeezed his nipples and smoothed the hair on his chest.

He oozed a faint odour of fresh sweat which emphasized his masculinity and which Celia found extremely erotic.

"Do we have to use Roger?" she murmured, sniffing and gently kissing the back of his neck.

"You'll be here to keep an eye on him."

"Oh joy. How did the planning meeting go?"

"Splendid." Shango was enjoying the feel of her breasts rubbing against his back. Every time she pulled at his nipples he became more aroused. "We're all set," he continued. "Radio Five Live at one pm. We think they're going to be fairly antagonistic so we're intending to counter it with a positive, calm approach, and then Premier FM at three pm."

"I hope they get the best out of you." Celia's tone was languorous, her mind only half on Shango's replies. With a little moan she tugged harder at his taut nipples and bit him gently several times on his firm back muscles. One of her hands strayed towards his belt and fiddled with the buckle.

"Sting FM?" Shango was also finding it hard to concentrate.

"Their emphasis is usually on sex, I mean, music, isn't it?" Celia felt her own nipples hardening.

"We've given them a line of...questioning....that should help...." Shango's body melted into a blissful state at Celia's touch and his breath came in short spurts.

"So you're all covered then?" Celia's voice was a whisper. Shango turned around so they were face to face.

"I believe we're covered here," his voice was low and sensuous as he lifted her light summer top, unclipped her bra and kissed one breast, "and we're covered here," he kissed and caressed the other breast, teasing the nipple, "and we're covered here..." he slid his hand between her thighs and kissed her full on the mouth. "Let's go upstairs."

● ● ● ● ● ●

It was six thirty am and already light outside. Celia slept peacefully while Shango logged on to MSN Hotmail.

> *Hi Sandra,*
> *It was good to see you again at the EBYN launch. Seeing as you're a media expert (!)*
> *Your support would be a great help with our radio interviews.*
> *Can you meet me at*

Pebble Mill Studios today at one pm? Here's my mobile number,
any problems, just
call.
Shango.

Shango deleted and re-wrote the message several times before finally clicking the "send" key. All the while he was listening out in case Celia woke up or came into their study and took him by surprise. Now that he'd sent the message he wasn't sure what to do. He couldn't stay logged on all morning but he was desperate to read Sandra's reply.

Shango really couldn't work out why Sandra affected him so deeply. Maybe they were lovers in a former life, but whatever the reason, seeing her again had awakened strong feelings he'd thought had died a long time ago. They hadn't touched at the wedding or the launch but he instinctively knew how it would feel to hold her again, to breathe in her scent and become one with her. He knew it would be like finding a part of himself that he'd long forgotten existed.

His hands behind his head, his feet up on the desk, Shango leant back and admired the view from the first floor window. He wore only boxer shorts and enjoyed the feel of the rays of the sun on his stomach, arms and chest. It promised to be another beautifully warm day.

Their spare bedroom, situated at the front of the house, was Celia's office and she'd decorated it well using soft yellows and muted beiges with accents of bright blue. She'd rearranged the furniture several times until she had an exterior view whether she sat at her desk or her computer. Celia also liked the fact that their house was only three years old and they were only the second occupants. Their neighbours were young couples with babies and small children, who'd initially been wary of the first black couple to move in amongst them.

Up the hill to the right was a cul-de- sac of bungalows inhabited by Senior Citizens, some of whom followed an early morning ritual of walking their dogs. Shango thought many of them looked suspiciously like their owners. He was always polite when they met but he noticed their gaze always strayed to his dreadlocks. To them, a black man with locks probably equalled trouble. He took comfort in the knowledge that come autumn, the same people who attached derogatory labels to him because of his hairstyle and skin colour, would be witness to him leaving the house every morning smartly dressed and weighed down with books and papers, as he endeavoured to influence intelligent, enquiring minds at one of the best universities in the country.

He didn't think it would be long before his neighbours realized that neither he nor Celia conformed to common stereotypes of how black people lived. Shango was independent in both ideas and action but what other people thought was his Achilles heel. Consequently, he strived to be seen as a capable and caring, hard working black man with integrity.

Shango glanced up at the clock to confirm his own estimation of the time. It was now nearly seven am and he was enjoying his solo early morning reflections which gave him a chance to get a clear perspective on the day ahead.

Once again his gaze drifted to the street. Unlike his old neighbourhood near Handsworth, this road was very quiet. People hardly drove down here unless they were coming to see a resident. That was another reason why Celia loved the house so much. She had plenty of peace to concentrate on her work. There was never any loud music or arguing couples or racing cars. Just like an advert on the TV, it was suburbia at it's best.

Shango compared this with the sheer "blackness" of where he used to live. There, a two-minute walk had taken him to black churches and black grocer's shops. A five-minute stroll had led to businesses run by the Khans, or the Singhs, whose sons he'd gone to school with. Ten minutes down the road and he'd have arrived at a community centre where the staff called him by name and let him have two hours of table tennis for the same price as half an hour. It had been impossible for him to drive around his old neighbourhood at any time of the day or night without hearing shouts of "hey big man!" All together it had formed a multiracial community that held on tightly to it's own, regardless of colour or belief. Now that Shango was on the outside he realized just how badly he missed its invisible, yet tangible, familiarity.

Here, on the north side of Erdington, a two-minute walk led to more houses, green park land and the local Spar, which was franchised by an impersonal white guy who never spoke to his customers. There were more private gyms in the area than council-run gyms and none of them offered basketball, table tennis or domino clubs for Caribbean Senior Citizens. The local Tesco sold Nutrament but Shango still had to travel inner city to get his Jamaican bun, hard dough bread and patties. That was the main difference with living in Erdington he noted, having to drive to get to all of the places he used to walk to. Like the barbers, or the black owned nightclubs on Soho Hill.

Of course none of this was life threatening but Shango wondered whether he'd ever get used to no longer being around his own people.

"You're up early." Celia stood in the doorway smiling at her husband.

Shango had been so engrossed in his own thoughts he hadn't even heard her get up. He smiled as he held out his arms to her and she moved into his embrace.

She looked beautiful; even first thing in the morning she was immaculate. She wore a satin pale-blue robe over a matching short nightdress and bare feet. She pulled off the scarf that kept her hair in place while she slept knowing Shango preferred her without it. She sat on his lap now and kissed him on the lips. Her breath smelt of Colgate toothpaste. Her clear, brown eyes and lucid complexion showed she'd enjoyed a good night's sleep. Shango snuggled close, enjoying her warmth.

"You were talking in your sleep again," he teased.

"Was I?" Celia laughed, embarrassed. "What did I say?"

"I don't know, I think it was in Greek as usual!"

"Why didn't you wake me up?" Celia slapped him playfully on the back of his head.

"I was waiting in case you mentioned a man's name!"

They both laughed and Shango ducked as Celia went to slap him again.

"What are you doing in here so early?" she asked following Shango's gaze to the window.

"I was wondering what it would be like if all of the houses around us were filled with black couples and families."

"It would be like the place we've just left." Celia's tone was serious.

"You mean we'd be surrounded by people who look like us and live like us?" Shango wanted to find out if Celia missed it as much as he did.

"I mean we'd have rubbish bags piling onto the street three days before collection. We'd have music blasting out of houses and cars at all times of the day and night. We'd have police raids on our next door neighbours and we'd have everybody chatting our business. Just because it's in the past doesn't mean it was all roses, Shango. We moved out here because we wanted something better to wake up to each day." Celia left Shango's lap and made herself comfortable on the settee, legs curled beneath her. "Aren't you happy here?"

"I think I will be. It's early days yet. I've spent my whole life in the inner city. This just takes a bit of adjustment that's all."

"You're a university lecturer Shango. The people you lived around only got out of bed to sign on or go clubbing. You couldn't stay in that environment and progress, you know that."

"But I went to school with them. I know their families and their children. They're my people, still a part of me."

"Of course they are. Your own parents left their family and friends in paradise to make a better way in this country, but that doesn't mean they ever forgot them or thought any less of them."

"You're right, darling."

"This is the best place for us right now, Shango. We gave a lot of thought to this move. Remember it's just one step in our future plans."

"Do you really like it here, Celia? When I start teaching again in the autumn you'll be in the house alone for hours, will you be okay?"

"When I'm writing, interviewing and doing research, three hours can seem like twenty minutes. I love working from home and I really like this neighbourhood."

"Good. I was thinking how nicely you'd decorated the study. It's comfortable but business-like at the same time."

"Don't get me started on decorating. Now that the launch is out of the way can we please make a start on some of the jobs around the house we said we'd get sorted?"

"No problem, tell me what you want done, I'll snap my fingers and Roger will take care of it."

"Not Roger again! Can he wallpaper?"

"He said he's done it before."

"Can he paint?"

"He says he can."

"Neatly?" Celia checked.

Shango rolled his eyes.

"Can he install light fittings?"

"Yes."

"Without blowing us up? Stop laughing, Shango, I'm serious."

"Don't worry! Everything is everything!" Shango was still laughing at the exasperated look on Celia's face.

"What about the leaky shower?"

"Roger said..."

"I know, I know, he's done it all before," Celia finished for him as she left the room to the sounds of his chuckling.

"Cup of tea?" she called over her shoulder as she went downstairs.

"Just juice, babe!" Shango called back.

He smiled as he made his way to the bathroom. Celia was definitely a one-off original and he knew that she'd always be there for him. But this morning he had another woman on his mind. He admitted to himself that since he'd seen Sandra at his wedding a year ago she'd been a constant figure in his thoughts. Seeing her at the launch had reinforced feelings that were already there. He half hoped that today would be the catalyst he needed to disprove his feelings for her so he could return to loving Celia honestly and whole-heartedly. By the end of the day he'd know how he felt for sure, assuming she came to the afternoon interviews.

Shango stood naked under the invigorating shower spray, which went from cold to hot, worrying in case his plans fell apart. What if Sandra didn't log on in time to read her e-mail? What if she was already tied up all day? What if she really didn't want to see him again? As Shango rinsed away the soap from his lean body he also rinsed away that last thought. His urge to kiss and caress her had been so strong he was sure she'd felt it too. Asking her to meet him on neutral grounds where they had to concentrate on something other than each other had to be the best way.

He was sure she'd come and mentally hold his hand because he'd asked nicely and because she was supportive of the network. They'd spend a couple of hours in a non-threatening environment and he'd go home happy, having finally had a chance to scratch his itch.

CHAPTER SIX

TEMPTATION. SHANGO SAW her as he locked his car in the small front car park. Sandra was waiting at the entrance to Pebble Mill radio and television studios. She looked good enough to eat.

Let her long relaxed hair fall loosely around her shoulders, Shango mused as he looked at her through half closed eyes. Lather her slowly all over with Olive Oil, place strawberries on each of her breasts and a mango in between her legs, drizzle with fresh cream and bite into it all. Sweet, holy temptation.

"Hi Shango, I got your message. It was a bit of a surprise." Sandra tiptoed to kiss him on the cheek. She smelt of velvet and satin. As she pulled away Shango caught a glimpse of her lacy bra where her white cotton blouse was unbuttoned. He let his gaze wander down, past her open lined chiffon skirt, to her slender legs and dainty clad feet in open toed sandals.

His mouth opened of it's own accord, "I like your shoes," he heard himself say stupidly.

"What?" Sandra was confused.

"Open toes, my favourite."

"Oh!" Sandra's laugh was a beautiful rippling sound. Shango admired her even white teeth. When she threw her head back he marveled that she hadn't got any fillings.

"I can see you've never had a sweet tooth." Shango was aware that he was still talking nonsense but he no longer cared. The drive to the radio station had been a torturous nightmare. He'd planned alternative scenarios in case Sandra did or didn't show. Now he realized that he couldn't remember either of his contingency plans.

"I can see why you needed my help today." Sandra was mystified by Shango's odd behaviour. He, meanwhile, was grinning like an idiot and unable to take his eyes off her. He couldn't believe that she was actually here! Angels were singing on high, the sun would shine forever more, Sandra had come to see him!

The beep from his mobile phone made him jump. With an

apologetic smile at Sandra he retrieved it from his waistband and checked the text. It was Rafi.

Caught in traffic, might not make it, will do my best, it read.

Shango beamed again, now he'd have Sandra all to himself, the day was turning out to be perfect.

"Ready?" he turned to her and asked.

"Sure," she replied.

••••••

"But why exactly do we need to En Blacken Ourselves? We've already got Black History Month, what more do you want?"

Sandra discreetly touched Shango's arm prompting him not to rush in with a rash answer. As expected, Radio Five Live were giving him a hard time. The presenter was at best antagonistic and at worst plain rude. Shango sipped his water and adjusted his headphones. He was hot and uncomfortable but he was determined not to let the presenter make a fool of him and his ideals.

"We live in a hemisphere which encourages the glorification of everything white and European often to the detriment of everything that isn't. Why not En Blacken Ourselves and add a bit of colour to a Western monochrome? Furthermore EBYN is not about a few weeks of retrospective contemplation of black history from a white perspective, EBYN is a dynamic, progressive, forward thinking, movement."

"But what good would it do me and my family and ninety-nine percent of our listeners?" The presenter refused to back off. "If it's no good to the wider community why should we encourage separatist ideals?"

"As I've mentioned previously, the network wasn't set up to change the lives of all men in the world. The network is there to facilitate a better way of life for black men and their families. However, for you to En Blacken yourself would still be a good thing because broadening your mind and seeing life from another perspective will help you develop and grow as a person. That's why men become explorers and travellers."

"I believe I'm developed enough. I've had a solid education. Why do I need to learn about black people? I live and work among them just as you live and work among white people. Do you need to En Lighten or En Whiten yourself, Mr Shango?"

Sandra and Shango exchanged glances. Their time was almost up and the presenter had been intent on making the discussion a racial one. Shango knew he only had a few minutes to put across the reason behind EBYN.

"I feel we're digressing a little," he began. All the way through the interview he'd kept his voice calm and an even smile on his face. Privately, he wanted to give the presenter a good thump.

"EBYN is not here to force anyone into a particular pattern of behaviour. It's simply a way of enabling African and Caribbean communities to progress under the leadership of the men in the families, thereby building a strong familial unit. Any sociologist will tell you that the family, in whatever form, is the base of society. Create stable families and you contribute to a stable income and a solid foundation for children and society as a whole."

"But–," the presenter interrupted.

"*If*," Shango spoke over him, "*if* you would like to know more about the aims and objectives of the network and how you, or your group, church, or organisation can become affiliated our website address is www......"

●●●●●●

"You socked it to him didn't you?" Sandra commented as they made their way to the front of the building.

"I wanted to sock him right between his eyes."

"He just kept going on about race and black and white. I was beginning to wonder why he'd invited you on. He was having a one way discussion with himself! I liked the way you kept your cool though."

"Really?" Shango was pleased at the unexpected compliment.

"Yeah, he was trying so hard to wind you up but you were ready for him."

"Where are you parked?" Shango asked as they stepped out into the afternoon heat.

"I took a taxi over from work, "Sandra replied. "Speaking of work I'd better call in; excuse me." She walked on a few feet ahead of him, her mobile phone already in her hand.

Shango looked around. They stood in the impeccable grounds of the Pebble Mill TV and Radio studio complex. On their left a crew was shooting the afternoon soap *Doctors*. Shango focused on the actors rehearsing, to mask his disappointment at the thought of Sandra leaving.

"All sorted."

ONCE UPON A LIE

"Do you have to go?" Shango hoped he wasn't whining.

"No, everything's clear so I've taken the rest of the afternoon off. Unless of course you don't need me for the next interview?"

Shango's heart did a little tap dance and angels serenaded them once again. *Need her? He never wanted to let her go!*

"We've got about an hour before we're due at Premier FM. Would you like an ice cream?" he asked.

They sauntered across the main road to Cannon Hill Park. Although situated in the heart of the city, it had a nature reserve with wild animals and activities for children. Amid its acres of rolling green grass stood the Midlands Arts Centre known affectionately in the area as *MAC*. It screened films, held exhibitions and hosted live music concerts. The couple walked by the huge lake which was being prepared for a forthcoming evening of fireworks and classical music. Shango bit his tongue so that he wouldn't ask Sandra on a date. He was trying desperately not to appear too eager. Cheeky Canadian geese left the water and followed them.

"I've got some old crackers in my bag."

"What are you doing with old crackers in your bag?"

The confused look on Shango's face made Sandra giggle. "Don't ask." She handed Shango four crackers wrapped in a plastic lunch bag.

"Not paying you much at the City Council are they?" he sympathised, prompting another burst of laughter from Sandra. Immediately one of the geese waddled up and snatched the biscuits right out of his hand. Triumphant, it waded back into the water with its meal, closely followed by its mate.

"Back foot!" Shango exclaimed. "Don't laugh, that could have been my finger!"

They strolled around for twenty minutes before it was time to drive over to Premier FM community radio station. Throughout their time at the park Shango marvelled at how peaceful he felt with this woman. Being with her was effortless. They didn't have to play mind games or watch their words. Their conversation, like the summer breeze, was light and easy. Sandra laughed often and Shango loved the way she fitted under his skin and into his space so comfortably. She seemed happy to talk about EBYN which suited him fine. He hadn't forgotten that they had history but he also didn't want to be reminded of how badly he'd treated her all those years ago.

As they walked through the miniature Welsh town that was

made up of houses no higher than their shins he fought back to the urge to ask her if she was seeing someone, not sure what he'd do if she said yes. As she laughed at another one of his jokes he found himself wishing with all his heart that he could be the special man in her life. He knew instinctively that he was heading for trouble but on this afternoon he didn't care. The hot summer's day was a backdrop to him falling in love with her all over again. He'd hopped willingly onto the roller coaster and now he was on for the duration.

• • • • • •

"Mobile phone switched off?" the producer reminded them as they entered the studio at Premier FM. Sandra nodded. Shango didn't even need to check. He'd purposely left his off in case Celia called while he was with Sandra; he reasoned that she could always leave him a message.

Chicken George was a veteran of Community radio and had gained a solid reputation as a presenter throughout the West Midlands. He guided Shango expertly through a half-hour interview that aimed to uncover the reasons behind the network and their future plans. Shango soaked up the opportunity to put a positive slant on his creation and enjoyed the following phone-in that allowed listeners to question him further.

• • • • • •

The sun had faded when Shango pulled up outside of Sandra's flat. She lived on the ground floor of a purpose built three-storey block in Moseley. It was three miles away from the city centre and just off Alcester Road, a busy commuter route that served the affluent south area of the city. Shango checked his watch, it was almost six. The five hours he'd spent in the company of this woman had passed like careless, wasted minutes.

"Time flies when you're having fun," Sandra said quietly.

"Yes indeed," was all Shango could manage above the sinking feeling in the pit of his stomach. It was finally time to say good bye and he was too disheartened to concoct any more excuses to hang around her.

"Drink?" she offered in little more than a whisper.

"Yeah, me too, take care then," Shango started up the engine and put the car into gear. He could hardly bear to look at Sandra, sure his misery at parting would show plainly on his face.

"Shango?" Sandra touched his arm. "I said would you like to come in for a drink?"

There it was again. Straight out of _Handel's Messiah_. A mighty chorus of angels singing "_Hallelujah!_"

Shango's depression vanished as he leapt out of the car and rushed to open Sandra's door for her.

"Make yourself at home. I'm just going to freshen up. The sun's lovely but it makes me feel a bit sticky. Would you like some juice, tea or something stronger?"

I want you, Shango thought, while out loud he said, "Grapefruit juice would be fine if you've got any."

"Some things haven't changed then," Sandra said.

Shango was taken by surprise. That was the first time she'd alluded to their past. They'd always joked about having to buy grapefruit juice just for him when all of their friends and family were happy with "normal" drinks like pineapple or tropical.

Sandra handed him a cool, iced drink and then went to get changed. Shango heard the sound of running water, which he guessed was coming from the bathroom. He fought the urge to go and see what she was doing, busying himself by looking through her coffee-table books. They were mainly pictures of black models. Looking around the walls of Sandra's twelve-foot lounge Shango noticed that the prints on her walls were originals.

"Do you like them?" Sandra had come back into the room. Her hair was pulled back into a pony tail and she wore a multi-coloured cotton sarong and white crocheted top. She wore barely any make up except for a little lip-gloss. In Shango's eyes she looked exquisite.

"They're brilliant, where did you get them from?"

"I took them myself!" Sandra announced proudly.

Shango stepped closer to the framed prints. They were pictures of beautiful children, loving couples, families and some lone adults. One picture stood out. It was a woman who bore a striking resemblance to Sandra. She looked at the camera over her shoulder. Her long hair had been dyed a dark blonde colour which matched beautifully with the sepia tones the photo was printed in.

"Is this you?" Shango was confused.

"It's my mom!" Sandra was delighted by the amazed look on Shango's face.

"But she looks so…"

"Young, vital, alive?" Sandra offered. "We got good genes in our family babe."

"I remember." Shango mused, struck by the picture in which Sandra's mom, Benita, looked at least ten years younger than her age. "How *is* Benita?"

"Fine, still cursing you."

"Cursing me!" Once again Shango was thrown off guard. "I thought she loved me, you all did!"

Sandra stood with her back to Shango looking out of her window to the park across the road.

"She loved you, my sisters loved you and my dad loved you," she said in almost a whisper. "We all loved you until you broke my heart."

"Sandra, I…" Shango knew his words were inadequate.

"Doesn't matter, it's in the past. We've both moved on."

"Sandra we don't have to avoid the past."

"Yes, we do," her tone was resolute. "Are you hungry?" Sandra threw another surprise straight at him.

"Are you inviting me for dinner?" Shango raised his eyebrows, even though she still had her back to him.

"I guess you need feeding after what you went through today." Sandra smiled as she approached him easily and gracefully; automatically all of his defences melted.

"Want a hand?" He bit his bottom lip as he followed her through to the kitchen.

"Do you know how to make zabaglione?" Sandra teased.

"Oh yeah, I cook it all the time!"

"Can you show me then?" Once again Sandra was laughing and once again the sound was music to Shango's ears.

"Thank you for your guidance at the studios and thank you for the crackers to feed the ducks, even though I nearly lost my finger, and thank you for a wonderful zabaglione." Shango punctuated each 'thank you' with alternate kisses on Sandra's cheeks. His touch made her smile.

"I'm glad you asked me to come along today," she leaned back against the doorway, and looked up at him.

They stood silently in her small hallway, delaying their goodbye. Shango could think of nothing more to say. Being so close to this woman made him feel like he was thinking underwater, or wading through thick mud. He was aware of her loveliness and her delicate femininity, but all speech had left his lips long ago.

"You're only leaving because you know I'll kick your ass at Scrabble," Sandra finally said.

"Is that a challenge?" Shango responded within the same moment.

"Might be!"

"Set it up!"

Sandra shut the window blinds and switched on the side lamps giving the room a cozy feel even thought it wasn't quite dark outside. She sat on the thickly carpeted floor a few feet away from Shango, the Scrabble board and score sheets between them. Sanchez sang quietly in the background.

"That's not a word!" she pointed to *Xiphoid* which Shango had placed on a triple word square. In conjunction with the adjoining word this would give him a score of sixty-five, putting him well ahead in the game.

"Look it up!" Shango's tone was triumphant.

"Xiphoid..." Sandra read aloud from the dictionary, "Sword shaped. How did you know that?"

"I'm not just a pretty face." Shango grinned.

"Game over, I'll let you have that one," Sandra conceded.

"Like you had a choice?"

Sandra mumbled good-naturedly. Their hands touched as they cleared away the letters and the board.

"I miss you Sandra." Shango held on to her fingers.

"No you don't. We've just had a nice day together that's all."

"We used to have lots of nice days together."

"Do you think I don't remember?"

"You don't show it."

"What good would it do? What we shared is in the past. You made your choice, Shango. We had four great years but you got bored with me and all Sensi had to do was wiggle her behind and off you went."

"Like a lamb to the slaughter."

"Maybe, but it was still your choice."

"I made a mistake."

"And you have to live with it."

"Did you ever forgive me?"

"No."

"*Could* you ever forgive me for being crazy enough to turn my back on what we had?"

"No."

"Then why am I here? Why did you agree to see me today? Why did you come to the launch knowing I'd be there?"

Sandra didn't trust herself to speak. Shango still held her hand but they sat a little apart. His questions made her uneasy and she wished she'd let him go earlier.

"Talk to me please." Shango's voice was soft. He placed his other hand under her chin. When he lifted her face he saw her tears.

"Oh baby, don't cry. I'm sorry, don't cry." He took her in his arms and kissed her gently all over her face. She clung to him remembering the many days and nights they'd shared when they were in love.

They'd first met at Bournville College in the late eighties. Shango was re-sitting GCSEs and was in the same General Studies A-Level group as Sandra, who was also studying A-Level Media and Communications. At first Sandra had ignored Shango. His friends, who took studying lightly, influenced him. They came to lessons late, neglected their homework and seemed intent on basically wasting time. Sandra's clique found them immature and irritating.

One day she and Shango had arrived late and found that the class had already left for a museum trip.

"I overslept," Shango explained shrugging nonchalantly and trying to excuse himself.

"I'm not the teacher." Sandra's response was curt.

"Why are *you* late?" Shango persisted. It was the first time they'd been alone and he decided to try and break down her defences.

"None of your business." She looked the other way.

"Probably had your nose stuck in library books." Shango studied her profile noticing how pretty she was.

"What's wrong with that?"

"Made you late didn't it?"

Sandra had laughed out loud at his response despite her determination to stay aloof from the class troublemaker.

Gradually they'd become friends. Sandra encouraged him to stop hiding his natural intelligence for fear of 'damaging his reputation.' Shango's competitiveness spurred him on as he couldn't bear to Sandra to constantly score better marks than him. They discovered a mutual love of sports, books and films and with the amount of time they spent together it was only natural for them to fall in love.

Ira and Ruby Katherine adored the gentle Sandra who brought out the best in their youngest son. Sandra's parents, Benita and Maestro loved Shango's forward thinking and the way he was so tender towards their youngest child.

Their relationship lasted almost five years during which Sandra began a Media degree at Birmingham Poly and Shango left education to go into sales. He wanted to have money in his pocket and to be able to buy nice things for Sandra.

It was during this time that Shango drifted heavily into the black nightlife in Birmingham and the surrounding cities. After working between forty and sixty hours a week to earn decent commissions, he grabbed the chance to wind down with a Guinness and reggae music booming from eight foot bass speakers which sent the rhythm pulsing though his whole body. Sandra rarely accompanied him as it wasn't her scene.

One night Shango was approached by a small, slim girl. She'd been watching him for a few weeks and noticed that he always came alone and only mixed with the men. At first Shango had ignored her as she'd whined and danced provocatively in front of him. When she'd finally made eye contact, Shango smiled at her brazenness. That was his first mistake.

His second mistake was to accept her offer to buy him a drink, knowing that she really wasn't his type and he was in love with Sandra. Sensi was far too skinny, wore dresses that revealed far too much and heels that were way too high. She also mistook Shango's politeness for genuine interest and once she had an opening she dug her claws in, determined to hold on.

A few weeks later Sensi asked Shango for a lift home, her taxi hadn't arrived and her friends had left without her. When they'd arrived at Sensi's flat in a run down area of Hockley she'd asked him to take a quick look at her faulty fridge. Once inside, Shango was impressed by how homely she'd made the dingy flat. They'd drank a lot, smoked a little and enjoyed the pre-sexual tension that filled the space between them. Sensi had a way of describing ordinary events that made them sound hilarious and Shango warmed to her. That was his third mistake.

The next thing Shango knew it was eight thirty the following morning and he was lying in bed with a naked Sensi draped across him. On the floor lay a used condom. The same brand that Shango used when he was with Sandra.

He'd left Sensi's flat feeling ashamed. He loved Sandra and had never even looked at another woman in all the time they'd been together. He'd given her numerous assurances that the club was just a means of winding down, that he wasn't interested in picking anybody up and she'd believed him. Now that he'd done the unthinkable, he knew there was no way he'd be able to hide it. Deep in his gut he'd known that this was the end between them.

Now, once again, Sandra was in his arms and it was the most natural thing in the world. They were wrapped up in each other where they belonged. Somehow, through kisses, caresses and tears they moved into the bedroom. As Sandra pulled at Shango's shirt and undid his buttons he gently held her at arms length.

"Are you sure?" He looked into her eyes for the true answer.

"Just keep kissing me," she whispered as she again sought the comfort of his arms and lips.

When they were both naked Shango drew back.

"Stand up," he breathed.

Sandra looked at him, unsure of what he wanted.

"Stand up," he repeated. "I want to see you, let me look at you and remember."

Sandra stood by the side of the bed. She moved back slowly so that Shango could see all of her. She wasn't embarrassed or ashamed to be standing naked in front of him. She loved the fact that she could still give him pleasure, that he still yearned for her after all this time.

Shango drank in her smooth, long neck, strong shoulders, graceful arms and tantalising breasts. Her flat stomach and taut thighs showed that she still worked out and her rich brown skin looked baby soft. His eyes settled on the crinkly hair between her legs and his desire surged. She was still so gorgeous, he knew he'd been a fool to throw it all away.

"Come here," his words were barely audible as he lay back and pulled her on top of him.

• • • • • •

Easing his arm from underneath her Shango slipped out of bed and dressed slowly. The illuminated numbers on the clock told him it was almost eleven. Celia would have been expecting him back hours ago; he had to leave. The thought made him sigh out loud.

His sigh disturbed Sandra who sat up and looked at him. The curtains were still open and the hurt expression on her face was half lit by street lamps.

"Is this it then? You got what you wanted, satisfied your lust?" She hated the words that were coming out of her mouth but she couldn't stop herself.

Shango turned to her wounded by the pain in her eyes. "I'll call you tomorrow, we can talk then." He finished dressing.

"Sure!" Sarcastic disbelief filled Sandra's voice. "What do you want from me, Shango? Is this a game to you? Did you make a bet with Rafi or something?"

"No!" Shango was astounded by the depth of her heartache. "I would never do anything like that, not to you."

"But you planned to just leave without an explanation or even a goodbye?"

"We'll talk it through tomorrow." Shango rubbed Sandra's arms but she shrugged him off.

"Look at the day we've had, look at what we've just done. How can you just get up and walk away as if it was nothing?"

Shango was quiet. He sat slumped on the edge of the bed realising from her words that she had no idea that he was married.

"Are you seeing someone, Shango?" Now she was reading his mind.

He stayed silent.

"How could you sleep with me if you're already with someone? All day you've been leading me on, I thought that maybe you wanted to try again. But you were just using me!" Sandra grabbed the pillow and started bashing Shango. She was crying and shouting, her voice hysterical, "Is it Sensi? Are you still with that tramp?"

"No, no, Sensi and I split up a while ago." Shango instinctively blocked the blows although they weren't hard enough to hurt him.

"Then who is it?"

"No one." Shango pulled her against his shoulder.

"No one?" Sandra questioned in a small voice, her eyes searching his face for reassurance.

"There's no one, only you." Shango comforted her until her sobs died down. They clung to each other for a long moment before Shango kissed her and gently broke free.

"I have to go. I will call you tomorrow. Don't worry about anything."

"Shango?"

"Yes, my darling," he was at the door.

"I love you."

"I know. I love you too."

The night air had turned crisply cold. Shango shivered as he walked to his car, grateful for the unexpected chill which helped to numb his thoughts. With no forethought or planning Sandra was once again lodged firmly in his heart. What had happened between them was so far beyond his comprehension he'd had to push it to the compartment of his mind marked "another time."

Shango was both elated and miserable at the timing. No matter what he felt for Sandra, his first love, his true love, he just wasn't the kind of man who could forget his wife. If he'd known that Sandra would again be in his life he would never have married Celia, but now it was too late. Sooner or later he'd have to tell Sandra he could no longer see her. Once again he'd break her heart and his punishment would be having to live with that for the rest of his life.

Shango drove through the dark streets of Birmingham along the dual carriageways that snaked from the south to the north of the city, torn between his love for his soulmate and his commitment to Celia. The mournful songs of Donny Hathaway in his CD player provided the backdrop to his pain.

He arrived home well after midnight. All through the journey Sandra had appeared before him, her luminescent smile a haunting picture. On the kitchen table was a piece of paper. In elegant script Celia had written:

Roger says he'll be here at 8:30 tomorrow morning. You deal with him. Your dinner's in the dog or it would be if we had one. Don't wake me.

CHAPTER SEVEN

STOP MESSING ABOUT. Go and clean your room!" Sensi was on a short fuse. It seemed like she'd been shouting at Kai all morning. Shango had phoned to say he was on his way over and Kai was overcome with excitement after not seeing him for a while.

"Daddy, Daddy!" he shouted finding it impossible to speak at a normal level and coordinate his limbs simultaneously.

"Do you want your dad to see how messy you are?" Sensi threatened.

"Mmm, mm." Kai shook his head.

"He'll be here in three minutes. How long does it take you to clear up?"

"Don't know." Kai shook his head again, his body was still dancing about.

"It takes you ten minutes!" Sensi pretended to look disgusted.

"Ten minutes!" Kai copied his mom's high-pitched voice, totally caught up in the game.

"You'd better get started if you want Daddy to see a tidy room!"

"Don't let him in yet!" Kai darted upstairs as if Shango was already outside.

Sensi smiled, amazed at how much nervous energy he had.

She did a last cursory sweep over the neat lounge and went through to the kitchen. She put the kettle to boil knowing Shango would appreciate a cup of peppermint tea with honey. It would be the first time she'd seen him since they met at Steele's on the night of the EBYN launch. She wasn't looking forward to it but she reasoned that at least after today it would all be over, and perhaps Shango would even be able to help her make other arrangements for Kai while she was at work.

Sensi put the teabag in the cup and placed the jar of honey next to it. Funny how after several years apart she still remembered Shango's preferences. She couldn't help wondering how well Celia knew him after just one year of marriage.

Sensi checked herself in the full-length mirror on the wall by the front door. She'd dressed conservatively knowing that was what Shango preferred. The "Office-Junior-White-Girl Look" didn't sit too easily with her, but it was only for a few hours. If she had to look the part of a repentant mother and ex partner for peace's sake then she would. She laid out Ebony, Pride and one of Kai's school textbooks on the coffee table. Neither magazine belonged to her but it all looked good. She heard the click of a car alarm and looked towards the window to see Shango's lean form walking up her small garden path.

Shango was about to ring the bell when the door swung open and he received an exuberant bear hug.

"Dad!" Kai threw himself into Shango's arms knocking him off his feet.

"I saw you on tele, Dad and I heard you on the radio!"

Shango smiled at his only child.

"Have you grown?" he stepped back and looked Kai up and down.

"I'll be as tall as you are soon!"

"No chance! Run and get your books for me, son."

"Now?" Kai questioned as he wriggled out of Shango's arms.

"Show me how intelligent and wonderful you are "cos I think I forgot."

"'kay!"

Kai sprinted off to find his end of term school report and Shango kissed Sensi on her cheek.

"How are you?" His voice was warm, a sign that he approved of the way she looked and the fact that she'd agreed to talk with him in her house. There'd been occasions when he'd made the thirty-minute journey along the M6 and the M5 from Erdington to West Bromwich, only to be met with cursing and a refused entry.

"We're fine, Kai's happy to see you…at long last."

"I can see that." Shango ignored the edge to her words. There was always a lingering attitude with Sensi. Once she bore a grudge she did so for life.

"Tea?" she offered without looking at him.

"Pepperm…" Shango began.

"–I know," Sensi interrupted rudely.

In the kitchen Sensi squeezed the teabag as if it had done something personal to her before dropping it into the bin. Damn, Shango, she thought. He looked so good in his cream jeans and

75

black shirt, his dreadlocks loosely flowing down his back. The combination was enough to make her weak at the knees. She wished that he'd turned up in the evening instead of the middle of the afternoon. Then she would have cooked him some parrotfish seasoned with lots of pepper. He could have put Kai to bed, they might have watched a film together and then after that who knows? But Sensi knew that there was no way she could tempt him into her bed in the middle of the day. Celia would be waiting for him, or maybe he'd have to meet Rafi.

Sensi sighed heavily, clenching and releasing her fists with a flick of her long fingernails. Just because Shango had decided on anther way of life didn't mean she was supposed to turn off her feelings did it? She wasn't sure if she was experiencing the dying pangs of love or wanton lust but she really didn't care. She just wished she could think of a way to get him naked and under her sheets. She'd never forget that Shango was the best lover she'd ever had.

When she re-entered the living room Kai was sitting on Shango's lap, his school paraphernalia to one side. Sensi placed the tray of tea and rum cake on the table and sat down.

"What did Nanny Hope say when you went to her house last time?" Shango was asking Kai.

"She said why are you two always coming here?" Kai replied. Shango glanced sideways at Sensi. His face was masked but she sensed the tension emanating from him.

"What else?" he continued, his voice soft.

Kai looked at his mom.

"It's okay," Shango encouraged him.

"She said she hoped that Mommy wasn't leaving me there again because she was fed-up of looking after me all night." Kai leant into Shango's chest and became silent.

Shango kissed him and stroked his cheek. He muttered soothing words to his son but the glare he gave Sensi spoke volumes. He was very, very angry.

"Drink your tea," she told him defensively before looking away.

Shango ignored her. After a few moments of silence he spoke to Kai.

"Are your friends playing out today?"

"Can I go and check, on my bike?"

"Sure, give me a kiss."

"How long Mom?" Kai looked at Sensi, with bright eyes that were shielded by thick, silky lashes. He was eager to get away from the tension that always seemed to bubble up between his parents.

"Ask your dad." Sensi couldn't bring herself to look at her son after his admission about Hope.

Kai turned expectantly to Shango who ran his hand tenderly along his son's head and rested it on his neck.

"Half an hour." He smiled. "Then you and me have got plans to make!"

"What's plans Dad?" Kai was already at the back gate, wheeling his bike through as he shouted the words over his shoulder.

"Summer holiday plans!" Shango replied, laughing in admiration at Kai's tenacity at wielding the large bike that was a size too big for him.

As soon as he was out of sight Sensi exhaled, she hadn't realized that she'd stopped breathing but she did know that she didn't have a single thing to say in her defence.

"How could you leave him with that witch?" His voice was an angry snarl. He stuck his hands in his pockets and stepped back, mindful that in his present state of mind, if he touched Sensi, he'd hurt her.

Sensi was quiet, the only sound an audible swallow, as she tried to calm her fears. She didn't know how to explain that after so many years of putting Kai first it felt good to do something that was just for her. She couldn't explain the half-formed plan she'd originally had, where Kai only stayed with Hope occasionally instead of every weekend. She couldn't find the words that justified her selfish and unthinkable cruelty to her own son, so she stayed silent, not realizing that her clenched lips and rigid posture were a catalyst to Shango's inner rage.

Shango paced the room, his peppermint tea untouched. He squeezed his eyelids together seeing a private panorama of times past when he'd witnessed the great love between a mother and son.

The atmosphere had sparkled as Kai and Sensi had laughed so easily at everyday things. When Kai had been fractious Sensi had soothed him by simply rubbing her cheek against his and their bedtime routine always ended with the same lullaby which they'd sung together.

With his eyes closed Shango could see it all. But when he stood still he was brought back to the present and was once again incredulous at Sensi's palpable guilt.

"Is it the money! Is that it?" he barked at her.

"No! I like the work, I like the club. Tony says..." Sensi was almost begging him to understand. She jumped and ran to the other side of the room when Shango threw his arms up in the air.

"You like the *work*?" Shango forced himself to stay still, afraid of obeying the urge that made him want to throw Sensi's slight figure against the wall. He knew deep down that he could never hurt the mother of his son. "Does your *work* mean more to you than Kai's happiness?"

"No!" Sensi withered under the look he shot at her.

"Then how could you do this to him? How you could you leave him there every week?"

"I couldn't let Tony down, he trusts me."

"And I trust you with Kai's well being. Shouldn't that mean more to you?"

"Of course it should! It does!"

"Then why?" With less than three steps Shango had crossed the room. He towered over Sensi, his eyes locked with hers as she trembled, too scared to move a muscle.

"I didn't know what else to do!" she cried.

"Please!" Shango's tone was mocking. "This is what you do. You find me a qualified babysitter with proper references. I give her fifty pounds a week so that my son can stay in his own bed in his own house while you go and please Tony Valentine."

"Thank you Shango." Sensi's voice was a small echo in the room.

"If I haven't had a chance to check her out by noon on Thursday, I'll ring Tony myself and tell him to find someone else to *trust*. Do you understand?" Shango's fingers closed around Sensi's wrist as he pulled her even nearer to him.

"Yes," she whispered unable to look away from him even though she didn't want him to see that she was on the verge of crying.

"I'm going outside to wait for Kai. I'm planning to see a lot of him over the holidays is that okay with you?" Shango moved away as he spoke, he'd stopped shouting but his tone was still harsh. He turned sharply back to Sensi awaiting her affirmative response. She nodded, rubbing the part of her wrist where his fingers had been and blinking to stop her tears from falling.

When Shango left the house she slumped onto the settee facing the bleak fact that he'd never again love her the way he used to. That part of him was dead and there seemed to be nothing she could do to bring it back.

Shango rested against the bonnet of his car, enjoying the hot afternoon sun which soaked away the tension knots stretching across his back and shoulders. He tried to regain focus after his outburst, admitting to himself that Sensi was the only woman who pushed him to the edge. Her stupidity and selfishness appalled and amazed him and he wondered why he'd never noticed it when they were together.

He looked around at the street where his son was growing up. West Bromwich Council had placed Sensi and Kai in a two bedroom house in a very pleasant area. The road was away from the main thoroughfares with the entrance to the park at one end and a small friendly all-purpose shop at the other.

Shango had never really liked West Bromwich. He'd always considered it to be a smaller, more crowded version of Birmingham, but this particular street could have come straight out of a middle class suburb. The houses were all double-glazed with lawns at the front. Some had long drives and some had linked garages. The occupants took pride in their homes and consequently the street looked well cared for. Most of the tenants and homeowners were South Asians with a handful of black families interspersed. The local primary school was within walking distance and there were plenty of children around the same age as Kai.

Shango was thankful that Kai was growing up in a decent area. He'd tried his best to be there for him and Sensi but it was becoming more and more difficult. Each encounter with his former lover left him feeling angry and out of control. The ideal situation would be for Kai to live with him and Celia, but he knew he'd probably have more chance of winning the lottery than getting the two women to agree to that.

He rolled his neck and leaned his head from side to side. He longed for a sip of the refreshing peppermint and honey tea that Sensi had made. He wished he'd taken a big bite from the thick slice of rum cake she'd set before him. He imagined it on the plate on top of the coffee table in Sensi's lounge, torturing him with it's juicy scent and rich brown hues. But the cost of going back into Sensi's house to enjoy the food was too high so Shango decided to stroll down to the park to look for his son.

CHAPTER EIGHT

GUNGU PEAS, RUM cake, curry goat and the fatted calf!" Shango pressed send and laughed out loud.

"What are you laughing at?" Celia was intrigued. She leant over from her desk and peered at the computer screen.

"This." Shango opened up the sent messages file and retrieved the last e-mail for Celia to read.

She mouthed the words silently. "What does that mean?" Her confusion made Shango laugh again.

"It's an invitation for Dad's seventieth birthday party."

"Who to?"

"Palmer." Shango's chuckles increased

"Will he understand it?"

"No!" Shango was in fits.

Celia looked at him sideways, her eyebrows furrowed, shaking her head in pity at his mirth.

"What time is it?" she asked, her nose back in her books, her pen in hand.

"You're sitting right in front of the clock!" Shango reminded her his eyes still on the computer screen.

"I can't be bothered to look up," Celia replied.

Shango gave her a withering look.

"I know what you're playing at," he mumbled, the trace of a smile on his lips, "asking me about the time!"

"Where is he then, Mister Jack of all Trades, Roger, who can't even get out of bed?"

"He'll be here."

"Will that be before or after the next millennium?"

"*Before or after the next millennium*?" Shango wiggled his head from side to side mimicking Celia.

"He should have started two weeks ago," she reminded him, her head down.

"*Two weeks ago*!" Shango teased again. He played a game of Backgammon against the computer while he waited for an e-mail reply from the States. The computer was winning.

"Watch it," Celia warned in a low menacing voice that made Shango laugh again.

"What time is it in Atlanta?" he queried through his chuckles.

"Ask Roger, he knows everything according to you." Celia turned a page.

"*He knows everything according to you!*" Shango couldn't desist from his mimicking game despite Celia's warning. Two seconds later he fell off his chair and was doubled up on the floor, screaming and laughing as Celia tickled him mercilessly.

"Say sorry!" she demanded.

"I'm sorry!" bawled Shango.

"I didn't hear you." Celia laughed. Her fingers found all the right spots, his ribs, his hips, the soles of his feet and his armpits.

"Then how come they heard me in Scotland!" Tears ran down Shango's cheeks and he lightly bumped his head on the study furniture as he desperately wriggled away from Celia's relentless hands. Soon his stomach muscles ached and his cheeks were sore from laughing. When the doorbell rang it was a welcome reprieve.

They struggled up from the floor, still giggling as they straightened out the room, while the buzzer rang continuously.

"Roger's here," Shango stated.

"I'm gonna break his fingers if he doesn't let go of my doorbell," Celia threatened, still smiling.

"Not if I reach him first!" Shango sprinted down the stairs two at a time mindful that Roger would need his hands intact to finish all of the left over DIY jobs around their house.

• • • • • •

"Roger can you turn the radio down please?"

"You've just asked me and I've just done it!"

"Er thanks." Celia was convinced that Roger hadn't lowered the dial once in the three times that she'd asked him to. Her patience had run out when she'd realised that she was typing the lyrics to Roger's reggae music rather than quotes for her newspaper article.

"Miss Celia?" Roger was in the doorway of her study.

"Roger, your brush is dripping paint onto the floor!"

"Sorry! Don't worry I'll clean it up."

Celia stifled a groan, Roger's "clean-ups" usually resulted in more mess.

"What's the problem, Roger?" she asked, careful to keep her

voice neutral. This was the umpteenth time Roger had disturbed her during the three days he'd been "working" in the house.

"Let me show you something." He gestured towards the stairs with his head.

Celia rolled her eyes in a silent plea to God as she followed him downstairs.

"I'm going to paint all the door frames black. Just give me the money." Roger's Jamaican accent became more pronounced as he saw the disbelieving look on Celia's face, "I'll go now to buy the paint."

"Black! You want to paint the frames black?" Celia's mouth started moving before her words came out, "Why?"

"Don't you see how it will look much better? I'll start early tomorrow."

Celia didn't know whether to laugh or cry. Roger was unbelievable. She was going to kill Shango when he came back from wherever he'd sloped off to.

"Roger, that's not what we wanted." Celia tried to be polite, but she was fighting a losing battle.

"You just give me the money and you will see, don't worry yourself about it."

"No leave it. It's fine, they're all fine!" she snapped.

"All right then," Roger grumbled.

Celia knew she'd offended him but he was getting on her nerves.

"Put the spotlights up in the study and sort the bedroom window lock please. I'll be back in a little while."

"Hmm." Roger was sulking.

Big baby, thought Celia to herself as she went to get her coat and her purse.

Roger's presence in the house was overwhelming. He left behind a decorator's odour of white spirits and sweat. His tiny radio belied its size by having the loudest speakers ever and everything Roger said he was taking care of ended up being in a worse state than when he started. The previous night Celia had tried to tell Shango how inept he was but he'd refused to sack Roger. Apparently Roger's gran in the West Indies was sick and he needed the money to pay for her treatment. Celia couldn't believe that Shango had fallen for the oldest trick in the book!

Her catalogue of complaints ranged from Roger hanging the bathroom blinds from the ceiling instead of the window frame, to putting up mismatched wallpaper in the dining room where she'd specified paint. Their formerly neat and tidy house resembled a war zone, with tools and paint cans everywhere as Roger started new jobs before completing old ones. His party trick were lights that came on and off at random. He called it a "chip-in". Shango joked that soon everyone would want a "chip-in feature" in their home.

When Roger announced that he'd rehung some of the downstairs doors–a job that definitely wasn't on the list–neither of them could bear to look and they'd drawn straws to see who'd get to check. As expected, the doors had been hung upside down.

It was approaching six pm and Celia was browsing the stores in Sutton Coldfield's high street. She loved the fact that there was no one blasting out a constant cornucopia of reggae, ragga and soul music. No heavy footsteps tramping up and down the stairs, and no-one constantly begging her to take a look at this and that. She'd go home in a bit, she decided, there was no rush. She'd just enjoy the cool evening air a little longer and then she'd have enough energy to return to face Roger and whatever else he'd done to spoil her lovely home.

"What the!" With one twist Shango's key broke off in the lock. He stared from the tiny piece left in his hand, back to the lock in disbelief. "Back foot!" he cried again. He rang the bell several times but no one came. He looked up at the study window wondering where Celia was. The absence of Roger's van told him that he'd left for the day.

He banged hard on the door in case Celia was near the back of the house before dialling her number from his mobile phone. The mechanical voice informed him: "The mobile phone you have called is switched off, please try later." Shango snapped his phone shut and went back to his car. In the glove box he found a small penknife which he used to try to gouge out the bit of key that was stuck in the lock. The more difficult it was the more tenacious Shango became.

After a few minutes he developed a cramp in his fingers. He checked the downstairs windows and rattled the locked gate that led to the back garden. Then he called Celia's mobile again, tutting in annoyance when he got the recorded message telling him to once again, try later. He didn't want to try later, it was after seven pm and he needed to wee. He didn't want to have to keep fiddling with his own front door lock and he didn't want to have to wait on his wife. He simply wanted to be inside his own house where he could use his own bathroom.

"Problem mate?"

Shango looked around as a police car pulled up. He held his phone with one hand and the penknife with the other. Between his lips was the remainder of the front door key. He knew it didn't look good.

The police car parked awkwardly, intentionally blocking in his BMW which was parked on the driveway. Shango sighed, wondering if they really thought he was going to try to make a run for it when he was so obviously tied up.

"We've had reports of a disturbance," the first officer said as he exited the car. His domed hat made his body look extra long and his skinny arms showed through his light summer uniform. Shango's eyebrows rose in disbelief at his words.

"What are you doing?" the second officer joined in, two steps behind his colleague.

Shango took the half key out of his mouth and faced them full on. They'd stopped less than two feet away from him. It was close enough for him to see the glint in their eyes that plainly said that they had power and he had none.

"I'm trying to get in," he said carefully, trying but not succeeding, in keeping the impatience out of his voice.

"Why are you trying to get in?" The officer's condescension dripped like a cold water tap.

"I live here." Shango bit his inner lip aware that the more information he gave them the more they'd try to trip him up.

"You live here?" the second officer echoed looking Shango up and down.

Shango said nothing. He wasn't in the mood for games, he was an innocent black man with a hungry belly being harassed by the police outside of his own house. It was a recipe for disaster.

"Got any proof of that, have you?"

"Inside," Shango said wearily. His hunger was making him lightheaded, "...all my ID's inside."

"I suppose this is your car?" The PC eyed the BMW.

Shango wished they'd get to the point. All they had to do was ask him his name and run a check on the car. The police computer would confirm his address in less than five minutes, then perhaps they could make themselves useful and help him get in. But the policemen were being purposely obtuse.

The officers began a slow patrol around Shango's car and the grounds of his house. They'd had another quiet midweek afternoon, but all summer their colleagues in Handsworth and

Sparkbrook spoke about black men resisting arrest, domestic violence and racial discord on the streets. Consequently they'd been happy to answer the call about a black man acting dubiously in a mainly white neighbourhood.

They looked up at the roof, ran their fingertips along the window seals, examined the car tyres, checked his windscreen and threw more pointless questions at him before finally making a decision.

"All right, cuff him!" The officer recited his lines with relish.

"What?" Shango was shocked. "You're arresting me? On what grounds?"

"Breaking and entering. Beats me why you'd try to burgle a house in broad daylight."

"Must be desperate times." The second officer couldn't keep the smile out of his voice as he approached Shango with the handcuffs.

"Listen, my decorator must have changed the locks, he's always making mistakes. My wife will be here in a bit, just hold on."

"Your *decorator*?" the officer sneered.

"He's probably only just left, you can call him!"

"Let's sort it out at the station." The officer grabbed his arm and pulled it behind his back.

Shango succumbed, unwilling to give them the satisfaction of a struggle as they snapped the handcuffs around his wrists.

Just as he was being led towards the police car Celia turned the corner. A few of their neighbours had come out to see what was going on. Celia followed their curious gazes to her own house.

"Hey!" she shouted involuntarily, surprised by the loudness of her own voice. The policemen looked up briefly and then ignored her.

"Oi!" Shango pulled away from their escort, "That's my wife!"

Celia panted, trying to get her breath back. She hated running and she'd just sprinted up the hill to their house to catch them before they drove off. Her bag was weighed down with three hardback books, a legacy of her leisurely afternoon's shopping.

"What's going on?" she gasped, one hand on the police car to support herself and her bags.

"Roger's done something to the locks and I couldn't get in," Shango started before the policemen could speak.

Celia flashed him a triumphant "I told you so" look.

"Tell them, Celia!" he implored.

"Is this your husband, madame?" the first officer asked, his words slow and reluctant.

"Depends, what's he done?" Celia asked ignoring the piercing look Shango gave her.

"Possible cause for breaking and entering." The disappointment in the officer's eyes was palpable. He was almost willing Celia to say that she'd never seen Shango before.

A stream of sexy thoughts went through Celia's mind as she glanced at Shango in handcuffs and appraised his lean, toned, body. His biceps bulged seductively from his short sleeved, plain white t-shirt. His abdomen was perfectly flat and his bottom round and firm in his jeans.

Celia nodded and the policemen released him. Now she knew for sure that Roger would not be setting foot in their house again.

By the middle of August the house was beginning to look like their home again. Celia had peace and space to write and Shango spent a lot of time with both Kai and Ira. In-between, he liaised with colleagues at work, drawing up syllabuses and finalising teaching plans for the autumn semester. The EBYN executive committee formed a well-respected advisory panel that drafted strategic recommendations for any organisation that involved black men and their children.

Sensi settled into her work at Steele's and Kai's new babysitter was working out well. Rafi interspersed his shifts as an AA patrolman with regular visits to Melody and was becoming more and more confident that she'd soon be home with him for good. He preferred to keep Paula at arm's length. When Shango asked him why, he used humour to change the subject. He couldn't explain that she was just a means of sexual relief for him. It was a cold hearted and unfair truth. Contentment hung in the air during the hot summer days and balmy evenings as Celia and Shango entertained their friends with barbecues on their back patio.

Through it all, however, Shango still had Sandra on his mind. In other circumstances he'd have given her the world, but he knew that even hearing her voice was a luxury that he couldn't afford. Breaking his marriage vows had caused him sleepless nights and he'd resolved to banish his love for Sandra to a deep and hidden part of himself. He suffered the dichotomy of disappointment and relief that Sandra hadn't contacted him either since their time together. But ultimately, he reasoned that the space in his heart he'd cleared for her would soon be filled and forgotten. All it took was time and he had plenty of that.

CHAPTER NINE

Hi Baby Bro',

By the time you read this I'll be on the plane. I'm flying straight to Birmingham International so you won't have to drive all the way to Heathrow to pick me up. Ain't I the considerate one! 'Cept that I don't get in until one am your time. (Ha!) I was wondering, what present should I bring to celebrate the old man's birthday? Hold off on the gungu peas but have the rum cake and the fatted calf ready. The prodigal son is returning home!
P.

PALMER EVEN WROTE with an American accent Shango thought, as he clicked on the small cross and exited from the net. "Celia!" his voice travelled across the upstairs hallway through to their room where Celia lay in bed reading in as usual.

"Yes, my King." she replied lazily.

"Are you busy, my queen above all queens?"

"Never too busy for you, my liege." Celia was smiling although her attention was still on the book.

"Well, your royal.......something......ness." Shango had run out of regal titles, "get your backside dressed and go and pick up your brother-in-law," he added the word please as he walked into the room and saw the look on Celia's face.

"Do you know what time it is?" she spluttered, gesturing at the clock as it if was a new item to the room.

"At least keep me company, he's flying in in an hour and I don't wanna go by myself," Shango whined as he flopped down on the bed beside her.

"I'm in my nightie," Celia protested, pointing to it in case Shango hadn't noticed.

"Pleeeeease."

"Whinge, whinge, whinge," she recited, her nose back in her book.

"Pleeeease," Shango continued in an annoying nasal tone.

"What do I get out of it?" Celia shut her book and laid it to one side.

"Huh?" Shango was caught off guard.

Celia licked her lips and eyed his crotch, a predatory gleam in her eyes.

"Make it worth my while." She raised an eyebrow and spoke in a fake Russian accent while her fingertips trailed the open entrance to his boxer shorts. Shango smiled, enjoying his arousal.

"Work first, fun later." Despite his denial he caressed her breast and kissed her lips.

"No, now!" Celia grabbed his bare shoulders and pulled him down on top of her.

"Just don't hurt me!" Shango conceded, succumbing helplessly.

"How long have we got?" Celia tugged at his boxers and tried to pull off her nightie.

"Ten minutes," Shango answered breathless with anticipation.

"We won't need that long!" Celia declared as they collapsed in giggles on the bed.

••••••

Thirty minutes later Celia double locked their front door while Shango switched on the ignition. The pair wore a glow that showed their lovemaking had hit it just right.

Although Celia had started off in control, Shango had soon taken over. Usually the loving between them was unhurried. They seduced each other in slow motion with playful nips, feather like touching and deep kisses. They allowed time for their sexual tension to become salacious desire, fuelled by a mutual admiration for each other's bodies. Shango called it chemistry, Celia called it raw sex. By which-ever name, it was something which they'd never experienced with other partners.

This evening, however, had been the antithesis of all that. Knowing that their time was limited, they'd ravaged each other frenziedly. Shango had turned Celia around until she was on all fours and then swiftly entered from behind, surprising her, as this wasn't one of their usual positions. When Celia had felt that he was close to the edge she'd wriggled free enjoying her chance to catch him by surprise. Satisfied that he wasn't about to come she'd given him a tantric kiss. Seven full seconds of nothing but their lips pressed together had sent shivers down Shango's spine and made his organ even more erect. With one eye on the clock, he'd pushed her back against the bed, lifted up both her knees, as if her legs were in stirrups, and entered her. They'd both come within seconds.

Shango glanced over at Celia. They were driving through the still night along the A34 road. After about twenty minutes they'd reach the A45 which would take them straight to the airport.

He'd dragged her out of bed past midnight and she still looked as fresh as if she'd had eight hours sleep. She was wearing a soft navy light woollen sweater that contoured itself around her generous bust. He could see black peep-toe sandals under her long, black jersey skirt. Her only make-up was a little lip gloss and the way she'd wrapped her hair with a silk scarf could only be described as elegant.

Her babyfaced prettiness warmed Shango's heart as he appraised her. Celia caught him looking and stuck out her tongue. They both laughed.

"What's Palmer like?" Celia asked in between singing along to Will Downing ballads.

"Male," Shango teased.

"Stop messing about, you know I've never met him!"

"It's been a long time since I've seen him myself," Shango admitted. "I was only twelve when he left."

"Are you anxious?"

"A little. I'm not sure we'll have anything in common."

Celia rubbed his thigh sympathetically before asking, "What does he do?"

Shango exhaled, "Good question. He's an exec for one of the Fortune 500 companies, I think."

"Fortune 500? Aren't they the ones with all of the money?"

"I think so."

"What's his role?"

"Financial analyst? I'm not exactly sure."

"Financial analyst in a private moneymaking company?" Celia looked at Shango, "Are you thinking what I'm thinking?"

"Nope," he admitted. He honestly didn't have a clue where Celia was going. She tutted in annoyance.

"Michelle," she said.

"Yes, that makes everything clear."

"Don't be sarcastic. Michelle does the same job!"

"So?"

"I give up!" Celia threw her hands in the air. For someone

who'd passed a MENSA test with flying colours, Shango could be particularly dense at times.

They fell silent as the BMW ate up the miles. All of the traffic lights seemed to be on their side, changing swiftly to green as they approached. Patrolling police cars left them alone. West Midlands police didn't view a black man and a black woman in a car late at night as a threat. Shango and Celia both knew it would have been a different story had Shango been on his own or with Palmer.

In the arrivals lounge of Terminal 1, Celia and Shango scanned the passengers alighting from flight CO 236 American Airlines from New York.

"What's he look like?" Celia wished she'd worn higher heels.

"Black man," Shango stated simply. He sounded terse but Celia understood that he was simply nervous. He'd soon be face to face with the elder brother who, under normal circumstances, could have been his closest ally. Instead Palmer had been sent to Atlanta at sixteen. Due to some unexplained family decision, Shango's only sibling was a stranger to him.

"I'm sure we'll know him when we see him."

"Either that or we drive home with a lucky stranger," Shango said and despite her seriousness Celia couldn't help laughing.

Palmer stood by the carousel waiting for his case. He noticed that even though it was after one am UK time, there were still plenty of people milling about in the second city airport. Liana, his girlfriend, had been right in suggesting the red wrap around seal would make it easier to identify his luggage, but he was convinced that leaving her behind had been a good idea.

She'd desperately wanted to come with him and be presented to his family, but Palmer needed space to think and time to breathe. He felt that a few weeks apart would slow down his unwilling descent towards the altar where Liana's parents, four aunts, five sisters and three brothers, were waiting for him. The beautiful Liana came as a very big package.

"Is that him?" Celia pointed to a slim man, the same height and skin tone as Shango. He stood in the center of the lounge looking around guardedly. His smart beige linen overshirt and same colour trousers were creased. Dark brown sandals and low cut hair prolific with waves completed his look. Shango approached him. They slapped hands and hugged briefly before sizing each other up behind warm but wary smiles.

"I can see you haven't changed a bit!" Palmer joked in an American accent so deep Celia went week at the knees. She noted the family resemblance immediately.

"This is my wife, Celia." Shango pulled her forward and she hugged her brother-in-law.

"Nice to finally meet you, how was your flight?" she asked.

"Goddam awful food, goddam turbulence, goddam cramped planes!"

Shango and Celia exchanged worried glances until Palmer tilted his head and they saw his deep dimples and twinkling eyes.

"Just kidding!"

All three laughed together as Shango reached for the luggage and they headed for the car park. Palmer was obviously on their wavelength, it was going to be a good trip.

• • • • • •

"You should be warm enough," Celia addressed Palmer. "I've left some spare blankets in the bottom of the wardrobe just in case. I'll see you both in the morning.

"Goodnight love," she kissed Shango warmly on the lips.

"Night sweetheart," Shango responded.

"Good night, Palmer, welcome to England; I hope you enjoy your stay." Celia kissed him on the cheek.

"I'm sure I will, thanks for making me feel so at home." Palmer smiled at Celia who smiled back as she left the room.

"More scotch?" Shango raised the bottle of JB's.

"Sure. I mainly drink JD at home but this is kinda nice."

"On the rocks or more soda?"

"On ice please. You guys have a nice home." Palmer looked around at the many books, and comfortable soft furnishings.

"Thanks. We haven't been here that long but it's definitely bigger than our old flat."

"Flat?"

"Apartment."

"Oh yeah, I forgot that's what you guys call it."

"Our decorator's just finished; be careful, some things might be a little loose."

"Loose?" Palmer was intrigued.

"Didn't quite finish the job. Whatever you do don't get Celia started on it." Shango chuckled at the memory of all of Roger's mistakes.

"If I see any wires hanging out shall I hide them?"

"Best not to touch them if you want to go back to the US with all of your fingers!"

The men were trying hard to ease the tension between them. They'd been apart for so long they were more like strangers than brothers.

They sat opposite each other– Shango in the leather reclining armchair and Palmer in the middle of the settee. Soft jazz played in the background and CNN was on the television with the sound turned off. Every now and then one of the men would glance at the headlines that moved across the bottom of the monitor.

"You think you guys can win the world cup this year?" Palmer commented on the silent TV report about the impending tournament.

"We've got a good chance as long as we don't crumble in front of Brazil."

"Everyone's depending on Beckham huh?"

"Yeah!" Shango looked at Palmer in respectful surprise.

"I know a little bit about football." Palmer's dimples appeared again.

The men sipped their drinks, Palmer watching the TV and Shango absorbing the music. He wished Celia hadn't left them alone.

"It's been a long time, little brother." Palmer was examining the drink in his hand. He looked at Shango and then back at his glass.

"I wasn't sure how you'd feel about me coming back after so long." Shango was relieved at Palmer's honesty.

"Me neither."

"Dad'll be glad to see you."

"How is the old man?"

"Wonderful. We can go over tomorrow."

"Anything you need me to do for the celebration? Seventy years is a real milestone."

"I'm sure Celia will have several jobs with your name on. She's done most of the organising. Well, she and Michelle."

"Michelle?"

"Celia's best friend, you'll meet her soon enough. She spends more time here than at her own place."

Palmer took a last swig of his scotch. "I'm all out. Think I'll hit the sack." He stood and stretched each limb in turn.

"No rush in the morning. Sleep as long as you need to."

Shango stood and the two men embraced briefly.

"Thanks for coming," Shango said.

"Thanks for asking," Palmer replied before making his way upstairs to bed.

●●●●●●

Palmer flicked on the light and checked his watch. It was four am and sleep was elusive on his first night back in England. He pulled up the wooden slatted blinds that shielded his window, it was a beautifully clear night. The constellations in the sky held his gaze as he thought about what his visit might bring. Tomorrow he'd be reunited with the father that had just stood back when his mom sent him to Atlanta. Palmer had never made much of an effort at keeping in touch with Ira or Shango. He'd mainly written to Ruby Katherine, desperate to hold onto his mother's love across the miles of separation, as the few letters he'd received from Ira had offered no comfort or hope that he'd be able to go back home soon.

He was apprehensive about seeing Ira. After twenty-two years he wasn't sure he could still hold in the bile of bitterness that rose from his stomach to his chest and lodged in the back of his throat. He couldn't help wondering if this trip would give him much needed answers or if Ira would just brush it all away like he had so many times before.

On the other side of the coin Shango's invitation couldn't have come at a better time. Lately it seemed that even in a city the size of Atlanta, there was still nowhere that he could hide when he needed to escape from Liana and her huge family.

It hadn't been difficult for him to start a relationship with his PA. When he'd first joined the company she'd been invaluable in showing him the ropes and making him feel at home. She looked like a pin-up from a magazine and, unlike many American women, she'd been reserved and quietly courteous which Palmer had found endearing. He'd hesitated about asking her out, unsure about mixing work with pleasure, but there were times when he couldn't help covertly watching her figure moving around the office. When her wavy hair gleamed jet black in the morning sunlight that streamed into his office, it seemed to be crying out to be stroked and Palmer had spent many minutes wondering what it would be like to caress her naked form, kiss her sensuous lips and satiate his growing desire.

Liana was extremely beautiful and smart. His colleagues couldn't understand why he was holding back but Palmer was not a man to rush into things. One night they'd all gone out to a jazz club to celebrate a co-workers birthday. Liana and Palmer had ended up sitting together and sharing a plate of food. After that it was natural to offer her a ride home and even more natural to kiss her at the end of the it. They'd made love on that first night and slipped comfortably into a rhythm of being boyfriend and girlfriend.

Soon after, Palmer had been invited to church and Sunday lunch with Liana and her family. They'd driven in a six-car convoy, each car filled with siblings and their children, aunts, uncles and cousins. They seemed to have a thousand questions about life in England and assumed that Palmer had grown up in London and met the Queen. They were curious about the tiny houses in Shakespeare's Stratford-on-Avon and wondered if he knew their distant relatives in Cardiff.

On that first occasion Liana had rescued him from the family interrogation but after that she'd seemed to welcome it. Palmer had soon noticed that Liana's parents treated him like a prospective son-in-law. Although they'd only known him a matter of weeks they involved him in major family decisions and called him freely at work or at home. Liana didn't see anything wrong when he questioned her about why she'd handed over his numbers.

When he visited Liana's parents the other husbands simply nodded sympathetically, having been through the same process, but it made Palmer feel as though he had a noose around his neck.

Perhaps, he ruminated, it was time to come home to England. He loved Liana, but it was more out of obligation than passion. She had everything he could ever hope for in a woman but she didn't make his socks roll up and down or float his boat. Being with her and her massive family was too much like hard work. England was where he'd spent the formative years of his life and where he still had a brother, sister-in-law, nephew and dad. He was a highly qualified financial analyst with a PhD from a top American university; he was thirty-eight with no dependents and financially solvent. If he was going to change his life then this trip would be the perfect time to make a decision.

Palmer anticipated that the awkwardness between himself

and Shango would resolve in time. They were brothers and had lived in the same house for twelve years; blood had to be thicker than water. As for Ira, the old man would have to face whatever ghosts came up while he was around. He was staying for a while so whatever happened, happened. All he had to do was take one day at a time.

The sky was no longer dark and the sun was rising. Palmer had been sitting up for over an hour. His head and shoulders drooped and his eyelids finally became heavy. Lying back onto the sheets he closed his eyes and welcomed sleep.

CHAPTER TEN

A WEEK LATER on Saturday afternoon the doorbell at 83 Matlock Road chimed for the umpteenth time. Ska music boomed out of the stereo speakers and heads nodded gently to the throbbing beat. Bottles of Babycham clinked against glasses half full with gin and other spirits. Party guests ate their fill of curry goat, mutton, rice and peas and coleslaw. They chose either rum and raisin ice cream, fruit salad, or a fat slice of rum cake to complete their sumptuous meal.

Ira wandered through each room demanding a birthday kiss and a rub-up dance from the ladies, and slapping hands with friends from the domino club. His wheezy laugh, raucous shouting and rude teasing indicated he was enjoying his special day immensely.

"You made it then?" Shango shouted above the din to Tony and Andrea Valentine as they squeezed through the crush of animated bodies into the hallway.

"He hasn't cut the cake yet, has he?" Tony responded jovially.

"Later." Shango handed him a bottle of Guinness and passed Andrea a glass of white wine.

"You look nice!" Celia came out from the kitchen and greeted Andrea with a kiss on the cheek. "Who are we wearing today? Dior? Chanel? Gucci?" she enquired looking Andrea up and down.

"Tesco, but don't tell anyone!" Andrea laughed.

"Really, those jeans and that top are from Tesco?" Celia hooked her arm through Andrea's and dragged her back down the hallway.

"Where are we going?" Andrea was curious.

"Food and gossip, what else!" Celia winked.

Keeping an eye on the hot food and dishing up desserts were Michelle and Paula who greeted Andrea with warm hugs.

"What's the news?" Andrea settled in at the small table and grabbed a meaty chicken drumstick.

"Palmer likes Michelle!" Celia and Paula chanted in unison like school girls in the playground. Michelle felt a warm flush creeping up her neck.

"For real?" Andrea questioned in a mock American accent.

"He's been eyeing her up all afternoon!"

"No!"

"Hey!" Michelle butted in, "I am quite desirable you know!"

"So's sexy Palmer," Paula piped up.

"I think they make a nice couple," Celia interjected. "Want us to fix you up love?"

"No thank you. If anything's going to happen it will happen naturally."

"You do think he's nice though?" Andrea checked in-between mouthfuls.

"He's not bad," Michelle said casually.

"Not bad!" The other women spluttered at the understatement.

"Next to my husband he's the most gorgeous man here!" Celia shouted.

"That's probably because most of the men are over sixty." Andrea's logic was faultless.

"But check out those dimples when he smiles!" Paula said as the women advanced on Michelle.

"There's nothing wrong with giving nature a helping hand," Celia laughed as she undid two more buttons on Michelle's purple silk shirt. Andrea pulled curly tresses of hair down from her bun and teased them around her forehead and the nape of her neck after which Paula sprayed a dash of Ralph Lauren perfume onto Michelle's open cleavage and wrists.

While Michelle protested half heartedly, she was actually enjoying all of the attention. Normally she stood back while Celia, Andrea, or even Paula took the spotlight. After more ribbing abut the wedding night and what the six children would look like, the women stood back and admired their handiwork.

"Very seductive," Celia murmured, twirling Michelle while Andrea and Paula nodded in agreement.

"Go get your man, girl!" Andrea ordered.

"Yeah right!" responded Michelle as once again everybody laughed.

Shango balanced his paper plate of food in one hand and held a plastic fork in the other. He sat in the living room with Ira, Preston and the men from Ira's domino club, enjoying their conversation which when the ladies were out of earshot bordered on the obscene. It had been a while since he'd heard big breasts described as great goolangas. Out of the corner of his eye he watched the man who'd travelled the furthest to be here today. Palmer wore a lightweight, casual but smart black suit and a simple white shirt underneath. His pose was relaxed and every now and again he'd laugh out loud at something said. Once or twice his gaze met with Shango's and he'd raise his eyebrows and nod.

Shango looked around and decided to go for a wander. The house was jam packed with men and women mainly of Ira's age group. Most of them were from Ira's church but some had come from the neighbouring cities of Leicester and Nottingham. Shango was touched and pleased that Ira's day was going so well.

His ears pricked up at the peals of laughter coming from the kitchen but as he popped his head around the door he was met by an immediate silence.

"What's going on, did I hear you mention the name Palmer?" Shango was being mischievous. He'd also noticed Palmer looking in Michelle's direction earlier on.

Celia, Paula and Andrea suddenly became very busy wiping surfaces as they strained to stay quiet.

"Michelle?" Shango addressed the only woman left who wasn't artificially busy, then he noticed that she suddenly looked very lovely.

"Have you done something to your...?" was as far as he got before Celia pushed him back through the door and the women convulsed in fits of laughter. Shango shook his head completely puzzled by their behaviour.

His plate of half eaten food still in his hand, Shango went to answer the ringing door bell. Opening the door wide with a welcoming smile on his face he froze when he saw Sandra standing there. A few seconds seemed like half an hour as Shango stood rooted to the spot.

"Are you going to let us in or what?"
Shango was confused. He could hear a voice but Sandra's lips weren't moving.

"Shango?" The voice was accompanied by an arm which touched his shoulder gently.

Shango looked automatically at Sandra's arms. They were filled with alcohol and presents. His confusion deepened. He looked back to the hand and followed it along from wrist to elbow to shoulder until his gaze was connected with a woman standing next to Sandra.

"Charmaine! Long time no see, how are you girl? Effusively Shango grabbed her up into a bear hug.

"Fine...just....can't.....breathe....." Charmaine gasped.

"Sorry." Shango let her go. "Dad's inside, go on through." His words were for Charmaine but the plea for understanding in his eyes was solely for Sandra.

She held his gaze for less than a second before following her sister into the house. Her message was clear. She had no interest in him, she was there just for Ira.

Shango felt as though he'd been punched in the chest though he fully understood the derision that had flashed from Sandra's eyes. He'd broken his promise to contact her and she could only infer now that he'd been interested in no more than sex. He'd probably caused her to hate him all over again, just like when he'd left her for Sensi.

Shango wondered how he was going to make it through the rest of the day. Once again his true love was close to him but now she despised him. The knowledge was like a knife stuck in his heart. He had to talk to her, explain and make things better. If her could kiss her just once he could make her pain go away and she'd know he meant it when he'd said he loved her.

Shango trailed miserably down the stairs that led from the front door to the small garden. It was separated from the pavement by a low brick wall which he sat on while he automatically reached for the inhaler in his shirt pocket.

As he shook the small canister and put it in his mouth he realized that seeing Sandra had made him forget all about Celia. In the presence of the other woman, his wife had simply ceased to exist.

"Everybody's wondering where you've disappeared to."
With his head hung down Shango saw Rafi's feet before he heard his voice.

"Why do you wear winter boots at the height of summer?" he asked him.

"Who are you avoiding?" Rafi posed his own question.

"Sandra's here."

"I know, so's your wife. What's your point?"

"She thinks I don't care." Shango looked up at Rafi.

"Who, Celia?"

"Sandra thinks I don't care, but I do, I'm in love with her."

"Do you still love Celia?"

"Of course, but not in the same way."

"Doesn't matter. Celia is who you made a promise to. Sandra is just a memory of a happy time. Remember who you are and what you stand for. Go back inside and support your dad on his birthday. Be with your wife and ignore Sandra. You do anything to embarrass Celia in public and I'll kill you myself."

With heavy footsteps and an even heavier heart Shango silently did as he was told knowing that this was Ira's time and his own emotional troubles would have to take a backseat.

"I was told to bring this in here?" Sandra handed the carrier bag of alcohol to Andrea who placed it on the kitchen table.

"Ooh goodies!" Paula looked up from the sink where she was washing up. Michelle and Celia continued their conversation with the other ladies who'd joined them.

"I hope it'll be enough."

"Enough? Girl there must be at least five bottles in here!" Andrea responded.

"Pour a double shot of Bells for the birthday boy and one for me!" Sandra requested as she rocked to the music getting into the spirit of things.

"There you go, give him a big kiss for me!" Andrea saw her off.

"She seemed nice," Andrea commented to Celia who was nosing in the carrier bag that Sandra had brought. "Who was she?"

"Haven't got a clue," said Celia.

Sandra walked gingerly from the kitchen back to the lounge, half expecting a tap on her shoulder from Shango. It had taken all of her courage to come to the party knowing he'd be there. After their day together Sandra had leapt to the phone every time it had rung, feeling the sting of disappointment when it was never him. Every morning and every night she'd checked her e-mail hoping to see a message with his signature. His silence was deafening but his signals were crystal clear. He didn't love her, he'd just used her for sex. Once again she'd let him in and once again he'd broken her heart.

She'd promised Charmaine that they wouldn't stay long at the party. Just a quick drink to be polite and they'd be on their way. Somehow she had to be strong enough to make it through the next hour.

"Hello husband what have you been up to?" Celia slid into Shango's arms as he entered the kitchen.

"Never mind me," Shango looked down at her as they moved in time to the music, "how much have you girls had to drink?"

"Not enough!" Paula waved her glass in the air causing everyone to laugh.

Disentangling himself from Celia, Shango picked up a white cardigan from the table.

"This could get messed up." He held it high so everyone could see, "Who's is it?"

"A woman came in with those drinks in that bag. I think it's hers, I'll ask her when she comes back," Andrea offered.

"Don't worry I got it." Shango swiftly left the room and dashed upstairs. From the time he'd seen it he'd already guessed that the delicately crocheted cardigan was Sandra's. It was exactly the type of thing she'd wear. In Ira's bedroom Shango held it to his face and breathed in her scent. God, he'd missed her.

Ninety minutes later all of the visitors were assembled in the lounge. There was an excited air of expectancy in the air.

"Ladies and gentlemen," Palmer's deep American lilt caused everyone to hush; he used the microphone from the Karaoke machine to help his voice carry through the downstairs rooms, "...distinguished guests..." Palmer nodded in Michelle's direction. Michelle could feel her temperature soar as he held her gaze for a second.

Celia looked up at Shango to see if he'd picked up the vibes but he was swatting at a wasp that had flown in from the back garden. She prodded him to stand still, but he used the excuse of squishing the pesky wasp to do a three hundred and sixty degree turn to scan the room. He noticed that Sandra was nowhere to be seen. He'd asked Charmaine to pass on her cardigan and prayed that she'd check her pockets and find the note he'd put there begging for another chance to explain. This could be his last window of opportunity and this time he wouldn't fail her.

"...on behalf of myself and my brother," Palmer continued, "I'd like to thank you all for coming here to celebrate with my dad who's seventy years young today! He's a special man with a great personality and we wish him many more happy birthdays!"

Palmer spoke over the spontaneous clapping and cheering that erupted. "Slow your roll, er......that means....hang on a minute. I'd like to introduce an extra special gift for Dad. He's already had the cigars and the Champagne, now here's something different."

"What is it?" Ira interrupted, curiosity getting the better of him.

"I can pre-empty it!" Rafi shouted out.

Palmer's infectious chuckles set off titters around the room. Enjoying the atmosphere Ira laughed loudest of all and slapped Palmer playfully on the arm.

"Did you mean, pre-empt?" Ira asked still grinning.

"That's what I said, pre-empty it," Rafi agreed causing another burst of laughter from the crowd.

Watching Palmer and Ira interact so well, made Shango proud and happy. Palmer had moved to Ira's house after spending three nights with himself and Celia. It was working out well. Ira was a sociable man and living alone didn't agree with him.

This afternoon his true personality came to the fore. He was lively, witty, handsome and gifted with a charismatic presence that filled the room. Thankfully the mental confusion that was cropping up so regularly was in abeyance today. Once again he was just normal Ira, the heart and soul of the party.

Celia glanced at Shango pleased to see the beaming smile on his face. Shango drew her to his chest and kissed her forehead. Despite his initial doubts about throwing a party for Ira, today had turned out exceptionally well. Across the room he noticed Paula sitting on Rafi's knee. They made a good looking couple and Paula had a kind heart, despite her loose reputation. He would have liked to see them make a go of it.

"Are you ready, Dad?" Palmer held his hand up for quiet. "Ladies and gentlemen, please give a big hand to *The Lilt Ladies Part Two: It Should A Been We!*"

Ska music metamorphosed into a rhythmic Calypso beat as Maida and Fay entered the room. Their heads wrapped in colourful bandanas, the two ladies, both in their sixties, wore fluorescent leotards in lime green and banana yellow. Waving orange feather boas they danced and cavorted with men, women and children. Familiar phrases such as; "Smile you boring little man," were succeeded by roars of laughter. After working through the crowd they salsa-ed their way over to a grinning Ira.

"I can't believe it's you two!" he exclaimed in disbelief.

"It's time to raise a glass to the birthday boy!" Maida patted Ira's belly while Fay draped herself across his lap.

For the next twenty minutes Ira, Shango, Palmer and all of

their friends and relatives laughed until tears ran down their cheeks. Maida and Fay worked the room grabbing and embarrassing whomever was in their path. Clothing, jewellery, hairstyles, partners, nothing was too sacred to send up. At the end of the night it was unanimously agreed, *The Lilt Ladies Part Two: It Should A Been We* were a great success.

"I've brought you a refill."

"Thank you." Michelle took the glass of dry white wine from Palmer. Apart from brief "hellos" in passing, this was the first chance they'd had to talk properly. All of a sudden her palms grew sweaty and she couldn't meet his eyes.

"It's gone really well." Palmer was happy to have such a beautiful woman all to himself. Around them people partied but he felt like she was the only person in the room.

"I've never seen him so happy." Michelle sipped her drink and fought the urge to fiddle nervously with her necklace .

"It's been a…" "I was wondering?" they spoke at the same time.

"Ladies first," Palmer offered.

"No, please, you go first," Michelle insisted.

Palmer noticed that she was even cuter when she was flustered. "Sorry." He laughed. "I was wondering if I could take you out this week?"

Michelle's heart screamed", Yes please, "but her response was characteristically demure.

"That might be nice."

"Can I call you?"

"Sure, if you can catch me."

• • • • • •

Shango stood in the doorway saying goodbye to the guests. The majority of people had gone but a few stragglers gathered their possessions and proposed one last toast to Ira.

"Shango, later!" Rafi fished out his car keys as he rushed past.

"What's up?" Shango called after him.

"That's my car!" Rafi shouted back.

"What?!" Shango was confused.

Rafi unlocked the door of his car and pointed towards the main road. Paula went running after him.

"Rafi, you said you'd give me a lift home!"

Shango watched as Paula was dragged in and the car took off at high speed.

When the last guest had finally gone and only Preston remained, Shango went to find Celia. She was talking with Palmer in the kitchen. "Ready babe?" he kissed her on the back of her neck and hugged her from behind.

"Yes love." She kissed Palmer's cheek. "See you soon."

"Later, bro." Shango and Palmer touched fists.

"Link with you tomorrow?" Shango checked. Palmer nodded as he took another sip of his Guinness.

"It's only nine o'clock and I'm shattered," Celia yawned as she drove home. "Ira had fun didn't he?" she smiled at the memory of Ira trying out his chat-up lines on the younger women.

"Hold on, phone's buzzing." Shango flipped open the receiver of his Nokia, "Yep?"

"It's me," Palmer sounded stressed.

"What's the matter?" Shango asked, glancing at Celia.

"It's Dad. He opened a birthday card, one of those musical ones and it sent him loco."

"What do you mean loco?"

"The music played, tinny and irritating and he ripped it up. He was shouting, no more noise! Then he put his hands on his head and just sat there rocking."

"Where is he now?"

"Lying down, I managed to get him upstairs."

"Where's Preston?"

"I asked him to make Dad some tea."

"I'm turning 'round." Shango gestured to Celia who frowned as she'd just turned onto a one way street.

"No need, man, he's calm now. I just wanted to know if he had any pills that he should take to help him relax?"

"Not that I know of. Are you sure he's okay?"

"I'll keep an eye on him. It's been a long day, maybe he's overtired."

"I don't mind coming back." Shango was still anxious.

"I got it, we'll talk tomorrow, okay?"

"Thanks for calling, when he wakes up give him our love."

"Roger that," Palmer signed off.

Shango hung up with a sigh. He'd hoped that Ira wouldn't experience any kinds of problems on his birthday. Celia rubbed his leg sympathetically.

"He'll be okay," she said softly, "it's been a long and busy day for him, you have to remember his age. Just let him get some rest and he'll be fine."

Shango nodded at Celia's comforting words but for some reason he couldn't quite fathom his heart was uneasy.

CHAPTER ELEVEN

Why?

SHANGO READ THE one word e-mail. He closed his eyes thinking of the most appropriate response. There was a knock on the door.

"Mr Shango here's those completed bibliographies that you requested. Just drop them on my desk when you've finished I'll distribute them. Oh, sorry, am I disturbing you?"

Shango politely shook his head. Linda, the department secretary, had a talent for blundering into situations and stating the obvious. He had a few minutes before picking up Kai. Celia was working in the office at home but at the university he could check and respond to his e-mail without interruptions. At least that was the grand theory, but he'd forgotten that the secretaries started back today.

Shango read the e-mail again. The single word could be referring to anything. Did Sandra want to know why he'd slipped the note into her cardigan at Ira's party? Or was it more than that? Did she wonder why he loved her, why he had to see her again, why he couldn't get her out of his system? Or conversely, was she asking why she should bother with him?

My dad's not doing so good. He typed the letters and pressed send. Then he absentmindedly scratched his head hoping for an immediate response. Using Ira's confused state of mind was a cheap shot but he was desperate to keep her attention.

What's wrong with him? The message flashed up in bright blue letters.

"*I'll tell you when we meet,*" he quickly typed in reply.

Why?

There it was again.

What do you mean why? Because I love you that's why.

Shango wiped his brow, he felt as though he was walking along a tight rope. He looked at the screen. Hope turned to impatience and wilted into despair as no new e-mails popped into his in-box.

After two long minutes he made himself a cup of coffee, still keeping an eye on the monitor. He sipped the hot liquid while leafing through a book of African Art and Design and raised his eyebrows toward the monitor. Still no message.

He walked over to the window and looked out onto the landscaped grounds. His office was on the first floor and he had a view of pink cherry blossom trees and deep red rose bushes. He admired them, grateful for their beauty as always. After weeks of glorious sunshine the dull August day was a mirror of his sinking feelings as he prayed for Sandra to write back. He approached his monitor and sat down before it, sending unconscious psychic messages to Sandra in her city centre office.

Shango rose and began angrily packing away his papers and books. He turned his back to the screen stifling the urge to throw it against the wall As he deliberated over sending Sandra one last message before he left for the day, a beep came from his computer speakers signaling a new message. He reeled around automatically checking the sender's name.

> *Wish I knew what you wanted from my life. Kiss Ira*
> *better for me.*
> *S.*

Sandra hadn't said that she loved him or wanted to see him but she hadn't brushed him off either. It was up to him to do the rest. He hummed to himself as he walked to the car park. This time he had no intention of letting her go. Whatever questions she asked, he'd answer. Whatever she wanted, he'd give her. She was already in his heart, now he just needed to find a way to keep her in his life.

••••••

"How was your day, babe?"

Shango smiled up at Celia as she came downstairs to meet him. He'd just dropped Kai home after taking him and his friends to the Sea Life Centre. It had been fun but now he was worn out.

"Busy but I still had time to miss you," he replied.

"Really?" Celia teased as they went through to the kitchen where Shango washed up in preparation for cooking. Celia handed him a towel to dry his hands.

"How did you get on with your articles today?" Shango's head was in the fridge where he was sorting out vegetables.

"Pretty good." Celia chomped on a raw carrot, "I had an e-mail from the editor of an American Journal. They've seen my work and they're interested in commissioning some articles from me."

"Excellent!" Shango kissed her on the cheek. "Any topic in particular?"

"Something along the lines of contrasting educational methodology for black girls here and in the US. You're dripping water!" she warned him as the pot in his hand tilted dangerously. "Are we having anything else with these vegetables?" Celia nosed around the pots, always happy for Shango to cook their evening meal. It meant he was a captive audience. After writing in solitary for several hours, she was grateful to have someone to talk to if Michelle wasn't around.

"What would you like?" Shango asked as he washed and picked the rice.

"No more fish, please."

Shango was eating less meat lately, consequently for most of the summer they'd dined on a variety of fish.

"Okay," Shango chuckled as Celia pulled a face.

The phone rang and Celia went into the living room to answer it. "It's for you," she called, "Rafi."

"Finish the rice for me please, honey." Shango left the kitchen to take the call.

Celia's heart sank. How could Shango forget that she couldn't cook rice to save her life? Sighing she put the kettle to boil. At least she'd remembered that rice needed hot water and not cold. But how much water? She filled the whole kettle and half a large saucepan just in case.

The sound of Shango's laughter reverberated along the corridor, through the kitchen and out in to the back garden where Celia pruned her plants while the water boiled. She shook her head wondering what Rafi'd been up to.

"So that's why you left Dad's in such a hurry," Shango said into the phone.

"I knew it was my car!" came Rafi's reply.

"But how could you spot it, if it went so fast?" Shango paced around the living room absentmindedly picking things up and putting them back while fully engrossed in Rafi's story.

"Trust me, I know my things."

"So what happened?"

"I sped after it!"

"What about Paula?"

"Paula?"

"I saw you drag her into the car."

"Woman was slowing me down! Anyway, I'm catching up to my stolen car speeding down Soho Road towards the lights at Grove Lane and Paula's screaming "Slow down, slow down!" Then I hear sirens and see flashing lights and Paula's going 'I told you so!'"

"Was it the fuzz?"

"Yeah, they let the driver get away!"

"Did you explain?"

"I tried to; they wouldn't listen."

"So what happened blood?"

"I got done for speeding. Immediate fine, three points on my licence."

"That's rough!" Shango was in fits.

"Stop laughing, it's not funny!"

"What's so hilarious?" asked Celia as she entered the room.

"Rafi got fined for speeding."

Celia frowned at him, not getting the joke.

"He was chasing his own car!" Shango could barely speak through his laughter.

"The one that got stolen?"

"Yeah!"

"You mean Rafi was chasing his own stolen car that was being driven by the thief and the police fined him for speeding and let the thief go?"

By now Shango was in bits on the floor where Celia joined him. Eventually their laughter died down when Celia remembered the food and Shango realized that Rafi was still on the line.

"Have you finished?" Rafi asked patiently.

"That's the funniest thing I've heard all year."

"It won't be funny if my insurance shoots up and I can't afford to drive. It would take me more than two hours on the bus to reach Melody and that's not even a return trip."

Shango listened silently to the regret in Rafi's voice.

"I can't let anything get in the way of seeing her. I shouldn't have been so reckless."

"You acted on impulse," Shango tried to console him." Anybody would have done what you did, it's a natural reaction."

"I'm all that Melody has, I should have been more careful. What if I'd had an accident?"

"It's over and you're okay, you and Paula, that's the main thing."

"I really think she might be with me soon, you know." Rafi's voice sounded brighter.

"Paula?" Shango was confused.

"Not Paula, Melody."

"Great! What have they said?"

"Nothing exactly, but she's doing so well."

"Don't get your hopes up Rafi, just in case. She's been in care a long time."

"She hardly has any fits these days. Her school reports say she's making progress."

"But the staff at the home haven't given any indication that she could move out to be with you?"

"Not in so many words, but everything points to that."

"Rafi I know you want Melody with you but…"

"–When she sees me she talks non-stop. We go for a drive or we watch a video or I play a game with her. Last week we even cooked together: scrambled eggs on toast with Tabasco sauce."

Shango listened as Rafi spoke of his dreams about what life would be like when he was reunited with his baby sister in their own house. He was prepared to give up work and the possibility of a relationship with Paula. The sacrifices came as nothing. He wanted Melody home with him where she belonged.

"Sometimes I just look at her, she's beautiful, you know, Shango. Thick, long hair like Mom's, smiley dimples just like Dad. Her skin's a kind of golden colour. Some days I just wish that I could give her my brain and send her off to be a model, or a secretary, or a mom with her own babies, whatever she wanted." Rafi's voice broke with emotion.

Shango stayed silent, there was nothing he could say to erase Rafi's pain.

"Maybe I shouldn't but I think about what she'd be like if she didn't have the fits and the slow learning. I bet she'd be really cheeky." Rafi chuckled. "She'd be looking at boys and wanting to go to dances. She'd probably never do as she was told." He carried on chuckling and Shango joined in, "I'd have to show my karate moves to those fresh boys."

"Karate! You?" Shango teased.

"You know what I mean!" Rafi laughed. "But how she *could* be doesn't matter, loving her is in my genes. She's all I have left and when I look at her I see Mom and that comforts me. Every time I get home after seeing her the house seems bigger and emptier. I can't wait to do up her bedroom, put up some Britney Spears and Beyonce posters. We can listen to their CDs at bedtime. She's left handed you know."

"She is?"

"Yeah, she's a star. A real star." Rafi went quiet. There was an ache in his chest at the familiar thought that his little sister might never come home. "Listen, man, I'll check you in the week. Basketball or something." He signalled an abrupt goodbye to his best friend.

"Stay strong, kiss Melody for me." Shango hung up.

The smell of burnt cooking drifted along the corridor. Shango heard the clattering of utensils and the splat of food being dropped onto the hard floor followed by a string of rude words. His heart weighed down with Rafi's anguish, he went to rescue what was left of the vegetables and rice.

●●●●●●

The phone rang once before Michelle snatched it up, pushing aside her piles of paperwork and long lists of figures in order to do so.

"Hey good looking," Palmer's sexy voice reverberated down the line. Michelle automatically checked her reflection in the huge mirror that hung over her fireplace. Then she blushed, feeling stupid, as she realized that Palmer couldn't actually see her.

"Hello, are you still there?"

Michelle had never heard such an appealing accent.

"This is a surprise, erm, hi!" she managed finally.

"I managed to catch you then?" Palmer joked.

"Yes, you did. How have you been?" she continued, doing her best to make her quivering voice sound normal and trying to remember when a man last had such an effect on her.

"Fine, you know. How about you?" Palmer sounded as though he was actually interested in what she'd been up to since they'd last met at Ira's party. But, despite her joy at hearing from him, Michelle still couldn't help wondering if he was genuine.

"I'm okay, just busy with work. I'm…"

"Aah!" Palmer interrupted.

"Sorry?" Michelle began.

"I love the way English people say that, 'sorry?'" Palmer laughed.

"Did I say something wrong?" Michelle asked.

"Oh, no," Palmer rushed to reassure her. "No, no, no. I'd love to know exactly what you do at work and much more, but not right now."

"Oh," Michelle was completely bewildered.

"I'm going up North for a couple of days to see some of Mom's relatives. I was actually calling to ask if you'd like to have dinner with me when I get back."

Palmer realized he was holding his breath as he waited for a reply. Michelle wasn't talking so he rushed to fill the uncomfortable silence. Michelle, meanwhile, had put the handset on the settee and was uncharacteristically jumping up and down in her stockinged feet and formal navy work suit. Just as she was getting breathless, she picked up the phone and wordlessly counted to three.

"If there's any particular food that you don't eat or if you'd rather watch a movie…" Palmer's nerves made him ramble.

"–Dinner would be lovely," Michelle interjected anxious to put him at ease, "and I'm not a fussy eater." She heard the smile in Palmer's voice when he responded.

"I'll pick you up about eight the day after I get back from Manchester."

"Bye then," said Michelle.

"Bye honey," said Palmer and he also heard the smile in Michelle's voice.

•••••••

The phone was on its fourth ring before Celia picked it up. She'd been lying on the thick rug in front of the television reading Black Hair and Beauty magazine. Unwilling to move from her comfortable position she'd willed Shango to answer the call but he'd just ignored it.

"Hello," Celia said.

"Celia, it's me, are you dressed?"

"No Michelle, I'm wandering around the house stark naked in fact we both are."

"Your neighbours will start complaining. How soon can you get to mine?"

"What's up?"

"We're going out."

"Where?"

"I'll explain on the way."

Michelle was glad she hadn't changed out of her work clothes as it saved her the bother of getting dressed all over again. In her bathroom she patted on a little more foundation to brighten her complexion. Then she cleaned her teeth and applied burgundy lipstick. She frowned as she looked in the mirror, unsure if the dark red colour suited her, but it was a change from the neutral lip-glosses she normally wore. She'd wanted something different and the Fashion Fair consultant had said this colour suited her skin tones. Michelle hoped it would grow on her. Finally, she smoothed light gel into her slicked back ponytail. In a couple of months she'd get extensions, but relaxed hair was always cooler in summer.

She glanced around her kitchen ensuring that nothing dangerous had been left on. Her coat, bag and car keys were piled neatly together near the front door. Michelle was fidgety as she waited for Celia to arrive. She calculated the drive from Celia's house to hers would take about twenty minutes, plus Celia had to get herself together, that alone could take ages. With restless fingers she dialled Celia's mobile but pressed the 'off' button before it rang. If she interrupted her she'd probably take even longer. She pressed the remote for the TV and turned the volume down. She lit a cigarette and tried to concentrate on the silent forms of Phil and Peggy Mitchell in the bustling surroundings of the Queen Vic. Anything to get her mind off the gorgeous Palmer.

"Babe are you going out tonight?" Celia turned to Shango who was stretched out on the settee skimming the local evening newspaper.

"Palmer's going up to Manchester in a bit. Dad'll be on his own again. I'll look in on him."

"Can you drop me to Michelle's?" Celia cushioned her request with a kiss on Shango's lips.

"Was that her on the phone?" Shango groaned.

"Yeah, she wants me to go somewhere with her."

"Where?"

"Don't know, she didn't say."

"When?"

"Now."

"She clicks her fingers and you go running?" Shango raised one eyebrow and looked directly at Celia.

"It's not like that, anyway you'd do it for Rafi."

"I'd do it if it was an emergency."

"But you can go to your dad's now and drop me off on the

way."

"It's in the opposite direction!"

"Thanks darling! I'll be two ticks!" Celia ran upstairs to get ready before Shango could protest any more.

He swung his legs wearily onto the floor, folded the newspaper neatly, checked his back pocket for the car keys and put the cushions back up on the settee.

"Come on then, woman, before I change my mind," he called up the stairs. "Will you need me to pick you up?" Shango pulled the curtains shut and switched on the side lamps. As an after thought he turned the radio on.

"I'll get Michelle to drop me back. Are you leaving that playing?" Celia heard the music as she came downstairs.

"Yeah, I think it creates a nice ambience." Shango smiled.

Celia pushed him playfully toward the door. "Nice ambience!" she mocked.

• • • • • •

"Hi, I'm Michelle Hamilton. I'm here to see Tanya."

"What time's your appointment?"

"I called about forty-five minutes ago and I was told I could see Tanya as soon as I arrived."

"I'll just her let you're here. Are you both having a reading?" The counter assistant glanced at Celia who frowned and shook her head vigorously.

"Can she come in with me?" Michelle asked.

"Should be all right, but check with Tanya when she calls you up."

"Thanks."

The girls had gone to the showcase canal area behind Birmingham's golden clubbing mile. It was packed with shops, hotels, restaurants and bars. Michelle stood patiently by the counter in the Zen New Age shop trying not to stare at another customer's clothes which were an eclectic mix of colourful patterns and fabrics; blonde spiked dreadlocks covered her head. The lengths some people go to for attention, Michelle mused.

Celia wandered around fascinated by her surroundings. Floor to ceiling bookshelves lined three quarters of one wall. The rest of the section was devoted to a fantastic variety of essential oils with neat handwritten tags, describing their purposes.

On the back wall of the shop were kits for spells and wishes along with "magic candles." Nearer the front of the shop were magnificent sculptured wax candles in a variety of colours some up to a foot high. These shelves were filled with a selection of oil burners and Feng Shui cures ranging from Chinese coins to wind chimes.

Celia eased past some tourists into the middle of the shop. The floor stands held bowls of crystals, some odd shaped, some smooth and flat. Charm bracelets made of precious stones with exotic names dangled from the ceiling. There were also more handwritten notes describing the qualities of the crystals. They advised the buyer to pick whichever stone they were drawn to. Celia couldn't decide between the pale rose quartz crystal for love, or the grey lodestone, which was supposed to aid in business transactions.

A colourful array of handwoven tapestries nailed to the walls led the way upstairs to the first floor. At the foot of the staircase was a stand which held glittering bookmarks The bookmarks detailed personality traits for each day of the month. Celia couldn't resist talking a peek at Shango's. She ran her finger along the markers, her tongue licking her top lip. Shango's birthday was the thirtieth of December.

You're a natural born charmer, it read, blessed with the ability to communicate with young and old of any nationality. Celia smiled at its accuracy.

"Michelle Hamilton!" Celia and Michelle followed the call to the top of the stairs where a middle aged black woman stood smiling down at them.

"Michelle?" she queried looking from one to the other.

"That's me."

"Please come up," Tanya invited.

Celia stood aside to let Michelle pass, she wanted to finish reading Shango's numerology bookmark but Michelle grabbed her arm and pulled her up the stairs.

"This is Celia, can she come in too?"

"It's your reading, whatever you want is fine by me." Tanya led the women into a small curtained off section of the upstairs floor. The dark purple interior walls were lit by a small round table lamp. A card table was positioned between two plastic chairs. Soothing pan pipe music played quietly in the background. Tanya pointed to a stool in the corner away from the table.

"Sit here, please, Celia."

"Okay." Celia's first impression of the petite dark skinned lady with the batik head-wrap and casual African overshirt, were favourable. She winked at Michelle.

Tanya sat opposite Michelle at the table and handed her a pack of Tarot cards.

"These are a little unwieldy because of their size, but I'd like you to shuffle them and then cut them into three."

Michelle's hands shook as she manoeuvred the cards.

"Take your time," Tanya said softly. "Place them on the table, that's it, now pick a pack."

Michelle chose the middle deck and placed it in Tanya's outstretched palm. Tanya laid out a spread in the shape of a cross. Some cards overlapped and some lay on their own.

"Interesting." Tanya nodded raising her eyes from the cards to Michelle, "What would you like to know?"

"She's in *lurve*!" Celia piped up from her corner.

Michelle flashed her a dark look, Tanya stifled a laugh.

"Sorry," Celia muttered.

"There is a man waiting to enter your life; he's not from here," Tanya said as she scanned the cards.

Celia inhaled, Michelle flashed her another stern look.

"Sorry," Celia mouthed.

"He's well off but he's not happy." Tanya glanced at Michelle who shrugged. "He has the Death card on his right. Don't be alarmed, it merely means change, and this change could come about very soon."

"Can you tell me about his personality? Is he a good man?" Michelle asked.

Tanya dealt another round from the second pack of cards that Michelle had shuffled. "He's a loyal and caring person with the ability to love deeply. But unresolved family conflicts affect him more than he realises. He stands at a crossroads and must decide whether to go back to the life he knows or whether to step forward to uncertainty."

"Which would work out best for him?"

"Ultimately only he can decide what to do." Tanya indicted the Strength card. "This woman either holds the Lion's mouth open or keeps it shut. It means that he has the inner courage to do what's right."

"Is there any room for me in the middle of all of this uncertainty?" Michelle asked the burning question, in response Tanya flipped another card.

"Is your birth sign Virgo?"

"Yes!" Michelle couldn't hide her surprise.

Celia rolled her eyes.

"There is a Virgo woman around this man. But there is also another woman, a Scorpio who feels she has a tight hold on him. She will be your greatest threat." Tanya pointed at another card, "This Cupid card is symbolic of a pairing; love and marriage await him. But with the wrong choice the marriage will not be happy."

Tanya checked her watch. Surprisingly half an hour had passed. All three women rose.

"Thank you so much." Michelle shook Tanya's hand.

"I hope I've been of some help to you. God bless and don't worry about anything."

••••••

"Looks like we'll be busy on Saturday then?" Celia poured boiling water over the tea bags and milk. She added sugar to her own but none for Michelle. They'd driven to her house in silence relistening to the reading on the tape Tanya had given them, Michelle intently absorbing every word.

"What's happening on Saturday?" Michelle asked.

"There's the bridesmaid's dresses to sort out, shoes, cake, reception venue, rings…"

"For who?"

"For you and Palmer!" Celia cracked up at the shocked expression on Michelle's face.

"Not so fast!" Michelle protested, "I never expected her to come out with anything like that."

"If you will play with fire!" Celia teased. "Let's settle in the lounge. Shango left the radio on, we can listen to it while we plan your guest list."

••••••

Sandra left -clicked the computer mouse looking for a distraction from her own melancholy. She'd waited until eleven thirty for the call that never came. She scrolled through the icons on screen considering her choices. Iyanla Vanzant, Jewel Diamond Taylor, Dr Bertice Berry and a plethora of other American psycho-analysts all there to help her focus on everything but the acute disappointment she felt. Shango had sent her an e-mail at one forty-five saying he'd call her later. Had he meant later that day or later in life? She tried to convince herself that she didn't care.

Sandra clicked onto a page that promised the wisdom of a

highly respected self-esteem counsellor. You promised me you'd be there for me, Shango, she mused. You said you needed one more chance to show me you were serious, but apart from a few rushed e-mails when have you had time for me? What are we doing? Where is this heading?

On the radio Gladys Knight sang, *"Take the ribbon from my hair...."* Sandra turned up the volume, her chest tight with emotion as she remembered the time when this used to be their song. She and Shango had held each other close many times while Gladys had sung their unspoken thoughts and feelings.

"Shango what do you want from my life?" Sandra wondered aloud as the DJ spoke.

"A treat tonight for fans of the great lady, Gladys Knight. This is from Shango to Sandra. He sends deep love and many apologies and asks for your forgiveness. He says he"ll make it up to you," the presenter continued, *"...sounds like someone's in the dog house. To Sandra from a repentant and loving Shango, here's Gladys."*

Sandra relaxed as the tension left her body. With a few simple words Shango had erased her anger and replaced it with love.

• • • • • •

Over at Ira's house Shango left a scribbled note on the kitchen table.

> *Hope you slept well Pops. I left at midnight. I'll call round tomorrow with Kai. If you've got other plans, just give me a call.*
>
> *Shango*

Treading softly, Shango locked the front door securely behind him.

• • • • • •

In the lounge of Celia and Shango's house Michelle switched off the radio and confronted her best friend.

"What are you going to do?"

"I'm not sure. I need to think about it."

"Girl you must be crazy! What is there to think about? Your

husband has just declared his love for another woman on national radio. He's humiliated you! Kick him to the kerb!"

"It's not that simple. I can't throw him out, it's his house too." Through her feeble protests Celia was remembering Shango switching on the radio before they left the house earlier.

"It's after midnight. Ira must be asleep by now. I'll wait till Shango comes in and we'll face him together. I've got some heavy words for him; the good for nothing, low down, sneaky, double crossing, lying…"

"There's no need, Michelle. Just go home."

"But!"

"Michelle this is my problem, I'll deal with it."

Angry at Celia's apathy Michelle grabbed her bag, stomped along the wooden hallway and turned at the front door.

"Love may be blind but don't let it make a fool of you Celia." Without waiting for a reply she turned the handle and was gone.

Celia rose from the settee and folded away the broadsheet newspaper, which carried her article *Education and Caribbean Girls*. She selected two meaty chicken legs, a generous helping of rice and peas, ready to be micro- waved, and placed cling film lightly over a side plate of salad. She set the table with condiments and a jug of juice, knowing her husband would be hungry when he came home. Then she went upstairs to shower and prepare for bed. She decided to wear the powder blue negligee and spray on Amarige de Givenchy perfume. They were Shango's favourites.

Shaking the rain off his umbrella as he entered his house twenty minutes later, Shango walked straight to the kitchen to eat the meal he knew Celia would have left for him. He placed the meat and rice in the microwave and set the dial to six minutes before taking off his damp coat. As he replaced his leather shoes with soft soled suede moccasins his mobile phone beeped. He glanced at the wall clock before retrieving the phone from his coat.

"Who's sending messages at this time of night?" he wondered aloud. He inhaled in anticipation at the smell of seasoned chicken permeating from the microwave. As the oven tinged Shango checked the screen on his Nokia. The envelope icon informed him he had a text message.

"WHO DA HELL IS SANDRA?" The letters assaulted his eyes. "DOES C NO BOUT ER?"

Shango checked the sender's number again. Sensi. She must have heard the request he made for Sandra but since when did she listen to anything but community radio? As he read the rest of the angry text Shango remembered that he'd left his own radio on earlier that night.

Reluctantly he walked along the passage to the living room. Stooping at the stereo he studied the fluorescent green line that indicated the various stations. His heart sank but even as he switched it on he hoped that he was still wrong.

"Welcome if you've just joined us," the DJ announced. *"We play the love songs you request every night from eleven pm until three am. Half an hour of back to back love classics coming up next."*

Shango sat on the sofa and rubbed the back of his neck. His appetite had vanished and he felt sick to his stomach. How could he have been so stupid? He didn't even know if Sandra had heard his request for her but now he was fairly certain that Celia and Sensi and goodness knows who else had. How foolish, how idiotic, how senseless. He was always advising the men of EBYN to stand in love and now he'd just fallen flat on his face.

"Shango have you eaten? Are you coming up?" Celia's voice travelled down the stairs.

Shango listened. There was no trace of anger or animosity in her tone. He had no idea how she'd repay his treachery, he'd just have to stay alert.

"Yes," he answered, "I'm on my way."

In the kitchen he scrapped the contents of his plate into the bin before clearing the table. He poured a stiff scotch over ice, leaned back against the counter top and sipped it slowly. The cold liquid refreshed him and calmed his nerves.

Upstairs in the bathroom Shango brushed his teeth and washed his face. In the silent dark of their bedroom he replaced his trousers and his t-shirt with light cotton boxer shorts. Then he crawled under the fresh smelling sheets and cuddled up to his wife. He nuzzled her neck and let his hands roam over the smoothness of her satin night gown.

"Is it the blue one?" he asked, trying to keep the guilt out of his voice.

"Yes," Celia replied softly. "How's Ira?"

"He's fine. I left him sleeping. How's Michelle?" Shango tried to match her tone.

"Same as usual," Celia answered. Both of them ignored the fact that Celia didn't elaborate about her time with Michelle as she normally would have. "Did you enjoy your supper?"

"It was very nice, thank you," Shango lied. "Good night, my

wife."

"Good night, my husband." Celia squeezed her eyes shut to stop the tears falling onto Shango's arm curled under her neck.

Shango closed his eyes and dreamt that he held Sandra in his embrace. Neither one stirred until morning.

CHAPTER TWELVE

"AS SOON AS…" Celia held onto the three tiny words as if she was clutching a safety net. She'd planned that *as soon as* she awoke she'd tell Shango that she'd heard the request and she'd demand to know exactly who Sandra was. He'd respond by saying that crazy Rafi was just playing a joke. He'd kiss her, make love to her and remind her that she was the only woman for him. But Shango had woken at six thirty and was gone by seven am.

Celia thought that *as soon as* she'd got through her morning's work she'd call Shango on his mobile, ask him to come home for lunch and then lightly mention what she'd heard with Michelle the night before. He'd say it was Kai being silly, they'd giggle at his son's antics and spend the rest of the day curled up on the settee watching Sky movies.

It was now four o'clock in the afternoon. Celia hadn't been able to reach Shango all day and she was getting hungry. She walked up the hill to the Marks and Spencer food outlet to get something to warm in the microwave. She decided that *as soon as* she'd eaten she'd call Shango to find out what time he'd be home. She might even ask him whether he'd had the radio on at Ira's last night. He'd say that the daft request was for one of the secretaries at Uni who was retiring. Celia would tease him about chasing after older women. Then they would get back to being a happily married couple.

As soon as…

"Excuse me!" The cashier shouted to her, but Celia was in a world of her own. She walked towards the entrance doors where someone pulled her arm startling her back to reality.

"That woman's calling you," a shopper pointed out. Celia looked around.

"You haven't paid!" the assistant yelled. All of the people queuing at the tills turned towards a dazed looking Celia.

"Miss?" A security guard appeared at her side. Celia looked up at him with dark eyes that were on the brink of tears. "I think you forgot to pay." The young black man's face was full of sympathy for the pretty woman who resembled his last girlfriend whom he'd really loved. He had no intention of letting her be embarrassed in a shop full of strangers.

"Over here." He guided her by the elbow. "How much is it?" he asked the girl when they reached the checkout. She looked at her till display.

"Seven forty-three," she said in a voice that was unnecessarily loud.

"Seven pounds and forty-three pence, Miss," the guard relayed the price in a soft tone to Celia who remained silent and didn't move. "Is your purse in your bag?" he prompted gently.

The mist that was shrouding Celia's mind cleared as she realised that she was the centre of all the commotion. She pulled her bag off her shoulder, opened her purse and handed the cashier her credit card. A few minutes later it was handed back to her with a reluctant, "Thanks."

"Would you like a hand to your car?" The guard was going out of his way to ensure she was all right. Celia's vulnerability had touched a soft spot within him.

"I walked up, it's not far, I'll be okay." Celia spoke slowly, gratitude inherent in her words. Then she began her walk back down the hill. *As soon as* she got home Shango would be waiting for her. He'd explain and then everything would be okay.

"Shango!" Celia called out when she opened the front door. She listened for his voice but the house felt cold and all she heard was silence. "Shango!" she called again willing him to shout back. But there was no reply. She'd returned to an empty shell.

In the kitchen Celia turned her shopping bags upside down and spilled the contents onto the table. She pushed the carrier bags to one side and appraised what she'd bought. Over seven pounds worth of chocolate biscuits, sponge cakes and boiled sweets glistened in front of her. There was nothing that she could heat up and call dinner. But as she looked at the sugary heap, Celia realised that neither comfort food nor proper nourishment could fill the aching hollow that had formed inside since she'd heard Shango's request.

Celia walked into the lounge and dialled his mobile. Again the recorded message told her to try later. Where the hell was he? What the hell was he doing and who was he with? Celia decided to check upstairs to see if he'd popped back while she was out.

At the foot of the stairs she caught sight of herself in the hallway mirror. She wore a dress that had long ago been consigned to the back of her wardrobe. How had she ended up putting it on today? It was made of wool that was too thick for the summer and it smelt of old sweat. It reached her calves and its outdated rust colour clashed with her skin tone.

Celia touched her hair realising that she hadn't combed it. It was spiky in some places and knotted in others. She had dried tear stains on her face and her lips were cracked as though she was dehydrated. She was appalled that she looked so disgusting but she didn't have the energy to do anything about it.

She wished Shango would come through the door and take her in his arms. Reassure her that she'd got it all wrong, call her silly while rubbing her down gently in a hot bath, cream her skin from head to toe, cover her with baby kisses and ease away her pain with slow lovemaking.

The phone rang and Celia rushed back to the lounge. At the last minute she stopped herself from picking it up realising that she didn't want to talk to anyone except Shango. Michelle's voice came through on the answering machine.

"Celia are you okay? This is the third message I've left. Where are you woman? Did you sort things out with him yet? I'm going to dinner with Palmer tonight but I'll keep my phone on. If you need me, call me. Don't worry okay? Just call me. Love you, bye."

Tears rolled down Celia's cheeks at the care and concern in Michelle's voice. Laboriously she climbed the stairs to her bedroom and pulled her suitcase from the top of the wardrobe. Shango had disappeared when she needed him most and the enforced solitude was overwhelming.

She selected a few things from each drawer, the bathroom and her closets. She moved without thinking. All she wanted now was to return to the home where she grew up so that her dad, Martin, could feed her soup and hold her hand until she fell asleep. So that for a few precious hours she could be a problem free little girl, instead of a grown woman deeply in love with a husband who loved someone else. So that she could be embraced by the love of her parents, knowing that whatever was wrong the three of them could fix together. She wanted to feel safe, secure and loved again, if just for a little while.

Michelle showered and dressed with meticulous care. The lace and satin of her brand new underwear lay sensuously against her skin. The expensive underwire bra from Agent Provocateur gave her small breasts a sexy cleavage, which was emphasized by her low cut pale chiffon blouse. She slipped on cream satin trousers over slim hips and pulled her hair up into a chic bun. A thin gold chain with matching earrings complimented the outfit perfectly. She sprayed on Emporio Armani's White perfume and surveyed the final result in the full-length bedroom mirror.

The spark between herself and Palmer was growing more tangible every time they spoke. Michelle hoped that tonight he would find her irresistible, the last thing she needed was to make a fool of herself in a relationship again.

She'd heard all the stories about men not maturing until they'd passed forty but she'd thought that she'd finally found a decent man in her last partner, Lyndon, though he was only thirty-six. Initially he was charm personified. Her wishes always came first and he seemed proud of her achievements at work. But it had only taken him three months to show his true colours.

He'd wanted them to move in together but Michelle had insisted that it was too soon. Then she realised that every time he visited her he brought a bag of laundry with him, and weekends spent at his flat seemed to involve her doing massive amounts of cleaning and vacuuming. At first she'd joked that he'd saved up all of his domestic work for her, but after a while she realised that it was true.

Lyndon's insecurities about her career and qualifications soon became the source of many arguments between them. He couldn't understand why she was intent on working instead of getting pregnant and staying at home, all without the benefit of a wedding ring. When he said she needed to readjust her bad attitude, Michelle readjusted her life to one without him. Whenever she allowed Lyndon to cross her mind the only regret she felt was in wasting so much time with him.

Palmer was still an enigma but everything felt different. She'd offered to meet him at the restaurant but he'd insisted on picking her up even though Birmingham had changed drastically since he'd last lived there. Michelle had become so used to making her own way to dates and paying her own taxi fares with Lyndon, that when Palmer had said he'd hired a Lexus jeep the day after he'd landed, it had been a glorious shock. Now Michelle glanced at the clock and prayed for the time to pass quickly. She couldn't wait to see him again.

Palmer stood in the lighted porch outside of Michelle's house and breathed quickly into his hand. He sniffed his palm once, then twice, then popped a soluble breath mint just in case. He'd parked the jeep on the road. The cul-de-sac where Michelle lived was a community of brand new gated town houses and he hadn't been able to recall Michelle's surname when he'd asked the warden to let him in. The grumpy man had insisted that he'd have to leave the car outside and meet Michelle on foot. Palmer hoped Michelle wouldn't mind the short walk back to the street. At least he'd remembered to spray the jeep to get rid of the new car smell. Unless, of course, Michelle liked that smell, then he'd have to find a way to get it back.

He was feeling slick in his stone coloured, three quarter length raincoat, under which he wore same coloured trousers and a short sleeved, black, zipneck cotton jumper. His finishing touch was a subtle splash of Diesel aftershave.

At precisely eight o'clock Michelle jumped up to answer her ringing doorbell and went sliding across the wooden floor. Flustered, she regained her balance and took three quick, deep, breaths before putting on her shoes and walking sedately to the front door. She did a quick check in the hallway mirror to make sure no lipstick was clinging to her teeth and no stray fluffs dangled from her nostrils. Satisfied that everything was okay she took one last breath and opened the door.

"Hi!" Michelle said, a little too brightly. She cleared her throat in an effort to get her voice back to it's normal pitch while Palmer kissed her hand.

"You look gorgeous." He slowly looked her over from head to toe, "Are you ready?"

"Yes, I'll just get my things. Can I give you one?"

Palmer looked at her perplexed at the question as she reddened in embarrassment.

"A drink, I mean...would you like one before we go?" she explained. Palmer couldn't help smiling, her confusion was charming. "I'm fine, thanks, let me help you with that." He took Michelle's wrap and placed it gently on her shoulders. Both of them felt the frisson of excitement when their fingers touched.

"You live in a nice area," Palmer commented as they drove off. "What's the name of this road again?"

"Pershore," Michelle informed him, "it leads to a place called Pershore, where the novelist Barbara Cartland grew up."

"Hmm." Palmer nodded thoughtfully.

"Do you like cricket?" Michelle asked.

"It's not really an American sport but Dad and Shango love

it."

"Most men in this country do. The Warwickshire County cricket ground is just around there. Maybe you'll get to see a match before you go back."

"Is that an invitation?" Palmer smiled.

"Could be." Michelle smiled back thinking she'd have to brush up on the game so she could explain it to him if they went.

Palmer drove Michelle to Birmingham's famous Balti Belt in Balsall Heath for a night of Indian food and music. He pointed out roads he used to be familiar with, noting how they'd changed. Since the early 1990's Birmingham had been undergoing a massive regeneration resulting in a European look and cosmopolitan atmosphere. Palmer seemed to like it. Michelle, meanwhile, was impressed with the way he navigated the unfamiliar streets and the admiring looks people gave the smart silver grey Lexus.

Over a meal of *Handi Gosth, Golda Chingri Madras* and to a background of Bollywood film hits, Michelle and Palmer talked and fell in love.

"What's your favourite time of year?" Palmer asked as he dipped his bread in *Pakora* sauce.

"That's an unusual question. I think it would have to be autumn or as you say, the fall."

"Why?"

"Because I always think of it as a time of new beginnings."

"Like New Year's?"

"Yes, but different. If you haven't done very well with your New Year's resolutions the autumn, marking the end of summer and the start of winter, gives you a second chance. Plus the colours of the trees and the leaves are so beautiful. It really lifts my spirits. What about you? What's your favourite time of year?"

"If you'd asked me first I would have said fall too."

"Really!"

"Sure, no kidding!"

"Why?"

"All of the reasons you've just said, plus, Atlanta is really beautiful in the fall."

"You're just messing about!" Michelle was incredulous.

"No I'm serious! Listening to you is like someone reading my mind."

They chatted and ate until well after eleven, discovering a mutual love of everything from maths to r&b and travel to technology.

For the first time Michelle felt relaxed enough to be her true self. There were no arguments, or power struggles, there was no need for her to put up a protective facade. She fully enjoyed the evening for what it was, no pressure, no problems.

Meanwhile, the headache of Liana and her family that had travelled with Palmer to England, had finally lifted. He was still worried about the confrontation with Ira that he knew was bound to come and the dilemma of whether to stay or go back to the States, but for one evening he was totally at peace. Michelle was smart, educated, considerate, unselfish and stunningly beautiful. He realised that he didn't want the night to end.

At last Palmer and Michelle stopped talking long enough to notice that they were the only people left in the restaurant. They laughed like children with a secret as the waiters coughed discreetly in the background. Bill please, Palmer signalled.

"I'll be right back." Michelle made her way to the ladies room. She reapplied her lipstick and squirted a dab of perfume on her pulse points. She felt a shiver of excitement at the thought of Palmer kissing where she'd just sprayed, her neck, her wrists and her breasts.

Palmer was silent on the drive back to Michelle's. This woman had provoked all kinds of unexpected feelings in him and now he wasn't sure how to act around her. On a whim he picked up her hand and held it in his. He was pleased to see a small smile on her lips even though, she too, remained silent.

"Is this it?" he asked as they turned into a road which looked familiar.

"Just a little further down, opposite the park," Michelle prompted.

When they arrived at the gates which opened onto the crescent of houses, Michelle handed Palmer her security card. He inserted it and the gates opened smoothly. He pulled up outside Michelle's two bedroom, three storey house.

"Thank you for a wonderful evening," he turned to her and said softly.

"Would you like to come in for coffee?" Michelle offered, her heart pounding.

"I can't tonight. Dad's on his own and he hasn't been feeling well," Palmer answered feeling Michelle's disappointment as she turned away.

The truth was that Ira had been fine that day. Shango had arrived early in the morning with Kai and they'd all had a good time. Ira had gone to bed just as he left for Michelle's and Shango had taken Kai back before making his own way home. Palmer knew that he couldn't go into Michelle's house. The urge he felt in his trousers told him that he wouldn't be able to keep his hands off her. But it was too soon and she was too special. He wanted to spend as much time as possible with her while he was here and having sex now would set the wrong tone for their relationship.

He saw the hurt in Michelle's eyes and sensed the rejection she felt at his refusal. He wanted to love it all away but the time wasn't right. Instead, he pulled her close and kissed her lips. A slow deep kiss that told her he cared for her.

"I'll call you as soon as I can," Palmer whispered at the end of their embrace.

"I'll look forward to it," Michelle replied.

●●●●●●

"Wife!" Shango called out cheerfully as he opened his front door. "Wi-fe! he sang the word as he picked up a pile of mail scattered on the hallway floor. "Baby love! Sugar dumpling!" he tried again and still got no reply.

Curious, he wandered from room to room. In the kitchen the untidy pile of cakes, sweets and biscuits on the table took him by surprise causing him to wonder just what was going on. He dumped the mail and sprinted up the stairs two at a time, his dreadlocks flying out behind him.

"Celia?" He pushed open the doors to the bedrooms and the study. In the bathroom he saw that half of the shelves were empty–the half where Celia kept her toiletries. His chest constricting, and his breathing getting heavier, he went back to their bedroom and pulled open draws and cupboards. Although not totally empty they were definitely more spacious than before.

Shango sat on the bed and fumbled in his shirt pocket for his inhaler. He breathed in the ventolin before looking up to confirm what he already knew. Celia's large suitcase was missing from the top of the wardrobe.

Shango thought hard. He guessed that she'd left because of the radio request but why hadn't she at least given him a chance to explain? She'd been fast asleep when he'd gone to get Kai that morning and he hadn't wanted to wake her.

He'd written a note to say that she could reach him at Ira's all day, but she hadn't called. Shango leaned over to see if the note had fallen onto the floor and heard a rustling in his back pocket. He reached in and pulled out the memo he should have left for Celia. He'd purposely kept his phone off all day so that he couldn't be reached by the University, expecting Celia to call him on Ira's number. But now he knew that he'd mistakenly taken the note with him. The pile of sugar in the kitchen gave a clue to her depressed state of mind. It was obvious that she couldn't handle his betrayal and now she must have thought that he'd abandoned her too.

With a heavy sigh, Shango wandered slowly back downstairs and into the kitchen. He tidied away the shopping from the table and automatically boiled water to cook rice and then began to season beef which he took from the refrigerator. He worked in total silence, sniffing and wiping his eyes which stung and watered as he chopped onions. His chest hurt and he felt mean and rotten inside. He'd never planned to hurt his wife. She was the ingredient that made their house a home and without her their home had lost its heart.

He put the meat into a dish and added the onions and gravy. Then he put the dish into the oven and set it to a low cooking temperature. He tasted the rice and satisfied that it was done, he turned off the gas beneath it.

Shango checked his watch and saw that he had less than five minutes to catch the corner shop before it shut for the night. He left the door on the latch and sprinted down the road.

"Just closing up, mate." The shopkeeper pressed the button by his feet that automatically unrolled the metal shutters.

"I know exactly what I want, I'll be two seconds!" Shango panted, slightly out of breath.

"Come on then," the shopkeeper relented and took his finger off the button.

"Flowers?" Shango scanned the interior of the shop hopefully.

"Only these left." The man indicated a bucket half full of wilted blooms. Shango looked at them, disappointed.

"I'll take that one." He picked out a rose which was fading fast, "How much?"

"Don't worry about it. Let's just hope it gets you out of trouble!" The shopkeeper laughed as he locked the door behind Shango.

In the sitting room back at home Shango tidied up and sprayed air freshener. He bounded up the steps, took two huge fluffy towels from the airing cupboard and placed them on the radiator to warm. Next, he closed the curtains in the bedroom, switched on the bedside lamp and put the electric blanket on a low setting. Finally, he splashed the rose with water before laying it on Celia's pillow.

Back downstairs Shango set the table for two, checked the beef once more and then grabbed his car keys before shutting the front door behind him. He was going to get his wife. His guilt weighed heavily on him and he couldn't let her continue to think that he'd abandoned her. He was going to find her and make everything all right.

•••••

Thirty minutes later Shango arrived at Angela's house. He rapped on the door, a mixture of emotions bubbling inside him. He was angry with Celia for not giving him a chance. He was furious with Angela and Martin for not calling to say Celia was with them. He was livid with himself for hurting her in the way he had. But even through his anger he still missed her welcoming smile, her gentle hugs, her terrible attempts at cooking and her joyful easy laugh. He decided then that he wasn't leaving without her.

Angela came to the door. "She's asleep." Her expression was stern and unwelcoming.

"Angela, may I come in?" Shango did his best to remain calm and polite.

"No." Angela shut the door leaving Shango fuming at her irrationality. He stubbornly rang the doorbell again.

"I've told you, she's asleep," Angela began as she opened the door.

"I have to see her, just for a few minutes," Shango pleaded.

"Just go!" Angela was on the verge of losing her temper with the man who had the power to hurt her only child.

"It's all right, Mom."

Angela turned at Celia's voice. "Darling are you okay?" she asked gently.

"Yes," Celia replied. "Have you come to take me home?" she addressed Shango who still stood outside.

"That's exactly why I'm here." Shango's loving gaze held Celia's eyes.

"That's all I want from you, I'll just get my things."

Ten minutes later Celia sat in the front seat of the BMW with her suitcase packed in the boot.

"Thanks Mom." She said a soft goodbye to Angela as they drove off.

Shango could hardly bare to see his wife in this condition. Normally so immaculate, her hair was uncombed, her dress crumpled and she had sleep lines on one side of her face. Her eyes were filled with pain and she sat totally still.

"What would you like when we get home?" Shango asked his voice filled with compassion.

"A bath, some food, a cuddle." The words came out in a whisper. Shango's heart turned over. Her requests were so simple. She just needed his love. That was all she'd ever asked for.

"No problem," he assured her. "Whatever you want, no problem."

Celia was asleep within minutes of them leaving Angela's. As dusk fell Shango was overcome with guilt. Rafi was right. Whatever he and Sandra had shared was in the past. He'd made a commitment to Celia and that was what had to stay uppermost on his mind. People were depending on him to provide an example. He had to show them that his marriage meant more to him than anything or anyone else.

CHAPTER THIRTEEN

SENSI HAD GONE straight back to bed as soon as Shango had left with Kai at seven thirty the previous morning. She wasn't pleased at having to be up so early. Shango's apology was that he wanted to show Kai how to cook a proper Caribbean breakfast for Ira. Even in her sleepy state she'd hassled him about the radio request but Shango had firmly brushed her off. Sensi vaguely remembered a Sandra from Shango's past and wanted to know if it was the same one but her derisive comments had only pushed Shango to wait outside in the car while she helped Kai to get ready.

When she'd surfaced again at eleven o'clock two important events had set the tone for her day. At noon she'd received a call from Ribs saying he was on his way. He was a casual acquaintance she'd met in one of the clubs. He called her infrequently but she always knew exactly what he wanted. Ribs had needs and he wanted her to satisfy them.

As soon as she'd hung up, the phone had rung again, this time it was Tony Valentine inviting her over later in the week to collect her wages from her weekend's work at Steele's. She'd called Ribs back and told him to come the following day, reasoning that he could give her a lift into Birmingham to Tony and Andrea's house. Ribs had been a little put out at having to wait but she'd promised that she'd make it worth his while. Then she'd enjoyed a leisurely day doing very little until Shango dropped Kai back early in the evening. He didn't hang around long enough for her to harass him again about the mysterious Sandra.

● ● ● ● ● ●

Today was the day that Ribs was due and she'd get her one hundred and fifty pounds from Tony. It was nearly ten o'clock. Time to get the day started. She dressed to make an impression on Ribs. He'd be driving her all the way to North Birmingham. She reasoned he might as well have something nice to look at during the trip.

"Morning honey." Sensi pulled back the curtains in Kai's room.

"Morning Mom, is it still night?" Kai crawled into his mother's arms for a hug.

"Very funny." Sensi kissed him, enjoying the baby sleepy scent of him. "Did you have fun with Granddad yesterday?" she asked, encouraging him to stand up so she could straighten out his bed.

"Yeah, Daddy kept making us laugh. Uncle Palmer talks funny!"

"That's cos he's American. Remember what I said we were going to do today?" Sensi selected clothes from Kai's wardrobe and underwear from his drawer while she spoke.

"Go to Birmingham?"

"Good boy, but what comes first?"

"I have to play at Jason's house till two o'clock then you'll come and get me."

"Well done." Sensi kissed and hugged him till he squirmed to be free, "Get dressed and I'll make you favourite breakfast cos you remembered so well."

At eleven forty-five Sensi arrived home after walking Kai to Jason's. Luckily it was just the other side of the park but at the last minute Kai had decided he didn't want to go. Sensi had pleaded, cajoled and finally threatened to leave him in West Brom instead of taking him over to Tony's. That was when Kai changed his mind, to Sensi's relief. There was no way she could manipulate Ribs with Kai hanging around.

Sensi put a peeled onion into a pot of boiling water and the pleasing aromas of seasoned food wafted through the small house. Ribs would be fooled into thinking she'd cooked just for him. He'd never know he was eating two day old leftovers from the dumpling shop in West Brom High Street.

At twelve thirty the door bell rang.

"Hello Sweetness," Ribs drawled.

"Don't just stand there, everyone can see you!" Sensi could feel her neighbours eyes on her and, like most gossips, she hated being the subject of derisory comments.

"Looking nice," Ribs continued. He moved in close to Sensi and ran his hand territorially down her neck, onto her breast and over her hips.

"Do you always have to grope me?" Sensi snapped again.

Dealing with Ribs was going to be harder than she'd thought.

"What's the matter with you?" Ribs shouted, his good mood vanishing. Sensi bit her lip to avoid retaliating. Her purse was empty and she was almost out of food. She needed the money that Tony held for her. She couldn't afford to antagonise Ribs.

"Sorry babe, all this heat is making me crabby." She leant her head into his chest and gently stroked his thigh. His blue cotton tracksuit bottoms emphasized the thickness of his legs. His white merino vest showed off his toned arms and broad chest.

"Let me cool you down." Once again Ribs' hand was on her breast. All of a sudden he looked up sniffing the air, "You cook?" he barked in Jamaican patios.

"I know you're a man that appreciates good food," Sensi replied coyly, glad that he'd stopped fondling her.

"I'm glad you know what I like." Ribs leered at her as she led him through the house towards the stairs, anxious to get the sex over with.

"Where are we going?" he asked pulling away from Sensi's grasp.

"I could give you a massage, help you to relax," Sensi teased. She was good at these games. Her eyes twinkled as she teased him, he had no idea he was making her feel sick with his smarmy ways.

"The food smells good. Let's eat!" Ribs slipped into Jamaican patios to emphasize his point. Straight away Sensi picked up that he was being serious. Good job she'd already transferred the food from its polystyrene container into a plate that sat in the microwave.

"You want a cup of tea with your lunch?" she offered.

"Beer," demanded the ever-charming Ribs. "You have a nice place here you know."

"Thanks." Sensi knew exactly what was coming next.

"Just you and the boy live here?"

"Hm, mm," she mumbled ambiguously while sorting out a tray and some napkins.

"Do you have a man that comes, regular?" Ribs wanted to confirm that the coast was clear.

"Only you handsome," Sensi called from the kitchen. She pulled a face but kept her voice sincere.

"So sometimes I could stay two or three nights?"

Over my dead body thought Sensi beginning to wonder what she'd ever seen in the odious Ribs. "But haven't you got a nice place?" she queried in a flattering tone of voice.

"The landlord tried to start a fight with me."

"About what?"

"I never do nothing!"

You mean you're getting thrown out because you haven't paid your rent, Sensi scoffed inwardly not hinting at her disgust as she turned off the fire under the onion and presented the stale food garnished with salad and hot sauce to Ribs.

"Come," was all he said when he'd finished eating.

Sensi smiled tantalisingly at him as he led her upstairs. I should have been an actress she thought, detesting the feel of Ribs sweaty palms on her backside as he followed her into the bedroom.

Ribs sat on the bed watching Sensi with his eyes narrowed. "You're a good cook," he said. "I wonder what else you're good at?" He cocked an eyebrow expectantly.

Oh my God, thought Sensi, he wants a show! When she remembered that she didn't have enough bus fare to get her and Kai all the way over to Tony's house in Wylde Green, her hesitation lasted less than a second. She had no choice but to finish what they'd started. She squashed down the revulsion that threatened to surge up from inside her, put on an old Teddy Pendergrass tape and swayed provocatively.

Ribs nodded his approval as Sensi slowly pulled off her top, wishing she'd worn more clothes. Her breasts were enhanced by her dainty underwire red bra. Lazily lifting one finger, Ribs beckoned her over. She approached him stepping in time to the music. "Stay close," he whispered, "I like it better when you're near."

Sensi forced a smile she didn't feel and cradled his head between her breasts. When she released him his wide grin showed off his gold capped teeth.

He ogled her body while pawing at her. By the time Sensi had wriggled enticingly out of her short skirt and peeled off her bra, Ribs couldn't hold back any longer. He pulled her down between his knees and gestured for her to unzip his trousers.

That's when Sensi mentally switched off.

As she freed his member from his boxer shorts she imagined that her body was only fulfilling a means to an end. Ribs grinned salaciously as he grabbed at Sensi's breasts. She nibbled at his testicles, then licked and sucked at his penis, slowly at first then faster, as Ribs became harder. She moaned and groaned in tandem with him hoping that this would hasten his climax. His hips jerked to and fro as his excitement mounted. Just when Sensi thought she'd be on her knees forever, Ribs shuddered and slumped back onto the bed, a sigh of pleasure escaping his lips. Sensi searched for a tissue to spit into. Turning away from him she wiped her face, grimacing.

"I could look for you more often." Ribs spoke as if he were offering her something irresistible, while Sensi thought to herself, this is it, never again.

Aloud she said in her sweetest voice, "Babe you were wonderful, even better than what they say."

"They talk about me?" Ribs asked proudly.

"Yeah, but they don't do you justice," Sensi lied.

Ribs lay back on the bed stroking his stomach like a lion that had just been fed.

"Budweiser?" Sensi asked as she pulled the last bit of her clothing back on.

"Oh yes," replied a sated Ribs.

• • • • • •

Loud music blared from the car as they turned into the road where Tony and Andrea lived.

"Turn it down a little Ribs," Sensi suggested lightly.

"Yes Sweetness." Ribs rubbed her leg with his hand.

Sensi turned around, ostensibly to talk to Kai, but effectively making Ribs' hand slide off her thigh.

"Remember your manners inside. These are nice people and I don't want you embarrassing me," she warned.

"Yes Mom," Kai answered.

"Stop here," Sensi directed Ribs. "Thanks for the lift."

"I'll call you." Ribs grabbed Sensi's hand as she left the car.

"Anytime you like," Sensi responded wondering how quickly she could get her number changed.

She'd made Ribs pull up at the end of the street. Looking at the numbers, she guessed Tony and Andrea lived about half-way down. Ribs had agreed immediately to drop her and Kai to Birmingham. He probably would have come in too, but Sensi reasoned that he'd got what he wanted and served his purpose. She didn't need him to get her home, soon she'd have money in her pocket.

"Mom, these houses are massive!" Kai exclaimed as they walked along the broad tree-lined road. Jaguars, Mercedes and top of the range BMWs sat in the gravel driveways, even though each house had two garages. Flower beds and well manicured lawns made the whole street look beautiful. Residents, dressed in clothes that were definitely not from ordinary high street shops, eyed Sensi and Kai as they strolled open mouthed along the road.

Sensi felt out of place in her black, high heeled, discount sandals, mini denim skirt embroidered with sequins and frilly one shouldered pink top. Unconsciously she touched her hair wishing that for once it was combed in a plain ponytail and without her usual fluorescent add-on pieces.

"Did you say number six-seven-two, Mom? Wow!" Kai looked in awe at the magnificent house.

"Stop shouting Kai," Sensi's voice faded as she stood next to him, "Wow," she echoed.

The detached house had a partial black and white mock Tudor frontage with light leaded windows. It was L-shaped and stood behind trees and a foreground of lawns, rockeries and potted flowers. The huge windows were dressed with luxurious curtains and blinds. Tony's black Jaguar XK8 was parked on the drive next to Andrea's red RAV 4 jeep. Sensi's knees buckled. She grabbed Kai's hand ready to make a run for it. No way could she enter this house and mix with those people.

"Now that you're here, you might as well come in!" Tony said brightly as he strolled across the lawn.

"Where did you come from?" Sensi was surprised.

"Over there." Tony pointed vaguely towards the back of the house.

"Have you got a garden?" Kai asked.
Sensi shook his arm to remind him of his manners.

"Hello young man," Tony greeted him and kissed Sensi on the cheek.

"This is my son. Say hello to Mr. Valentine, Kai."
Kai shyly shook Tony's hand his eyes fixed on the grassy trail to the back garden.

"Hello Mr Valentine, have you got any children?"

"Kai!" Sensi shook his arm again, "Sorry Tony, he's curious."

"No problem. He looks just like his dad."

"You know my dad?" Kai was impressed.

"Come on in. Andrea's cooking dinner, let's see if we can find someone for you to play with Kai."

"You're having dinner? We won't stay long. We don't want to disturb you," Sensi spluttered wishing she could just take the money and run.

"Don't be silly!" Tony put his arm around her compelling her towards the house.

"Hi Sensi," Andrea greeted her warmly as she entered the huge kitchen.

"How are you Andrea?" Sensi tried not to stare at her surroundings.

The units were a mix of lime oak wood and glass. The floor was a shiny slate black. Sensi guessed that the fridge and dishwasher were integrated into the cupboards. There was a matching island in the centre of the room where Andrea sat chopping and peeling with her daughter, Natalie. Off a side door Sensi noticed a utility room full of Bosch appliances. Through the windows Kai spotted the large garden complete with mini basketball court and cricket strip where Romeo and Omar, their two boys, were playing.

"Can I go outside, Mom?" Kai asked.

"I'll show you," Natalie offered. Her pretty round face, large eyes and thick curly eyelashes made Kai's stomach leap. Even though at thirteen, she was at least a head taller than him, he put his arm around her waist like he'd seen Shango do with his Aunty Celia. Andrea and Sensi exchanged looks with raised eyebrows.

"You can play with us if you want to." Kai made Natalie an offer she couldn't refuse.

"Looks like I'm cooking dinner for my future son-in-law!" Andrea quipped as Kai and Natalie left the room.

"I don't know what's got into him," Sensi added.

"The child's in love!" Tony laughed.

"You have a beautiful home," Sensi complimented Andrea. The light-hearted banter had helped her to relax.

"Thanks." Andrea gestured to the chair next to her. Sensi washed her hands in the double sink and joined her. Then she began peeling husks off a large pile of corn.

"Would you like to see the house?" Andrea asked Sensi. Tony was playing in the garden with the children. Sensi and Andrea had seasoned the curry goat and finished all of the vegetables and rice. The different foods were either in the oven or bubbling on the stove. It was time for a break.

Number 672 Oakwood Close was as huge inside as it looked from the outside. Andrea led Sensi into all the rooms off the spacious hallway chatting about the mishaps they'd had with the kids and the trials of keeping the place clean. Noticing Sensi's intimidation

Andrea declined from mentioning the cleaning lady who came twice a week.

Sensi's breath was taken away by the twenty-two foot lounge and TV room. Tony's study was beautifully serene, lined with full bookshelves. A small stereo played Classic FM. On the other side of the hallway, next to the elegant eight-seater dining room, was the music room. A little larger than the study, it housed guitars, music stands and an upright piano.

"Who's learning?" Sensi asked running her fingers over the ivory keys.

"Me!" Andrea laughed, "and Tony!"

"Really!" Sensi was intrigued.

"We couldn't get the kids to keep up their practice and they hated lessons, we thought that if they saw us doing it they'd be inspired."

"How're you getting on?"

"Terrible. I'm tone deaf and Tony refuses to use the right fingers in the right places, but we don't tell the kids that. We just make sure they see us practising everyday and enjoying our lessons."

"What about the guitars?"

"That's the one thing the kids do enjoy."

"Kai says he wants to learn the guitar," Sensi said wistfully. Andrea nodded but said nothing. A compact cloakroom was the final downstairs room.

"Upstairs?" Andrea said brightly.

"Okay," Sensi replied.

As they walked up the galleried staircase Andrea pointed out various family photos including people Tony insisted on displaying in case they ever "popped in."

"Where do they live?" asked Sensi.

"Barbados, LA, fairly local!" laughed Andrea.

She guided Sensi through all five bedrooms making humorous comments as they went. Sensi was overawed by the en-suite bathroom with jacuzzi and Andrea's own private dressing room.

"How do you do it? How do you manage to have such a lovely home and such well behaved children?" They were in the upstairs computer room now as Sensi stared out of the window watching the boys running around in the back garden. Kai stayed near Natalie. To him the afternoon was obviously his idea of a hot date.

"Years and years of hard work. Everyday we get back on the

treadmill just to maintain what we have and provide security for the kids. Sometimes I think it would be easier if we just went to live on a desert island."

"Why don't you?"

"Easy is boring. We like challenges, keeps the blood pumping. Makes you feel alive. I'll just check the food. Would you like a drink?"

Tea please."

"What's wrong?" Andrea had come back in to find Sensi wiping her eyes.

"Nothing, I'm okay."

"Then why the tears?" Andrea placed the tray of teacups on the desk and stood close to Sensi.

"I want so much for Kai and it seems like I'm just going round in circles. Look how happy he is here. I never seem to have enough money and sometimes it's so difficult being on my own with him."

"Kai seems happy enough. He's a wonderful little boy. Polite, charming, bubbly, intelligent."

"I don't think that I can give him everything he needs."

"What else does he need except your love? He knows that you'll always be there for him. That's the best gift you can give." Andrea put her arm around Sensi's shoulders.

"I feel like I'm just putting on a front, like everyone else is better at this than me," Sensi sobbed.

"Better at what?" Andrea probed gently.

"Life."

"We all put on a front. None of us knows how to do it perfectly. We just take each day as it comes, try to plan for the future and do our best."

"You and Tony don't have any problems." Sensi blew her nose with the tissue Andrea handed her.

"Of course we do! You think that running a house like this, bringing up three kids, taking care of the club and training to be a magistrate doesn't give problems? Not to mention Tony's other businesses."

"But you still manage!"

"That's because we've made a commitment to see it through whatever happens. We're determined to reach our goals and that means taking the rough with the smooth. That's just how life is."

"At least you're not doing it on your own."

"Shango doesn't seem like the kind of man who'd ignore his

child."

Sensi was on the verge of saying that Shango rarely saw her or Kai, let alone make child care payments, but when she looked into Andrea's sincere face, her lies fell by the wayside.

"Shango is a wonderful dad, but I don't think he likes me very much."

"You have to get on with him for Kai's sake."

"I try but I just wind him up. We go from one argument to the next, I feel…" Sensi searched for the right word, "…inadequate compared to him."

"Why?"

"Because I don't teach at a university and I'm never likely to."

"You don't have to prove yourself to anybody. In Kai's eyes you're already a star.

"Why?"

"Because you're his mom. You don't have to be anything else."

"I want him to be really great just like his dad."

"You're proud of everything Shango's accomplished aren't you, Sensi?"

"Yes and you're the only person I'm telling."

"You should tell him."

"Why?"

"It might help to build the bridges between you two, get rid of some of the animosity. It can't be good for Kai to see you two arguing all the time."

"We try not to fight in front of him but sometimes it gets a bit tense."

"You're not still in love with him, are you Sensi?"

"A little," Sensi started to sob again.

Andrea held her close while moving her away from the window so that Kai wouldn't look up and see.

"When we were together I thought it would last forever, but then he started to plan a life without me. One that I couldn't fit into. He's changed so much. Sometimes I hardly recognise him. If only we could just turn the clock back."

"That's one thing none of us can do, Sensi."

"I know." Sensi wiped her eyes. "With Shango I felt as if I would always be loved. That there would always be somebody there for me."

"What about your family?"

"There's only me and Hope."

143

"Is Hope your sister?"

"No Hope's my mom. We don't talk much."

"Why not?"

"She's not a nice woman, Andrea. Nothing that I do is ever good enough for her and she hates Kai."

"She hates Kai!" Andrea was shocked. "He's the most gentle, most caring child, I've ever seen." She gestured towards the window, "Look at him out there, all he wants to do is make sure that everyone gets a turn. I wish my boys were as thoughtful as that. What is there to hate about him?"

"She's a bitter woman. She has no happiness in her life so she doesn't want anyone else to be happy."

"What's made her like this?"

"Who knows? When I was fifteen I left home because I couldn't take anymore of her insults and put downs. She criticized everything about me. Told me I didn't have enough sense to pass my exams, that all I was good for was walking the street. She told me that I'd end up whoring for England."

Andrea was speechless. She held Sensi as the tears fell again and she cried her heart out.

"I can't do anything to please her. Kai and I are better off without her."

"No one has a perfect family, but look how wonderful you are with Kai."

"I don't think I am."

"Of course you are. Just look at your son." Andrea turned Sensi towards the window. "He's happy, well dressed, obviously well loved and well looked after. He's a very lucky boy."

"I wish I was smart, like Shango, or even Celia, just so that I could help Kai more."

"Sensi you are smart."

"No I'm not. I didn't even get any GSEs."

"All that measures is whether you're good at passing exams. It's no bearing on your level of intelligence. "

"If I was clever I'd be in a good job and I wouldn't have to do.....things....to get money."

"What things, you mean working at the club, what's wrong with that?"

"That's not what I mean. Sometimes when Kai's at school....when I haven't got anything for his dinner...or when I need money to put in the electricity meter..."

Andrea was silent knowing it was important for Sensi to say what was on her mind but dreading what she was going to hear.

144

"Afterwards I hate myself and I hate them too for being so weak."

"Who do you hate Sensi?" Andrea's voice was a whisper.

"The men. I hate the men that give me whatever I want as long as I make them feel good."

"Feel good?"

"It's so easy, it's stupid!" Sensi spat out. "You just utter a few words about how masterful they are, how they rock your world, how they're the best you've ever had. Want to make a man squeal? Just flick your tongue back and forth on the ridge under his penis. Want him to think you're the sexiest thing since Cleopatra? Put both his balls in your mouth at the same time and give them a tongue lashing. Want him to worship your body? Tie his hands with silk and stand inches away from him while slowly putting your hands down the front of your pants or peeling off your bra." Sensi spoke bitterly. "You know I can make a man come in under a minute? How's that for being good at something!"

A fresh torrent of tears followed Sensi's confession. Andrea hugged her and stroked her hair, muttering soothing words until Sensi's tears abated. Eventually Sensi looked up. Her eyes begged for understanding.

"Now you think I'm tramp," she said.

"I think you're a very intelligent woman who's never had the guidance and nurturing that she deserves." Andrea was close to tears.

"I suppose you're wondering why I don't just ask Shango for more money?"

"You don't ask Shango for more money because you want to be independent," Andrea stated simply. "You want to prove to him that you can survive. Sensi what do you want to do with your life?"

"Me?" Sensi was surprised.

"What sorts of things do you enjoy?"

"Erm," Sensi sighed and dried away the last of her tears, "I don't know."

"Let's look on the internet." Andrea sat down in front of the computer.

"What for?"

"Let's see," Andrea logged onto AOL, "what are your hobbies?" she looked up at Sensi.

Brow furrowed, Sensi thought for a moment. "Oils," she said finally.

"Oils?"

"Those....what are they called....homepath, homeost...aromapath...?"

"Homeopathic oils? You mean aromatherapy?"

"Yeah."

"Tell me what you know about aromatherapy," Andrea encouraged while she tapped the words *aromatherapy courses* into the search engine.

"How long have you got!" Sensi cheered up at the thought of discussing something she loved.

"Fire away!" Andrea laughed.

"When Kai has a cold I rub eucalyptus into his chest. When he can't sleep I burn basil in an oil burner in his room. For headaches the best thing is chamomile and rosemary either in the bath or on a tissue. Ginger and peppermint for constipation, lemon and geranium for diarrhoea. Marjoram rubbed into joints helps if you've got arthritis…" Sensi stopped as she realised that Andrea was staring at her.

"Girl you know your stuff!"

"You think so?"

"Is the sky blue, is grass green, is the Pope Catholic? That was amazing. How did you learn all that?"

"I don't know. I just experiment and when I'm not sure of something I look it up."

"Have you ever thought about doing it professionally?"

"How do you mean?"

"Running your own aromatherapy business."

"Me a business woman!" Sensi scoffed.

"Why not? You could make good money doing something that comes naturally to you."

"But I wouldn't know where to start."

"Look at this." Andrea moved over and Sensi leaned into the monitor. Together they looked at a range of courses in Sensi's home area covering aromatherapy. Then they searched for courses in business management. They were so engrossed in the information that they didn't notice the time passing.

"Ladies how burnt would you like your dinner?" Tony eventually called upstairs.

"Coming, babe." Andrea pressed print and the pages of information spilled out. "You can make a success of this, Sensi, just believe in yourself and hold onto the bigger picture."

"Do it for Kai?" Sensi asked putting the sheets into an envelope.

"Do it for yourself," Andrea affirmed. "Come on, time to feed the five thousand."

CHAPTER FOURTEEN

WHERE SHALL I put his bed?"

Shango, Palmer, Ira and Preston looked up. The coarse voice foreshadowed the broad, bulky figure of Maureen Clarence. Her curly, black, synthetic wig had slipped to one side underneath her plastic rain hat, exposing short, grey plaits. The belt of her brown mac stretched and strained where it was buckled across her rotund belly. As she stomped towards the centre of the room in broken down shoes that had seen better days, the West Handsworth Domino Society prepared itself for a showdown.

Satisfied that she had everybody's attention, Maureen continued her tirade, her dentures clacking together.

"He's never at home, he might as well sleep here!"

Men cradling their dominoes and bottles of Guinness shrank sheepishly into their seats or looked the other way trying to avoid Maureen's onslaught.

"Cuthbert!" she screeched, causing the men closest to her to wince. "Where's he hiding? The damn coward!"

From her vantage point in the centre of the hall Maureen scanned the room with mean eyes. With difficulty she doubled over and inspected under the tables. Some of the men sniggered as her ample backside spread to twice its size, while the huge rolls of fat around her belly wobbled. Maureen cut her eyes at them and kissed her teeth. She was in no mood for games.

"Mrs Woman, what's the matter with you today?" Ira spoke in an amenable tone as he approached Maureen.

"I sick of he! He never at home, might as well I bring his things here!" Maureen snapped, her accent an odd mix of English and Grenadian patios.

"He's not here now," Ira said calmly knowing full well Cuthbert had left earlier with his nineteen-year-old girlfriend, Tanika. He lowered his voice. "Don't let the man make you lose your cool in front of all of these people. Come have a drink. We'll sort it out."

Maureen smiled at Ira as if in agreement before bursting out,

"You as bad as he, Ira Shango! You all does just stick up for each other! Take me for a fool. If he's not here I know he's in bed with that skinny, buck teet' miss! The one with the false hair long down she back, pretend it does be real! Fo - fool old man. He think that going to help him get it up, after all these years! When he comes back tell him those bags outside belong to him. I done had enough of his nonsense!"

Maureen's voice boomed across the centre. The women tidying away the lunch plates in the kitchen came out to see what was going on. They gathered her to one side leaving the men to bring in Cuthbert's belongings from off the street.

"When you said 'never a dull moment' you weren't kidding were you Dad?" Palmer laughed as Ira returned to his seat.

"What's next Dad? Clowns, magicians, singing and dancing?" Shango added as he checked his domino cards.

That woman has always been mad. Just like all Grenadians," Preston said.

"You can't say that man," Ira pulled him up on the racist comment.

"You didn't know my uncle," said Preston gravely causing everyone at the table to laugh.

It was a wet Wednesday afternoon and Shango and Palmer had stopped off at the domino club for a quick game before going back to Ira's. They'd only been there for a short while before Maureen's outburst but Shango could feel a difference in the atmosphere compared to his previous visits.

As he'd wandered around the room nodding to the older men, he'd had to strain to catch the eye of some of them and their acknowledgements were curt and brief. Other men had looked at him knowingly. One even whispering obscurely, "*You've joined the gang now!*" Shango was perplexed but the man had just winked and moved on.

Prior to today the men had always greeted Shango with warm respect. They asked him how the network was doing and offered help with contacts, equipment or information. Some of them still teased him about being a newly wed and asked for "*his lovely wife*", but today that camaraderie was missing. Shango didn't want to believe that the grapevine was buzzing with news about him and Sandra but he knew there was no other reason for their behaviour.

Standing alone in a corner of the room he watched as Ira introduced Palmer to those who hadn't met him already. It was interesting, thought Shango, that Ira was so detached around Palmer. There was none of the proud boasting that he'd expected along the lines of "*My first born has finally come home*".

Apart from a brief hug when they'd first been reunited he'd never seen them touch and Ira certainly didn't treat Palmer as though he'd been away for over twenty years. Ira obviously enjoyed Palmer's company around the house but there was no apparent joy that he was home. On the other hand, Palmer didn't seem disappointed by Ira's lack of excitement either. Perhaps, Shango concluded, it would take more than two weeks to make up for such a long parting.

Shango smiled at Miss Madge and Miss Elaine as they approached him on their way to the kitchen. He turned towards them ready for his usual fussing and motherly embrace but the woman's eyes slid over him and they continued on their way.

Shango felt cold.

He started to call after them but stopped. They'd frozen him out and there was no point in hassling them. Or maybe, Shango hoped, maybe he was just imagining things. Sure he was spending a lot of time by himself there today, which had never happened before, but it hadn't been an ordinary day. Mad Maureen Clarence had diverted everyone's attention.

Looking around for someone to talk to he spotted Fudge, Stanford, Milford and Jerome at a table near the bar with a spare seat between them. These men were some of Ira's old sparring partners from his days as a boxer. They'd known Shango since he was a little boy and he'd grown up calling them all "uncle." He decided to sit with them until Ira and Palmer were ready to leave.

"What are you guys drinking?" Shango addressed the group affably. Jerome and Milford looked up eagerly.

"Whatever you're buying....stud," Miford answered while Jerome nodded.

Shango could have sworn Milford had a glint in his eye.

"Uncle Fudge, Uncle Stanford?" Shango looked at the other two men.

"Nothing," replied Fudge. Stanford kept his gaze on his poker cards.

"Be back in a minute." Shango walked over to the bar. Unconsciously his shoulders slumped and his feet dragged. His head felt heavy and his chest was beginning to feel tight. He felt the snub from Fudge and Stanford and the disrespect from Milford and Jerome. He dredged up a smile for the barmaid Linette, but wasn't surprised when she ignored it and served him his drinks without their usual friendly banter.

"If you guys have something to say, then just say it," Shango said when he returned with the drinks.

"In the abundance of water the fool is thirsty," Fudge mumbled. He still didn't look up.

"You can't bamboozle the university professor!" Milford sneered.

Shango sat looking from one to the other. The men continued to talk about him as is he was wasn't there.

"You know, my father always said to me, 'The Queen might have an idea about the harem, but she doesn't really need to *know* about the harem,' I think it was good advice." Jerome looked around the table staring extra long at Shango before laying down his cards and gathering in his chips. Stanford sipped his Red Stripe and dealt a new hand making sure he excluded Shango.

"In some societies, unfortunate men who are stuck with ugly woman are expected to.....*misbehave*," all of the men chuckled except Shango, "raise you seven," Stanford motioned to Fudge.

"But if your woman isn't ugly, fat or old....." Fudge passed Stanford a card, "raise you six, well....." he let the rest of his sentence hang unspoken in the air.

"In African villages a woman does not know what goes on in the hut of her husband's other wife," Jerome puffed on his cigar and drank his Guinness, "there's a reason for that," he continued.

"The King must keep his own counsel. It's the law of the jungle," Fudge pointed out.

"There's a song all the young people sing," chimed in Milford again, "Something about if you can't be with the one you love ....I fold." He laid down his hand of cards and stood.

"I fold."

"I fold."

"I fold."

One by one the men put down their cards, stubbed out their smokes, picked up their drinks and left Shango alone and humiliated at the table.

"I'm not going to be single forever!" Aldephia was sitting on Ira's lap, her hand caressing his chest.

"Senior Citizens falling in love, I don't believe what I'm seeing," Palmer joined their banter. He'd been trying to get Ira to say his goodbyes for the last twenty minutes and they were still no closer to the door.

"Adelphia you know I'm not walking down the aisle again, not unless it leads to the bar!" Ira laughed heartily at his joke. He held tightly onto Adelphia's waist. At sixty, she had chocolate smooth skin, clear eyes and still lustrous black hair. She wasn't exactly pretty, but she certainly wasn't a bad catch. Ira enjoyed the tingling feeling in his crotch from her sitting on his lap. Occasionally his hand would stray towards Adelphia's full breast, grabbing a quick, covert, squeeze.

"Ira, I'm only going to remind you one more time of my credentials." Adelphia tactfully moved Ira's groping hand and pulled a face at Palmer that had him in stitches. "I can cook your stew beef and dumplings, I can darn your socks, I keep a tidy house, I go to church regular, I'm not bad looking and from when you put the ring on my finger, you would never find me looking at no other man!" Adelphia rocked back, roaring with laughter, flinging her leg up in the air. "Course you have to get rid of this beer belly." Adelphia rubbed Ira's rotund stomach.

He placed his hand on top of hers shouting, "This is what makes you a man!"

"Sounds like a match made in heaven!" Palmer declared enjoying himself as much as they were.

"Not like some people's marriages," Adelphia pointed. The men followed her finger across the room to where Shango sat in forlorn solitude. "I hear him and Celia mash up and it's not even a year?"

Ira pushed her off his lap and Palmer looked at her coldly.

"What else did you hear?" Palmer asked, his calm voice belying the fury that was rising within him on behalf of his brother.

"They say he has another woman and the wife is just there for show," Adelphia elaborated. "No wonder he looks so miserable. His wife must have kicked him out?" She looked to Ira for confirmation, anxious to give her friends a full update.

"That's why you can't get married." Ira's voice was full of scorn. "Get your brother," he ordered Palmer. Turning his back on Adelphia he snatched up his coat, hat and newspaper, nodded to his friends and strode towards the entrance. He'd been enjoying several late nights with Adelphia. But now that she'd shown him how big her mouth was it would be a long time before she saw him at her doorstep again.

• • • • • •

The three men sat drinking in Ira's lounge. Shango's depression pervaded the atmosphere. He cradled his Heineken in one hand and held his chin with the other. Every few minutes he emitted a self-pitying sigh. The television was tuned to a rained off cricket match. Ira stared at the green canvas that covered the pitch as if willing the rain to stop and the teams to resume play solely for his pleasure.

"Anybody hungry?"

Neither Shango nor Ira bothered to answer Palmer.

"Anybody want a drink?" Palmer tried again.

There was still no response.

"Tea, coffee, arsenic?" Palmer stood between the two men and waved his hands around in front of their faces. "Lighten up guys, it's like somebody died in here."

"You're blocking the TV," was Ira's only comment.

"You're getting on my nerves," was Shango's.

"Don't blame me, just cos you've been an idiot," Palmer replied moving aside so Ira could continue to watch the green canvas floor of the cricket ground.

"Is that Edgbaston?" Palmer looked at the TV. "Me and Michelle might go there. Would that be a good place for a date? Dad? Shango?"

"Women don't understand cricket," Ira mumbled.

"Michelle doesn't understand anything, she's from outer space," Shango said unkindly.

"What's eating you?" Palmer asked him.

"Just shut up about stupid Michelle, stupid food and stupid drink!" Shango shouted. "Some of us have got more important things on our minds."

"Like what? Being stupid enough to broadcast your love for your mistress on the radio?" Palmer retorted, tired of Shango's attitude.

"What did you say?" Shango stood up and pushed Palmer's shoulder.

"Oh, sit down," Palmer shrugged him off.

"Don't tell me what to do. You can't just come in and act the big man all of a sudden." Shango stepped closer to Palmer until their faces were less than an inch apart.

"Just chill, man." Palmer took a step back.

"I said, don't tell me what to do!" Shango stepped forward and hissed in Palmer's face.

"Or what?" Palmer spoke through clenched teeth. "You'll

153

handle me as badly as you handle your women?"

"I'm not telling you again, back off!" Shango lost his temper and pushed Palmer who fell awkwardly onto Ira. It felt good to be have someone to take out his bad mood on.

"Enough!" Ira pushed Palmer off his legs and stood up. "You all carrying on like two babies. Sort yourselves out! You wouldn't go on like this if your mother was still alive."

Palmer looked up in surprise. It was the first time Ira had mentioned Ruby Katherine since he'd arrived. "What's Mom got to do with this?" he asked.

Once again Shango and Ira ignored him.

"Don't you dare mention her to me after what you did," Palmer spoke directly to Ira, his voice shaking with pain and anger.

"Easy man," Shango immediately forgot about his own misery and tried to pre-empt the argument he saw coming. He touched Palmer's arm gently.

"Get off me, you're as bad as him." Palmer shook off Shango's hand.

"What are you on about?" Shango was confused, "What's got into you?" He looked directly at Palmer but now it was his turn to be ignored by the other two men.

Ira sat back down and lit his pipe keeping his eyes on the screen. They had begun showing highlights from previous matches. The great batsman, Tendulkar, formed the backbone of the Indian innings with a masterful score of one hundred and twenty not out, against England.

"You want a drink, man?" Shango asked Palmer, still hoping to keep him calm.

"Bourbon on ice," Palmer snapped.

"Dad?"

"Just tell this man to stop his ranting in my head," Ira retorted. "Telling me I can't talk about my own wife in my house! Who does he think he is?"

His inflammatory comments shattered the peace Shango was trying to build.

"When you talk about my mother after shutting me out in the cold for so long I will rant at you, old man!" Palmer snarled.

Shango poured Palmer's bourbon and a shot of Teacher's whisky for Ira. He added ice to the bourbon and water to the whisky. He handed each man his drink and then sat apart from them. Shango could see that they were both ready to boil but he said nothing.

Give it time, he thought, just give it time.

Almost immediately Palmer burst out, "I was only sixteen! How could you send me off to 'relatives?' I didn't even know those people!" He switched off the TV and faced Ira squarely, determined to force an answer out of him.

"Man, stop your noise," Ira pressed the remote but Palmer stood in front of him, blocking the signal.

"I asked you a question." Palmer's face was distorted with anger. He banged his glass down on the table, keeping his eyes on Ira.

"It was the best thing at the time." There was no hint of submission in Ira's voice but he couldn't look Palmer in the eye.

"What do you mean people you didn't know, of course you knew them, they were Mom's family," Shango interjected.

"Mom's family?" Palmer shifted from leg to leg as he answered Shango's question but still aimed a deadly glare at Ira. "Have you ever wondered why none of them came over to visit or even phoned once in a while?" Palmer spat the words out remembering again how he'd emigrated to Atlanta while Ruby Katherine, Ira and Shango had just carried on with their lives, filling the gap as if he'd never been there.

Shango put his fist to his mouth, and leant his elbow on the table, frowning as he looked from one man to the other. The tension in the room was almost unbearable. "What's going on ?" he asked.

"While you were basking in the love and comfort of home, I was having to adjust to a new life hundreds of miles away from everything and everyone that was familiar to me. You, Shango, were a spoilt brat who never cared about anyone except yourself. Now that you're stuck with the burden of an ageing father, you suddenly need me!"

Palmer's harsh and uncensored words hit Shango like a slap in the face. Shango stared hard at him trying to understand where the deep well of anger was coming from.

"Dad?" Shango looked to Ira.

"Don't ask me, Shango. Some things should be left to lie." Ira turned to Palmer, "What's the point, man?" he asked plaintively.

The phone rang, shattering the silence that followed the poignant question. Ira looked awkward and uncomfortable, Palmer seemed ready to explode, Shango was mystified, but no one moved. Meanwhile, the phone on the hallway table continued to ring.

"Answer the phone man!" Ira snapped at Shango.

"It can wait." Shango kept his voice calm and even.

"Now!" Ira roared at him.

Shango left the room. Damn the phone.

"Speak." Shango's tone was brusque.

"Shango what time are you coming home? I expected you ages ago." Celia was surprised at the harshness in his voice.

"I can't talk, I have to go."

"But what time...?"

"Later." Shango hung up and headed back to the small living room. Ira and Palmer were talking, their agitated voices drifting from beyond the half open door. Shango lingered in the hallway, leaned back against the blue flock wallpaper and listened.

●●●●●●

Celia was annoyed. She placed the phone in its rest and turned back to her manuscript. She was trying to meet a deadline for her article about stereotypes in education. She scanned over what she'd written and switched on the computer so she could e mail the finished draft to her editor.

Celia typed automatically, her mind fixed on what had just transpired between her and her husband. After all his promises of making everything right between them Shango shouldn't have been so rough with her on the phone. She'd asked him a simple question and he'd bitten her head off. As far as she was concerned he was lucky that she allowed him near her, how could he forget so easily what he'd almost lost with that stupid radio request.

She decided to call him at Ira's again once she'd finished her assignment, if he didn't like it, tough. He needed to be reminded that he was still on thin ice with her.

●●●●●●

"You shouldn't have sent me away!" Palmer was angry. "I didn't do anything wrong. You just wanted me out of your sight. You were happy to pretend that I never existed. Why? Didn't I do everything that was expected of me and more? I respected you, I minded mom, I watched over my younger brother–*the family favourite*– I excelled at school, I went to church every Sunday, what more could I have done?"

"Palmer you have to look at the whole picture," Ira remonstrated.

"Why don't you call me son? You've never called me son! You've never held me when I was sick, never comforted me when I was hurt, never bragged to your friends about how well I was doing, never once said you were proud of me." Tears welled up in Palmer's eyes. He moved closer to Ira who sat rigid, still unable to look at him.

"Too much water under the bridge. Too late now, man, too late, just leave it," he whispered.

But Palmer couldn't.

"Why did you send me away? You broke my heart, you broke Mom's heart. I know she didn't want me to go and I never got to see her alive again. How could you do that to us?"

Ira was silent. His chest felt heavy and his head began to pound. He looked around for Shango.

"Son?" he called out to him.

"No Dad, this time it's just you and me." Palmer knelt by Ira's chair and held Ira's face gently between his hands, "Look at my tears, even grown men cry. I've waited twenty-two years for an answer. We have to finish it Dad, you have to tell me why. Please."

Shango held his breath and gripped his knees. His conciliatory instincts urged him to go in and solve the family crisis, but he knew that if he did that, the dynamics would change, and Ira and Palmer might never resolve their conflict. He was so used to being in control he was finding it impossible to be a fly on the wall. He considered going home and calling them later, but remembered that he'd left his car keys in the lounge.

He shifted on the thin carpet, ran his hands backwards over his locks and arched his stiff back. He was caught dead in the middle. He couldn't leave and he couldn't participate. This was Palmer's battle. The waiting was killing him but he had no choice but to remain sitting on the stairs in Ira's dim hallway.

Ira finally reached out and stroked Palmer's head, neck and shoulders. "It's not your fault," he whispered. "It was never your fault. You're a good boy, you made your mother proud."

"I don't understand," Palmer said.

Ira was silent for along time before he spoke again. "Before you were born I had a best friend. His name was Mack and I loved him like a brother. We came over together on the boat from Jamaica. We had plans, hopes, big dreams and great ideas. We were going to make a fortune in England and return home while we were still young enough to enjoy it. Mack was my right arm, we watched out for each other. Pass me my pipe."

Palmer picked up the rosewood pipe from the coffee table. He slowly filled it with tobacco and handed it to Ira along with a lighter. Then he sat in the middle of the two seater settee and stared into the bars of the electric fire while Ira talked. The rain falling against the windows provided a rhythmic backdrop to Ira's story while the dark clouds mirrored Palmer's pain.

"We came over in the late fifties. At first there was plenty of work, in factories, on the buses, at British Leyland making cars. But by the seventies it was beginning to dry up. Even the menial jobs were going to whites or Indians and I went from being a working man to a kept man. It was a blow I wasn't expecting. I thought I'd be back home by then, not still here in this cold, racist country. I had too much time on my hands. Mack and I stayed in the bookies all day or else we drank ourselves stupid in his rented room.

In the evenings I took out my frustrations on Ruby Katherine. I couldn't help it. She was so beautiful and understanding, but I was too proud. I couldn't face not being the breadwinner, watching while Ruby Katherine left early in the morning to clean stinking toilets for white people. She'd never had to work and look at the position I'd put her in."

"What do you mean, you took it out on Mom?"

"Man, don't ask me those questions."

"What did you do to her!?" Palmer was shouting.

"I was the man of the house!" Ira shouted back.

"What did you do?" Palmer continued his interrogation. "Humiliate her? Beat her?"

Ira was silent.

"You beat her! Jesus!" Palmer was incredulous.

"You don't know what it was like back then! Spending hours down the Labour Exchange only to be told to come back tomorrow just to beg a few pennies from the white man's government. The constant fear that my woman was going to end up on the street. Having to watch her come in night after night, knowing she was a queen and she'd had to spend the day cleaning up someone else's shit. I had no money, no job, no pride in myself but I still had to be the man."

"So you beat her!"

"It was all I had left!"

Shango gripped the banister. His stomach turned and his blood boiled as he heard Ira's confession for the first time. He closed his eyes, wishing he could undo the last five minutes and everything that had been said. He breathed hard, wiped his face with his hands and clenched and unclenched his fists. He willed himself to resist storming in and strangling the man who'd laid a hand on his mother. He had to let Ira live so that Palmer could have some restitution.

"How could you?" Palmer roared.

"Fix me another drink!" Ira held out his glass and gestured towards the bottle of Teacher's near to Palmer. "More!" he barked when Palmer handed him one shot.

"We'd had a miserable day," he continued, ignoring the fury on Palmer's face. "We'd spent hours in line hoping for work, only to be told after they'd picked all the white men, that they weren't hiring after all. We were sick and tired of rejections. It was soul destroying being constantly told we weren't needed after they asked us to come here in the first place. Took away your dignity, made you feel like less of a man. My woman could just smile and say please and get a job and I, a skilled labourer and Army chef, couldn't get nothing."

"She cleaned toilets," Palmer interjected remorsefully.

"She had a job! She had _money in her pocket_, she could pay the bills. I was the man and I had nothing! Not even two shillings to rub together.

Mack and I spent the rest of that day drinking and gambling away what little money we had on the horses. The more we drank the more it seemed to be the answer to everything. I got uncontrollably drunk. Inebriated to the point where I didn't know or care what I was doing or saying. I should never have come home like that, I should have stayed out, slept it off, come home in a better mood. But I didn't, I was just as stubborn then as I am now."

It wasn't until Ira paused to take a long sip of his drink that Palmer realised that he'd been holding his breath. He exhaled and his whole body shook with tension. He tried to relax and quell the urge to shake the rest of the story out of Ira. He wanted to use his strength and power to make him admit that he was wrong and then hear him beg for forgiveness. Instead, he paced around the room, not daring to look at the old man in case the urge to attack him grew too strong.

On the stairs Shango's breath came short and shallow. He fumbled in his pocket for his inhaler, took two puffs and rubbed his eyes. The strain of not interfering was almost unbearable.

"Your mother tried to calm me down," Ira continued at last. "She'd never seen me like that before. She was worried that I was going to hurt myself. But I couldn't take any orders from her. Why should I be silenced, made impotent in my own house?"

"I don't want to hear this." Palmer stared into his hall full glass of scotch.

"You will hear it! You wanted to know, you came all the way from America complaining that you couldn't wait any longer, you just shut-up and listen! She was nagging me constantly: be quiet, sit down, go to sleep, drink some tea! I couldn't stand her voice whining in my ears. I pushed her, she started screaming and carrying on, said she didn't know what got into me. I couldn't take the noise."

"So what happened?"

"I had the empty beer bottle in my hand when I swung at her."

"Were you crazy?"

"Shut up man, you weren't there! She ran out of the house, all the way to Mack's. You don't think she could have gone somewhere else for refuge instead of to Mack!" Ira scoffed.

"You scared her," Palmer rushed to her defence. "She'd have thought that Mack was the only one who could talk to you, get you to calm down."

"Yes, you're your mother's son all right," sneered Ira.

"What happened?" Palmer's voice trembled.

"One month she stayed with him. I never saw either of them, he kept her away from me, said she didn't want to see me, for one whole month."

"What are you saying?" Palmer whispered already knowing the answer to his question.

"How could I ever love you..." Ira's voice trailed off, he looked through the window to the pouring rain and grey skies.

"Mack and Mom? But how can you be sure that..." Palmer couldn't believe what Ira was saying to him.

"We never lay together when I was unemployed. Not for over a year. I gave you my name because she begged me to. You were bright and brilliant, a model child but you're not my son. That was always the one thing that you couldn't be."

"You couldn't stand the sight of me so you sent me to the other side of the world?" Palmer tried to shout but his voice came out in a whisper.

"For sixteen years you were a constant reminder of how my wife and my best friend betrayed me. I had to give Ruby

160

Katherine an ultimatum: I would divorce her and take Shango or you could go to live with her relatives in Atlanta. The final decision was hers."

"You left her with no choice!" Tears fell from Palmer's eyes and he sank onto the carpet. He felt as though his body had turned to stone and he couldn't move. He bowed his head and stared for a long time at nothing.

In the heavy silence Ira smoked his pipe. The day he'd dreaded had finally come and it was worse than he'd ever imagined it would be. He'd finally had to admit his unprovoked cruelty to the only woman he'd ever loved and now his sons knew of the dark, violent side that he'd always kept so well hidden. Now they also knew about the shame he'd felt in Palmer because his beautiful Ruby Katherine had betrayed him.

He was weary. He wanted to go to bed with Ruby Katherine beside him, smelling of the Lilac and Lavender scent that she'd always bought from the Avon lady. He wanted to lay his head on her breast, feel the silk of her sheer nightdress and finally ask for her forgiveness. He'd been deeply sorry for over twenty years, but his pride hadn't allowed him to say so. He'd loved her enough to give Palmer his name and she'd agreed never to see Mack again. He should never have made her send the boy away. That was unforgivable. In between each puff of his pipe, he tried to find the courage to tell Palmer that he was sorry but the words wouldn't come.

A few minutes later Shango entered the room. He gave no sign of the pent-up fury that raged inside him. He stooped and kissed Ira on his forehead but Ira made no response. Then he walked across the room to Palmer who stood up to meet him. Slowly they touched fists, then shook hands. Shango put both arms around his older brother and drew him close. Each action was filled with emotion.

After a little while Shango released Palmer with a whispered, "I love you man." He grabbed his jacket and checked the pockets for his car keys. As he walked through the hallway the phone rang again. He picked up the receiver. "I'm on my way," was all he said. Then he walked out of the house leaving Palmer and Ira alone together.

CHAPTER FIFTEEN

"Ready?"

"LIKE A LAMB to the slaughter," Shango replied so softly that Rafi almost didn't hear him. "What exactly was the message they gave you?" Shango asked.

"It's probably nothing. The EBYN exec committee just said they thought it was time for a consolidating talk," Rafi reassured him with a conviction that he didn't really feel.

"And you think that it's perfectly normal for my executive panel, from the organisation that I founded and of which I'm Chair, to summon *me* to a meeting?"

"It's not exactly about you," Rafi hedged.

"So it's about you, then is it?" Shango snapped.

"No," Rafi answered slowly.

"Well, what else? Our last scheduled meeting was only a couple of weeks ago, we've got no formalities to go over, somebody is trying to stir up trouble."

Shango ran his hand over his locks from back to front and sighed. He squeezed his eyes shut and massaged his temples. He was bone weary. The confrontation that lay ahead was the last thing he needed. As he stood in Rafi's front garden debating whether or not to go inside, nurse a scotch and delay the inevitable, his phone buzzed. He fished in his pocket and checked the caller's number on screen before answering.

"Prisoner 101," Shango answered.

"Is that supposed to be a joke?" Celia's stone was sharp. "I was just calling to find out what time you'd be home for dinner."

"Are you cooking?" Shango asked.

"No, *you're* cooking."

"So it doesn't matter what time I get in then, does it?"

"Don't be clever with me Shango. I just want to know what time we're eating."

"You mean you just want to know where I am and what I'm doing."

"Do you blame me?"

162

"Celia, how many more times? We've been through all of this over and over and over again!"

"Oh shut up! It's bad enough that you can't keep your pants zipped up, but you're not even discreet about it."

"Celia I've told you a thousand times, it was nothing serious."

"Nothing serious, you sure? That's okay then." Celia's voice was heavy with sarcasm. "What time will I see you?"

"The prisoner will be reporting in at six pm, if that's okay with you."

"I wouldn't be making comments like that if I was in your shoes." Celia hung up.

Shango snapped his phone shut and looked glumly at Rafi he rolled his head back and looked up to the sky.

"What are you doing?" Rafi asked cautiously.

"Praying."

"For who?"

"Myself."

"Bit late for that isn't it?"

"No need to state the obvious."

As Shango watched the evening sunset through half closed eyelids, he realised he was glad that he was approaching the end of his day, of his week in fact. It had been exceedingly tough.

From the snubs and snide remarks at Ira's domino club to the condescending text messages and bad looks in the streets, his love for Sandra had made him a pariah.

"It's not because you love her, it's because you were stupid enough to announce it," Rafi spoke into the silence.

"I love it when you read my mind."

"Shango what happened to your love life, man?" Rafi could hardly believe that his friend had been brought so low.

Shango shrugged, he couldn't even begin to answer that question. He turned his phone over and over in his hand enjoying the smooth feel of its satin silver casing. Rafi reached out for it.

"If these mobile phones get any smaller you'll be able to wear them as earrings." Rafi stopped mid-chuckle, "That was a joke. Things must be bad if I can't make you laugh." He paused and look upwards into the darkening sky, "Looks like there's going to be a storm tonight."

"That's one way of looking at it I suppose." Shango shrugged again.

"Look, are we going to this meeting or what?"

"Whatever, I'll take my car," said Shango.

"Right behind you, man."

Handsworth Leisure Centre was only fifteen minutes from Rafi's house but as they pulled into the car park Shango felt as he'd been driving for hours. He checked his reflection in the rearview mirror and was dismayed at what he saw. He had dark circles under his eyes and the grey that normally just tinged the roots of his locks seemed to be have spread. His skin looked sallow and his normally trim beard was in disarray.

He was no longer a man in control of his destiny. Instead, all of the fabric that he'd worked so hard to weave together was unravelling. The rock solid foundation on which he'd based his marriage and his vision for EBYN was crumbling and Shango didn't know how to pull it back together.

His radio request for Sandra had created a huge chasm between him and and his wife. Since collecting her from Angela's, Celia had asked him to sleep in the spare room until they'd resolved the issue. Shango had had no choice but to agree. And although Celia pushed him away at nights, in other ways she'd become excessively clingy. He was sure that if they just talked without recriminations, long stony silences, or appointing blame, they'd eventually be able to move forward.

Shango was trying hard to show his love but he wasn't sure that he was getting through. He was home every night, he made sure there were never any unexplained phone calls going in or out of the house, he did his best to shield her from gossip and speculation and he'd gone from being a free agent to virtually giving her a written itinerary of his whereabouts. But still it wasn't enough. The gulf between them grew wider every day, but until Celia was ready to talk, there was nothing more Shango could do.

Celia stood in front of her wardrobe enjoying the feel of the fabrics against her fingertips. She loved to wear velvets, silks and brushed cotton. The type of material that fell in graceful folds around her soft curves when she moved and was most comfortable for sitting in for long hours, when writing articles at her computer.

She felt angry with herself for being so churlish with Shango on the phone. He'd sounded like he'd had enough, almost as if he wished he could undo the request he'd made that had turned their lives upside down. He'd sounded like a little boy that was tired of standing in the corner and wanted to be allowed to play again.

Celia was also tired. Being constantly angry was mentally exhausting. Every day Shango faced her hostility and every night he slept alone in a cold, unwelcoming bed. But in punishing him, Celia punished herself too. Whereas once she'd had the refuge and comfort of Shango's arms when she was low, now she had nothing. She hated the situation but what choice did she have? She'd put her trust in him and he'd hurt her to the core. They lived together but now she couldn't allow herself to touch him, hold him, kiss or make love to him.

It was a torturous loneliness. At night she placed her hands between her legs to quell the longing that was there for him. During the day she spoke to him in curt sentences and she avoided his gaze lest her eyes reveal her deep love for him.

Since he'd brought her back from Angela's he hadn't given her a single reason to doubt him. Perhaps it was time to forgive. Maybe not forget, but certainly to forgive.

Celia's hand rested against her clothes. She pulled out one of her newest and most elegant long dresses and held it against her skin. Yes, she decided, admiring her reflection in the mirror, it was definitely time to forgive.

The faces of the members of the EBYN network were sombre. Shango nodded to each of them as he walked into the centre of the room with Rafi at his side. The men returned his greeting but there was none of the usual exuberant back slapping, fist touching or handshakes. Tonight, with serious business to attend to, there was no room for levity.

"Brother Shango," Ras Reuben approached calling out as if Shango was still in the car park. "thank you for coming here tonight," he continued. The smile on his face did nothing to hide the insincerity of his words.

"There's no need to thank me for coming to a meeting of my own organisation," Shango responded dryly still wondering exactly what was going on. The men had formed a circle around him and Rafi, making him feel trapped. He decided that it was time to take the initiative. "What's all this about?"

"Brother Shango, the members and I," Ras Reuben began as Shango raised his eyebrows in surprise, *the members and I*? "..are starting to feel that the fox is amok loosely amongst the hungry chickens," the elder continued with a greasy smile.

"I beg your pardon?" Shango struggled to keep his temper under control and not punch the condescending grin right off Ras Reuben's smug face.

"Because of recent happenings, "Ras paused for effect, "we must be prepared to be upstanding for the common good of all black men and women, including the children. The community has whispered, not silently but with a loud roar, and now we have our authority ready." Ras Reuben finished his elaborate speech and waited expectantly.

Shango looked sideways at Rafi and then around at the group quizzically. Was he the only one who hadn't understood a word Ras had just said?

"I beg your pardon?" he repeated.

"Look man," Tayshan Webber stepped forward, "I'm not quite as eloquent as the Ras but I think what he's trying to say is that we believe in the principles of this network and we care about how we're represented. You know you haven't exactly been what you'd call *'upstanding'* lately with your wife and your girlfriends. Sorry Shango but it's got to be said, everybody knows and it makes everyone think that we're all like that."

"What?" Rafi started, but Shango gestured for him to be quiet.

"Look, just stand down, then we can publicly elect another leader, make it seem like he's just covering for a while, 'till you get back on your feet. Sorry man."

Tayshan's speech was humble and apologetic but it's impact still left Shango reeling.

"Does everybody feel like this?" he asked looking around the room.

"Not me." Rafi's was a lone voice.

"Brother we all have our needs but how we handle them is another matter. We expected more from you and we're well disappointed."

"Ras shut up man!" Rafi had had enough.

"It's okay, Rafi, thanks." Shango moved from the centre of the circle and walked to the front of the room.

"As far as I know we're a properly constituted body with procedures which we agreed on right from the very beginning. Has a vote been taken on this yet?"

Several of the men muttered, "No."

"Then let's do this properly. All I ask for is an opportunity to put my side of the story in a non-judgemental atmosphere. Ignore the rumours and bad mindedness that's followed me like a bad smell for the last week. Allow me ten minutes, then, we'll vote and if you ask me to stand down then I will do so. But remember, this network was formed from my dreams and my vision and one day I will come back and I will lead again. Remember any man can make a mistake, but only those with strength of character and no thought of failure, can rise like a Phoenix from the ashes."

Some of the men had the grace to look ashamed at Shango's words. They took their seats while Shango puffed on his inhaler, breathed deeply and prepared his mind to produce the words his men needed to hear.

● ● ● ● ● ●

Sandra pressed print on her computer keyboard, pulled the sheet of paper from the printer and laid it on the table. Ever since she'd discovered how quickly she could type she'd spent hours keeping an electronic journal. When her mind was overflowing her keyboard provided a necessary relief. But this evening Shango had invaded her thoughts and something just didn't feel right. Whether her eyes were open or shut, whether she was working, eating, sleeping or doing nothing he was always uppermost on her mind.

When she hadn't heard from him after they'd first made love she'd spent a day in bed with tissues and a huge box of chocolates, mourning his loss all over again. It was nothing less than sheer willpower that had enabled her to go to Ira's party, just for Ira's sake. She'd thought that this same strength would be sufficient to shield her from Shango's advances, but she had to admit to herself that she was fighting a losing battle.

Shango was in her heart and soul, the space he'd carved there years before still had his name on it. She longed to see him but her pride wouldn't allow her to call. If he wanted her, then this time around he had to do all the running. He had to prove himself because she refused to meet him even halfway. When Shango could show that he was prepared to be a fool for her then she'd be able to fully let him into her mind as well as her body.

Sandra stood at her window in her short satin nightie and matching dressing gown. She sipped iced Bailey's while looking at the view. The storm clouds over the park were dark and foreboding, lonely and comfortless, matching her mood exactly. Turning away from them she decided to read in bed for a while, too restless to sit in front of the TV.

But before settling down she took the page she'd printed out earlier, sprayed it with perfume and put it inside a rose coloured envelope. In black ink she wrote; *"To Shango"* then she pinned it to the outside of her front door and went to sleep.

● ● ● ● ● ●

From deep inside his pocket Shango felt his mobile phone vibrating again. He knew without looking that it was Celia on the line calling again to find out where he was. It was half past seven, he'd said he'd be home at six.

He'd just completed his seventh circuit walking slowly around the perimeter of the outdoor basketball court at the leisure centre. He'd put everything he had into a passionate speech as he fought to keep control of his group. On occasion many of the men had nodded in accordance with his words and at the end some of them had even applauded him. But he knew that there were still others, such as Ras Reuben and his cronies, who'd be happy to take his crown.

Afterwards he'd left the room while they debated his suitability as a leader in light of his marital infidelity. After that, they'd vote. There was nothing more he could do except wait.

"Hello wife," he said wearily into his handset.

"Hello darling, are you okay?"

The warmth in Celia's voice took Shango by surprise; he'd expected another battle.

"To be honest with you, I've been better. The guys are giving me a hard time." Shango hadn't meant to be so open, but he was tired of fake nonchalance.

"I was thinking, why don't I cook tonight?"

"You, cook?" Shango burst out laughing but his tone was gentle.

"Yes, me cook for a change, and I'm not talking Marks and Spencer's ready-meals, I mean really cook, a whole meal from scratch. How about it?"

"Yes please!" Shango felt better already. "Celia?..." he began but stopped, fearing another rebuff.

"I know," she said, "It's time for us to talk. I love you Shango and I want you back. Let's start again tonight with dinner."

"I love you too, Celia, that's never changed. I want you to know that."

"I do, see you later?"

"Definitely."

"But not too late?"

"I'll do my best, just remember that when I get there I'm all yours." Shango squinted at the sky. The storm was still threatening but now he could finally see a chink of evening sunlight. He looked on it as a good omen.

"Yo!" Rafi called to Shango across the courtyard. "Time."

Shango walked slowly back to the building to hear the group's verdict. It was all over and done in minutes. Less than two hours ago Shango had been architect and chair of the En Blacken Yourself Network. Now, as the night drew in, he was just another member. Rafi and a few of the men had suggested that Shango be put on probation in an effort to circumvent his total demotion, but the majority had voted against them feeling that this was the only way to keep public confidence in the network.

Shango felt as though he'd been punched in the chest. The punishment was harsher than anything he'd expected but the worst part was having to sit silently while Ras Reuben was elected as the new leader. As he shook hands and wished Ras well his expression was neutral but inside he was burning up with rage.

Afterwards Shango stood alone in the carpark while the men said their goodbyes.

Rafi approached him. "Want to come back to mine for a bit?" He felt bad for his friend. "I'm sorry man, they wouldn't listen to me," he tried to explain when Shango stayed silent.

"No problem. I have to take what's coming to me," Shango said slowly, his mind far away, thinking of other things from another time.

"You gonna follow me home, then?" Rafi asked.

"No."

"You going home to Celia?"

"Maybe."

"Don't tell me you're going to see Sandra! Shango, you've got to get that woman out of your mind. What has she ever done except cause you trouble?"

"It's not like that, man."

"That must be why you're still head of the network– oh, excuse me, you're not! You got carried away by new sex with an old flame and life went down the pan. Get a grip man!"

Shango held up a warning finger. "Leave it," he growled.

"I'm the one who's watching you suffer and trying to help you pick up the pieces. You've lost EBYN and you and Celia are hanging on by a thread. You wanted to set an example, what the hell kind of example is that?"

Shango turned and headed for the car park. He couldn't face the truth that Rafi spoke. There was a pounding between his ears and his chest was tight. He needed space to think and to escape his from his own conscience.

"You know I'm talking sense," Rafi caught up to Shango and grabbed his arm but Shango pulled away. He stopped at the door of his BMW and glowered at Rafi.

"Not now." His voice was low and forbidding but Rafi was heedless.

"Then when!" Sheer anger made him push Shango backwards against the car. Shango stumbled, but pulled himself upright.

"Leave the bitch alone, man! She ain't got nothing for you except destruction!"
The force of Shango's fist against his cheekbone caused Rafi to stagger and fall backwards.

"What the hell?..." He lay on the ground looking at Shango in shock. It was the first time they'd ever come to blows.

"I'm sorry." Shango took a step towards Rafi, "I'm...sorry." He stepped back, guilt etched into his face. He was remorseful, but he didn't stop to help his friend. Instead he got into his car and drove off at high speed.

Shango didn't notice the dark settle all around him as he sped across the city. He pressed the pedal to the metal and imagined that it was only his will that propelled the car. After a day of losses it felt good to finally be in control.

As he drove, a montage of pictures flashed through his mind: Ira and Palmer never a real father and son; Ruby Katherine and Mack, illicit lovers; his wife, bereft and unkempt seeking solace in her parents arms; a scantily dressed Sensi looking for validation in a club full of leering men; a hurt Sandra ignoring him at Ira's party; the humiliation he'd suffered at the domino club; Rafi, his best friend, felled by his own hand.

It was all too much, too many faces, too many hurt people, too many plans gone awry. He blinked to dismiss the awful images and realised that the wetness on his cheeks was his own tears.

Twenty minutes later Shango sat silently in the car park outside of Sandra's block. There were no lights on in her flat. He was disappointed at the thought that she was probably asleep. He turned up the radio to drown out his conscience which nagged him to go home to his wife.

Sitting in the middle of Moseley he was surrounded by the

essence of the woman he wanted to be with. He was less than twenty feet from her front door and when he closed his eyes, that was close enough to sense her, even feel her.

After a few minutes he left his car and headed for Sandra's building. As he neared the door someone came out and he seized the window of opportunity to slip inside. Sandra's flat was opposite the main entrance. It was after ten and didn't intend to wake her so he hadn't pressed the intercom. He just wanted to be as close to her as possible before he went home to hear what Celia had to say about the state of their marriage.

As he approached her door he saw the note with his name on it. His spirit soared to know that she'd been thinking of him. He opened the envelope enjoying it's perfumed scent and leaned against the wall while he read.

> *Dear Sweetheart,*
> *I've tried so hard to write you out of my life, tried to write away this pain that is the other side of your love, I fill my days from morning till night with people, appointments, parties; I have to keep moving because every time I stand still I miss you. Baby, I wish I could truly believe what your eyes tell me every time we kiss, what your fingertips tell me every time we make love, what your heart tells me every time I hear it beating. I wish you really knew, that you are my love and I can't breath without you....*
>
> *S...... x*

By the time Shango had knocked once Sandra was in his arms and his life with Celia was nothing more than a distant memory.

CHAPTER SIXTEEN

AFTER THEY HAD made love Shango rolled over onto the cold side of the bed. Flat on his back he pulled Sandra to him. She snuggled close, laying her head on his broad chest.

"Always remember that I love you," he whispered as he kissed her.

"I love you too," Sandra whispered back.

Their juices saturated the bed and filled the room with the smell of sex. Sandra inhaled, savouring the scent.

"What is it, babe?" Shango murmured sleepily.

"I love the way we smell after sex," replied Sandra. She closed her eyes wanting to recapture the contentment she felt when he'd entered her and rocked her deliciously. With a skilful movement of his hips against hers he'd blocked out her cares and concerns. Her mind and body were filled with love for him when they came together in a passionate denouement. There wasn't a part of her that didn't feel him, didn't long for him and hadn't clung to him as they'd satisfied their mutual desires.

Just as she'd succumbed to sleep, Shango's snoring became louder. Carefully, Sandra removed Shango's pillow and placed it over his nose, then panicked fearing she'd suffocate him. She pulled it away in time for the next deafening snore to emerge.

Sandra reflected that once Shango opened his eyes he'd be as good as gone. She simply nodded when Shango said he didn't like to leave his house empty all night while struggling between wanting to confront him and not wanting to provoke him into saying things she didn't want to hear. Like, maybe, there was another, more important woman in his life.

The bright red numbers on the digital bedside clock said twelve forty-five am. Soon he'd drag himself sluggishly from the bed, yawn his way through getting dressed and then leave bleary eyed. She'd be alone trying to work out how to fill the hole he'd left.

In the hallway of her flat she clung to him.

"Get some rest, I'll call you later." He kissed her goodbye.

"I wish you could stay."

"So do I, but you know how things are right now."

No, thought Sandra, to be honest I don't think I do. Her thoughts remained unspoken, a silent barrier between them.

Shango sensed her upset but he knew he had to leave. It was late, he had no idea what he'd say to Celia. He only hoped she'd be asleep so he could shower away his betrayal before climbing into their bed. He looked back at Sandra. She stood in the moonlit doorway wearing a short, sheer, baby blue dressing gown that skimmed her knees. She looked gorgeous. The sight of her tousled hair, captivating eyes and beautiful curves made his nature rise. For a minute Shango fought the urge to lead her back inside, enter her precious, secret place and hold her all night long. He had to leave, he was already very late.

Sandra waved at him as he opened his car door and got in. She turned off all the lights in her flat and double-checked the locks on the window and the front door. In her bedroom she blew out the scented candles that had added to the fragrance of their lovemaking. She discarded her light robe and wrapped herself in Shango's pyjama top. As she closed her eyes the doorbell rang. Sandra threw off the covers and leapt off the bed, grinning.

"Five minutes, that's all, just five minutes." Shango mumbled while kissing, caressing and half carrying her back to the bedroom.

Fifty minutes later Shango steered his sleek BMW away from Sandra's flat in Moseley, South Birmingham. He wondered if it was possible to do a thirty-five minute drive in less than ten minutes. Mentally he was kicking himself, he must have been mad to go back to Sandra just so that they could hold each other, swap sweet kisses and drink wine. So simple and so perfect. With Sandra he could relax and be himself, not someone's son, mentor, lecturer, or even husband. Sandra was an extension of him. He wished he was still with her, but he had a wife and a house on the other side of the city where he should have been hours ago. Now was the time to concentrated on what lay ahead.

● ● ● ● ● ●

At ten o'clock the music on the radio stopped as the news chimes started. The presenter read the headlines out loud as if nothing else was going on in the world. Celia remained seated at the dining table. Her tears obscured the roast chicken in front of her and she could no longer smell the delicious aroma of sweet potatoes, snapper, plantain and calalloo, that she'd prepared for her husband.

On the kitchen counter lay the Caribbean cookbook that she'd dug up from the back of Shango's bookcase. She'd been determined that tonight would prove once and for all that she could cook for her man. She didn't remember the two hours of work that had gone into the meal. How she'd almost given up and asked Michelle to show her just one more time how to season and mix and mash and saute and grill and bake and roast. But then, drawing on a strength so deep within she almost didn't know it was there, she'd reminded herself of this self-imposed torture. She needed Shango to eat food so well made that it blew his mind. She wanted him to taste the love in each mouthful.

Sitting at the table Celia didn't hear the new radio programme begin. She stared into the yellow flame of the candle but didn't see it flickering. She rubbed her hands on the lap of her burgundy dress, soft velvet, Shango's favourite. She crossed and uncrossed her legs clad in silky black stockings and suspenders. Her leather strappy sandals with three inch heels chafed against the rug under her feet.

She forgot that she'd dressed exactly as Shango had always asked her to. It no longer mattered that if he came in now and saw her sitting there serene and gorgeous, her short natural hair adorned with a real rose, that he'd catch his breath and think that she was the most beautiful woman he'd ever seen. It didn't occur to Celia that Shango would tilt her chin and examine every inch of her doll-like face, glad that she wore hardly any make-up.

Celia could no longer picture him kissing her tenderly, caressing her breast and holding her close, savouring her beautifully presented, delicious meal and then leading her in a slow dance to their song - Lionel Richie's *Three Times a Lady* - before taking her in upstairs to seal the evening with a perfect expression of his love and gratitude.

As Celia sat at the table she didn't hear the chimes of the eleven, twelve and one o'clock news. Through her silent tears all Celia could see was Shango in the arms of someone else. Louder than her own heartbeat, Celia heard the cries of her husband in the throes of orgasm with that woman. A despised, invisible, bitch. The one who would always be known as the faceless, hated Sandra.

All Celia knew was that Shango was loving someone else

while the wife he'd promised to love and cherish was forgotten and cast aside, left sitting at a table filled with expressions of her love for him. All Celia understood was that Shango didn't care and that she was truly alone in their marriage.

At two am Celia heard the key turn in the lock. Outside, Shango fiddled frantically and twisted the stubborn piece of metal until realisation dawned. Celia had pushed down the latch and purposely locked him out! Now he'd have to ring the doorbell to get her to open up. It was the early hours of the morning, he had no alibi and he smelt of another woman. If he had to wake up Celia there was no way he was going to get to the bathroom to wash without being seen.

He kicked the step and banged his head against his fist, cursing his weakness. Why had he allowed this to happen? He should have been home by nine, ten at the latest, but he'd craved Sandra just as she'd yearned for him. Their passion had overwhelmed them both and he'd forgotten all about Celia.

The memory of Sandra in his arms made him too weak for a battle. He prayed that Celia would be too tired to argue so that he could appease her in the morning. He'd bring her breakfast in bed, mow the lawn, take her to see a slushy film, or even, as a last resort, spend an evening with Martin and Angela discussing some boring Russian philosopher. He'd do whatever it took as long as he didn't have to deal with her tonight.

Shango pressed the bell. His hand shook and his upper lip was sweating. He heard Celia's footsteps pause before she lifted the latch, then the door opened. Shango steeped inside trying to look apologetic. The pain in Celia's eyes told him he'd failed.

"Babe," he offered a conciliatory hand. Celia moved back and Shango noticed how captivatingly gorgeous she looked. While he was admiring her, Celia turned to the side and picked up a large tureen that she'd placed on the hall table just before opening the door. She held it high above her head threatening to spill its contents all over him. She still hadn't said a word.

"Darling," his tone was placatory.

"Don't come near me you bastard."

"Sweetheart, I can explain." Shango took small steps towards his wife.

"I said don't come near me!" Celia was on the verge of losing control, the dish shook in her hands.

"What are you going to do, throw that at me?" Shango's tone

was disbelieving.

Enraged, Celia aimed high and tipped the contents over him. Calalloo and sauce splashed onto his face, neck and chest and dripped onto the floor.

"Woman are you crazy?" Vegetables slopped off his chin and nose. The stone cold liquid squelched between his shirt collar and his neck, dripped down his chest and stained his light coloured shirt red and green. He pulled at string beans and carrots that settled around his eyes and in his hair. He was not happy.

"Now I don't have to smell that bitch on you," Celia stared at him with fire in her eyes. The dish crashed to the floor and shattered as Celia unleashed blow after blow on her husband. "Bring her home, so I can see her!" she shouted.

Shango held up his arms for protection as Celia thumped, slapped and pinched him. He tried to swerve away from her vicious attack and she pounded his back until the pain made him suddenly turn with his hand raised high in the air. Celia stopped immediately.

Shango caught sight of himself in the hallway mirror. His face was a mask of pure anger, his body heaped in a threatening pose and his hand clenched into a fist ready to deliver a heavy punch.

"Do it you bastard, do it!" Celia taunted, "Can't bring yourself to hit me but you can sleep with another woman!" she pushed him against the wall, using the full force of her body.

As Shango stumbled backwards he grabbed her arm, she lost her footing and fell against him. He held her for a brief moment, her head on his chest, his arm around her, their hearts beating rapidly, then Celia stepped back and slapped him hard across his cheek. Shango put his hand up to soothe the searing pain and felt something wet and sticky. He looked at his fingers, Celia's wedding ring had ripped through his skin causing him to bleed.

For the first time that evening Shango really looked at his beautiful wife. Through her large brown eyes shone a magnitude of pain. Her body, so exquisitely dressed, was half turned away from him. Her fists were clenched, her jaws tight, her stance defiant. He saw what he was doing to her. He loved another woman, he wanted to be with another woman. He couldn't, wouldn't admit it, but she knew and it was killing her.

Celia considered her husband's sorry state. He was covered in cold soup and blood dripped from his cheek. There would probably be bruises in the morning where she'd hit him. Worst of all her handsome, darling, beautiful man was caught in a lie with no way out. For the first time in their marriage she called the shots. Whatever happened next would be totally up to her. For several long minutes, they stood contemplating one another. Then Celia turned and started up the stairs. She was exhausted.

"Come," was all she said as Shango stood looking after her.

In the semi dark of their bedroom Celia bathed Shango's face with cotton wool dipped in aloe lotion. With even strokes she repaired the damage her hands had inflicted. Shango sat on a cushioned stool, his face turned upwards, grateful for Celia's care as she smoothed cocoa butter oil into his aching back and shoulders.

"Turn around," Celia spoke softly.

Shango swivelled so he was again facing Celia. She poured basil and sweet almond oil into her palm, rubbed her hands together and massaged his scalp. Shango rested his head against her breasts, put his hands gently on her hips and inhaled her scent. She'd changed into a black satin nightdress whilst Shango wore only his boxer shorts. As her hands roamed over his head he felt a warm stirring between his legs. He clutched Celia tighter and moaned softly. She made no response but continued to work her way around his head and the back of his neck. Her touch was light and comforting.

"Head up, "she said. Again, there was no malice in her tone. It was a simple instruction with which Shango immediately complied. His lips were level with her nipples now as she rubbed his ear lobes and the sides of his neck. His shorts grew tighter as his arousal became obvious, He wanted to take Celia's hand and place it right there, feel her fingers close around him, gently moving up and down, bringing him to the point of no return. But instead he closed his eyes and sat in deference as Celia's caresses soothed his bruises.

"Finished, how does that feel?" Celia asked.

"Very good thanks." Shango was frustrated. He wanted more of the sweet massage. He wanted her to undress and let him rest his lips against her full breasts, his hands cupping her buttocks while she continued to tenderly stroke his head, neck and chest, going further and further down until...

"Turn off the light." Celia interrupted his reverie with a sharp tone. She was in bed, still clothed he noted, disappointed. Sighing, he put the stool under the dresser then flicked the switch that plunged the room into darkness.

"You can make up the bed in the spare room, can't you?"

"The what?" questioned Shango.

"I've got an early start. Deadline for my article for *The Voice Education Supplement*, so don't make any noise while you're getting settled."

Celia sounded resolute but Shango just kissed his teeth. He'd had enough. This was his wife, in his bed, in his house. He was going to take control. Shango flung away the quilt. Deftly he ripped Celia's nightdress at the seam and pulled it clean off. Then he lay right on top of her, nose to nose, hip to hip, toe to toe.

"Shango, what the?" Celia trembled at his actions.

"Woman!" Shango silenced her as he twisted his hips, manoeuvring his shorts down to his ankles. Celia gasped as his hardness pushed against the top of her thighs. Using his knee he nudged her legs open while his hands gathered her breasts together enabling his tongue to lap first one nipple then the other. She cried out as Shango teased her nipples into hardness feeling herself growing wet with desire as his fingers fondled and caressed her most intimate place, claiming it as his own. She held her breath as his head followed his hand.

Her orgasm was building as Shango willingly gave her the pleasure she deserved. He wanted to say sorry, not with flowers or a fancy meal, diamonds or a holiday but with pure love and affection. He would give her as many orgasms as she could handle, deferring his own pleasure until he was sure she was satiated and loved.

"Shango, Shango…" Celia grabbed the top of Shango's head as he thirstily drank her juices. She parted her legs even further allowing him to push his tongue deeper inside her. His fingers still teased her nipples and squeezed her swollen breasts. The intensity was almost unbearable making her forget how much she had hated this man just a few short hours ago. Now, the sweet delight of his touch reinforced the love that was in her heart for him and compelled her to overlook his weaknesses. As Shango moved against her in that special way she arched her back and bit her lip as waves of orgasmic bliss swept over her.

Shango looked up, his mouth moist and smelling of her. "Come here," she whispered. He moved towards her and she wrapped her arms around his neck and thrust her tongue deep into his mouth. With her free hand she guided his penis towards her special place. She was ready for him. His stiffness strained to be inside her and the thought of filling her up sent erotic impulses screaming through his body but still he took it slow. He had to make her realise that this wasn't just sex, it was a declaration of love from a contrite heart. Shango had never wanted to cause his wife so much pain. He couldn't help loving Sandra, but still he desired to make Celia happy and this was his opportunity.

Looking right into his eyes, he entered her. Her cry in response was music to his ears. "Whine for me, baby," he encouraged as he penetrated her deeply. She rolled her hips backwards and forwards until he could feel every part of her. The sensations sent blood rushing to his member until at last he rocked her for the final time.

Celia lay naked with her head on Shango's chest. His arm was wrapped around her shoulders. He'd retrieved the cast off quilt and covered them up to their waists. He listened to her quiet, even, breathing amazed that everything she did was feminine and discreet. She carried herself with a regal air, looked stunning in whatever she wore. She kept their house immaculately clean yet comfortable. She was a brilliant journalist, considered to be an expert in the field of education and black youth. She loved to laugh and had masses of patience for Michelle, who he always thought was a bit sad. She was beautiful and he knew that many other men would love to be with her. If she'd been able to cook then she would have been perfect. In fact she probably was perfect, she just wasn't the woman for him.

Deep down he knew that his love for her was growing weaker not stronger. But he couldn't voice his thoughts. Spoken out loud it would mean the end of everything they'd been building together. It would give too many people the chance to say "We knew she wasn't right for you." More importantly Shango would be letting himself down. He believed that marriage was for life. He'd been stumbling along waiting for the situation with Sandra to somehow right itself, but he'd never considered leaving Celia. She was his wife, he was committed to her. Their marriage meant more to him than just a piece of paper.

In her sleep Celia hugged him tighter. Shango kissed her forehead and started at the ceiling. He had no idea what he was going to do.

CHAPTER SEVENTEEN

ADDICTED. PALMER WONDERED if that was the best way to describe his feelings for his sister-in-law's best friend, Michelle Hamilton. Smitten, besotted, bewitched, captivated. He tossed the words backwards and forwards in his mind as he stared out of the window at the rain soaked day.

He admitted to himself that he was consumed by all of her. By her beautiful hair which fell in soft wisps around her neck, by the curve of her breasts beneath her tailored suits and blouses, by her petite ankles that led to finely curved calves and firm thighs. This woman, more than any other, had gotten under his skin. He remembered the delight he'd felt when she'd laughed at his jokes. He smiled at the thought of her dainty footsteps and the way her petite hand fitted into his. He wanted to wrap her up in his arms and never let her go. He closed his eyes knowing that when he did so all he'd see would be more pictures of her. Sweet and wonderful Michelle.

In the kitchen, Ira played Ella Fitzgerald songs on the tape deck of the small stereo radio whilst filleting fish. The smells of seasoning drifted through the house along with the trumpet solo from Ella's band. When Ira remembered the words he sang along to Ella and the Duke, when he forgot he just hummed. His hands prepared the fish with the skill honed from his days as an army chef, while his mind sorted memories of when he was a young man, sharply dressed in the fashion of the forties and fifties. His smile broadened as he recalled feeling so proud to be walking down the street with the elegant and beautiful Ruby Katherine by his side.

Upstairs Palmer roused himself from his daydreaming. He flicked backwards and forwards through his wardrobe several times, looking for a suitable outfit. Then he checked and double checked the shirt and trousers that he finally chose, making sure that there were no creases or loose threads. He did everything with determined precision, taking his time in deciding which shoes and even which socks finished off the outfit. He couldn't help the dismal weather but today he was meeting the woman of his dream so everything else had to be perfect.

Michelle looked outside with dismay. It had rained for three days straight and it seemed like the brilliant sunshine that had heralded August was gone for good. She's taken the day off work especially to be with Palmer and her supervisor Don had done a double take when she'd handed in her request for leave.

"Are you ill?" he'd asked, puzzled.

Michelle had given him a scathing look, "Do you mean am I planning to be ill on Wednesday? Of course not. I just need some time to myself that's all. Is that going to be a problem."

"No! Gosh, usually we have to pay you to take time off."

"Don't worry, I'll still be getting paid!" Michelle had laughed. She understood Don's surprise. Normally she hated taking days off. She considered her assistant to be just short of incompetent and she didn't like the way the work piled up until she got back. It was just easier and more efficient to always be around. But today work was the last thing on her mind.

Michelle didn't have to think twice about being available for Palmer. After all, he wouldn't be in England for much longer. She could hardly ask him to wait until the firm closed down over Christmas although she knew she'd like it if he was still around then. She didn't know where they were going today. He'd said he wanted to surprise her. Ordinarily Michelle didn't like surprises; they made her feel out of control but knowing that Palmer had organised it made it seem okay, even special. She wished for his sake that the rain would stop. She'd feel disappointed for him if their options were severely limited by the weather.

Michelle put on her favourite Sweet Honey in the Rock CD and checked her appearance yet again in the mirror on the inside of her wardrobe door. The master bedroom was her favourite room. She liked the restful honey colour of the fitted wall-to-wall units which housed spacious floor-to-ceiling wardrobes, with a range of modern storage options including hidden baskets, half-height rails and pull-out draws.

Turning from left to right, looking at her reflection over her shoulder, something just wasn't quite right. Her navy trouser suit looked too much like an office uniform. She stripped down to her underwear and inspected her rows of clothes. It would be the third time she'd changed outfits while waiting for Palmer.

Pretty good, Palmer mused, inspecting himself in the mirror. He patted his hair and squirted Diesel aftershave on his neck. He picked up his mac from the bedroom chair along with an oversized umbrella, just big enough for two, he thought with a smile, checked his shoes to make sure there was no mud or dirt on them and finally made his way downstairs.

"You look happy!" Ira commented when Palmer walked into the kitchen.

"That's because I'm the luckiest man in this town," Palmer replied, chuckling. Ira joined in and their deep laughter drowned out Ella's sweet singing.

"Are you a lucky man or is Michelle a lucky girl?" Ira teased.

"The answer to that would be yes!" Palmer was enjoying the banter. It lifted his spirits to see Ira in such good humour. Things hadn't been easy for them since he'd found out about Ruby Katherine's infidelity but they were both just taking things day by day.

"You know, I would never have pictured you two together," Ira commented.

"They do say love is blind." Palmer was still smiling.

"Love might be blind but it ain't deaf, what are you going to do about the other one?"

"The other one?" Palmer was flummoxed. He'd totally forgotten all about Liana.

"The one with the nice voice. She keeps calling here but you're never in." Ira stirred the soup with his right hand and gestured impatiently with his left.

Palmer studied the red stains on Ira's apron, wondering if fish bled, while he waited for Ira to explain.

"Who, Dad? Who's got a nice voice and when did she call?" he prompted realising that if Ira took much longer he was going to be late for Michelle. Palmer hated tardiness.

"Ahm, Joanne?" Ira struggled to remember Liana's name.

"Joanne?" Palmer was lost.

"No, not Joanne," Ira tried again, "You know the one I mean, ahm, Leslie."

"Leslie? Dad!" Palmer checked his watch, he was becoming exasperated.

"You just go about your business. When I remember I'll write it down." Ira's smile was replaced by a look of anxiety and confusion. He stirred the soup erratically causing some of it to slop over onto the cooker. Mindful of the old man's age Palmer felt guilty for harassing him.

"It's no problem, Dad, just sit down a minute." He took the wooden spoon from Ira's grasp and led him to the chair. When Ira was seated Palmer poured him a glass of water.

"Sip this slowly for me."

"Don't talk to me like that, I ain't no baby!" Ira snapped.

"Okay," Palmer replied calmly.

Since his birthday party Ira became easily agitated and could sometimes take a while to calm down. Palmer didn't like leaving him on his own when he was in this state of mind.

"I can't even remember the woman's name!" Ira slammed the glass on the table in frustration.

"Dad it doesn't matter," Palmer tried to reassure him.

"Nothing matters does it?" Ira had a faraway look in his eyes. "You're right, Ruby Katherine left me and now nothing matters, not the damn woman's name or the blasted fish soup!"

Ira sat silently after his outburst. He still hadn't drunk any of his water. After a while he looked at Palmer as if surprised to see him there.

"What about your lady friend?"

"I'll call her and cancel." In the pit of his stomach Palmer felt raw disappointment at not seeing Michelle but he knew that his responsibilities lay with Ira.

"You go, Sensi will be here soon."

"Sensi's coming?" Palmer was surprised. He hadn't seen Kai's mom since he'd arrived in England.

"She's bringing Kai, I cooked the soup for them. You go to your woman. Sensi's a good mother to that boy, Shango should open his eyes and see that. I'm tired, have to lie down, leave the back door open for her when you go." Ira ended his instructions by nodding at the stereo, "Put that tape upstairs for me," then he left the room.

Palmer turned off the gas fire underneath the fish soup. He tidied away Ira's cooking utensils, wiped down the kitchen surfaces and left the back door closed but unlocked. Then he followed Ira up to his bedroom. When he got there Ira was fast asleep on top of the covers still wearing his stained white apron and his slippers. Palmer plugged in the stereo and pressed play then he turned the volume down low. He covered Ira with a light blanket and left the house shutting the front door quietly behind him. It was a relief to know that Ira was resting safely and that Sensi would arrive soon. Meanwhile he was anxious to get going. In a smart house on the south side of the city, the girl who had his heart was waiting for him.

"Hello." Palmer greeted Michelle with a warm kiss which sent an unexpected shiver down her back.

"Lost your tongue?" Palmer teased still holding her close.

Michelle knew that if she was ever going to speak again she'd have to extricate herself from his grip.

"Drink?" her voice came out in little more than a whisper. Palmer was looking straight into her eyes and the effect was intoxicating.

"Okay." Palmer reluctantly let her go. His eyes followed her as she walked across the open plan lounge into the kitchen. He admired the way her skirt hung on her slim hips and her kitten heels emphasized her tiny feet. She'd put her hair up and the elegant style suited her perfectly.

"Where shall I put my coat? It's a little bit wet."

"Here," Michelle responded wondering why she still couldn't speak in complete sentences. She frowned, feeling flustered and uncomfortable.

"How about I mix the drinks and you hang this up for me?" Palmer came to her rescue thinking how charming Michelle looked when she was vulnerable.

"Thanks." Michelle prayed silently for her ability to use the English language to reappear.

"So what would you like to do this afternoon?" Palmer called out as he poured a glass of dry white wine for Michelle and a rum and brandy for himself.

Standing in the hallway cloakroom Michelle took a deep breath before opening her mouth, "Whatever you like." Thank God I can speak again she thought to herself.

"Pick a hand." Palmer left the drinks on the table and walked over to her.

"Pardon?" Michelle knitted her brows in confusion. Palmer fought the urge to kiss her again.

"Pick a hand, it's okay," he encouraged. He held both arms out straight in front of him and gestured with his head, "left or right?" His broad smile finally put Michelle at ease. Tilting her head and smiling back at him she playfully tapped his right hand.

"Now how did I know you were going to pick that one?"

"You must be reading my mind."

"Would it make me happy if I did?"

"You'd have to read it and see!"

"The right hand says we stay in, talk, get to really know each other and later, when we're both hungry, I'll cook dinner for you. Something with a real Atlanta flavour."

"What would have happened if I'd picked the left one?" Michelle was curious.

"You'll have to choose that one next time to find out."

Palmer leaned forward and planted a light kiss on Michelle's nose. As she smiled up at him he pulled her into his arms. When he kissed her long and hard he took her breath away. Eventually their lips parted and Michelle said what was really on her mind.

"Palmer, is there anyone in Atlanta?" she laid her head against his chest in case his eyes revealed what she was dreading.

"Not any more."

Michelle felt the relief wash over her but there was more she had to know.

"Was there someone special?"

This time Palmer's silence lasted several moments. Michelle pulled away and sat on the sofa. She shivered as the warm feeling she'd felt in Palmer's arms dissipated.

"I see," she said.

The cold formal tone of her voice made Palmer's heart plummet. He moved over to her but held back from touching her.

"There was someone," he began.

"What's her name?"

"Liana."

"Pretty name," Michelle said without malice, "What's she like?"

"Not as beautiful as you," Palmer's voice came out in a whisper. His heart ached as he realised that he was losing the first and only woman he'd ever loved. "Darling…" he sat by Michelle and held her hand but she looked away.

"How'd you meet her?" she asked in a flat, resigned tone.

"She's my PA." Palmer hoped that being truthful would be the best and quickest way to get Michelle back in his arms.

"How convenient." Michelle avoided his eyes and left her hand limply in his.

"It's over," Palmer said, "…it was over from the day I met you."

"Does Liana know that?" Michelle spat out.

Palmer's silence was her answer.

"I didn't think so," she said bitterly.

"She doesn't know because I haven't spoken to her since I've been here."

"You haven't spoken to her?" Michelle's tone was full of disbelief.

"That's right. I haven't even thought about her, because every day and every night all I can think about is you."

"Oh really."

"Goddammit, look at me, woman!" Palmer pulled Michelle up from the sofa and held her tight forcing him to look into her eyes. "Can't you see that all I long for is you?"

Standing so close to him, Michelle felt the power of his muscles and the strength of his lean, toned body, She also felt his erection pushing against her.

"I'm not just an easy lay!" she shouted pushing him away. "I'm not going to be a souvenir of your trip so you can compare notes when you get back to your woman!"

"I would never, ever treat you so disrespectfully, I *care* about you."

The passion in Palmer's voice took Michelle by surprise. She moved away from him wishing she could believe what she heard. She began to cry because it was all too much. Palmer seemed like the man of her dreams, the one behind the door at the end of the long corridor who she never got to see because she never finished the dream. But now he openly admitted that until recently he'd been in love with another woman. Might still be for all she knew.

"I think you should leave," she said through her tears.

"You want me to go?" Palmer's voice was soft.

Michelle nodded.

"I'm not leaving." Palmer walked slowly towards her, "Who broke your heart, Michelle?"

At last he was holding her again and she offered no resistance. They stood together, bodies touching from shoulder to hip.

"What did he do to hurt you so badly?"

Michelle relaxed as she felt Palmer's warm breath on the back of her neck.

"I'm scared that it's all going to go wrong," she whispered as he gently stroked her hair and kissed her face.

"I won't hurt you Michelle, I could never hurt you." Palmer's tenderness was overwhelming. A sob caught in Michelle's throat.

"I'll be here for as long as you let me," he promised.

Sensi and Kai locked the back door behind them as they entered Ira's house.

"Grandad!" Kai called out as he ran from room to room.

"Kai, stop making so much noise," Sensi warned, "Go quietly and see if Granddad's in his room."

Kai sprinted up the stairs two at a time, ran in and out of the three small bedrooms and then bounded back to the kitchen where Sensi was putting on the kettle.

"Nope!" he said.

"No what? Can't you talk to me in a proper sentence?"

"That's what Dad says."

"Well?" Sensi spooned sugar and poured milk into two cups and prepared hot chocolate for Kai while she spoke.

"I didn't see him," Kai responded, "Can I watch TV?"

"What do you mean you didn't see him. Is he up there or not?"

"Don't know. Can I have a biscuit please?" Kai was still bounding around the small room.

"Biscuits and hot chocolate in a minute. Stay still before you knock something over!" Sensi was getting impatient. She made a mental note to mix some calming herbal oils for Kai's bedtime bath before he wore her out.

"Come." Taking Kai's hand she led him upstairs. They checked all of the rooms including the bathroom. Just as he'd said, Ira was nowhere to be seen.

"Has Granddad gone out?" Kai asked.

"I don't know. I'm sure he knew we were coming, I don't think we're late," Sensi mused aloud. "Let's see if granddad"s made any fruit cake to go with our tea. He's probably just gone to the shop."

Sensi tried to calm the disquiet that was growing inside her. If Ira didn't show up soon she'd have to call Shango, but no one ever seemed to know where he was these days and Celia was becoming impossible to deal with.

Thirty minutes later Sensi was worried. Kai was watching TV while she ran backwards and forwards out to the street to see if Ira was on his way home. When they'd arrived earlier the rain had eased off, but now it had started to fall hard and steady. Sensi noticed that Ira's coat, umbrella and hat were still hanging in the closet. She also noticed that his everyday shoes were with them but his house slippers were nowhere to be seen. She decided to wait another twenty minutes before ringing Shango.

"Why did you come to England?" asked Michelle.

Palmer was stretched along her huge couch and she lay contented in his arms. He stroked her skin and nuzzled her neck affectionately. Michelle felt as if she was in heaven.

"To be with you."

"Good answer," Michelle smiled, "but I want the truth."

"I had some issues with my dad; I wanted to see Shango again."

"And you needed some breathing space?"

"You're too clever for me," Palmer kissed Michelle.

"Tell me."

"What?"

"Everything. About you and Ira, about you and Shango, about why you live in Atlanta."

"Anything else?"

"Tell me about you and Liana, then give me her address so I can go and kick her butt!"

Palmer laughed, kissed Michelle again and then opened his heart for the first time in his life without reservations or restraint.

Another hour had passed. The rain pelted down and Sensi was seriously concerned about Ira. Normally he put Kai at the top of his list of priorities. Sensi flicked through Ira's phone book which lay on the old-fashioned phone stand, not knowing who she should call. She stopped at the name Adelphia because it was ringed in stars. On impulse she dialled the number.

"Hello," a woman answered.

"Hello, is that Miss Adelphia?" Sensi tried to use the professional voice Tony had taught her to use whenever she answered the phone at the club.

"Who's this?" Adelphia had no such pretensions.

"I'm Ira's daughter-in-law," Sensi flinched at the slight misrepresentation, "I just wandered if you'd seen him because he's late for our appointment."

"Are you the one with the footloose husband?" Once again Adelphia's mouth ran away with her.

"Excuse me?" Sensi was taken by surprise.

"Don't worry, it happens to us all. I know someone who can give you something to put in his food!"

"No thank you, sorry to bother you!" Sensi put the phone down in disbelief. Now she knew that she couldn't put off calling Shango any longer.

"They really made you tell them all the names of the royal family?" Michelle was shaking with laughter.

"All the ones I could remember, after a while I just made them up!"

"And that was the first time you met Liana's parents?"

"Yeah, they took my phone number, my cell number, my pager number, even my gym number."

"No!"

"Seriously! They showed me around their huge place and practically gave me my own room, with toothbrush and pyjamas!"

Michelle doubled up and Palmer chuckled glad to be free of Liana's overbearing parents.

"Why are you calling here Sensi?"

"Celia I don't want to argue with you, can you just tell me where Shango is?"

"Why do you want him?"

"It's important."

"Is it about Kai, the child you tricked him into having?"

"Look, bitch, I never tricked anyone, you tricked him into getting married with your fake pregnancy and that so-called miscarriage."

"I'm going to hang up on you now."

"Don't you....!" but Sensi's words were lost to the dial tone.

Sensi had called Shango's mobile several times but it was always on ansa-phone. They'd been in the house for two hours and there was still no sign of Ira. She exhaled loudly. Something was very wrong. She gathered her thoughts wondering what she should do.

"Where did you learn to cook so well?" Michelle sat opposite Palmer at the candle-lit dining table in her sparkling kitchen. She loved the granite surfaces of the worktops and the shiny black tiles on the floor, the candles and the flowers which enhanced the food, but most of all she loved having Palmer there with her. A variety of dishes lay between them with delicious smells coming from each.

"Single men in Atlanta learn to be self-sufficient."

"You mean you realised that you had the Pizza delivery on speed dial?"

"Your eyes twinkle when you laugh."

"No one's ever said that to me before."

"I could say it every day and never get tired."

"I'd never get tired of hearing it."

"More wine?" Palmer offered. In the candle's ivory flame she looked stunning and he couldn't take his eyes off her.

With tears in her eyes Sensi dialled yet another number in her desperate quest to find Ira. The phone was picked up on the forth ring.

"Andrea?"

"Sensi, how are you?"

"I'm sorry to bother you, but I need your help."

"What's the matter? Sensi, don't cry, it's all right."

"He's out in his slippers, he's left his coat and it's raining so hard."

"Who? Kai?"

"No, Ira. I'm really worried, he's out in the rain."

"Who with?"

"I don't know, no one, I think he's lost."

Andrea was silent while she absorbed Sensi's words. She remembered Tony mentioning that Shango was concerned about Ira's increasing confusion.

"Where's Shango?"

"I can't find him, and Celia won't tell me."

"Where's Palmer?"

"I don't know, there was nobody here when we came."

Andrea swiftly assessed the situation. "I'm coming over," she said.

"No, you don't have to do that."

"Get a pen, Sensi, take my mobile number, stay by the phone. Where's Kai?"

Sensi looked up to see Kai standing right in front of her. "He's with me. What if something's happened to Ira?"

"Don't cry, Sensi, I'm on my way, we'll sort it out, it'll be okay." Andrea hung up. "Natalie!" she called to her daughter, "Mind the boys till your dad gets back. I won't be long."

Meanwhile Kai wiped the tears from his mom's face with the sleeve of his shirt.

"Is Granddad dead, Mom?"

"Granddad's not dead, but he's missing and Aunty Andrea's going to help us find him." Sensi held her son tightly, "Can you be brave and help me and Aunty Andrea think about what to do?"

Kai nodded.

"Good boy," Sensi said holding him close.

Beres Hammond sang a love song and time finally stood still as Michelle and Palmer danced, entwined in each other"s arms.

"I don't think I'll ever forget this evening," Michelle murmured.

"It doesn't have to end."

"It doesn't?"

"Have you ever seen Atlanta in the fall?"

"Is that an invitation?"

"It could be. You could come over, we could have some down time."

"Don't tempt me."

"Why not?"

"Because I might say yes."

"I wish you would."

"Persuade me with a kiss," Michelle's tone was soft and endearing.

Palmer was happy to oblige.

CHAPTER EIGHTEEN

HI KAI, HOW'RE you doing?" Andrea breezed into the house bringing an air of calm confidence.

"I'm hungry and I'm worried about Granddad," Kai replied honestly.

"Don't worry, we"ll find your granddad. Where's your mom?"

"She's in the kitchen."

"Sensi how are you holding up?" Andrea greeted her with a hug.

"I feel as though as I'm going out of my mind," Sensi responded, anguish written all over her face. Aware that Kai was right behind her, Andrea flashed a warning look at Sensi before turning to him.

"What would you like to eat?"

"Sausages and chips, please."

"Why don't you watch some TV while your mom and I sort that out for you?"

"Okay," said Kai skipping back to the lounge.

"He's such a lovely child, you're very blessed," Andrea commented as Sensi started to cry again. "Tell me what happened." Andrea passed her the box of tissues and made herself a cup of tea.

"What about Kai's dinner? Sensi sniffed.

"Cook and talk, it'll be therapeutic," Andrea advised.

An hour later Kai had eaten and there was still no sign of Ira.

"I think we'd better call the police," Andrea suggested.

"I don't know what to say to them," Sensi admitted.

"It's okay," Andrea reassured her as she dialled the number. "We don't know what he was wearing, we weren't here when he left.......yes, he's been a bit confused at times, but not every day.....no he doesn't have dementia, yes he's just turned seventy.....no, we can't think of anywhere he might have gone.....but we're sure he's only in his slippers because his shoes and his coat, hat and umbrella are still here......send somebody round......half an hour....okay....... pardon?.......No, I hadn't thought of that.....thank you, Officer."

Sensi and Kai looked at Andrea expectantly as she hung up.

"They're sending somebody round but they suggested we call the hospitals in the meantime," Andrea explained.

"Why?" Sensi queried.

"In case..." Andrea looked at Kai, "...someone might have brought him in," she finished.

"We've got to get in touch with Shango," Sensi said. "Call Celia, she'll talk to you."

Celia picked up the phone on the first ring. She'd been watching television while listening to the radio and reading a magazine. None of it was helping to keep her mind off her absent husband.

"Celia, it's Andrea, you okay?"

"I've been better, what's up?"

"I'm at Ira's with Sensi and Kai."

"What are you doing there with her?"

"We've got a problem, Celia, Ira's been missing all evening and we can't find Shango or Palmer."

"What do you mean missing?"

"Sensi arranged to bring Kai over to spend time with Ira but he was already out when she got here."

"Did he leave a note?"

"Good question, hold on." Andrea turned to Sensi, "Did you look for a note?"

"Yes," Sensi mouthed, "...but I didn't see one."

"No."

"He might have just forgot and gone to Preston's or something."

"That's the worrying bit. Ira's outdoor stuff is all here, but his slippers aren't.

Celia glanced outside as the rain lashed against the windows, her heart sinking at the thought of Ira wandering around unprotected against the elements.

"Poor Ira," she said, "I didn't want to tell Sensi, but me and Shango have been having so many problems lately, I've no idea where he is. What about Palmer?"

"We think he might be with Michelle."

"I'll call him and tell him what's going on. Call me if you hear anything."

"I will."

"Andrea?"

"Yeah."

"Tell Sensi I'm sorry, I didn't realise."

"Okay."

Ten minutes later Celia's phone rang again.

"Hello?"

"Celia, it's Andrea."

"I couldn't reach Palmer, I think he's out with Michelle. I left messages on his mobile and her answering machine."

"That's why I'm calling you, we've found him."

"Shango?"

"No, Ira."

"He's come back?"

"He's in hospital."

"Oh my God, which one?"

"City, we're going over there now."

"I'll leave another message for Palmer and Michelle, then I'll meet you there."

"Phone's ringing," Michelle said dreamily as she rested her head against Palmer's chest. They had been slow dancing for more than twenty minutes.

"Let it ring," Palmer replied lazily.

"It could be my other lover," Michelle teased.

"Tell him I got here first and I'm not going anywhere."

"Music to my ears," said Michelle smiling.

• • • • • •

There were at least fifteen people already queuing at the desk of the Accident and Emergency Department.

"Go in and wait while I find somewhere to park," Andrea directed, but once inside Kai spoke to the first nurse he saw.

"Have you seen my granddad?"

"What's his name?" the nurse asked smiling down at Kai.

"Granddad Ira Shango," Kai replied looking hopefully at the nurse.

"Why don't you wait here and I'll just go and look in our special book."

Sensi smiled her thanks and led Kai over to the waiting area.

"Sensi!" Celia came rushing through the doors towards them, "Have you seen him yet?"

"No." Sensi felt uncomfortable at being face to face with Celia, it was rare for them to be in such close proximity.

"Hello Kai," Celia greeted him. "Don't cry, they'll take good care of your granddad in here. Where's Andrea?" she asked Sensi trying to avoid the awkward silence that was building between them.

"Parking the jeep." Sensi refused to look Celia in the eye.

"Sensi, I'm sorry about earlier, I should have been more helpful."

"Yes, you should have; I'm not your enemy Celia, don't take out your problems on me."

"Celia! You made it, thanks for coming." Andrea embraced her. "Parking was murder but I got a space in the end. Have they told us anything?"

Watching them made Sensi feel shabby and inferior. Although she was only a size ten and Celia was a size sixteen, she noticed how at ease Celia was in a light summer dress and shawl and she wished that she was wearing more than faded jeans with an old denim jacket. Self consciously she touched her extra large, bright, dangly earrings as she eyed Celia's discreet gold ones. Her hand moved automatically to her hair, as she noticed Andrea's neat and sophisticated slicked back style. She regretted choosing a synthetic wig with gold and yellow highlights because she couldn't be bothered to style her hair.

As she watched the light reflecting off Andrea and Celia's lightly painted manicures, she curled her fingers and stuck them in her pockets to hide her bitten off fingernails. Andrea had been right, she could do so much better.

"Your grandfather is on ward D42, third floor," the nurse informed the group.

"Thank you," Andrea said as they all made their way along the corridor to the lifts.

"Mr Shango is resting now. He was brought in about an hour and a half ago by a couple who said they'd seen him wandering through Winson Green. They were a bit worried because he was wearing his slippers and his apron."

"This is his grandson, how is he?" Sensi asked the ward sister.

"We'd like to keep him in overnight, just for observation. Is his wife at home?"

"Ruby Katherine? She passed away," Celia informed her.

"Apparently that's who he was looking for. Does he have any other close relatives?" The sister looked at the three women.

"I'm, we're his daughters-in-law," Celia gestured at herself and Sensi, "this is a family friend," she added looking toward Andrea. "He does have two sons who we're still trying to reach, can we see him?"

"Of course, but bear in mind he's a little drowsy and he'll need his rest."

"Hey!" Palmer's voice attracted their attention. He strode through the ward to where they stood, Michelle close behind him.

"I just got your message. I can't believe it, is he okay?" Palmer hugged all the women and Kai. Michelle did the same but just nodded politely at Sensi.

"We're going to see him now," Celia said.

"Is Shango…?" Palmer began.

"–No one can find him," Celia cut him off before he could finish his query. She didn't want to think about what Shango might be doing or who he might have been doing it with.

In the taxi on the way to the hospital she'd rung his mobile repeatedly, finally giving up when she'd realised that she was torturing herself with images of him and Sandra together. She couldn't decide whether the fact that she'd never seen the other woman's face was a curse or a blessing. Either way, she was in their lives and Celia was about to reach the end of her rope.

Andrea, Celia, Sensi, Kai, Michelle and Palmer stood around Ira's bed as he slept, a serene expression on his face. They'd pulled the curtains closed for extra privacy and in the dim light Ira looked small and childlike.

"How was he when he came in?" Palmer spoke in a whisper.

"The sister said he was asking for Ruby Katherine, they think that's why he went missing," Celia replied in a soft voice.

"He was out looking for Mom, oh no!" Palmer said, obviously distressed as Michelle squeezed his hand comfortingly. "Where the hell is Shango?" Despite his anger Palmer's voice rose only a little.

"There's no point in worrying about that now," Andrea soothed. "The main thing is that we've found him and he's all right. Listen, I have to get back to Tony and the kids."

"Thanks for everything." Palmer kissed Andrea on the cheek and hugged her briefly.

"It's no problem. I'll call you tomorrow, see how he's doing.

Tell him I expect to be sharing a glass of whisky with him by the end of the week. Sensi would you like a lift?"

"I'm a bit out of your way."

"Don't be silly."

"Thanks, say goodbye, Kai."

Celia sat down next to Ira and held his hand. Palmer sat in the other chair across the bed watching while Ira slept on.

"I'm going to get some coffee, I won't be long," Michelle said.

Thanks babe," Palmer kissed her hand before she walked away then he turned to his sister-in law. "Celia I'm sorry I didn't get your messages earlier, I should have left the damn phone on."

"It doesn't matter, at least you're here."

Palmer understood that Celia was referring to Shango's absence. For once he was unable to defend his brother knowing that there was nothing more important than this right now.

"He'll turn up," he muttered, but he knew that he was convincing no one.

• • • • • •

"Ira Shango?" Shango asked quietly.

"And you are?" the nurse enquired.

"His son," Shango replied before following the direction the nurse pointed him in.

Shango paused a few feet from the bed and took in the tableau of sleeping bodies belonging to his wife, his brother and apparently his brother's new woman, Michelle. Then he saw Ira in the middle of the bed looking small and helpless. He felt a stabbing pain in his heart at the thought of his beloved father wandering the streets, alone and confused, looking for a dead wife. He moved a step closer and that's when Celia opened her eyes.

"I–" he began but stopped, totally shocked when Celia rose and spat in his face.

"Palmer," she hissed giving Shango a vicious look, "Palmer, I'm ready to go home now."

"What!" Palmer jerked awake, momentarily forgetting where he was. The weight of Michelle curled up in the chair with him made him smile. As he glanced at his watch he noticed Shango on the opposite side of the bed.

"Palmer would you take me home please?" Urgency edged Celia's voice. Michelle opened her eyes and stretched cat-like, watching the interaction between Celia and the two men. She was too tired to speak.

"Palmer I–" Shango tried again, this time looking directly at his brother.

"Save it!" Palmer snapped, "I'm too weary." With a last glance at Ira he took Michelle's hand and walked away.

"Celia, please…" Shango began again.

"Go to hell and take your bitch with you!" Celia pushed past him and rushed to catch up with Michelle and Palmer.

Shango sank wearily into the chair where Celia had been sitting, ran his hand across his hair and then rubbed his forehead. He was exhausted. He waited for a while and then, noting that Ira was sleeping peacefully, he decided to go home, snatch a few hours sleep and return in the morning.

Celia stared at the pile she'd made that filled up most of the hallway. She'd packed three suitcases, seven bin liners and four cardboard boxes with Shango's clothes, books and personal effects. Satisfied that there was nothing left, she then carried, pushed and pulled them all out onto the wet driveway. She didn't stop until the hallway was clear and all traces of her cheating husband were out on the driveway where she felt they belonged.

An hour later Shango pulled up onto the drive and stopped abruptly when his wheels hit one of the suitcases. With slow, weary movements he got out of the car, stood in the pouring rain and viewed all that Celia had done with an expression of disbelief. He moved all of the bags, suitcases and boxes into the garage. Then he reversed and drove off. From a darkened upstairs room of the house Celia watched him clear the baggage and felt her heart crumble as he drove away.

Shango let himself into Ira's cold and empty house. It was almost three am. He stumbled into the kitchen, picked up an almost empty bottle of scotch and tipped the remains into a glass. Then he swallowed it neat in one gulp hoping to numb his senses. Eyes half closed he crawled upstairs and staggered into Ira's room. The scotch warmed his chest and clouded his thoughts, a sign that blessed sleep was finally on it's way.

In Ira's bedroom Shango stripped down to his boxer shorts. Then he opened the wardrobe and looked, bleary eyed, at Ruby Katherine's dresses which Ira still hadn't thrown away. He pulled a red one from its hanger and breathed in its scent pretending he could still smell his mom's perfume. He imagined that she was holding him in an embrace, just like when he was little. He heard her soothing voice, telling him everything would be okay, then he felt her soft hands stroking his face lovingly and gently.

Eventually Shango lay down on the bed and fell fast asleep clutching Ruby Katherine's favourite red dress.

CHAPTER NINETEEN

SHANGO'S SLEEP WAS filled with dreams of the day before. The day he'd stopped his best friend from committing murder.

Rafi had called him early in the afternoon. Shango had been working at the University but he'd left his papers and gone around straight away. The letter that Rafi had been waiting for from Melody's care home had finally come. After almost two years of assessments, visits and reports, the Social Services Department had finally made a decision about Melody's permanent place of residence. Rafi wanted Shango to be there to share the good news when he opened the letter.

"Remember," Shango had kept a smile on his face while he'd cautioned his friend, "it might not say exactly what you want to hear."

"It'll be safe, I can feel it." Rafi had beamed while waving the white envelope.

"But just in case," Shango couldn't bear the thought of seeing Rafi's hopes dashed, "just in case, why don't you expect the worse and then that way you might get a nice surprise," he'd cautioned.

"I'm ready for this," Rafi insisted, "and I know what's in this envelope." His hands shook, "You open it." Nervously he'd handed it to Shango.

"Okay," Shango had said, "here we go."

"No, I'll do it!" Rafi's exuberance had been infectious.

"Sit," Shango had ordered laughing, "now take a deep breath."

Rafi had inhaled, the bright smile still on his face.

"When you're ready."

On Shango's command, Rafi had ripped open the letter. Shango had watched as Rafi's face turned ashen and his expression changed from joy to horror. "Oh no," he'd whispered as Rafi had screwed up the letter and hurled it across the room.

"The bastards!" Rafi had shouted as his body trembled with rage and disappointment. "They're taking her away from me!

They can't do this!"

Shango had retrieved the letter from where it fell. Dear Mr Burton, he'd read:

> *Thank you for your constant and valued input regarding the care and well being of your sister Melody Burton. We are certain that your efforts have been a significant factor in your sister"s continuous improvement.*
>
> *However, after careful consideration I must regretfully decline your request for Melody to live with you in your family home.*
>
> *Due to factors which cannot be revealed at present we feel that Melody"s interests would be best served if she were to remain living where she is for the foreseeable future.*
>
> *Please be assured that the care team will continue to liaise with you on a regular basis to ensure Melody continues to receive the best possible package of care.*
>
> *Thank you for your application.,*
> *Yours sincerely,*
> *Laura Hurst.*
> *Chair,*
> *Birmingham Social Services.*

"I'm sorry, man." Shango had sat on the sofa next to Rafi, "We knew this was a possibility." He'd spoken softly, his eyes filled with concern.

"Who knew?" Rafi had shouted, "Who's *we*? That bitch Laura Hurst? The staff at the home? Were you in on it too? Did everybody already know except me?"

"Calm down, man, this won't help." Shango had looked up at Rafi who was pacing the floor.

"This is my life, this is my sister, she's all I have left. How can they keep us apart?" Rafi was still shouting. When he'd walked as far as he could go he'd balled his hand into a fist and punched the wall continuously until Shango had pulled him away.

"We can appeal," he'd suggested as Rafi'd shrugged him off and sucked the blood that was dripping from his knuckle.

"Appeal to who? She's the top lady!" Rafi was pacing again and his relentless shouting had given Shango a headache.

"We can take them to court." Shango had tried to get his friend to see reason.

At these words Rafi had stopped and turned giving Shango his full attention.

"What did you say? he'd asked, frowning.

"We can take them to court," Shango had repeated sitting down, hoping that Rafi would do the same.

● ● ● ● ● ●

"Are you okay man?" Twenty minutes had passed since Shango had mentioned the possibility of suing Social Services. Since Rafi had sat down he hadn't said a word. "You want a drink?" Shango tried again to elicit a response but Rafi had just stared sullenly at the floor. His black mood had filled the small room with a heavy atmosphere.

"Cigarette," he'd finally muttered.

"Where are they?"

"I'm going to get some." Rafi had stood and walked towards the door but something in his tone had alerted Shango.

"I'll go," he'd said quickly. "Rothmans blue, right?"

"I'll sort it, I'm not coming straight back, you might as well go back to work."

Rafi had spoken with a steely edge and a hard look in his eyes that had sent a chill through Shango. "I might pass by Brick's," he'd said confirming Shango's fears.

"No man," Shango had tried to reason with him, "Brick's the last person you need right now." Shango had grabbed Rafi's arm and locked eyes with him. He'd been prepared to hit him again if that's what it took to stop Rafi from going to Brick's place to see about an illegal gun.

"That Laura Hurst, I'm not going to hurt her, I just want to make her change her mind. Maybe she doesn't realise Melody's all I've got."

Rafi's words had been tender but his voice was still hard and unfeeling. Shango knew then that he'd stay with him as long as necessary to make sure that Rafi stayed away from Brick and guns and Laura Hurst.

By night time Rafi had sunk into a deep depression. Shango had found a full pack of cigarettes in the kitchen and had opened all the windows so he could breath more easily while Rafi chain smoked. Leaving Rafi alone, even for a few minutes, had been too great a risk so he'd simply inhaled air at the window through the pouring rain and prayed for the constriction in his chest to ease.

As the hours had passed Rafi had raged, sworn, shouted and then quietly reminisced about the happy times with Melody and his mom before she'd died. He'd vowed to hunt down his father and aim a single shot at his head before going on to do the same with Laura Hurst. At one point he'd pushed Shango to the ground in an effort to leave the house to find Brick. Shango had struggled to his feet and blocked the door. He would've taken a beating from his friend if he'd had to. As long as Rafi was kept in the house, he wouldn't be able to do anything stupid.

At eleven o'clock Shango had checked his mobile phone. There were thirteen missed calls and his message box was full. Shango had guessed that most of them were from Celia but he'd put her on the back burner. At that moment Rafi had been his main priority.

"Hungry?" Rafi had asked at eleven thirty. He'd been staring at the television for hours without really watching it.

"I'll cook." Shango had been glad for something concrete to do. He'd felt that there were no more words of comfort to offer his friend.

"I'll help."

Shango had smiled at the thought of Rafi helping him to cook. They were usually a disaster together in the kitchen, but the desolate tone in his friend's voice had torn him apart.

After they'd eaten a simple meal of fried dumplings, baked beans and egg, Rafi had gone to bed. Shango had waited to make sure that he was really asleep. When he'd left at half past midnight he'd taken Rafi's car keys just in case Rafi had later decided to pay Brick a visit after all.

The first thing Shango did before he'd driven away from Rafi's house was to listen to his messages. The knife that twisted in his heart when he'd heard that Ira was missing had twisted even deeper when the following messages said that Ira had been taken to hospital. Exhausted and afraid of what he might find he'd driven through every red light to get to his dad.

Now Shango jumped and murmured in his sleep as he re-lived being frozen out by his wife and his brother at his father's bedside. He opened his eyes and looked at the clock. He'd slept for four hours. As he rubbed the sleep out of his eyes he felt the soft, silky material of Ruby Katherine's dress that he still clutched in his hand.

After yesterday's storms the sun was finally breaking through the clouds. Shango forced himself to get up. The last few days had seen events slipping out of his control. Now he resolved it was time to turn things around.

CHAPTER TWENTY

SHANGO WAS BACK at City Hospital at nine thirty am. The nurse appraised him briefly noticing his firm muscles, long legs and broad chest, before recognizing him from the night before.

"I was just finishing my shift," she said as she buzzed him in, "and now I've got a gorgeous man to see me home!"

Shango laughed along with the nurse and her colleagues. He acted as if he hadn't noticed that she was twice as old as him with a face that was as plump and round as her figure and dull black hair that had the texture of straw.

"How's my dad today, has he been behaving himself?" Shango asked with a smile still on his face. He was hoping that his joviality might distract from the fact that it wasn't even ten o'clock yet and visiting time didn't start until two pm.

"I can see that flirting runs in the family," the straw haired nurse continued, "...you're a little early for visiting," she added taking Shango by surprise.

"Nurse Connor," he cajoled, quickly glancing at her name badge that rested on her large protruding breast, "...the early bird catches the worm!" Inwardly Shango cringed at the awful cliche but it was all he could think of at short notice and with only a few hours sleep.

"Handsome *and* witty." Nurse Connor laughed. "Just what I need at this time of the morning!" She waved him along.

Shango felt as if he was being watched as he walked to the opposite end of the ward. He turned around and found Nurse Connor studying his hips and bottom. When he caught her eye she winked suggestively at him and blew a kiss.

"Morning Pops." Shango kissed the old man on the cheek and sat down on the bed. Ira was propped up against the his pillows listening to hospital radio through plastic headphones. He opened his eyes and smiled at Shango.

"You listening to Jim Reeves again?" Shango teased, happy to see his dad refreshed again.

"What do you know about Jim Reeves?" Ira answered. Although his eyes were bright his voice sounded thin and weak.

"I know that he's not as good as Desmond Decker," Shango teased while gently bouncing Ira's hand between his own.

"Desmond Decker can't touch this!" Ira responded with another smile.

"You gave us all a fright last night, Dad," Shango continued.

"I frightened myself."

"They said you got really wet. How're you feeling?"

"Fine man, don't fuss," was all Ira managed before he was overcome by a lengthy bout of wheezy coughing.

"I'll call the nurse." Shango was alarmed as the coughing fit went on.

"No," Ira gasped, "when Ruby Katherine gets here she can look after me, it won't be long."

Dismayed Shango stood back as the nurses swiftly moved in. They placed an oxygen mask over Ira's nose and mouth to help him breath and laid him in a prone position. Shango stayed silent while Ira closed his eyes and the nurses attached a drip to his arm.

"He still needs a lot of fluids," one of them explained kindly.

When the nurses withdrew Shango sat by the bed watching Ira sleep peacefully; a myriad of questions ran through his mind. At eleven thirty the doctors came on their rounds. Shango stood as they approached Ira's bed. He tried to work out which one was the senior consultant. The two doctors nodded a good afternoon to him before addressing Ira who was just waking up again.

"How are you feeling today Mr Shango?" the younger doctor asked leaning over him. The older doctor checked Ira's charts at the foot of the bed as Shango looked from one to the other.

"Is my wife here yet?" Ira asked, his voice a little hoarse. Shango felt his heart plummet as the doctors looked from Ira to him.

"Mom's not coming Dad." Shango kept his voice light.

"What do you mean? Of course she's coming!" Ira was distressed.

"No Dad, Mom's...." Shango began but stopped when the older doctor cleared his throat.

"You're Ira's son?" he asked, his eyes warning Shango not to say anything else about Ruby Katherine.

"Yes, I'm his youngest son," Shango replied.

"Perhaps we can have a word?" The older doctor led Shango

away from Ira's bed.

"Do I take it that there is no Ruby Katherine?" the doctor spoke quietly.

"There was," Shango replied with a sigh, "but she died, almost two years ago. Lately Dad seems to keep forgetting, I don't understand why."

"I see." The medic was thoughtful, "your father recently turned seventy, is that right?"

Shango glanced at Ira before nodding.

"He was found wandering in heavy rain wearing his slippers and no overcoat?" the doctor continued.

"Yes, the family couldn't reach me, I was dealing with a crisis and I had to turn my phone off you see." Guilt overwhelmed Shango as he fumbled for an explanation.

"None of this is your fault." The doctor touched Shango's arm in a gesture of reassurance.

"I should have been around but I didn't know," Shango continued.

"It's a bit early to make a full and proper diagnosis but I think that your father may be suffering from the onset of Alzheimer's disease." The doctor delivered the devastating news in a calm, soothing tone.

"What!" Shango was speechless.

"As I said, I'd like to carry out further tests before I make an official diagnosis, but I think that's what we might find out."

"How?" Shango blurted out.

"We can't be sure, sometimes it's genetic, sometimes not."

"I don't think there's anyone else in the family who's had it. But Dad is so fit, surely…"

"–Studies have shown that many Alzheimer's sufferers remain physically fit and healthy until the end of their lives."

"What happens now?"

"He can go home later today and we'll make an appointment for him to see a specialist."

"Will he be all right?"

"It's early days yet, but we'll do everything we can."

After discussing medication with Shango and the nurses, the two doctors left him alone with his father. Ira was now more lucid than before.

"Am I going mad son?" he asked with a note of vulnerability.

"No madder than usual Dad." Shango forced himself to smile.

"That's all right then," Ira responded before going back to

sleep.

• • • • • •

Shango jingled the bundle of twenty pence pieces in his hand as he stood in front of the public phone in the foyer of City Hospital. A second later he listened to the phone in his house ringing. Celia picked it up.

"Hello."

Shango smiled, he'd forgotten how alluring Celia's voice sounded on the phone.

"Don't hang up," he said gently.

"Why shouldn't I?" Celia's tone instantly became harsh and unfeeling, "Your dad could have died yesterday while you were in another woman's bed!"

"Celia please."

"You disgust me and you ought to be ashamed of yourself!"

"Celia!" Shango tried again but his words were cut short by the dialling tone ringing in his ear. Celia had hung up on him.

He counted to three and glanced at the piece of paper in his hand. Mentally he ticked off numbers one and two which read:

1) Spend some time with Dad
2) Call your wife

He breathed deeply and pressed redial.

"I don't want to talk you Shango," Celia answered on the first ring. She was calm, but still angry.

"Celia we have to talk, we have to sort this whole mess out."

"You made the mess you sort it out!" Celia shouted, annoyed with herself for losing control.

"You're right and I take full responsibility." Shango deliberately kept his voice calm and loving and Celia hated the effect it had on her.

"You're making me cry," she reached for the tissues on the top of the television.

Shango ran his hand over his locks which were as immaculate as always. "I only ever wanted to make you smile. You have the world's most beautiful smile," he whispered with his eyes closed, picturing her face and speaking from his heart.

"How can I believe a word you say?"

"I still love you," Shango promised.

"But you're in *love* with her aren't you?" the sound of Celia's sobs tore into Shango.

"Not on the phone, Celia, we have to talk, but not like this."

Shango tried to soothe her.

"You can't even call me 'darling' anymore can you?" Celia was still sobbing.

"I'll be over later, will you let me in?"

"Just give me a little time to get myself together."

"I'll be there in two hours."

"Make it three," Celia said before she murmured a soft goodbye.

Shango turned away from the phone. His feelings were indescribable. His love for Sandra, the best thing in his life, was killing the woman to whom he'd made the most solemn vow.

At their home Celia dried her tears. Her face grew hard and expressionless as she went upstairs into the bedroom. She flicked open his briefcase, glad that he'd never bothered with the combination lock, and threw his files and papers on the floor until she found what she was looking for.

With a small black notebook, marked PERSONAL in her hand, Celia went downstairs into the kitchen. She made a cup of tea with three sugars and no milk which she carried into the sitting room and rested on the coffee table near the window.

Whilst waiting for the tea to cool Celia carefully turned the pages of Shango's diary. Eventually she found a number with no name but she recognized the code. It began with 0121 449... the area code was Moseley in Birmingham. She dialled the full number three times, listening carefully to the voice of the woman who answered. Celia hung up each time without speaking, her silences getting longer with each call.

Slowly sipping her tea and folding her legs beneath her, she continued her search through the journal. Within a few minutes she'd found what she was looking for. Celia's lips moved silently as she mouthed the numbers she was dialling. Unwittingly she held her breath as the phone rang four times before it was answered by a young woman with a strong Birmingham accent.

"Yes?" the girl questioned.

"I'd like to speak to Brick please," Celia replied, her voice steady.

"What's it in connection with?"

Celia was impressed, the young woman had obviously been well trained.

"Tell him it's in connection with..."Celia paused wanting to make sure she said exactly the right thing, "the usual business."

"He'll call you back in a bit, has he got your number?" The girl didn't miss a beat.

"Ask him to call me immediately on this number." Celia repeated her mobile phone number before hanging up.

Brilliant sunshine lit up the whole street as Celia sat and waited patiently for Brick's call. She stared out of the window as her neighbours went about their daily routine, seeing and feeling nothing but her own pain.

● ● ● ● ● ●

Shango held the money in one hand as he turned over his page of lists and dialled the second number. The phone rang several times before Sensi picked up the receiver. Panting slightly she breathed a short hello while wiping her hands on a tea towel.

"Is this a bad time?"

"Shango?" Sensi automatically sat down on the nearest chair, shocked at hearing Shango's voice.

"Were you busy?" Shango asked anxiously,

"Kai's out playing," Sensi rushed to explain.

"So he should be on a day like this. I'm at the hospital with my dad."

"I wanted to call but I got busy."

"He's not great."

"Oh no."

"But he's much better than last night."

"Good."

"Sensi?"

Sensi held her breath during the pause that followed.

"Can I come over?" Shango blurted out hoping he sounded more confident than he felt. He glanced at the piece of paper in his hand while waiting for Sensi's reply and licked away the beads of sweat from the top of his lip.

3) Go to see Sensi
4) Call Rafi

He superstitiously avoided looking at the rest of his list.

"Yeah!" Sensi got her voice back, "Kai will be happy anyway."

"I need to spend some time alone with you."

"Why?" Sensi was baffled by Shango's friendly but strange behaviour.

"I want to say thanks for last night, that's all. I'll see you soon."

Shango hung up quickly wanting to hold onto the advantage he'd gained in taking Sensi by surprise.

Meanwhile Sensi stared at the receiver in her hand as if it could provide the answers to all of the questions that now ran through her mind. Shango wanted to see her? To say thanks? What was going on she wondered.

Smiling, Shango dropped another twenty pence into the slot and dialled again. This time the phone rang only twice.

"Hello."

"Rafi! what's up?"

"Yo!" Rafi tried to match the bright cheeriness of Shango's tone but his head felt foggy and his limbs were heavy, a combination of a late night and too many cigarettes and beers.

"Have you seen my car keys, man?" he remembered to ask.

"Right here," Shango shook them while mentally ticking off numbers three and four on his list before checking numbers five and six.

5) Call Palmer

6) Kiss and hug and hold her tight, all night, tonight, my darling Sandra

"You dropping them off then or what?" Rafi had slept deeply through the night and for most of the day so far. His body felt sluggish and unwilling to cooperate.

"Later, how're you feeling man?" the concern in Shango's voice brought back harsh memories of the day before when Rafi had had his hopes of living with Melody destroyed by uncaring bureaucrats. As he relived the vicious pangs of disappointment, the fog in his mind lifted. Meanwhile Shango pushed two more twenty pence pieces into the slot as the pips signalled that his money was about to run out.

"Hello?" Shango checked to make sure that Rafi was still there.

"I'm going to appeal," Rafi spoke with certainty.

"Good for you."

"We need each other, she's the only family I've got left. We have to be together they've kept us apart for too long."

"I know a good Solicitor, we'll get you sorted."

"Thanks man."

"In the meantime," Shango continued, "there's something I need you to do for me."

"Anything, as long as I don't have to drive."

Shango chuckled. "Have you still got the list of phone

numbers for all the EBYN members?"

"It's here somewhere." Rafi looked around at the cluttered and messy room.

"Set up a meeting for me."

"When and where?"

"My dad's tonight at six. No excuses from anyone."

"It's done."

"Aren't you going to ask me what it's about?"

"No need, man. Whatever's going on I've got your back."

"Thanks man."

"*Now* can I have my car keys please?"

"I told you, later!" Shango chuckled as he hung up the phone. He opened his hand and was pleased to see that he still had lots of change left. Once again he put two more coins in the slot and waited patiently until the phone was answered on the other end.

"Yeah?" Palmer's voice gave the impression that whoever he was with had made him extremely comfortable.

"Boy she's got you tightly wrapped up," Shango laughed into the phone.

"And very wonderful it is too," Palmer laughed back. "Hey, are we okay now?" he asked in the silence that followed.

"I hope so, man. I'm sorry I couldn't be there for Dad last night, I'm just glad you guys were."

"We'll talk about it." Palmer was no longer angry but he didn't intend to let Shango completely off the hook, "Have you been up to the hospital yet?" he asked.

"I'm at the hospital now," Shango explained; he hated Palmer to think badly of him.

"Oh!" Palmer was surprised. "Did you speak to the medics yet?"

"Briefly."

"What did they say?"

"It could be Alzheimer's."

"What!" Palmer was stunned.

"They're not totally sure, it's an unconfirmed diagnosis."

"They gotta do some tests, right?"

"That's it."

"Oh my God, poor Dad. Did you talk to him?"

"I spent some time with him, made him laugh, held his hand."

"You're always there for him."

"Just like you were last night."

"Just like you've been for the last twenty years."

"Is Michelle going to let you go anytime soon?"

"I hope not. I've already persuaded her to call in sick today."

"Michelle call in sick! That's a first!"

"That's the effect I have on her, what can I say?" Palmer was laughing again.

"Listen.....thanks for dropping Celia home last night."

"That's no problem but you two should talk."

"I went back to the house and she'd piled all my things up on the drive."

"In the rain?"

"I didn't think she'd let me in so I stayed at Dad's."

"How did you sleep?"

"Badly."

"Look, I'll be up there soon."

"That's good because I have to go but I didn't want to leave Dad alone, they'll probably discharge him later."

"I'm on my way."

"Thanks bro'. I'll see you at Dad's later tonight, I'm holding an EBYN meeting."

"For real? Why?"

"Palmer, once you've worked hard to realise your dreams you shouldn't let any man take them away from you."

"I hear you, bro', I hear you."

"I lost control and let my heart rule my head. Now I have to remain strong and analytical."

"You don't seem like the kind of man who gets blown about by the breeze."

"Exactly."

"So you're taking back your name?"

"I'm definitely taking back my name."

"What about your love life, man?"

"What about yours?" Shango laughed.

"I've finally found the missing piece."

"Really, you feel that strongly about Michelle."

"Yep. I'm just not sure if I should stay here or ask her to come back to Atlanta with me."

"What does your heart tell you?"

"I want to take her home to the States."

"Go ahead then."

"Hold on Shango, it's not so easy, how can I ask her to leave behind everything she has here?"

"Like what?"

"Family, a beautiful home, you guys, her work."

"You mean sisters and a mother who're so jealous they can't

be around her for longer than five minutes, an immaculate house that's cold and lonely, a career that's full of petty back stabbing? A country that struggles to recognise her brilliance and achievements because she's not a white male? I guess you're right, you can't possibly ask her to leave all that behind."

"When you put it like that."

"Talk to her, find out what she wants and then you'd better to be ready to take that long walk."

"Long walk?"

"Down the aisle!"

"I'm ready."

"Boy you've got it bad!" Shango laughed and Palmer joined in.

"Listen, we're going to have make some arrangements about Dad, you know...if it *is* Alzheimer's...." Palmer was serious again.

"Let's cross that bridge when we come to it. See you later."

"Later."

Shango hung up and put the rest of the coins back in his pocket. As he walked briskly across the car park he glanced up at the sky. It was turning out to be a bright and sunny day. Just the day for a man like him to once again put the world to rights.

CHAPTER TWENTY ONE

STOP FUSSING, IT'S only Shango," Sensi told herself. But still she automatically picked up invisible bits of fluff from the clean carpets.

"He's coming to see Kai, anyway......I know he *said* he wants to see me, but really it's his son, it's got to be....who am I talking to?" Sensi asked her reflection in the mirror, "Oh God, look at the state of my hair!" she shouted aloud before dashing up the stairs to the bathroom where she grabbed handfuls of gel and slavered it onto her slicked back pony tail.

"Hello!" Shango's voice travelled through the house and up to the bathroom. Sensi cursed under her breath, she'd forgotten that she'd left the front door ajar for Kai.

"Be with you in a minute!" she called back still smoothing down her hair with frantic movements.

"No need, I'll come up." Shango took the stairs two at a time and reached the landing before Sensi could call out a protest, but his unexpected tap on the bathroom door still startled her.

"Er, one second," she said just as Shango opened the door and entered the small room.

"Hey nice do!" admiration shone from Shango's eyes as he gazed at Sensi's new hairstyle, "All one colour for a change, really suits you!" he continued staring hard at the glossy black plait which rested lightly on her shoulders.

"Er thanks." Sensi glowed inwardly with pride but refused to let Shango see the effect he was having on her. They stood looking at each other for a few seconds until Sensi began to feel that the room was getting smaller and smaller.

"I'll put the kettle on," she said edging past him wondering why her heart was beating so fast, "Kai should be back in a minute or you can go down to the park, I think he's playing basketball or cricket or.....something." Sensi stopped talking aware that she was rambling. She was sure she could feel Shango's breath on the back of her neck as they came downstairs and she turned back to

215

look. Sure enough he was right behind her, practically on the same step and still staring at her ponytail. Sensi quickened her pace and almost jogged into the kitchen.

In the living room Shango stretched out on the sofa and put his feet up on the coffee table.

"What are you smiling about?" Sensi put her head around the door, the kettle in her hand.

"I'm smiling," Shango replied slowly, "because the world is finally beginning to turn in the right direction!"

Okay.....then." Sensi went back to making the tea realising that she didn't know what Shango was on about.

"Sensi leave the tea, come here please." Shango was still smiling but there was a different tone to his voice.

"I was just going to cut some rum cake," Sensi called back wondering why she was delaying being around him.

"Bring the cake and come please," Shango asked again.

"You're very polite today." Sensi handed him a tray which held a large slice of rum cake on a small plate with a fork and a napkin folded into a triangular shape. Next to it was a glass of grapefruit juice with generous amounts of ice and a cocktail umbrella. Shango looked at the tray in surprise.

"And you're very..." he searched for the right word, "cultured."

"What do you mean?" Sensi was wary.

"I mean that this looks wonderful, thank you." Shango leaned over and kissed her cheek. Sensi sat in stunned silence.

"Have you been smoking something?" she eventually asked causing Shango to burst out laughing. It was so infectious that she joined.

"I'll be mean and horrible if you'd prefer." Shango was still laughing.

"What's the matter with you today?" Sensi wiped away the tears of laughter from her eyes.

"This feels good doesn't it?" Shango's laughter subsided and he held Sensi"s hand and looked straight into her eyes. Once again she felt her temperature rise and her palms go sweaty.

"What feels good?" she asked, still confused.

"Laughing and joking, enjoying each other's company, like the old days." Shango explained.

"It's better than us arguing all the time, even though it's mostly your fault," Sensi teased.

In that instant Shango noticed that her smile was perfect and her eyes twinkled. Her flawless dark brown skin glowed, complimented by something else that was new, her understated make-up. For the first time ever Shango regarded Sensi as beautiful. He pulled her close and kissed her deeply.

For a brief moment that seemed to last forever Sensi revelled in the touch of Shango's hand against her skin, she breathed in the sweet, sexy scent of him and arched her back as he pulled aside her top and sought her breast, caressing her nipple. When he bent his head to replace his hand with his tongue she gasped in delight and stroked his locks before pushing them aside, so she could touch the smooth skin on the back of his neck. She yielded easily when Shango pushed her gently down on the settee and stroked her belly button with his tongue. As she lifted her hips to entice him to go even lower their eyes met and Shango saw the love in Sensi's and knew that she would only see lust in his. Abruptly they stopped and Sensi turned away.

"Was that what you wanted? Is that why you're being so charming today?" she spat out.

Shango rubbed her back, "I'm sorry, that wasn't supposed to happen."

Sensi shrugged him off, "You dangle your wife on a string, you're in bed with your woman while your Dad's out walking the streets, and now you come all the way out here to grope me! Are you trying to win some sort of competition?"

"Sensi I–"

"You make me sick! No wonder you never wanted to see Kai. You bastard! Do I look like some cheap tart that you can just add to your list?"

"Sensi I actually came to say thanks for everything you did for my dad last night and for doing such a good job with our son."

"That's a funny way to say thanks. Where were you yesterday? What happened to your phone? I hope you enjoyed whatever she was giving you, your dad could have died while you were getting your rocks off." Sensi stopped suddenly as Shango gave her a murderous look.

"I wasn't with any woman last night," he hissed, "I was helping out a friend in need and I've always been there when Dad's needed me."

Sensi bit her lip. The angry undertones of Shango's voice scared her and she didn't want to risk arguing with him anymore. For a short but powerful moment she'd had the man of her dreams in her arms and the love she'd buried inside her had almost been let loose until she'd seen in his eyes that he didn't feel the same way. She felt like an idiot.

After seeing Andrea and Michelle at the hospital Sensi had decided to make a change, make more of an effort to look like a lady, the way they did, but now she felt that she'd chosen the wrong time. Shango obviously thought she'd made an effort just for him. No wonder he'd come on to her.

"Sensi," Shango spoke softly his voice a mixture of regret and respect, "how come you're different today?"

"I didn't do it for you." Sensi wiped her eyes with a tissue.

"You look wonderful and there's something about you, I can't put my finger on it."

"Like you said, Shango," Sensi turned to face him, "it's time for the world to start turning the right way."

"Are you changing your life?" he asked.

"I can't keep on down a dead end road."

"What will you do?"

"I want to do aromatherapy, maybe one day even have my own salon." Sensi spoke defensively, ready with a sharp retort in case Shango ridiculed her.

"That's fantastic, no one can give massages like you." Shango's enthusiasm was genuine.

"I'm going to go to college and do a course in it and one in bookkeeping, then I'll get a job as an assistant before I branch off on my own."

"I'm really pleased for you and I think you'll do great." Once again, Shango was beaming.

"Can you see me running my own shop?" Sensi asked excitedly.

"Of course!" Shango didn't hesitate, "What would you call it?"

"I don't know! Something really sophisticated." Sensi laughed.

"When you start your course, let me know what I can do. Whatever you need, tuition fees, books, Kai out of your hair so you can study in peace. I want to help, Sensi, I think this is fantastic."

"I can't wait, but I'm really scared."

"Why?"

"Girls like me don't usually run businesses."

"What do you truly want for your life, Sensi?"

"I want better. I want to own my own home, so that if anything happens to us Kai's got a roof over his head, I want to do better and be better. Shango it's time for a change."

Shango smiled as he hugged Sensi and kissed her forehead, "I hope you get everything you want and deserve, I'm always here for you. They hugged once more before Sensi pulled away and smoothed her hair and clothes. Shango checked his watch, "Kai's been out for a long time," he commented.

"That boy forgets the meaning of time once he starts playing."

"I'll fetch him, then I'll have to get going."

"Thanks. What about you and Celia?" Sensi asked with genuine concern.

"We'll work things out."

"I know you will, Shango, but be honest with her, don't string her along if it's really the other woman you want to be with."

"I'll see you soon." Shango kissed Sensi on her cheek and held her close.

"Here, you know you want this!" Sensi handed him the fragrant rum cake wrapped in the napkin and laughed as he licked his lips.

• • • • • •

"Thanks for coming.....hey it's good to see you.......come in.......glad to see you brought your son....there's soft drinks on the table, help yourself........"

Shango stood in the doorway of Ira's house and greeted the members of EBYN as they arrived. Some of the men looked confused, others wary, one or two outwardly hostile but Shango treated them all to a genuine smile and a firm handshake. By six fifteen the lounge was overflowing and Rafi signalled that they were ready to start. Just as Shango was shutting the door Ras Reuben strode up with two men flanking him. Shango swung the door open and smiled at the three of them.

"Brother Ras," he began,

"Shango what's this all about?" Ras Reuben demanded standing inches away from him.

"This is all about peace and restoration," Shango replied cryptically, "Please come in."

Ras scowled at his accomplices as they followed Shango into the house. He couldn't prevent the shocked look on his face when he saw that just about every single member of the network was in the room.

"Outside!" he hissed as he quickly pushed his men back into the hallway. "I told you to make sure no one came!" Ras addressed the shorter of the two men.

"I called everyone I knew," Shortie whimpered feebly.

"So what happened?" Ras fumed.

"I couldn't *make* them stay away!" the man protested.

"Did you even try?" Ras Reuben's other accomplice asked angrily.

"Gentlemen!" Palmer strode confidently towards the group. He'd been watching them for several seconds and now spoke up, "Would you like some lemonade on this warm evening, or perhaps some iced tea? I know you English men like your tea." Without waiting for an answer he put his arm around Shortie and led him back into the lounge. Ras and his friend were forced to end their interrogation and follow.

Shango silently surveyed the lounge, comparing tonight's gathering with the first official meeting they'd had at the beginning of the summer. There was an hint of discontent in the air, but Shango didn't feel as though it was directed at him. He glanced over to the far corner where Brother Ras stood with his two henchmen. He'd noticed that no one else had approached them and they were surrounded by a veil of hostility. Shango was pleased. If the members were restless under Ras Reuben's leadership it would make his attempt to regain his throne much easier. He closed his eyes and briefly prayed for understanding, compassion and wisdom to descend upon the room.

"Gentlemen," he began a second later in a low, authoritative tone that immediately gained everyone's full attention. The men stopped chatting and held their cups and glasses still. Rafi moved away from Shango's side allowing the spotlight to be totally on him.

"It's such a beautiful evening, warm sunshine, a cool breeze and instead of spending it with your loved ones and families, you choose to spend it here with me. Thank you from the bottom of my heart."

Shango looked into the eyes of each man as he spoke. They all looked back unflinchingly, even Ras, but his was a glare that was filled with hate. Instead of cowering under it Shango directed his next comment to him.

"Thank you especially to Brother Ras who took this network under his wing and guided it whilst it seemed I was losing my mind. We are indebted to him." His words fell into silence until Rafi, picking up an invisible clue from Shango, began a tentative round of applause; the rest of the men gradually joined in. "EBYN, the organisation that I founded, with a vision for the twenty-first century, was in critical condition," Shango spoke emphatically over the growing applause, "…and this is the man that brought you through!" he finished as the clapping died down.

With all eyes upon him Ras had no choice but to nod respectfully at Shango and acknowledge the applause from the men. But a subtle aura of ill will still emanated from him and his cronies.

"Brothers," Shango continued, "a short time ago you decided that the integrity of the EBYN community was more important than my ego and reputation. The result was that I had to relinquish my role as leader. I'll admit, at the time it was a heavy loss to bear. Instead of seeing it as a natural consequence to my actions, I took it personally and lashed out at those who were there for me. Rafi I apologise." Shango looked directly at his friend as Rafi nodded to him. "And to those of you who took time out to call me during those dark days to make sure I was okay and to whom I was less than courteous, I also apologise. But, as many of you know, it is a fool who does not let experience teach him and I am honestly glad that you made that decision because it shows that the network is on the right track. It shows that our purpose will be served and it shows that we will make a positive difference in the lives of our families and our community!"

Shango was forced into silence by the thunderous applause that greeted his words. Rafi and Palmer exchanged grins as Shango worked his magic across the room.

"Excuse me!" Ras roughly pushed past the men to get to Shango's side. "Brother Shango! Are you trying to say that you've learnt your lesson and you want your toy back?" The smile on Ras' face belied the threat in his voice. It was an open challenge to Shango for the leadership of EBYN.

Shango held Ras' gaze. He was in no hurry. He looked around at the members, back to Ras, at Rafi and Palmer and then at Ras' henchmen. He stood in a relaxed pose, hands easy by his side, his breath deep and sure. In stark contrast, Ras stood erect, his fists clenched and his feet apart, he was ready to do battle.

Shango dragged over an empty chair, offered it to Ras and sat on another, legs astride, the chair turned back to front. As he leaned forward he noted the tension in the atmosphere. Ras shifted impatiently in his seat, regretting his impulsive sarcasm.

Slowly nodding his head at no one in particular, Shango affirmed to himself that he'd already won. It was there in the empathetic eyes of the members. It was apparent in the forgiving vibes that reverberated invisibly around the room. Shango's victory hung in the air waiting to descend upon his shoulders, he knew it and Ras knew it.

"Just like we did it before, Brother Ras." Shango faced his opponent letting the words spill slowly from his lips.

"Stop talking in riddles!" Ras anger erupted as he realised that he was fighting a losing battle.

"Just like we did it before," Shango repeated. "Put it to the vote."

"No!" Shortie burst out knowing they'd be easily out voted.

"Sounds like a good idea to me." Tayshan Webber looked directly at Ras Reuben as he spoke, "Shango's right, that's exactly how we've always done it. As it begins so shall it end."

Shango and Ras Reuben stood simultaneously knowing they'd be expected to leave the room. Reuben stomped through the hallway and straight out of the house closely followed by his two men.

"Skills like yours are always welcome in the network, he called out sincerely."

"You may have won this battle but you haven't won the war!" Ras and his men took off in a jeep with darkened windows.

"You're better off without him, bro'." Palmer and Rafi were standing behind Shango.

"He won't trouble us again," Rafi assured.

Shango turned to them and allowed his triumphant grin to shine through. "Gentlemen, I do believe we have a reason to celebrate!" he declared as they went back inside. Shango relaxed as his impromptu party began to swing. He luxuriated in the fact that once again he was on top and in control, guiding events instead of being dragged along by them.

In the middle of the fun Shango felt the familiar vibration of his mobile phone. He snapped it open to see that he had a text message. Quickly he pressed the envelope key. Sandra's mobile number flashed up followed by her message.

> I CAN'T TAKE THIS ANYMORE. I DON'T KNOW WHAT YOU WANT. I HAVE TO GET AWAY TONIGHT. DON'T TRY AND STOP ME.

Shango read the words twice not really understanding them. He tried to ignore the hollow feeling in the pit of his stomach as he looked around. Finding a quiet corner in the house wasn't easy, music resonated from the downstairs rooms and everywhere he went members toasted him with whatever drink they had in their hands, welcoming him back. Shango's elation was fading fast and he was desperate to contact Sandra. Eventually he went into the bathroom and locked the door behind him. The signal from his phone was weak and he prayed it would last until he'd finished. He called Sandra at home, her phone went straight to answer machine. Shango knew that she was there screening his call.

"Babe," he was tentative, not wanting to beg, "...sweetheart, I know you're there. If you don't want to pick up the phone, that's fine, just listen. I love you and I will always love you. I'm on my way and we'll do whatever you want when I get there. Just wait for me."

"Everything okay?" Palmer stood at the foot of the stairs as Shango left the bathroom and came down.

"I have to go."

"Leave and go where?" Rafi joined them.

"I got a message, something doesn't feel right."

"Celia?" Palmer asked, then tutted when he saw the answer in Shango's eyes.

"When will you learn?" Rafi kissed his teeth in annoyance.

"Listen I spoke to Celia already, I'm seeing her later, she's cool."

"She's cool about you loving another woman?" Palmer was sceptical.

"Sandra needs me now."

"Never mind Sandra," Palmer interjected, "What about you, who do you want, who do you need? Maybe if you answer that, when you get your life back on track you'll stay on track."

"Sandra," Shango said. "She's the one I want and she's the one I need. It's as simple as that." He scooped up his car keys from the hallway table and headed for the door.

"Hey, what shall we tell..." but Shango was in his car before Rafi could finish his sentence. He looked at Palmer. "Everyone seems to be having a good time."

"It's still early."

"Seems a shame to break up the party now."

"Another beer?" offered Palmer.

"Lead me to it! Hey, he's still got my car keys!"

"Where else do you need to be?"

"You're right! Let's get back to the fun!" Rafi laughed slapping Palmer on his back.

● ● ● ● ● ●

In the immaculate living room in Sandra's Moseley flat, Celia coolly aimed the compact gun steadily at her rival. Brick had taken two hours to call her back, then he'd skirted around the real issue for another twenty minutes, wanting to be certain that Celia was who she purported to be and wanted exactly what she said she did. By remaining calm and unemotional Celia passed his test with flying colours.

Brick had eventually arranged for one of his associates to meet her in a public park. He'd stipulated that she bring five hundred pounds in cash, along with a deposit of two hundred and fifty pounds to ensure the safe return of the weapon. Celia doubted that she'd see her deposit again but she was past caring. Shango had pushed her to her limit and for the first time she was about to experience life on the edge.

She'd read through Shango's e-mails and found Sandra's address amongst the many love letters she'd sent him. Then she'd taken a taxi to Sandra's flat keeping the gun concealed in a small handbag that hung from her shoulder. She'd instructed the driver to wait, throwing a ten pound note at him to make it worth his while.

Getting into the flat had been almost too easy, all she'd had to do was ring the bell, speak into the intercom and then push Sandra back in at gunpoint when she'd opened the door. Sandra, of course had no idea who she was, so Celia had the upper hand. She'd never taken any type of drugs but from the rush of adrenaline through her veins she now understood exactly what she'd been missing.

Every time Sandra had tried to speak Celia had cocked the gun at one of her limbs, enjoying the surge of power she felt when Sandra trembled. Then Celia had stood over her and dictated the text message to Shango which Sandra had sent with shaking fingers.

The fact that it all seemed so easy made Celia regret taking so long to fight for her man. She held the life of this bitch in her hands. All she had to do was squeeze the tiny lever and put an end to it so that she and Shango could be together again. The small gun in her hands that glistened with her sweat was assurance that her plans couldn't be stopped or altered.

Celia wasn't surprised at Shango's phone call which came after they'd sent the text. Celia had kept her eye on Sandra throughout the whole of Shango's plea. Sandra had glanced repeatedly from the answering machine to Celia's tense face, hardly taking in a word Shango was saying.

"Give me the tape from the machine," Celia had ordered when Shango had hung up. Her voice had been emotionless. It didn't matter that she'd just heard her husband telling another woman that he loved her. Soon the dirty hussy would be gone and Shango would forget all about his "fling" and once again only have eyes for her.

"Why don't you give me the gun?" Sandra coaxed in a soft tone trying to project a bravery that she hadn't felt.

"Shut up bitch." Celia stood and motioned Sandra toward the bedroom. She pointed with the gun as Sandra got to her feet, "Time for you to pack. You're leaving."

"Leaving?"

"Get a move on!" she'd barked when Sandra had stood rooted to the spot. "We've got a taxi waiting."

CHAPTER TWENTY TWO

SHANGO PULLED UP outside of Sandra's flat. He was halfway to the building when he realised that he hadn't switched off his engine or locked the car. He ran back, dialling Sandra's number with one hand while pulling the keys out of the ignition with the other. As her house phone switched to the answer machine Shango tried to quell the feeling of dread that was growing inside him. His free hand dialled Sandra's mobile number, praying that she was still at home.

"Oi!" someone shouted through the intercom, "who is it?"

Shango looked at the number-plate nailed to the wall. He was pressing thirty five instead of thirty three. He switched over immediately.

"She's not in!" The voice followed the creaking sound of a window being opened somewhere above him. Shango ignored it. He held onto the buzzer, while listening to the message on Sandra's mobile and wondering where the hell she was.

"Are you deaf?" the voice called again, "I've told you, she's not in!"

Shango stepped backwards and looked up. An older lady leaned out of her third floor window chewing tobacco which fell in dirty, brown blobs from her mouth as she spoke.

"You're after that black girl, aren't ya? The slim one. I used to have a figure like that."

"You're dripping," Shango said in obvious distaste.

"If you're going to be rude, then you can stand there all day."

"Look, I'm in a hurry, where is she?" He couldn't find any charm for this woman.

"How would I know?" the woman wiped loose spit from her mouth with the back of a liver spotted hand and gazed upwards, "Turned out nice again, considering."

"Lady," Shango used the term loosely, "can you help me or not?"

"I *am* helping you and look what I get for my trouble, people just don't appreciate good intentions." The woman withdrew and

226

closed the window firmly behind her.

Shango exhaled and tried to ignore the familiar tightening of his chest. Frustration gnawed at him, something was amiss. He fired up the three litre engine of his BMW, selected first gear and held the car steady between the clutch and the accelerator ready to move in an instant. He turned down the radio station and pressed redial on his phone. Eventually a familiar voice said "Hello." Shango looked at the phone, brows knitted in surprise, "Celia?" he questioned, wondering if he'd rung her phone by mistake.

"Darling," Celia answered, not at all surprised, her voice syrupy thick with sentimentality.

"Celia!" Shango repeated, his voice rising a tone higher.

"Don't worry, love, Sandra's with me." Celia smiled into the phone whilst poking the gun into Sandra's side. "I just have to sort her out and then I'll be home."

Shango listened carefully to the background sounds, he heard a diesel engine amidst heavy traffic. "Celia, why don't I come over," he offered casually, masking his anxiety. The women must be together. But why? And where were they going?

"No!" shouted Celia.

"I'll pick you up, we'll get something nice for dinner? How about that?" Shango forced himself to speak softly.

"There's more to life than food!" Celia shrieked through the phone causing Shango to wince in pain as he held it away from his ear.

"Celia wait!" he shouted.

"I'm busy!" she looked into Sandra's eyes and her pulse raced excitedly at the fear in them.

"Let me speak to Sandra." Shango knew he'd stepped onto dangerous ground but he had to take the risk.

"I suppose a last goodbye won't hurt, be quick!" As she placed the phone next to Sandra's ear a warning flashed behind the triumph in her eyes.

Sandra seized the moment and shouted into the mouth piece, "Airport!" Enraged Celia struck her across the cheek with the phone. Sandra screamed as the pain lashed through her. The startled taxi driver swerved sharply, hitting the kerb. Celia yelled at him to keep moving, the line went dead and Shango found that he could hear no more.

With one movement he released his hand brake, reversed out of the car park and headed for the A45, the road that led straight to Birmingham Airport.

• • • • • •

"Looks like you'll be coming home with us, Ira!" Tony Valentine joked as he sat at Ira's bedside and wondered where everyone was.

"Are you sure Shango and Palmer knew you were being discharged tonight?" Andrea queried, frowning at her husband's attempt at levity.

"Yes I think so, maybe they forgot?" Ira tried to hide his disappointment and growing confusion.

"They'll be here, probably just caught in traffic," Andrea soothed, "You certainly look much better anyway, got some colour back in your cheeks."

"I didn't get to thank them," was Ira's strange response.

"Who?" asked Tony, "Thank who, Ira?" he asked again into the silence wondering why Andrea had flashed him a disapproving look.

"You ask too many questions, Valentine, leave Ira alone," she warned.

"We're just talking," Tony defended himself.

"You can talk without asking questions all the time."

"I wasn't hurting him."

"Now you're whinging."

"I'm not whinging."

"Stop it, it's irritating."

Andrea and Tony were in the comfortable zone of two people who didn't really need words but spoke out loud for the simple pleasure of hearing each other's voices. Their harmless bantering was a blanket of reassurance that their friend, this confused, old man called Ira, was going to be okay.

"You started it by giving me those looks," Tony continued, "You know I hate it when you do that."

"I did not give you a look," Andrea countered.

"You're always doing it."

"Only when you need to shut up"

"I don't need to shut up."

"You do when you're embarrassing me."

"All I said was...."

Ira sat on top of his newly made bed. He wore smart clothes that Michelle had picked out for him so he wouldn't have to leave the hospital in the sodden rags he'd been wearing when he came in. The collar of his bright white shirt was stiffly starched, his trousers beautifully pressed and his black shoes gleaming. Michelle had made him look a million dollars but she wasn't here to see it. He wondered where she was, where they all were.

He smiled indulgently at Andrea and Tony knowing that their amiable bickering was merely saying "I love you". The sound of their voices was comforting, and soon his sons would arrive. He lay back against the pillows allowing his mind to wander.

It was the early sixties and he was with his friends, Preston, Fudge, Commentator and Mack at a bottle party. To wind down on a Saturday night, they'd all gather at someone's house and bring a bottle or two of alcohol, some cigars and cigarettes and dance to Blue Spot reggae records. The men covertly watched a group of women on the other side of the room before making their move, trying to decide who had the shapeliest hips, or the largest breasts or the firmest bottom, but Ira only had eyes for the prettiest one, Ruby Katherine.

As the night wore on the music got louder, the booze flowed, the women relaxed and the men made a sport of trying to outdo each other.

"I mean to have that one for my bride," Ira declared loudly, nodding at Ruby Katherine.

"You'd marry her?" Preston challenged.

"Yes man!"

"When?" Fudge demanded,

"Now?" suggested Commentator,

"Right now?" Preston urged.

"Right now!" Ira refused to back down, "I would take her by the hand and marry her right now in front of all of you, and every single one of you would wish you were me!"

The men slapped him on the back as he approached Ruby Katherine and led her onto the dance floor. He'd planned to wink at his mates over her shoulder, a sign that he'd netted his bait, but he found that once he had this exquisite beauty in his arms nothing else mattered. A slow record came on and she laid her head on his shoulder. She felt so tiny in his arms and her Lavender perfume mixed with her own scent had delighted him. He held her tightly, sure that their feet weren't touching the floor. When the song ended he couldn't let her go.

Ira drifted back to the present aware that Tony and Andrea were regarding him silently.

"Happy memories?" Andrea asked reaching for his hand.

"The best," Ira's eyes twinkled, "I was just about to ask Ruby Katherine to marry me.

"Tell us how you proposed," Tony urged, sitting back in his seat, ready for a good story.

••••••

Michelle started to dial Celia's number for the second time but stopped herself. She wanted to share the joy of being in love for the first time, but hesitated because Celia's own love was causing her so much pain. She couldn't believe the ironic timing.

Michelle left the phone on the settee and went into her back garden. She'd never really spent much time there until these last few days when Palmer had stayed with her. A gardener came once a fortnight to mow the lawn, trim the bushes and tidy away the weeds. She'd look over his work and write him a cheque, apart from that the garden may as well have belonged to someone else for all the notice she took of it. It was simply a piece of green land that came with the house.

Now Michelle experienced it with new eyes. She'd stood in Palmer's arms in the middle of her lawn at sunset as he'd described his garden in Atlanta. She'd closed her eyes seeing the places where Palmer had planted his roses, grown his herbs and put his sun lounger. He'd illustrated it so vividly she'd almost felt the sun on her back and smelt the fragrance of his flowers. She realised that his garden was his oasis of peace which he'd yet to share with any woman.

"Liana." Michelle said the name out loud and waited but she felt no pangs of jealousy, no desire to kick the bitch out of town, nothing, except maybe an ounce of pity. Liana was young and attractive, she'd soon find someone else for her huge family to adopt now that she'd lost Palmer.

Michelle decided to go ahead and ring Celia. True love not withstanding, her friend was going through a hard time and she needed her. She'd offer to keep her company and provide a listening ear, they could talk about the wonders of Palmer another day.

••••••

"How much further?" Celia spoke to the taxi driver but kept her eyes firmly on Sandra who steadily returned her gaze, a purple bruise marking her cheekbone where Celia had hit her with the phone.

"Just a few miles," he responded in a thick Middle Eastern accent, glancing at them in his rear view mirror.

"Keep your eye on the road!" Celia ordered.

"All right, keep your hair on, missus," he mumbled under his breath in Arabic.

"We don't have to do this, I'll talk if that's what you want." Sandra's voice was calm but her stomach was churning. She ignored the desire to rest her head in her hands and soothe away the pain from her wounds. She could still feel the metal of the gun against her side, and Celia eyes carried a manic look.

"*Now* you care what I want?" Celia mocked, she leaned close to Sandra's ear, "It's amazing what a bit of metal and gunpowder can do isn't it? Maybe this'll stop you trying to take my man!?"

"I didn't know," Sandra pleaded, "He never said; I didn't know."

"You're not that stupid! Didn't it occur to you even once that he had a wife? Who do you think he was running away to all of those nights when he didn't stay with you? God, I've have given Shango more credit for choosing a bitch with brains instead of a dumb whore like you."

Sandra sat back in horrified silence. This woman was Shango's wife? Her thoughts scattered in a dozen different directions and her head pounded as though Celia had just hit her again.

"W- w -wife," she stuttered.

"You didn't know!" Celia laughed crazily, her head thrown back and her eyes blazing, "You really didn't know!" Celia cradled Sandra in her arms, the gun swung loosely from her hand but neither of them paid it any mind. Sandra sat limply as Celia patted her gently. "Poor, silly, little girl," Celia kissed Sandra's head, "you really didn't have a clue that he was loving me all along, that you were only second best, you thought it was real love."

As Celia rambled on the driver caught a glimpse the gun. His eyes slid over to Sandra who blinked twice at him hoping he would grasp the situation. The driver nodded silently and looked ahead for a gap in the heavy traffic. He didn't want any trouble. As far as he was concerned the sooner he got rid of his two crazy passengers the better. He steered away from the upcoming police station. No police meant no chance of exposing his illegal immigration status.

"No guns, no trouble, no more black people," he said in rapid Arabic as he desperately searched for an exit off the main road.

Shango hit the wheel in sheer frustration. He'd criss-crossed the city and reached the A45 in record time, but had since moved less than a mile in the last fifteen minutes. The radio travel bulletins warned of tailbacks up ahead and he realised he was going nowhere fast. He glanced around quickly and, satisfied that there were no police in the area, furtively pressed redial on his phone.

"The mobile phone you are calling is not responding, please try again later," the recorded message said. Shango swore and banged the steering wheel again wondering why he always seemed to end up in the lane of traffic that was inert. He watched as the cars next to him progressed steadily forwards.

"White Ford Escort, silver Subaru, *nice* Rav 4," he noted their details, looking for a way to keep his mind occupied, "…green Mondeo, new Mini Cooper, taxi…" His gaze followed the taxi whose blurry figures seemed oddly familiar. At that moment the sun broke through the cloud and illuminated the passengers.

Shango shivered as his common sense raged against what his instincts told him. The passengers could have been male or female and of any race but through his heightened intuition he *sensed* that it was Celia and Sandra. He blew his horn, attracting the attention of everybody except them. The driver in front of him, unhappy at being beeped, gave him the finger.

Finally the traffic ahead of him surged forward. Shango jerked the car from first to second and finally into third gear. He wiped his sweating palms alternately on his jeans, fumbled in his pocket for his inhaler and squirted two sprays into his mouth in quick succession. His eyes barely left the taxi, which tantalised like a carrot on a stick, just out of his reach. Beads of sweat formed across his forehead which he wiped with the back of his hand. He ignored the drops he felt trickling down the back of his neck, it took all his effort just to think clearly.

He surmised that Sandra and Celia were both in the taxi. Celia was obviously not in a rational frame of mind, Sandra must be extremely frightened, but he couldn't fathom why they were heading for the airport. What would Celia gain from that? Shango's frown deepened as he tried to figure out Celia's logic. He needed to confront Celia, reassure Sandra and make them both feel safe again. But for now he had no option but to follow wherever it was that Celia was leading.

Michelle was growing anxious, she'd called Celia at home, on her mobile and now she'd just called Shango's mobile, all to no avail. It was as if the pair had disappeared into thin air. She paced her living room trying to decide what to do next. She had a nervous feeling in the pit of her stomach that wouldn't settle, something was going on and Celia was at the centre of it. She dialled Palmer's number.

"Hi." His rich deep voice always made Michelle smile. She felt better already and he'd only said one word.

"Hey baby," she cooed.

"Hey sweetheart, what's up?" Palmer responded warmly unable to stop the grin that spread over his face at hearing Michelle's voice.

"Sounds like you're in the middle of a party." Michelle stalled for time unsure how to begin describing her fears for Celia.

"The guys are getting into it, drinking and slapping those dominoes but it's not really a party without you, why don't you come on over?" Michelle's brief hesitation was enough for Palmer to become concerned. "What's wrong, babe?" he moved from the hallway into the quieter kitchen, "Are you okay?"

"Darling I'm fine, just a little bit worried about Celia."

"She should be okay, Shango's arranged to see her tonight, I think they're going to have a *long* talk."

"Do you know if he's with her now?"

"Could be, he left here earlier, why?"

"It's nothing I can put my finger on, but I've got a bad feeling. I can't reach her or Shango."

"Shango said that today was the day he was going to sort out his business, maybe that's what he's doing."

"What does that mean for Celia?"

"It could mean that she might need a friend soon."

"But I can't reach her, what if?....."

"Hey come on," Palmer soothed, "we've got to stay positive."

"What should we do?"

"I'll keep trying Shango till I get him, and I'll see what Rafi knows. Stay by the phone in case Celia calls, then you can go straight to her. Okay?"

"Okay."

"Sit tight, and don't worry, I'll call you back."

● ● ● ● ● ●

"Are you still here, Mr Shango?" the nurse smiled at Ira, Tony and Andrea as she tended to the patient in the next bed, "We've made you feel so welcome you don't want to go!" she laughed and the trio laughed with her.

"My sons are too busy with their women to bother with me," Ira casually commented though his eyes appeared heavy.

"Something must have come up, Ira, I'm sure they wouldn't have just forgotten you like this." Andrea was disturbed by the look of abandonment on Ira's face. "We'll take you home," she decided, ignoring the frown that Tony flashed her.

"Darling, what about the club?" he protested moving close to her so Ira wouldn't hear, "We've got to open up in a couple of hours."

"It's only fifteen minutes to Ira's from here by car. If the guys don't show up I'll stay with him, you open the club and I'll catch up with you later."

Andrea and Tony exchanged a long look that encompassed Tony's dissatisfaction with Andrea's decision and her refusal to capitulate. It was also a subconscious acknowledgement that no more would be said until they were alone as they'd made a pact never to argue in public.

"Did they give you any pills, Ira?" Andrea asked as she helped him off the bed and motioned for Tony to carry his overnight bag.

"They're packed away," Ira said.

"Good, let's get you home to your bed."

"My own bed, my own house, my sweet Ruby Katherine," Ira whispered to himself as they left the ward while Andrea and Tony glared at each other behind his back.

CHAPTER TWENTY THREE

"YES!" SHOUTED SHANGO on realising that he was finally gaining ground on the taxi that had begun to slip away from him. His expression was icily grim as he pulled alongside the cab and pipped his horn several times to get the driver's attention.

At first the driver ignored him, the only thing on his mind being that fact that in the back of his cab was a woman with a gun. He cursed himself for getting such an unlucky fare, for such horrendous traffic and for ending up in a country that never wanted him in the first place. Perhaps, he deliberated, these were all signs from Allah that he was supposed to have stayed in the country of his birth and become an Imam.

By the fifth time Shango had pressed his horn, the driver had decided that he was being chased by a Jamaican Yardie Rastafarian, who was probably in league with the mad black woman wielding the gun. The omens were getting stronger, Allah definitely wanted him to return to his mosque back home. He sent up a silent prayer that if his life was spared he would be the best mosque leader in the business.

"Pull over!" Shango shouted as his window wound slowly down to reveal his face contorted with anger and confusion. The driver looked from him to the women and back to him again before deciding to ignore him.

"Pull over! Now! Are you stupid or something!" Shango swore as his car almost lurched into the taxi. He held the steering wheel with his left hand and gestured frantically with his right. His patience had run out and he wondered if the taxi driver was deaf. "Yo!" he tried again, beeping his horn and shouting and waving. He pointed to an upcoming side road, "Turn there!" he ordered before flipping his indicator on and making the turn himself.

From inside the cab Celia watched horrified through the shadowy glass as Shango appeared. Her head pounded and nausea rose from her stomach to her throat as she realised she was losing control. She broke out in a sweat that made her face shine, wetted her palms and loosened her grip on the gun which fell to her feet. With a lightening reaction Sandra kicked it away before Celia could retrieve it. Incensed Celia swung her arm back ready to whack Sandra but she was knocked off balance as the cab took the turn. Her head banged against the window and she cried out in pain.

"What are you doing?" she screamed at the driver.

"No English, no English!" he shouted back, his hand raised in a gesture of submission.

"Stop the taxi!" Sandra shouted catching sight of Shango, "Stop!" she reached forward and banged on the glass partition.

"No English, *yar Allah*, no English!" the driver kept up his charade hoping that his god would somehow deliver him from his insane passengers and their accomplice in the BMW who was flashing his headlights at him.

Shango pulled into the car park of a derelict pub. Dusty gravel flew up from under his wheels as he stopped abruptly. A few yards behind him the black cab also came to a halt. Seconds later the driver alighted and flung himself on the ground, face down, near Shango's feet.

"No English," he was petrified, "No shoot, you Yardie, sell drugs, I no tell police, no shoot!" the man rambled on.

"Shut up." Shango wasn't in the mood to accommodate the man's foolish fears. "Get up," he said more gently when he saw that the driver was actually shaking, "I'm not going to hurt you, I just need to see the girls. Let them out and go home."

The driver looked up at him dubiously. Shango responded with a benign look. "I just need to see the women, I'm not armed, see?" he patted his pockets slowly and lifted the bottoms of his jeans.

The driver was now crouching on his knees. His eyes betrayed his unease and spit dribbled from the corner of his mouth as he looked from Shango to the cab. Shango followed his gaze and watched as Celia walked towards him pushing Sandra in front of her. As they neared, Shango could clearly see the gun that she pointed at his lover.

"I no tell police, please no shoot," the driver begged Shango.

"Go," Shango told him a flat voice, his eyes locking with Sandra's and noting the dullness in them, the blue-black bruise on her face and the tears that flowed freely down her cheeks. "No drugs, no Yardies. That's my wife, that's my lover and I'm breaking their hearts. You go."

With a last look at Shango the driver stumbled back to his taxi, keeping as far away from the women as he could. He took off without a backward look envisaging his new life as a priest in God's house back in the Sudan.

"Celia please, put down the gun." Shango held out his hand but stayed where he was. His eyes filled with compassion and his heart twisted with the pain he felt emanating from the women. "I'm sorry." His words were soft and his voice low. "I never meant it to come to this, I'm sorry."

"What did you mean, then, sweetheart?" Celia spoke bitterly. She stared at Shango but kept the gun firmly fixed on Sandra. "What exactly did you have planned when you hopped from my bed into hers?"

"I loved you, Celia, I love you still, please, put down the gun," Shango pleaded.

"You bastard!" Sandra cried out surprising both Celia and Shango, "I should have known you were just playing more of your stupid games. Let her shoot me, I don't care, she's your wife, you still love her, I was just a diversion. Let her kill me, because then you won't be able to break my heart anymore."

"Sandra, I..." Shango moved towards her, his arms open.

"–No!" Celia shouted, "You're not going to stand there and console this bitch. What about me?!" she screamed hysterically, "What about what you've done to me!"

"All right!" Shango held his palms upwards and took a step back, "Let's all stay calm."

"You think I won't shoot her if we're calm?" Celia scoffed.

"She didn't know about you, Celia. I wasn't man enough to tell her. I let her think that I was free. I couldn't give you what you deserved and needed, I strung you both along when I should have been honest from the start. It's me you should be aiming at, shoot me." Shango raised his arms in submission and waited. His heart was beating at twice it's normal rate and his t-shirt was drenched in sweat.

Celia held tightly onto Sandra's arm but her eyes were locked onto Shango as she considered his words.

"Why?" Sandra spoke into the silence, "Why Shango?"

"Because I loved you Sandra, I've never stopped loving you. But I made a promise to my wife which I couldn't just ignore."

"You bastard!" Sandra spat bitterly, " I would have done anything for you, anything."

"Enough!" Celia shouted. She shook Sandra's arm, spinning her around and causing her to lose her footing. She fell heavily and screamed out in pain when Celia stomped on her side to prevent her from getting up.

"Was this the reason you left me alone at the hospital on our wedding day, cos you were with this bitch?"

"No!" Shango shouted and ran towards them. "Celia stop!" Shango was drowned out by Celia's ranting and Sandra's screams as she felt the searing pain from Celia's rapid kicks to her ribs, hips and back. Then Celia aimed the gun at Sandra's head and pulled the trigger, just before Shango grabbed her and dragged her away fromm Sandra's prone form. From the corner of her eye Sandra saw the barrel and automatically curled into a foetal position, knees to her chest, her arms wrapped protectively around her head. Meanwhile Shango flung Celia aside, her legs twisted and she dropped to the floor.

Celia felt as if her world was moving in slow motion. She pulled the trigger and waited for the loud bang that would signal that she'd won, that it was all over, the bitch was dead and she could once again have Shango all to herself. But when her cheek collided with the gravel stones she was shocked back into realising that she'd been shoved aside. She tried to make sense of what was happening aware that she'd shot the gun but there'd been no bang.

Shango knelt next to Sandra and turned her over checking her face, neck and chest for blood and open wounds but he couldn't find any. Frantically he felt her neck for a pulse then searched again for the bullet hole. Meanwhile, Sandra lay unconscious in his arms.

Celia rubbed the side of her face as she slowly sat up. She looked at the blood on her palm and blinked, trying to focus. She felt dizzy and awkward as she tried to stand. Her left ankle buckled beneath her causing her to bite her lip as the pain from it flashed through her whole body. Her silky summer dress was ripped where she'd fallen. The strap of her sandal had come loose at the stitching, and gravel and dirt clung to the blood where her cheek was cut open. Her silk headscarf had slipped off revealing uncombed clumps of matted hair.

Celia's eyes were bright as she spotted the gun. She walked over to it unsteadily and picked it up. She reasoned to herself that it must have misfired, that was why she hadn't heard the bang. She smiled wryly as she realised that Sandra was now a sitting duck in Shango's arms. All she had to do was point the gun, pull the trigger and kill the bitch, how hard could it be?

She paused for a brief second as she realised the possibility that Shango could get shot too. Her head cocked to one side and her eyes narrowed as she contemplated the tableau before her. Her husband of less than two years was weeping over the woman she intended to kill. He'd followed them across the city, and demanded that the taxi driver eject them, so that he could save this stinking hussy. He was a stupid man, she decided. If he'd just let her get to the airport his whore would have been safely on a plane and that would have been the end of the matter. But Shango always had to be the knight in shining armour, the one to save the day, the hero. Didn't he know that heroes ended up alone? Celia raised the gun and took aim.

"Shango move," she said without emotion.

"Don't do it, Celia," he looked over his shoulder at her, there were tears in his eyes, "this isn't you."

"How would you know?" Celia hissed as she limped around him to get a clearer shot at Sandra. Before Shango could jump up to knock the gun out of her hand, she fired straight at Sandra's face. She smiled in triumph as she heard the click of the trigger and watched to see the blood stream from Sandra's head. Shango held his breath, his eyes closed as he'd realised there was no way he could stop Celia. Instead he'd leant over Sandra hoping to absorb the bullet with his own body. He'd heard the click but felt nothing. He sat up and watched Celia pull the trigger again and again, coming closer each time until she was just inches away from him and Sandra. When she finally spoke Shango smelt her stale breath.

"He tricked me," Celia cried, "that bastard took my money and tricked me. It's empty, there's no bullets, it's empty."

● ● ● ● ● ●

"Why are you parking all the way down here?" The sharp edge to Tony's words indicated his underlying irritation with Andrea.

"Look at all of the cars parked along the street. I can't get near the house. Is something going on?" Andrea directed her question to Ira who shook his head. She refused to rise to the bait set by Tony. As far as she was concerned he was being unnecessarily unreasonable and she wasn't in the mood to play games.

"Don't know how you expect him to walk so far, he has just come out of hospital you know." Tony deliberately spoke his thoughts aloud.

"You've always like walking, haven't you?" Andrea asked Ira who looked sideways from husband to wife and decided not to get involved.

"It's walking that put him in hospital in the first place," Tony muttered.

"Walking calms the spirit doesn't it Ira?" Andrea was determined not to be beaten.

"Might as well have left the jeep at the hospital," Tony continued, sulking, as it seemed that Andrea was winning.

Andrea put the jeep into neutral and pulled up the handbrake. "There you go, Ira, I've parked as close as I *can*," she stressed the words glancing at Tony. "Seems like there's a party going on at yours, no wonder we've had a little bit of a walk."

"I don't understand why some people always have to have the last word." Tony touched Ira's arm but looked over his head at Andrea.

Once again Ira pretended that he was lost in his own world rather than risk coming between this pair.

"My God, I can't believe I forgot!" Palmer embraced Ira and shook hands with Tony before kissing Andrea. "Everything's been kind of crazy with the re-launch of the network and all the guys here partying. Welcome home Dad, how're you feeling?"

Ira looked around before replying, absorbing the sight of all the young men in his home, laughing, drinking and smoking. They were all members of EBYN but to his mind they looked just like his friends of forty years ago, down to the sharp zoot suits, haircuts and winkle picker shoes.

"My mates have come to see me?" he looked to Palmer for confirmation.

"Yes Dad," Palmer agreed, "They're all here, happy to see you well again."

"Commentator?" Ira grabbed the arm of a young man who was passing by, "What are you doing here? Does your wife know you're out this late?" Ira laughed and shook the man's hand vigorously.

The man looked from him to Palmer who nodded his head. "Good to see you Mr Shango," the young man greeted him before moving on.

"Is Jerome here? Stanford?" Ira looked up into Palmer's face wanting to know who else he'd meet in his house that day.

Palmer forced himself to smile down at his dad, forced

himself to keep the light in his eyes that had appeared when Ira first arrived, forced himself not to show the disappointment and heartache he felt at Ira's obvious confusion.

"You tired Dad?" he asked. "Come and sit down with the guys, I'll bring you a whisky. How does that sound?"

"And dominoes!" Ira slapped Palmer's arm. "Whisky and dominoes. Who can I give brush to tonight!" Ira's laughter lingered behind him as he eased through the crowd into his lounge and sat in his favourite chair.

"Are you okay?" Tony interlocked his fingers with his wife's. They were united once again in their empathy for Palmer.

"He was a little quiet on the way home, but I'm sure they wouldn't have let him out of he wasn't totally well," Andrea consoled.

"It could be the beginning of Alzheimer's," Palmer told them.

"I'm so sorry," Andrea replied shocked. "*We're* so sorry," she amended as Tony squeezed her hand.

"It's his age, it's not an official diagnosis, but we're prepared for, you know, whatever," Palmer said quietly. "Hey, I'm forgetting my manners. Why don't you guys come through and let me fix you a drink."

"Sure, where's Shango?" Tony wondered.

"I was going to ask you that. Ice?"

"Please," Andrea said. "If this is an EBYN party then how come he's not here?"

"He was, but he left a little while ago. I think he's with Celia, Michelle's been ringing there but couldn't reach her either. Mixer?"

"Coke for me," said Tony. "Do you think they're okay?"

"Sure. Shango's sorting out his business and putting his world to rights. He hasn't got an easy road but if anyone can handle it he can. You guys hungry? Rafi cooked chicken."

"Rafi!" Andrea and Tony burst out laughing at the thought of Rafi in a pinafore frying chicken.

"Try not to worry over Ira," Andrea said when the laughter died down, "He knows your life is in the States, he's got the best family here and a whole community of friends, including us."

"I know, you guys are great," Palmer thanked them.

• • • • • •

Shango reached up and took the gun from Celia's hand. She looked down as it slid through her fingers, but she made no

241

protest. Shango laid it on the ground next to where he sat Sandra's head still in his lap.

"Is she okay?" Celia asked quietly but before Shango could respond Sandra opened her eyes. She squinted at the vague shapes of Shango and Celia, trying to understand why the world seemed to be the wrong way round. As things came into focus she struggled to sit up and free herself from Shango's embrace.

"What happened to your face?" she asked Celia, eyeing the drying blood on her cheek that was mixed with the remnants of small stones. Her voice carried no malice, only curiosity.

"I fell," was all Celia said.

"You two wait here." Shango picked up the gun and eased himself up slowly. His body was stiff and awkward and he felt as though he was developing the mother of all headaches. "I'll bring the car over."

"Then what?" Celia asked,

"Then we'd better get you two checked out."

"As simple as that?" Celia persisted. "I tried to kill her, Shango, I really wanted her dead."

"I know," he responded, one hand on her shoulder and looking straight into her eyes, "but thank God, you didn't."

Celia rested her head on his chest for a brief second before he released her and walked over to the car. Then she turned to Sandra.

"Are you okay?" She was tearful.

"I think so; just a few bruises where your foot argued with my ribs." Sandra tried to smile but found that she was crying also.

"I love him so much but I'm not enough for him, even though I tried so hard," Celia explained, not sure if her words were making sense. "He's special, he has everything and he is my everything. Do you understand why I couldn't just let him go?"

"I didn't know," Sandra said.

Celia helped her up and the two women fell into an embrace.

"I didn't know about you, otherwise I would never have...Shango made me believe that we could go back in time, but it's impossible."

Shango pulled up alongside Celia and Sandra. Wordlessly he opened the rear car doors for them to enter but neither woman moved. Shango watched as they cried and clung together, drawing strength from each other to somehow go forward after the last few emotionally wrought hours. He was the cause for their despair but at this moment he was outside of their circle and there was nothing that he could say or do. The women shared a common bond of heartache caused by him and where it had once driven them apart, it now united them.

JULY 2003

SHANGO ROLLED UP the blinds in the study. It was six thirty am and the sun was already out, promising a beautiful bright start to a gloriously warm day. He stood at the open window in only his boxer shorts, string vest and bare feet, surveying the quiet neighbourhood. The breeze that blew across his face was soft and refreshing, just right for the month of July.

He looked up the road to the bungalows on his right, remembering with mixed feelings, the day the senior citizens had reported him to the police for trying to break into his own home. His gaze wandered to the three houses opposite whose occupants had recently had babies. He smiled to think that in a few years time the tranquillity of the street would be eclipsed by the boisterous enthusiasm of teenagers driving their parents mad. He thought about his next door neighbours, a mixed race couple, Carl, black and Freya, Swedish, his smile broadening as he recalled Freya teaching him and Rafi Swedish phrases at a barbecue Celia had organised the previous summer. He couldn't get his tongue around the sing song accent but Rafi had driven them all mad for weeks afterwards showing off his new "bi-lingual" talent.

Shango turned back to the interior of the room. He stood still for a moment enjoying the feel of the warm sun on the back of his neck. He hadn't changed the decor of the room, happy to be reminded of Celia's good taste, but since she'd gone the room had lost its soul and its walls were bare without her books, calendars, pictures and yellow post-it notes.

She'd left her computer and he could still picture her typing away, her tongue poking shapes in her cheek, an old childhood habit. When she'd told him her plans he'd gone out and bought her a laptop. She'd protested, saying it was far too expensive at nearly three thousand pounds, but he'd insisted on buying her the best possible specification. Now, when he lay alone in the bed they'd once made love in, the radio drowned out the taunts that said he'd only given her the laptop to ease his conscience.

Shango sighed and went into the bathroom. He examined his chin in the mirror, noting the hairs that had sprouted overnight, before opening the cabinet to select his shaving cream, toothbrush and toothpaste. He stared for a while at the empty shelves that used to be filled with Celia's things. Then he pulled a towel out of the airing cupboard and automatically held it to his face, his actions were in vain, Celia's essence was gone from the house for good.

Shango turned the power shower on full blast gasping as the icy water pounded his skin. He remembered Celia's shrieks when he'd re-set her shower to cold while she was still under it. His shoulders shook as he recalled how she'd jumped out of the shower, threw on shorts and a t-shirt and chased him all around the house, through the back garden and up and down the street, in her bare feet, until they'd both collapsed laughing on the front lawn.

Shango eased the soapy cloth along his arms, over his taut stomach and down between his thighs. He soaped his penis slowly and waited to see if thoughts of his ex-wife would cause it to rise but there was no immediate reaction.

He closed his eyes and pictured Celia wearing a short, silky nightie as she stood at the cooker burning their breakfast, he imagined her in naked in bed writhing sensuously beneath him as he brought her to orgasm, he felt her taking him in her mouth and sucking him hard, but from the waist down he felt nothing for her. She no longer stirred his passions and made him desire her. She'd become like a close friend who he thought of with fond memories but wasn't particularly in a hurry to see again. He would always care about her but he was no longer in love with her.

Shango lay on the bed with a towel slung casually across his waist. Barely an hour had passed since he'd been awake and he was restless. He wanted to be interacting with people, playing with Kai, teasing Sensi and cooking with Ira, but it was too early. Shango looked up at the ceiling for inspiration trying to work out what he could do with this spare time. While his eyes examined the light bulb, his left hand reached for his to-do notepad that lay on the bedside table. He read it while still lying on his back, it had a checklist of at least twenty things and they were all crossed off.

Replacing the pad, Shango tried to decide if he was hungry, he settled for a no. Was he thirsty? Also no. He tried to remember if he had any more course papers or essays to mark but that was a non starter. He was always up to date with his academic timetable and now that term was over he was more or less free. He sat up and looked around the room thinking that he could do a bit of dusting. But every surface gleamed back at him courtesy of Michelle and Rafi who'd had an *"anything you can do, I can do better"* competition. To the amusement of himself and Palmer they'd vacuumed, dusted, mopped and shined the whole house relentlessly, neither wanting to be the first to give in. Michelle was certainly a lot more relaxed since she'd fallen in love.

Shango pulled on a clean pair of shorts and went downstairs into the living room. He refused to slump in front of the TV, determined instead to find something that would stimulate his mind. Wandering around the room he stopped at the large rosewood bookcase that he'd chosen with Celia. He loved it's design, classical yet modern, while she'd been attracted to the richness of its dark wood veneer. They'd initially claimed alternate shelves until Celia had mixed them all up saying that that's what married people did with their possessions. Now the majority of the books that lined the shelves were his. Celia had left only a couple behind. He ran his finger along the spines trying to arouse an interest that wasn't really there. He stopped at a hardback book of photographs and essays titled *Another Africa*. Sitting down in the easy chair by the window, he turned each page slowly, absorbing the content and trying to see the pictures from a new perspective.

Twenty minutes later Shango was awakened by his own snoring. Putting the book to one side he checked the time on the video recorder. Eight o'clock. Shango stretched and slapped his hands together. Finally the world was awake and he could have some company.

"Rise and shine!" Shango called out as he kicked open the door to the spare bedroom, "The early bird gets the worm!" he continued as he opened the curtains and wooden blinds with a flourish, "He who hesitates is lost!" he said even louder.

"All right, already!" Palmer was not pleased at being woken up so harshly.

"Orange juice, coffee, bagels, and scrambled egg with lots of hot sauce," Shango announced as he laid the tray down next to Palmer.

"Who's that for?" Palmer asked. He kept the sheets pulled up to his neck and squinted at Shango out of one eye.

"Do you know what time it is?" Shango asked sipping Palmer's juice.

"Do *you*?" Palmer threatened. "I can't eat all of this food, man," he winced as he looked at the tray.

"Don't hurt my feelings now. I cooked this with love and affection. It may be the last time I ever get to do it." Shango pretended to be upset.

"Come back in an hour." Palmer put his head under the covers as he waved Shango away.

"Nope!"

"Okay, fifteen minutes?" Palmer pleaded as Shango pulled him up to a sitting position and wafted the cup of coffee under his nose. "Hmm, that smells good," he conceded. "What?" he asked aware that Shango was studying him.

"Do you remember what you're supposed to be doing today?" Shango asked slowly.

"Hey, one of us has to stay calm," Palmer smiled.

"Calm? Is that how you're feeling?" Shango was baffled.

"Nah, I'm just winding you up. I'm as nervous as hell!" Palmer finally admitted as both men laughed. "I've got so many things running through my head. What do I do first?" Palmer took a bite out of his scrambled egg and bagels.

"Panic, unless you've already done that," Shango advised finishing off the last of the orange juice.

"Check, did it all night long. Think I only fell asleep five minutes before you came in."

"Think about all the things you've forgotten."

"Like what?"

"The ring, the speech, collecting your suit from the tailor's."

"Okay, I'm doing that now, anything else?"

"Panic some more?"

"How much panicking can a man do?"

"On his wedding day? As much as he wants." Shango chuckled, "This is it man, are you ready?"

"I have to be ready?"

"For a woman like Michelle? Absolutely!"

"Huh, I just hope she's ready for me. By the way did you enjoy my juice?"

"Highly refreshing. Are you getting up now or are you going to stay there stuffing your face?"

"Do I have a choice?"

"That's what I want to hear. I'll run you a shower," Shango offered mischievously.

"No thanks. I like mine hot so I'll fix it myself." Palmer stretched and flexed his muscles as he rose. "Is this all a dream?" he looked at Shango a serious expression on his face.

"It's the best dream you could ever have," Shango replied. "This is one dream you won't want to wake up from."

"Do you think Michelle feels the same way?"

"She said yes, didn't she?" Shango laughed slapping Palmer on the back just at the moment that he slurped his coffee.

"Did you sleep well?" Angela smiled at Michelle who blinked her eyes at the morning sunlight that streamed into the room with Angela's entrance.

"I don't think I slept at all, I've probably got huge bags under my eyes. One look at me and Palmer will change his mind!" Michelle was only half joking.

"You'll look as gorgeous as you always do. In fact, even more so, Palmer won't be able to keep his eyes off you," Angela reassured her.

"I can't believe this is really happening." Michelle sat up and rubbed the sleep out of her eyes.

"Then you're like ninety-nine percent of brides. How do you feel?"

"Like I'm caught up in someone else's fantasy. Like if I go back to sleep and wake up it'll all disappear and I'll be alone again."

"You're on the verge of major changes, getting married and starting a new life in Atlanta. It's quite exciting."

"And scary. I wish Celia could be here today."

"Me too, but she's here in spirit, you know that."

"She sent me an e-mail to say she's thinking of going to Nigeria."

"That's where her dad's family is from. Her birth dad, Olayeni I mean, not Martin, of course."

"Do you mind her looking for him?"

"No, but obviously I'm hoping that she won't feel like she no longer needs us."

"I'm sure that would never happen."

"Perhaps if she gets in touch with her roots she'll find the self worth that she's always looked for in other people."

"You think that Celia tried to validate herself through others?"

"Celia always felt that she wasn't black enough or white

enough. She seemed to think that if she gave her power over to strong people like you and Shango it would fill the hole inside her."

"I always thought that she was the strong one in our friendship."

"She probably was, she just didn't know it."

"Do you think that she should never have married Shango?"

"I know she adored him but I don't think they were suited as man and wife."

"Why not?"

"They were at different stages in their lives, both looking for something that the other didn't have to give."

"So right from the beginning you never thought it would work?"

"I don't think they stood a fair chance. It just wasn't the right time for them. At least now Celia's following her heart. She's doing things she always wanted to do, like seeing America and going to find her Nigerian relatives. Maybe when she's finished travelling she'll get round to writing that bestseller."

"Unless someone else sweeps her off her feet."

"I think that next time around she'll be wiser about who she lets into her heart."

"You know that Palmer's asked Shango to be his best man?"

"They're brothers, who else would he ask? What about you, are any of your family coming?"

"I doubt it." Michelle looked away and sighed heavily, "You should have seen their faces when I told them. I really hoped that this time they'd be pleased for me, but all they had to offer was criticism and negativity."

"That must have been hard for you."

"It was more embarrassing than anything else."

"In what way?"

"When I took Palmer to meet them all they wanted to know was what kind of car he drove and how much money he made, oh yeah, and could he get them green cards and put them up in the States. Not a single word of congratulations for us, they only wanted to know what they could get out of it."

"How did Palmer handle it?"

"Superbly. He was polite and genuine and thankfully he didn't use them to judge me."

"So they're definitely not coming to the wedding?"

"Mom said she can't afford to take time off just for fun and my sisters won't come without her, they're like a pack of wolves, they all stick together."

"People can only be who they are, Michelle, they've allowed their jealousy to override their love for you for so long they've forgotten how to show that they care."

"I don't know how I would have got through today without you and Martin to support me. Do you think we'll be okay, me and Palmer?"

"How could you not be?" Angela responded without hesitation. "Do you remember the dream you used to tell me about? The one where you'd always wake up just before you saw the face of your true love?"

"Yes."

"Close your eyes." Angela sat on the edge of the bed and took Michelle's hand in hers, "Imagine that long corridor with the door half open at the end, see it?"

"Yes."

"Now imagine that door opening all the way."

"Okay."

"Keep your eyes closed. For the first time you can see who's standing on the other side, your true love, the man who'll adore you, love you and protect you forever. He's overjoyed at the thought of spending his life with you. Who do you see Michelle?"

"Michelle found that when she tried to speak she was crying. Palmer's face appeared clearly in her mind. She leant forwards into Angela's arms.

"Tears of joy?" the older woman asked.

Michelle nodded.

●●●●●●

"Very handsome," Sensi appraised as Shango stood on her doorstep. He looked magnificent in a well cut navy blue tailored suit with a sparkling white shirt and burgundy silk tie. The pointed edge of a silk burgundy handkerchief peeped from his breast pocket. His locks were tied back with a matching burgundy silk ribbon and he wore expensive crocodile-skin loafers and black silk socks. "You better mind one of the bridesmaids doesn't carry you off to have her wicked way," she added playfully.

"If only," Shango joked as he kissed Sensi on the cheek. "Is Kai ready?" he asked as he walked inside. "Hmm, that smells nice," Shango commented on the perfume that drifted around the interior.

"I'm burning ylang ylang incense for Kai. He's polishing his shoes again. He's so excited about being a page boy for Palmer, I was hoping the scent might calm him down."

"I'll see to him. Young man!" Shango called out from the foot of the stairs, "Let me have a good look at those shoes!"

"One more polish, Dad!"

Shango and Sensi laughed at the excitement in Kai's voice. "Speaking of relaxing aromas." Sensi picked up a small package that lay on the table, "Could you give this to the happy couple for me?"

"That's beautiful." Shango examined the carefully wrapped box, admiring the shiny, silver paper and delicate white bows. "What is it?"

"His and hers fragrances which I mixed and bottled myself."

"You made these yourself?" Shango was impressed.

"Yep, tell them I said good luck."

"That's really thoughtful, Sensi."

"Don't make a fuss." Sensi was a little embarrassed at the way Shango was looking at her, but pleased that she'd surprised him.

"Here's your post." Shango handed her a slim brown envelope that had fallen to the floor just inside the doorway. Sensi took it reluctantly. "What's up?" Shango asked, noting her mood change.

"It's my results, from the aromatherapy course. If I pass I might be able to get a job; it's the first step to getting my own shop. But what if…"

"–Why are you worried?" Shango interrupted. "I've watched you work your butt off over the last year on this course. Wasn't it me who took Kai all those nights so you could study for your exams? And wasn't it you who showed me your reading list and said you'd never get through it and then six months later showed me all the books you'd ticked off cos you'd read them?"

"Yes, but…"

"–No buts. You've given this everything you've got, open the envelope."

"It's not as simple as that."

"Yes it is, now open up so I can congratulate you."

"I've got to sit down," Sensi said.

"Drum roll!" with exaggerated movements Shango beat a fast rhythm on the back of a wooden dining chair.

"Be quiet, you're making me nervous!" Sensi laughed. She ran her fingers over the envelope but couldn't bring herself to open it.

"Woman!" exasperated Shango snatched it out of her hands and ripped it open. He held her at arms length while he quickly scanned the content, ignoring her attempts to snatch it back.

"Yes!" Shango threw the letter on the floor and lifted Sensi off her feet.

"What does it say, what does it say?" she screamed as he twirled her around and planted kisses on her cheeks.

"I'm getting dizzy," she squealed, laughing.

"You two are very noisy." Kai ran into the room looking extremely smart in a miniature version of his dad's suit.

"You've got the cleverest mom in the world!" Shango shouted dropping Sensi on the settee and picking up Kai, who laughed, delighted to be swirled around so high up.

Sensi sat on the settee shaking. "Does it really say that?" she asked in a quiet voice as reality sank in.

Shango put Kai down and handed her the letter. "See, I told you you could do it, well done, you've passed, well done."

• • • • • •

"Bad memories?" Rafi stood at Shango's side as they watched Michelle and Palmer pose for photographs with Kai and their bridesmaids. Like Shango, Rafi was dressed in navy blue but he'd discarded his jacket as the day had grown warmer and now sported a patterned satin waistcoat, white shirt and sharply pressed trousers.

"Only good ones," Shango reassured him.

"You sure?" There was genuine concern in Rafi's voice.

Shango looked around at the elegant guests gathered on the lawn outside of the church. Ira, in top hat and tails, his mental confusion temporarily abated, was once again in his element. The wedding brought out the best in him and he laughed, joked and proudly boasted of his first-born and his new daughter-in-law. Tony and Andrea kept one eye on Natalie and the boys, while liaising with their staff to ensure that the reception, which they were catering, would run smoothly.

Rafi nodded towards Palmer and Michelle. "Reminds me of you and Celia, like that French thing."

"Deja vu?"

"That's Spanish isn't it?" Rafi frowned.

"Never mind," Shango chuckled before continuing more soberly, "I always knew that Celia and I weren't quite on the same page, but I honestly thought we'd go the distance."

"You knew she wasn't the woman of your dreams?"
Shango nodded in affirmation.

"So why'd do marry her? Because she was pregnant?"

Shango tutted. "Because she was special. I just couldn't give her what she really wanted."

"You gave her a home, you gave her a name.....you almost gave her a kid.....what more is there?" Rafi was distracted as a pretty woman walked past him and winked.

"Me. I loved her but I kept a part of myself in reserve and I don't think I even realized that I'd done it but she always knew."

"Did she give you everything? All of her I mean." Rafi tried to see where the pretty lady had gone.

"Over and over again, she said it was impossible for her to love me any other way."

"Do you miss her?"

"Sometimes, mainly because of the house."

"You could move or just redecorate."

"I don't want to. She sent me a letter, you know. Not very long, but more than I expected or deserved."

"What did she say?"

"That she's writing, travelling, doing okay and that she hopes to forgive me in time because she doesn't want to spend her life hating me."

"When's she coming home?"

"No idea. She's thinking about going to the Caribbean and then maybe to Nigeria to look for her real dad."

"Do you think she's running away?"

"No, I actually think that for the first time in her life, maybe she's going in the right direction."

"How do you mean?"

"When she's done travelling she'll find that she's always had everything she needs."

"Everything except you."

"She doesn't need me, I think she realises that now."

"Tell her that no matter where she is, she's still my girl," Rafi said.

"Will you two get over here and be in my wedding pictures?" Palmer shouted across the lawn to the men.

"Thought you'd never ask!" Rafi and Shango squeezed in either side of Palmer and Michelle and smiled for the camera.

● ● ● ● ● ●

Shango loosened his tie and the collar of his shirt as he stood in the doorway watching the children playing outside. He'd just finished his obligatory dance with his brother's new bride and found that he'd really meant it when he'd kissed her cheek and wished her a lifetime of happiness with Palmer.

"I'm sorry your best friend couldn't share your special day," he'd said, holding her close as they'd danced to James Ingram's *One Hundred Ways*. "Do you blame me for chasing her away?"

"You broke her heart and almost destroyed her, Shango, she didn't deserve that. No-one does. Just promise me you'll let her get on with her life now."

"I just want her to be happy and if that means leaving her alone, then that's what I'll do."

As the song came to an end, Shango gave Michelle a last hug before leaving her contented in Palmer's arms.

Now he walked along the grassy path that circled the community centre, retracing the same steps he'd taken on his own wedding day two years before. It was a warm July evening and the air was filled with the mild, soothing scents of English flowers. Shango inhaled and exhaled deeply, thankful that for once his chest wasn't constricted and he could breathe easily.

At the corner where the paths converged he felt her before he saw her.

"Hi," was all she said in a voice that melted his heart.

"I'm glad you came," he spoke softly as he led her to a bench shaded by willow trees, "let's sit."

Sandra let Shango take her hand and lead her to a nearby bench. Her flowing skirt swished and her feet, clad in flat leather sandals, padded softly. Shango looked her over slowly, admiring her shiny black hair which fell to just below her chin, his eyes resting on the single silver chain around her smooth brown neck, before dropping down to the soft curve of her breasts where her blouse was slightly open. Evening birdsong mingled with chatter from the reception hall and a gentle breeze was the only movement between them.

Sandra had sat silently throughout Shango's appraisal, but when the passion in his eyes became too much she spoke up.

"Sounds like they're all having a good time." Her voice was edged with nervousness.

"The happiest man in Birmingham is right here with you," Shango responded still gazing intently at her, "you look beautiful." He was still holding her hand.

"You're only saying that because it's true!" she laughed lightly and looked away.

Shango held her chin and turned her face to his. He looked deep into her eyes until she broke contact.

"You lied to me," she said quietly.

"Many times and I'm not proud of that," Shango admitted.

"I don't know if I can ever forgive you."

"I understand."

"Your wife could have killed me."

"She would have had to shoot me first."

"You hurt me badly; really, really, badly."

"I've lost sleep over what I did to you."

"You broke my heart."

"Breaking your heart broke mine too."

"You might hurt me again."

"I might, there are no guarantees."

"I'd be a fool to let you back in."

"I'd be a fool to let you go."

"You're a bastard."

"You're a Queen."

"I deserve better."

"I want to give you the best."

"Stop it!" Sandra pulled her hand away from Shango and rubbed her nose, "Stop playing games with me! What exactly do you expect after everything that's gone on?" She stood up and walked away. She couldn't think clearly without being overwhelmed by the love that churned inside her for this man. Shango caught up with her and held her close, ignoring her attempts to push him away.

"Why *did* you come, Sandra?"

"I don't know!" she shouted, struggling to get out of his grasp.

"Ssh." He held her tighter. "Why did you come?" he whispered and his strong arms around her made her stop fighting him. "You've spent a year avoiding me. You wouldn't answer my e-mails, you even moved house so I couldn't find you. You've had twelve months away from me, but I never gave up on you, I never gave up on us, but I thought you did. Why are you here?"

"Ira invited me."

"Then why didn't you come to the wedding?"

"I..." Sandra faltered,

"They make a beautiful couple, my brother and his new wife.

That's what every one used to say about us, remember?"

"No."

"You're lying." Shango's voice was a whisper in her ear, his breath a soft caress on her cheek. "Why did you come?" he asked again, longing to hear her answer.

"You know why I came." Sandra rested her head on his chest and held him close, "Don't make me say it, you know why I'm here."

"It's you and me, Sandra," Shango touched her head, arms and shoulders with gentle fingertips before lifting her chin so their lips could meet. "I would cut off my right arm if it would take away all of the pain I've caused you." He pressed his lips to hers tenderly. "You're on my mind day and night, wherever I am and whatever I'm doing; I can't breathe without you. Give me a chance to make you happy, just give me a chance."

"Shango I can't." Sandra tried to pull away from him but he held her tight.

"Yes you can."

"I can't, I shouldn't," Sandra cried in his arms.

"I want you, Sandra." Shango kissed away her tears, "I've always wanted you, I can't live without you. This past year has been empty and lonely; last summer, the time we had together, before.......Celia found out..., that was the happiest time of my life. I can't go back to being without you."

"You have to," Sandra murmured. "We had the right love Shango but it was the wrong time, it's always been the wrong time."

"I can't believe that. You're the other half of me Sandra. Say yes and save us both."

"From what?" Sandra looked up at him through her tears.

"From emptiness, loneliness, everything bad, everything sad, all that my life is without you. Save me, Sandra, please."

"I can't take any more heartache, Shango."

"You won't have to."

"How can you be sure?"

"My heart tells me."

"I'm worried that..."

"Don't worry about anything anymore, just love me." Shango silenced her fears with a soft, reassuring kiss that spoke a thousand words telling of his eternal love and devotion. A kiss that sealed their union and bound them together, forever, body and soul.

END